Jo Beverley's

ROMANCES ARE

"Wickedly delicious."
—Teresa Medeiros

"Delightfully wicked."
—*Library Journal*

"Romance at its best."
—*Publishers Weekly*

continued . . .

Lady Beware

"Jo Beverley carries off a remarkable achievement in *Lady Beware*, the latest and possibly last in her Company of Rogues novels. . . . It is the unusual combination of familial comfort and risqué pleasure that makes this book a winner. . . . No doubt about it, *Lady Beware* is yet another jewel in Beverley's heavily decorated crown."　　　　　*—The Romance Reader*

"[E]nchanting . . . a delightful blend of wit (with banter between Thea and Darien), intrigue (as evil lurks throughout), and emotional victories (as love prevails in the end). . . . Watching Thea and Darien spar is entertaining, and watching them succumb to the simmering love and passion is satisfying."
　　　　　—The State (Columbia, SC)

To Rescue a Rogue

"Beverley brings the Regency period to life in this highly romantic story [with] vividly portrayed characters. [Readers] will be engrossed by this emotionally packed story of great love, tremendous courage, and the return of those attractive and dangerous men known as the Rogues. Her Company of Rogues series is well crafted, delicious, and wickedly captivating."　　　　　*—Joan Hammond*

"With her usual beautifully nuanced characters and lyrical writing, RITA Award winner Beverley brings her popular Company of Rogues Regency historical series to a triumphant conclusion . . . [a] quietly powerful romance."　　　*—Booklist*

The Rogue's Return

"Beverley beautifully blends complex characters, an exquisitely sensual love story, and a refreshingly different Regency setting into one sublime romance."　　　　　*—Booklist*

"Jo Beverley has written an excellent character study. One of the best books I've read this season."　　　*—Affaire de Coeur*

A Most Unsuitable Man

"Beverley brings back some of the characters from *Winter Fire* as she takes her readers into the dangerous, intriguing, and opulent world of Georgian England. Her strong characters and finely honed dialogue, combined with a captivating love story, are a pleasure to read."　　　　　*—Romantic Times*

An Unlikely Countess

Jo Beverley

A SIGNET BOOK

SIGNET

Published by New American Library, a division of
Penguin Group (USA) Inc., 375 Hudson Street,
New York, New York 10014, USA
Penguin Group (Canada), 90 Eglinton Avenue East, Suite 700, Toronto,
Ontario M4P 2Y3, Canada (a division of Pearson Penguin Canada Inc.)
Penguin Books Ltd., 80 Strand, London WC2R 0RL, England
Penguin Ireland, 25 St. Stephen's Green, Dublin 2,
Ireland (a division of Penguin Books Ltd.)
Penguin Group (Australia), 250 Camberwell Road, Camberwell, Victoria 3124,
Australia (a division of Pearson Australia Group Pty. Ltd.)
Penguin Books India Pvt. Ltd., 11 Community Centre, Panchsheel Park,
New Delhi - 110 017, India
Penguin Group (NZ), 67 Apollo Drive, Rosedale, North Shore 0632,
New Zealand (a division of Pearson New Zealand Ltd.)
Penguin Books (South Africa) (Pty.) Ltd., 24 Sturdee Avenue,
Rosebank, Johannesburg 2196, South Africa

Penguin Books Ltd., Registered Offices:
80 Strand, London WC2R 0RL, England

First published by Signet, an imprint of New American Library,
a division of Penguin Group (USA) Inc.

First Printing, March 2011
10 9 8 7 6 5 4 3 2 1

An Unlikely
Countess

Chapter 1

Northallerton, Yorkshire
March 1765

He was drunk, but could still see well enough in the dimly lit street. Well enough to detect ruffians at work. And that the victim was a woman.

Catesby Burgoyne grinned, drew his sword, and charged. At his battle cry the ruffians whirled toward him, eyes white rimmed, mouths agape. And then they fled.

Cate staggered to a halt, flailing his sword. "Come back!" he roared. "Come back, you scum, and meet my blade!"

Only their fleeing footsteps answered.

"Damn your blasted eyes," he muttered. "A bit of slaughter's just what I need."

A breathy sound made him turn, sword rising again, but it was only the woman, leaning against a house wall, staring at him.

The narrow street was lit only by two feeble householder lamps, so all he could see was pallor and shadows. Pale face surrounded by loose, pale hair. A dark gown that covered her neck to toe. Gown was respectable. Hair wasn't. Couldn't be respectable, could she, out alone at night?

He shoved his sword back into its scabbard. "You must be new to the trade, sweetheart, to dress so dully." Damnation, where were his manners? No need to be crass because she was a whore and he was at odds with the world.

He bowed. "Catesby Burgoyne, ma'am, at your service. May I escort you to your destination?"

She shook her head, mute.

He walked closer to see her better. She tried to shrink back, but the wall was relentless.

"Please . . ." she whispered. A thin hand clutched a shawl at her chest as if it could be a breastplate.

Cate was trying to come up with reassurance when a door opened nearby and a flat Yorkshire voice asked, "Wot's going on 'ere, then?"

The stocky man carried a candle that illuminated his face and straggling hair more than them. Even so, the woman turned away as if to hide her face.

She had a reputation to lose?

"The lady was attacked, sir," Cate said, striving to hide all trace of gin from his voice. "The villains have fled and I'll see her safely home."

The man peered, but like all sane people, he didn't go looking for trouble. Probably Cate's aristocratic tone helped him along that path. "Good night to ye, then," he said, and shut his door.

Cate turned back to the woman. She still stared at him, but the intervention of someone from the ordinary world seemed to have restored her voice.

"I must thank you, Mr. Burgoyne," she said on uneven breaths. "But, please, there's no need to delay you longer."

A well-bred voice. Her left hand bore no ring. Where was her father or brother to permit this?

"I may not be the most perfect of gentlemen, ma'am, but I cannot leave a lady to walk the night streets alone."

"I live very close by. . . ."

"Then this will delay me little."

He gestured her onward. He'd commanded men in battle. Surely he could command one ordinary woman. She did move forward, stiff with wariness.

Or anger?

Now, that was interesting. He assessed her as best he could in the gloom. Hard to judge her looks, but her features seemed set in . . . resentment. Yes, that was it. Resentment. She might have reason to be wary of him, but why in Hades should she resent him? She was also dawdling, but he would not be put off.

"Your direction, ma'am?"

She quickened her steps as if she might outpace him—a thin, sour thing, all sharp angles and antipathy.

He kept up without effort. "Unwise to venture out alone so late, ma'am."

"I merely wished to walk."

"I have no pressing engagements. If you desire a stroll, I could escort you for miles."

Her angles became harder, which vaguely amused him. A blessing that, on such a dismal day.

They'd arrived at the main street of the town. He saw no one else on foot, but this was also the Great North Road, lined with inns, all still open, hoping for late trade. A coach rattled by and turned through the arch to the Golden Lion, the best inn in town.

To the left lay the Queen's Head, a mangy, ill-run place where he'd failed to drown his sorrows. He'd escaped into fresh air, but fresh March air was cold up here in Yorkshire, and the next London coach didn't pass by until early morning. He'd need a bed for the night somewhere, but could only afford to share a room with others.

The woman was simply standing there.

"Forgotten where you live, ma'am?" he drawled.

She turned sharply to face him. "Why are *you* walking the streets at night?"

"A man is allowed to, ma'am. Especially one with a sword, who knows how to use it."

"Men are allowed anything, whilst we poor women have no rights at all."

Ah. "What man in particular has offended you? I have a sword and know how to use it."

She gave a short laugh. "You'll not call out my brother."

"He wouldn't fight?"

"Only in court. He's a lawyer."

"The lowest form of scum."

He meant it as the general, common gibe, but she said, "He is indeed."

What had the fraternal scum done to her? Something he could avenge? He was done with war, but at this moment bloody violence would be immensely satisfying.

"His name and location?" he demanded.

"You're ridiculous."

"Perhaps he has an excuse for scumminess if you flail him with such a razor tongue."

"You'd be sharp if . . . *Oh!*" It was pure exasperation. "I suppose, being a man, you'll insist on having your way. Very well."

She marched across the street and into a lane lined by rows of small cottages, where she stopped by the fourth door. "Good night, sir."

The breathy hiss was angry, but cautious. So, she didn't want to alert the neighbors to her improper behavior. The only light here escaped from a couple of shuttered windows, but Cate could tell her small house probably had only two rooms on each floor. From her bearing and speech, she'd come down in the world.

"Is your brother inside?" he asked quietly.

"No, thank God."

"Will he be back soon?"

"Live *here*? Aaron?" She laughed, but quickly covered her mouth with her hand.

Something was wrong here, and he found lame ducks so hard to ignore. It was the bane of his life.

"If you were to invite me in, ma'am, perhaps I could advise you."

"Invite you in?" She looked around frantically, seeking listeners. "Go away."

"I'm not planning a rape. You need help, but we can't discuss your situation here."

"We can't discuss it anywhere. Go away or I'll scream."

"Truly?"

She hissed in a breath. "You wretched, drunken—"

A door opened nearby. "Whosur? Woyeruptuh?"

The old man's accent was so thick Cate could hardly understand the words, and he was Yorkshire born and bred. The meaning was clear enough, however.

He pressed down the latch and pushed her inside. He followed, having to duck to save his head, and shut the door. They both froze in place, listening, and Cate was aware of her bony angles conflicting with a sweet smell. She took the trouble to store her clothes with herbs.

A dog whined.

Cate turned to face new danger, but the small dog looked to be a spaniel, a gentle breed. Hard to tell its mood when it stood in front of the candlelit back room, but dogs didn't whine a threat.

The woman pushed past Cate and hurried to the dog. "It's all right, Toby." She fondled its floppy ears and the tail wagged.

Woman and dog went into the kitchen and so Cate followed, instinctively hunching, even though the beams cleared his head—just. The floor was beaten earth, the air damp, and the front room held only one dip-seated chair.

Had all the rest been sold off so she could survive?

What was the story here?

He ducked into the kitchen—to face a knife, held firmly in a bony hand. It was only a short kitchen knife, but probably sharp enough to do some damage.

The dog only whined again, the cowardly cur, but she, with her weapon and her fierce, determined eyes, pale hair glowing in the candlelight—she was magnificent.

Cate raised both hands. "I intend no harm, ma'am. My word on it."

"And why should I trust your word? Leave. Now."

"Why?" he asked, taking evidence from the room.

The tallow candle gave too little light and too much odor, but it illuminated poverty well enough. The tiny kitchen, like the whole house, was cold. If there'd been a cooking fire in the hearth it had long since burned to ashes. He saw no sign of food.

The only furniture here was a deal table with two chairs at it, and a rough sort of sideboard holding cheap pottery. Alongside pots, however, sat a few pieces of pretty china and glass. Remnants of the better life that showed in her well-bred accent and proud demeanor?

Why was this goddess alone and in such desperate straits? Why was she bedraggled and dressed so poorly?

Her encompassing gown was a particularly dismal shade of black, her knitted shawl an ugly brown.

Had she truly been out on the streets attempting to earn some pennies in the only way available?

Her thinness told of hunger, but it etched strength into a face worthy of a Roman empress—high brow, long straight nose, perfectly curved lips, and a square chin. Not a face to conquer the fashionable world, but, by God, it was in danger of conquering him.

"Go!" she commanded again, but without confidence. The cowardly cur whined again, somewhere amid her skirts.

He realized his height was frightening her and sat, placing his hands on the table. Holding her eyes, he said, "I admire your courage, ma'am, but you won't scare me away, and if it comes to a fight you'll give me no more than a scratch. Simpler by far to sit down and tell me your story."

She tried to hold on to her strength, but her lips quivered.

Oh, 'struth.

Cate quickly took the leather flask from his pocket and put it on the table. "Have some of this."

"What is it?"

"Dutch courage."

"What?"

"Geneva. Gin."

"Gin!"

"Have you never indulged? It can sweeten bile."

She changed her grip on the knife. Startled, he half rose to defend himself, but then she drove it, two-handed, deep into the rickety table.

"My, my," he said after an appreciative moment. "Do please sit, drink, and tell."

"You've already had too much to drink, sirrah."

"It's never too much unless I'm unconscious. You have glasses, I see. We could even be elegant."

Suddenly she laughed. It was ugly, but a release of sorts. She pushed straggling hair off her face, then took two glass tumblers and slammed them on the table. She went back to open a low cupboard and returned with a bottle.

"Brandy," she said, putting it beside the glasses. "My mother's medicinal supply. I'll get some water."

"Seems a shame to dilute it." Cate picked up the bottle and unstoppered it. "Your mother is abed upstairs?"

"My mother is dead."

"My condolences."

"Four months ago."

Cate cursed his drink-blurred mind. He was being tossed pieces of a picture but couldn't quite put them together.

She sat down opposite him, straight and proud. "Pour me some, then."

The knife stood upright between them. Some vague reference to the sword of Damocles struggled to form, and failed.

He sniffed at the brandy. Not good stuff, but perhaps not atrocious. He poured half an inch into one glass and pushed it over to her. He poured the same into the other. He'd normally take more, but even half an inch might be enough to send her under the table. He didn't want her sozzled, only loose tongued.

And in his arms?

No, he had no place in his life for folly like that, but he'd help her if he could.

The spaniel appeared at his knee, whining again, but this time begging for attention.

"Away with you, coward."

"Don't be cruel," she said. "Toby, come here."

The dog slid away and only then did Cate notice that it was missing a hind leg. Devil take it, a lame dog to add to a lame duck—though falcon seemed more worthy for the goddess. He picked up his glass and drank, knowing he should leave before he was entangled.

She sipped and grimaced. But then she sipped again, thoughtfully. A woman willing to explore new experiences. Another hook in his heart.

"Will you give me your name, ma'am?"

"No."

"I've given you mine."

"Then I've forgotten it."

He hesitated, for the Burgoyne family home, Keynings, was less than twenty miles away, but he preferred honesty.

"Castesby Burgoyne, at your service."

She cradled the glass as if it might warm her. "An odd name, Catesby."

"My mother's family name. Yes, the line of Robert Catesby who led the papist Gunpowder Plot to blow up King James the First and take his Parliament with him."

"The Guy Fawkes affair? A strange heritage to pass on to a son."

"I've often thought so, but she sees the name as representing one who stands firm to his principles."

"Are you papist, then?"

"No, and nor is she, or her parents or grandparents."

Her lips twitched, and humor sparked in her heavy-lidded eyes. Another hook. Or rather, two. A ready sense of humor and striking eyes. Would she laugh during the passion her eyes promised? That too was what he liked.

He toasted her. "I didn't claim my mother was a rational woman. Does your name have such grisly connotations? Judith, perhaps, who cut off the head of invading Holofernes? Boadicea who led her armies against the Romans?"

She merely smiled.

"You hold your silence? Then I christen you Hera."

"Wife of Zeus?"

"Queen of the gods."

"By virtue of marriage, however. I would rather be Judith, who acted on her own."

"There's a man you wish to behead?"

She merely sipped more brandy, but all humor had left her as she contemplated the knife.

"Your brother, perhaps? A lawyer—and a gamester?"

She looked at him, startled. "What made you think that?"

"Poverty."

"Aaron's not poor."

"Then he's unkind."

She took another sip of her brandy. She'd be swigging it soon, but it hadn't loosened her tongue. He poured a little more into her glass and topped up his own.

"I have a brother," he said to encourage her, "but he's a prince among men. A tender son, a devoted husband, a loving but firm father."

"You're fortunate, then."

"I'm sure I am."

She cocked her head. "He's not all that he appears?"

"He is."

"But you resent it. Because you are none of those things?"

As sharp as her knife, damn her, but it added to his admiration.

"Your brother?" he insisted. "How can he see you in this state? You were clearly born to better things."

"He doesn't see me. He doesn't visit. Not since

Mother died, and we lived elsewhere then." She drank more brandy and then cradled her glass, staring at the play of candle flame on spirit. "I thought him a tender son. A good brother."

The brandy was doing its work at last. Cate could dimly remember when such a small amount had made him babble. Long, long ago.

"Until?" he prompted.

"Yesterday. Yesterday, I still clung to hope. Today I received his letter." She looked at an unfolded sheet of paper lying on the floor. "He sent it by a traveler. Thoughtful, perhaps, to spare me the pennies of the usual post, but it came late. Everything always seems worse at night."

"What does it say?"

"That the responsibilities consequent to his upcoming marriage make it impossible for him to increase the amount he sends me for my support."

"That doesn't seem entirely unreasonable."

"Does it not?" Her eyes met his over the knife. "He sends three guineas a month."

"That is very little," he agreed.

"While writing of the fine house he will soon have, and the carriage and pair for his future wife."

"Ah."

She slammed her glass down on the table so hard that brandy splashed. "He *owes* me a decent life. He owes it to me. And to my mother if she were still alive. Everything he is, everything he has, is because of our unstinting labor and sacrifice over ten long years. We've gone without every elegance and indulgence, and often without necessities as well."

Cate was almost breathless at her warlike intensity.

She swept her hand around. "I live *here*. Once we had a lovely home, but . . . we've moved to poorer and poorer places in order to support him. My sweet mother died in poverty. All so my brother could be educated and establish himself in his profession. So that he could return Mother to a decent, comfortable life. So he could help me make a good marriage."

"And now?"

"Now he throws money away and says I must wait."

"You went out tonight to visit him?"

"He lives in Darlington." She took another drink, seeming to savor it now. "When I read that letter I couldn't believe what he was saying—wait, wait, wait. This place was supposed to be only for a little while. For my first mourning, and while Aaron completed his training. He's practicing law. He's soon to make a good marriage to a woman who brings money. What need is there to wait? I was shocked. Then angry. So very, very angry. It felt . . . it felt like this brandy makes me feel." She stared at the knife as if envisioning a deadly purpose for it.

Plague take it. Shock he could believe, tears he would expect, but her anger was of another order, especially when it drove a blade deep into wood. She might be headed for a madhouse, or even the gallows.

"But why go out? What did you intend?"

She blinked at him. "Intend? I simply couldn't stay inside. I was suffocating in here, surrounded by darkness, dampness, and evidence of all our privations. Remembering the tender promises he made to my mother, his tears at her graveside because his prosperity had come too late. It was partly Mother's fault. She always resolutely made the best of things, even when . . ."

Cate poured a little more brandy into her glass, wishing she'd complete that sentence. This wasn't a new tragedy. What were the roots?

"He was always so grateful for the extra coins we'd

scrimped," she said, "but he never realized their cost. Mother would have us dress in our best and serve him tea from the few pieces of china. There was decent furniture then, but I had to sell it to pay for the funeral. Mother made me promise. Aaron mustn't pay, not when he needed every penny to set up in business."

"Then perhaps he can't bear all the blame."

"If he had an ounce of sense, if he ever looked beyond his own comforts . . . But I never imagined. I read that letter, and it was all too much. I was choking. I needed air. I simply walked the streets. . . ."

"Until you were attacked."

"Until then."

Fire quenched, she put a thin finger into the spilled brandy to trace a pattern on the table. A work-worn finger with a broken nail. Three guineas a month. It would pay her rent, and buy fuel and food, but little more.

"What do you think to do about your brother?"

"Do?" She straightened. "I shall write to him again. I'm at fault for following my mother's pattern and not making the situation clear."

"And if he doesn't respond as you wish?"

"He must."

She couldn't be as certain as she tried to sound. She had no weapons in this fight and must know it. Out of sight, out of mind was a powerful force, and if her brother chose selfishness, she would live here like this forever.

Something about her caught him so powerfully that he wanted to sweep her away to a better life, but what did he have to offer? He had no profession. He'd been forcefully advised to sell his commission in the army and told he wouldn't be welcome back there. His history in other enterprises was dismal.

His brother might have given him an allowance if

they hadn't almost come to blows a few hours ago. He could never return to Keynings now.

His only course seemed to be to find a rich wife. He didn't have much to recommend him to a family of his own class, but perhaps being the second son of an earl would count with a rich merchant or such.

No, he had nothing to offer Hera.

"Wouldn't you be better off as a governess or companion?" he suggested.

"Become a *servant*? Never. I will have my right. I will be a wife with a home of my own."

"Boadicea," he said with a grimace. "She led her armies against the Romans—and was slaughtered along with nearly all her people."

"I hardly think I'm in such danger, Mr. Burgoyne."

"I hope not. But you must know that our world isn't kind to demanding women, no matter how just their cause." Cate downed his brandy and rose. "I regret your situation, ma'am, but there's nothing I can do to assist you."

She rose too, needing to steady herself on the back of her chair. "I never expected it, Mr. Burgoyne. I thank you for driving off those ruffians and wish you well."

Her hand was so thin and she was so alone. There was one small way to help. He took two shillings out of his pocket.

"I have only enough money to get me to London on the stage with the simplest food and lodging along the way, but I can spare this if you'll let me sleep here. I'll have privacy and less fear of fleas, and you'll double your day's allowance."

She eyed the shillings, licking her lips. The coins held value to him at the moment, but he had money in London and could earn shillings, and even guineas, in any number of ways. She, being a woman, could not.

"What if anyone found out? I'd be ruined."

Those licked lips could lead to her ruin if he were a different kind of man. Dammit, she shouldn't be alone and unprotected. Perhaps he could seek out her brother. . . .

Insanity. He didn't know the man's surname or location, and had no means of forcing him to do the right thing. And he wanted an uncomplicated life from now on.

"I promise to leave early and carefully," he said.

She bit her lip, clearly fighting with herself, but brandy was a great loosener of standards.

"Very well." She picked up the candle. "I'll show you to my mother's room. I regret that the bed is unaired."

"I've slept rougher."

Before leaving, Cate grasped the hilt of the knife and began to work it out. She stepped away from him, eyes fearful, but he simply freed it and put it down.

"A lesson for you, Hera. You'd have found that hard to do. Be sure you can deal with any results of your angry actions."

She turned and led the way up steep, narrow stairs, resentment in every line of her back.

The road was never smooth for a brave, rebellious woman.

They arrived in a tiny hallway between two doors, dangerously confined in the small space. She opened the door on the right and went in, allowing him to breathe again. Damnation, he hadn't felt such instant, powerful attraction to a woman in years.

She lit the stub of a candle to reveal another almost bare room. The narrow bed would be too short, but it would do.

"Thank you. If I'm gone before you rise, I wish you well, Hera."

"As I do you . . . Catesby."

The flickering light of two candles played strange games with her features and with his mind.

"My friends," he said, "call me Cate."

That ready humor showed. "Does that not cause you embarrassment?"

"I have a sword, remember, and know how to use it."

Again, humor died. "Lucky man."

He wanted to lead her onto primrose paths. Back onto them. She'd been light and merry once; he knew it. Back before whatever disaster had brought her family low. He wanted easy days for her, and frivolity, and ready laughter.

In that, however, he was impotent.

She hadn't left. Cate became breathless again, half hoping, half fearing her intent. Desire stirred, and in that he wasn't impotent at all, but she promised nothing but trouble, and a liaison with a stranger would be disastrous for her.

When she raised her chin and looked him in the eyes, he was still frantically fighting his baser nature.

"Will you kiss me?"

Devil take it, Cate. Don't do this.

"I thought you saw me as a threat."

"We're drinking comrades," she said flippantly, staring at a wall, but then met his eyes again. "I've never been kissed, you see, and now it seems I never will be, so I thought . . ."

He couldn't resist her gallant need.

"The men of Northallerton are fools."

He took the candle from her hand and placed it with the other, and then cradled her face with his right hand. He'd like to run his fingers into her loose hair, but she was already tense and he was too desirous, so he simply kissed her.

One of her hands gripped his wrist, but she didn't protest. Too late he realized she might panic and cry rape and he'd have no defense that anyone would believe.

But she didn't, and he wanted to give her this.

He had no idea how much of a kiss she wanted and doubted she did, either, so he kissed her again, teasing at her lips, hoping she'd open them. She pressed her lips back against his but clearly had no notion what to do.

He could use his thumb to coax her jaw down, to open the way, but instead he simply played his lips against hers. She relaxed, but showed no sign of wanting more. At length, he slid his lips to kiss her cheek, intending to end it there.

Some instinct made him draw her into his arms.

Perhaps he needed that as much as she did.

She was stiff—until she suddenly slumped against his chest, her head tucked down, strength gone. He stroked her back, feeling the thinness of her spine and shoulder blades. It was the gauntness of chronic hunger and it infuriated him.

There's nothing you can do, Cate.

He gently separated them, making sure she was steady on her feet.

One of her hands rose, perhaps to touch her lips, but instead went to her hair, as if she feared it had run wild. "Thank you," she said, not meeting his eyes.

"We should celebrate your first kiss with a feast. I'll go and get some food from one of the inns."

Her eyes shot to him. "You can't come and go," she insisted in a whisper. "People on this street notice things."

"When did you last eat?" he asked.

"A few hours ago."

"You don't eat enough."

"Are you being uncomplimentary about my appearance, Mr. Burgoyne?"

Her high-and-mighty manner made him want to laugh, but none of this was funny.

"I want to help you. Tell me your name and I'll send you money from London."

That had her straight-spined again. "You will not. I'm no charity case, especially of yours. It is for my brother to assist me, and I'm sure he will."

"And if he doesn't?"

"I'm managing, and will continue to do so."

He wanted to shake her.

"Then good night," he said.

"Yes. Good night."

Despite her firmness, she hesitated, and Cate wondered what he'd do if she asked for more, perhaps even for everything.

But she grasped her candle and hurried out, closing the door behind her.

Damn her for a proud, imperious queen, but it was better so. He needed no more trouble in his life.

He pinched out the precious candle, doing his best to pinch out all tender feelings at the same time. A budding Boadicea was no business of his.

Chapter 2

Prudence Youlgrave extinguished the candle to save it, but then sat on the edge of her bed for a long time. All the pain and fury of her brother's betrayal still roiled in her, but on top flowed the soothing sweetness of that kiss.

It had meant nothing. She knew that and didn't wish it otherwise, but it soothed like ointment on a burn. Perhaps the magic came from its being her first kiss, or even from the brandy. If so, she could become addicted.

Perhaps the true magic had been the embrace. Such a feeling of being safe, of warmth within strong arms and a tender hand stroking her.

Her mother had held her tenderly when she'd been a child, but that had ended as she'd grown older. Unhappily, she remembered, at about the time they'd been exiled from paradise. Mother had embraced a positive attitude like a weapon. Perhaps hugs would have weakened her.

In the last months of her mother's life, in nursing her, any tenderness, any protectiveness had been for her to give. In the four months since, she'd relished her independence. She'd lived her days completely as she wished, at no one's beck and call, free to read and to

take country walks as she passed the time before joining
Aaron in Darlington.

Now she had to face the truth. She wasn't independent
at all. She was very dependent on Aaron's three guineas
a month. Without that she'd be in the workhouse—if
she were lucky. They didn't harbor the healthy, so either
they'd find her menial work or she'd be on the streets,
surviving the only way women did in that situation.

Aaron would never let it come to that, but then, she'd
never imagined he could refuse her direct appeal.

She had to press her eyes to stop tears.

Only brandy tears. She'd probably wake in a bad
state as payment, but she couldn't regret the comfort it
had brought. Or the scandalous contact she'd petitioned
from that man.

She hadn't realized how sensitive her lips could be,
that they could tingle like that. She'd not expected the
effect when her lips had parted a little, when they'd
breathed together. When something—something tightly
coiled inside her—had stirred in a most disturbing way.

She'd wanted to press closer then, to try to kiss more
deeply. Thank heavens he'd stopped. But then he'd
drawn her into his arms. Oh, it was heaven to feel so
safe and secure for the first time in ten years. Perhaps, in
that particular way, for the first time in her life.

"A foolish illusion," she muttered, shocking herself
out of madness with sound. Impoverished, drunken
Catesby Burgoyne was no source of security.

That embrace, however, was a reminder of her purpose.

She would have a husband. That was her right, the
unspoken debt that Aaron owed her. She would be a
married woman, with a respectable position in decent
society, a home to manage, and children to cherish.

And a man to protect her, kiss her, love her, and embrace her. A sensible, worthy man, she reminded herself as she undressed down to her shift and got into bed. Not a drunken adventurer. A solicitor like Aaron. A doctor or clergyman. She might not mind a merchant of the more respectable sort.

A gentleman of the gentry, with a country property? A country property like the one in which she'd once lived ...

No, she would not be a foolish dreamer. Those days were gone. A decent gentleman of Darlington would suit her very well.

She woke to sunlight shooting through the ill-fitting shutters. Awoke to awareness of complete folly. She'd let a man into the house. Let him *stay* in the house overnight! She must have been brandy-mad to do that.

And to do the other.

She touched her lips as if they might be different, but then rushed into her simple clothes and peered out. The door of the other bedchamber stood open and the room was empty. A pang of sadness brought the sting of tears.

Idiot!

The question was, what had he stolen? Or was stealing now—she heard a noise below.

She crept downstairs armed with only her wooden candlestick, but there was no sign of the dangerous Mr. Burgoyne. Only Toby, wagging his tail.

Rather than stealing, her scandalous guest had added to the two silver shillings that lay on the table. She picked up the silver tiepin, turning it in the sunlight. The head was formed like a tiny dagger.

She studied it as if it could reveal something about him, but if it did, it was only that he enjoyed violence.

She should be angry that he'd left it when she'd declined his charity, but she closed her hand more tightly around it—almost as if it were a loving gift.

A rascal and probably a gamester to be in such straits, but . . . at the awareness he was gone, never to be seen again, something pressed inside her that was almost like pain.

Cate Burgoyne.

A ne'er-do-well, but so tall and strong. So fearless and quick with his sword. The memory of him racing to the attack still made her breathless. So handsome.

What created that quality, handsome? Clean-cut features, a firm mouth, lean cheeks—but it was more than that. It was the whole of him, including the confidence in every line.

He claimed to be short of money, but he wasn't accustomed to poverty. His clothing was finely made and in a good state, including a neckcloth trimmed with expensive lace. She knew the value of lace, having slowly sold all they had. He could probably pay his way to London in luxury by selling his bits and pieces and didn't know it.

She shook away all thought of him, put the shillings in her pocket, and hid the pin in the back of a drawer. Then she built a small fire in the hearth to boil the kettle. After some bread and a cup of dandelion tea, she took out one of her last sheets of writing paper, trimmed the pen, and sat to compose exactly the right letter to Aaron.

She'd completed only one careful sentence when Hetty Larn came in through the back door. "Here's yer bread, Miss Youlgrave."

Prudence put her letter aside. "Thank you, Hetty."

"It's no trouble, miss."

Hetty was slim and homely, but had a brightness about her that astonished Prudence. How could anyone be bright when living in the poverty of White Rose Yard? Perhaps Aaron saw it as draped with roses, even in March, but the name came from the property on the High Street whose land this was.

The tavern called the White Rose.

Hetty lived next door with her husband, Will, and her two young children, who were grinning from against their mother's skirts. Toby trotted over, tail wagging. Giggling, the children knelt to play with him.

Prudence's mother had had a kind heart, but even so, wherever they'd lived, she'd insisted on keeping a distance between them and their lower-born neighbors. On her own, Prudence had been unable to be discourteous. This row of cottages in White Rose Yard all backed onto a narrow common area where some grew vegetables or kept chickens, and everyone hung out washing. Front and back doors stood open in fair weather, and neighbors came and went.

The day after Prudence had moved in, Hetty Larn had knocked at the front door. Prudence had learned that was appropriate for a first visit. There was etiquette, even in White Rose Yard.

Hetty had offered a small pile of fresh haverbread, the oat pancakes eaten by the poor here more often than wheat bread. Prudence had been taken aback, but she'd known it was kindly meant, so she'd accepted the gift with thanks.

From there she'd slid—downhill, her mother would say—into familiarity. It was a kind of business arrangement, however. Hetty baked extra haverbread for her, and Prudence looked after her children for an hour or so now and then.

She'd found children a surprising amount of work and had come up with the idea of teaching them their letters to keep them out of mischief. To her surprise, they enjoyed it, and the boy, Willie, was quick and clever. Hetty was over the moon.

Prudence took down the package of teaching materials she'd made, and the children ran over to scramble up onto two stools at the table.

"It's good of ye to teach 'em, miss."

"It's good of you to bake for me, Hetty. I've never quite found the way of it."

"'Tis easy enough. I could teach ye."

Prudence smiled, but it covered a spurt of outrage. She'd never need to know how to make haverbread, or any sort of bread. She was destined for better things.

"I could teach you to read, Hetty."

"Me! Lawks, miss, there's no point in that. But there's likely other parents here who'd be happy for ye to teach their little 'uns."

"Set up a *school*?"

Hetty stared, as well she might when she had to know Prudence's poverty. But to set up a school would be even worse than becoming a governess. It would confirm eternal, scrimping spinsterhood. It would be defeat.

"I don't expect to be here much longer," Prudence said. "Now that the first part of my mourning is over, I'll soon be moving to live with my brother in Darlington."

"Oh, that's a shame, miss."

Prudence bit back a response and turned to the table, where she unfolded the package to reveal the alphabet. Each square of paper held a letter and a little picture. There were other pieces of paper with words on them.

She gave each child a word. "Now find the letters that make up the word, dears." She put a brown pottery dish in front of each child, sprinkled it with flour, and put a pen-size stick beside it. "When you've made your word, try to write it in the flour."

Willie immediately took the stick and carefully formed "cat."

Hetty looked on adoringly. "Such a treat t'see them making letters, miss."

"They're both clever children." In fact little Sarah showed no great signs of cleverness, but Willie was clearly capable of achievement if he'd been born into another station in life.

"Oh, I meant to ask," Hetty said. "Are y'all right after last night?"

Prudence froze and turned slowly to face the other woman. "What do you mean?"

"We 'eard old Mr. Brown calling for sum'un to stop what they were doing. Will looked out, but there was no one to be seen. But this morning old Brown said as 'e were sure people 'ad been lurking in the shadows outside our 'ouse and whispering as if up to no good."

"Truly?" Prudence said, eyes as wide as she could make them. "Has anyone's house been broken into?"

"Not so far as I know, miss, and I'm glad you weren't disturbed. Well, I'll be off. Some jobs are so much easier without little 'uns around. You be good, young Willie and Sarie!"

She left and Prudence blew out a breath. She'd been slow in writing her letter because her mind had wandered so often to dashing Cate Burgoyne, but he'd been part of her insanity. Last night could so easily have left her with a tarnished reputation, which would have meant the ruination of all her hopes.

She sat down with the children, resolved to think no more of him. She'd finish her letter and send it off. Aaron would see the justice of her complaints and invite her to live with him in Darlington after his marriage. There, she would be able to find a suitable husband.

A good, worthy man of her own station, not a high-born wastrel like Cate Burgoyne.

Two weeks after she'd sent her letter, Prudence accepted that her brother was ignoring it.

Now she couldn't see why she'd thought he'd do otherwise. He'd always been able to put inconvenient obligations out of mind. The number of times she'd had to nag him into doing his schoolwork!

She'd never imagined that he could ignore her plight, however.

When he'd attended their mother's funeral, he'd been disparaging about their little house on Romanby Court, as if its limitations had been their fault. When he'd made a similar remark about the furniture, she'd told him directly that the better pieces had been sold to pay the doctor's fees.

His response? That she should have managed better.

Prudence knew now she should have demanded more at the time, but she was accustomed to "investing in his profession," as their mother had put it, and she'd been sure it would be for only a little while. . . .

She'd moved to White Rose Yard—the cheapest place she could find—to wait out the earliest months of mourning and the final months of Aaron's training. She'd been careless with money until recently, when Aaron's silence had begun to worry her.

Toby, always sensitive to trouble, whined, looking up at her so sadly, so fearfully. She didn't know if he'd been timid before the accident that had taken his leg, for that was when she'd given him a home, but he now seemed always to fear the worst. She would *not* be a Toby. She'd write again. Aaron had always needed things put straight to him. She took down the writing materials, but Toby whined again, eyes pitying.

"You're right. What point in repeating myself?"

But where did that leave her? Scraping by in White Rose Yard on a guinea a month, or setting up a dame school, where she'd teach the rudiments of letters and numbers in her home and be paid in eggs, bread, and cabbages.

"Y'all right, miss?" Hetty asked cheerfully, in the universal local greeting.

Prudence brushed away tears. "What are you doing here, Hetty?"

Hetty flinched at the sharp tone. "I just popped in with some extra greens from me dad." She was holding a big spring cabbage.

Prudence almost snapped something about charity cabbage, but manners stopped her, and after that, common sense. She needed charity.

"I'm sorry, Hetty. I was just . . . upset. Thank you. You're very kind."

"It's not much, miss. Growing well this spring, the greens." She cocked her head. "I don't mean to intrude, miss, but is there anything I can do to help?"

Prudence deflected. "Where are the children?"

"Me mother came with the greens. She's 'appy to look after them. Have you had bad news?"

Prudence wanted to say no, to smile, to protect her pride, but the truth burst out. "I've had *no* news. My brother is ignoring me."

"Yer brother? The one in Darlington?"

"He's a solicitor."

Prudence had said it with defensive pride, but instantly saw her mistake.

Hetty's jaw dropped. "Why're ye living 'ere, then?"

Prudence wanted to pour out her grievances, but pride, burdensome pride, made her say, "He doesn't have room at the moment. He's to marry and then he'll have a house provided by his father-in-law."

"Still an' all, ye should be living better than this."

"It's costly to set up as a lawyer."

"I suppose that's likely, miss. But he's to marry, you say. All'll be right then. He and his wife'll welcome you there, especially when there're little 'uns."

"You mean they'll want an unpaid nursery nurse."

"Family to 'elp out and be company," Hetty explained.

"Would you?" Prudence asked.

"Have one of me sisters living with us? Or Will's sister? It'd be company, wouldn't it, whilst Will's at work, and a sharing of the tasks. But they're all settled on their own—all but little Jessie, who's a maid over at the 'all."

Impossible to explain that life for Prudence in her brother's house would not be such a cheerful blending. She'd be happy to be company for his bride, a Miss Susan Tallbridge, but not to be a poor relation, destined to be grateful and to prove it by taking on any task given her.

"When's the wedding, then?" Hetty asked.

Another startling question. Prudence had no idea. "Soon," she said, but with growing excitement.

The wedding! Why hadn't she thought of that? Aaron would have to send her the money to travel to the wedding and to buy new clothes so she wouldn't shame him. The wedding would correct everything. She'd mingle in the best Darlington society, for Aaron's bride was the daughter of a well-to-do merchant.

Her lighter spirits made her sorry for being sharp earlier. "Will you call me Prudence, Hetty? And would you rather I call you Hesther?"

The young woman laughed. "Don't ye go doing that, miss. I mean, Prudence. I'd not know who ye meant."

She was blushing. Was it wrong to suggest such intimacy? "If you'd rather not . . ."

"Nay, I'm 'appy to be 'etty." Then she giggled. "'appy to be 'etty!"

A wife, a mother of two, and still four years younger than Prudence's twenty-six and able to giggle like a girl.

Hetty cocked her head. "Sorry if ye don't like me mentioning this, Prudence, but yer 'ands are rough for a lady. Can I give you some of me cream?"

"Cream?"

"Mother makes it. Fleece oil and 'erbs, mostly. A bit smelly-like, but it softens rough skin right well."

"You already give me enough for the little I do."

"This is just friendly-like. If that's not presuming too far."

When it was put like that, Prudence couldn't refuse, and she noticed that Hetty's hands were in better condition than her own. Hetty did a great deal more rough work.

"No, of course not."

Hetty beamed. "I'll go and get ye some right now."

When she'd gone, Prudence smiled with new hope.

The wedding. Her doorway to a better life. When she went to Darlington for that, there'd be no point in returning here. Her life would change overnight.

She'd need a new gown, more than one, but probably Aaron truly was still short of money.

As soon as Hetty brought the pot of cream and left again, Prudence went upstairs to take her one good gown out of the wooden chest where it lay carefully folded in muslin among herbs. She'd plunged all her other gowns into a black dye bath to provide mourning, but held this blue one back.

Her one good gown, but four years old.

She spread it on her bed and considered it. She'd

worn it only for church and for Aaron's rare visits, so it was fairly well preserved. The hem was worn, but if she turned it up just a little that would be hidden. She held it to the light of the small window. The cloth was faded from the bright blue it had once been, but perhaps that wouldn't be obvious, and the muted color was more suitable for mourning. It would be less than six months since Mother's death.

She should stay in black, but the blue gown was plain, and clearly Aaron thought their time of mourning was past. Could she even add some pretty trimming? Braid, beads, and ribbons were expensive, but if she bought thread, she could embroider the gown. Black and another shade of blue.

Even thread and good needles cost money, however.

She took out the shillings, considering them as if they were talismans. Then she nodded, put on her shawl, and went out to the shops.

Three weeks later, Prudence stormed out of her back door and in through the open one next door. It was the first time she'd entered Hetty's house, and she would never have imagined doing so uninvited, but she had to speak to someone.

Hetty was on her knees attacking a big tub of some sort of laundry. She blinked up at Prudence and then began to rise.

"No, don't . . ." Prudence said, but it was all wrong to have Hetty on her knees. "I mean, please, if you want. I'm sorry. I shouldn't have just barged in."

Hetty was already standing, wiping her hands on her apron. "Course you should. The blankets can soak."

"Blankets."

"Nice warm, windy day. Good for the blankets' annual wash. Is something up, luv?"

That was still new to Prudence, Hetty's use of the casual "love." It seemed to suck her deeper into White Rose Yard, but she'd been so sure she'd soon leave that it hadn't mattered.

She sat on one of the stools at the plain table. There was only one chair and she knew that would be for Will, the man of the house. Men—the masters of all.

"My brother is married."

Hetty looked at her blankly, but then gasped. "Without you there! Why would he do that?"

"Why would he not?" Prudence said bitterly.

"But you've been working so 'ard on that gown."

Prudence wished she'd not come here, not revealed her hurt.

Hetty took down a couple of pottery beakers and a stoppered jug from which she poured.

"That's not gin, is it?" Prudence asked, assailed by memories. Since that night, she'd drunk what remained of the brandy in guilty sips at her lowest moments.

"Gin?" Hetty exclaimed. "As if I would! It's me mother's cordial. It'll raise yer spirits." She sat down opposite Prudence, pushing one beaker over.

Prudence sniffed and smelled mostly herbs. She sipped and first tasted a sickly sweetness, but then she coughed. "Raise my spirits. It's full of spirits!"

"Just Mother's 'omemade wine. It's the 'erbs that do you good, though."

Prudence swallowed some more. "I'll be a tosspot at this rate."

"Go on with ye. Now, tell me wot's wot. You 'ad a letter?"

Prudence took another drink. "From, would you believe it, my brother's wife. Regretting that I was unable to attend, but desirous of relating all the delights of the day."

"That's good of 'er, then."

"Good! It's a taunt, pure and simple. Every detail of the fine company, the elegant wedding breakfast, her gown, Aaron's new suit of clothes, their new home . . . All were pins aimed at my heart."

"Oh." Hetty sipped more of the cordial.

"It's true. She'll have been the one who said who could and could not be at her wedding. She must be the one who doesn't want me in Darlington."

"Yer brother could stand up to 'er if he wanted."

"Maybe not. She brings a good sum of money, and her father's influential in Darlington."

"Still, your brother's the man of the house."

Prudence sighed. "Am I still making excuses for him? I'm being foolish all around, aren't I?" She sipped some more of the sweet drink. "I'd pinned hopes on the wedding, you see. I would be a lady there and I'd meet his fine circle. I might even . . ."

She stopped her revelations, thank heavens, before admitting her dream of meeting a gentleman who admired her.

She frowned at her cup. "This is a powerful concoction."

"Cures a cold nicely, and the rheumatics."

And a broken heart? Her heart wasn't broken, however, only battered and bruised. It was her dreams that were shattered beyond repair, taking her hopes with them.

She cradled the cup and drank more. "I don't want to live like this, Hetty." She realized that could seem insulting. "I mean . . . it's not the place or the people I mind, but I want more. I want . . ."

"A husband. Every woman does, and every man a wife. But I know it's not easy for a lady like you. Ye can't marry a simple man, but ye need money to marry a gentleman."

"Did you bring money to your match?"

"I brought some linen and me new clothes. And I'm 'ealthy and a good worker, as is Will. He knows 'is trade, and I know how to run a home and care for all in it."

"I know how to run a home."

"With servants," Hetty said, without any apparent intent to insult.

"I run this house," Prudence protested, but then thought of the bread she didn't bake, the blankets she'd never washed, and the moth holes spreading in them. She did dust and scrub, but she didn't make a hand cream, roast her own dandelions for a hot drink, or keep chickens.

"I do know how to run a house with servants," she agreed. "When we lived at Blytheby Manor I helped run our part of it. I helped to care for the finer items, such as the best linen, the glass and china."

All of which was gone. Except her mother's favorite vase, and the two glasses out of which she'd drunk brandy with a rascally rake . . .

Hetty was staring at her, wide-eyed. She topped up their pottery cups. "You lived in a *manor* house?"

"What? Oh, Blytheby Manor. Yes, but not as you think. My father was the librarian there."

"How the 'eck did you come to be 'ere? A manor house. Only think on it!"

Prudence did, too often. She thought of the suite of rooms in which her family had lived, and the estate on which she'd been free to wander. She remembered the feeling of belonging there, almost as if part of Sir Joshua Jenkin's family, and her comfortable acquaintance with the daughters of nearby families. She'd seen herself as part of their society.

After all, though she'd not been born at Blytheby, she'd known no other home. Her parents had moved there when she was two years old. When Sir Joshua had gambled away his money and shot himself, and her family had had to leave Blytheby with only days' notice, it had felt like being cast out of paradise.

She couldn't bear to relive all that, however.

"How did I come to be here?" she asked. "A series of misfortunes."

"How old were ye when this all 'appened?"

Disaster hadn't been completed in an instant, but Prudence said, "Fifteen."

Old enough to glimpse a happy future but not old enough to have embarked on the path. Sir Joshua had promised to hold a party for her when she reached sixteen. Not a ball, of course, but there would be dancing. He'd arranged dancing lessons for her. . . .

She drank some more cordial, swallowing some tears.

Hetty said, "It must be hard to live so grand and 'ave it all taken away. Easier to be where you're born to."

Prudence wasn't convinced that being born to White Rose Yard was an enviable fate, but Hetty had a point. Prudence didn't envy the great of the land—the dukes and earls with their mansions and vast estates. That wasn't her place to be any more than Hetty's would be Blytheby Manor. She simply wanted, needed, to return to her rightful level of society, comfortably one of the middling sort, as her parents had been. If she were a man, like Aaron, she could achieve that through the right employment, but for a woman it must be marriage. The only employment open to her would be the genteel servitude of governess or companion, with no time or place to call her own.

"This is no life for you," Hetty stated. "So what're ye going to do?"

Prudence sighed and stood. "Wash my blankets, maybe."

"I don't mean that! You don't want t'live your life 'ere and it's not right that you do. So what're ye going to do about it?"

"There's nothing I *can* do."

"There's always summat. Why not go to Darlington and talk to your brother face-to-face? There's many a man who'll slide by what's right until brought face-to-face with it."

Prudence remembered thinking the same thing.

"It's sixteen miles. I can't afford the coach fare."

Hetty screwed her face up over this. "Will's uncle Frank drives a cart up there and back three times a week. He'd take ye along for a couple of pence."

"I couldn't...."

What if Aaron rebuffed her? She wasn't sure she could survive such heartlessness, such obliteration of hope.

But she suddenly remembered the Burgoyne man rushing at her attackers. Then later, the way he'd swiftly opened the door to her house and pushed her in, thus avoiding their being caught whispering together in the street.

Fearlessness.

Prompt action.

Attack.

Her innards quivered, and it was probably the cordial speaking, but she said, "I'll do it, then. I'll go to Darlington. I will have my justice."

Hetty grinned and toasted her. "That's the way of it, Pru. You go and tell 'im wot's wot."

Chapter 3

Darlington

It rained on the way to Darlington. Not heavily, but
enough to dampen Prudence's spirits and her clothes.
Frank Jobson gave her some sacks to cover herself, but
rain spotted the skirt of her blue gown.

Prudence had thought carefully about how and where
to confront her brother. Not at his home, where he'd be
under the eye of his wife. Not at his office, either. She'd
relish shaming him before others, but it wouldn't serve
her purpose.

Thus, she would wait in the street at the time he would
emerge to walk home for his dinner. Her sister-in-law's
letter had obliged with the information that dear Aaron
came home every day to dine with her at one.

If he rebuffed her, she would not be put off. She
would find out where his father-in-law, Mr. Tallbridge,
lived and try to speak to him. If Tallbridge wasn't available, she'd leave the letter she'd carefully composed,
laying out the injustices of her situation. She'd tried to
phrase it without bitter complaints against her brother,
but she'd made a point of the possibility of embarrass-

ment for Tallbridge's daughter if her husband's sister came to grief.

She was fully prepared, and was even wearing Catesby Burgoyne's silver pin for courage, but she dearly wished she weren't arriving in Darlington damp.

She said farewell to the carter and set about learning her way around the town, enjoying strolling through the streets just like anyone else. No one here knew she lived in White Rose Yard, and her clothing was of decent quality. In the eyes of strangers she was a respectable woman going about her respectable day.

She found the tall, terraced building that housed the legal firm where her brother was employed, and then, having time to spare, sought out his new home.

It was a small house, almost a cottage, and the front door opened directly onto the pavement without steps or railings, but it looked neatly made and suitable for a young couple starting out in life.

It would suit Prudence too, and surely now, before children, there was space. In such a house there would be ample food and she could regain her looks. From such a house she could move in Darlington society and find a husband, especially if Aaron provided a dowry.

He clearly wasn't at all penny-pinched. In fact, he would now control his wife's money.

She pushed away anger at that and concentrated on her future.

She returned to the busier streets looking at the goods displayed in shop windows and making imaginary purchases for her future home. That pretty flowered china. That striped material for curtains. That lovely carpet for the drawing room.

She mentally bought more trivial indulgences—a needle case, a book of poetry, a bouquet of flowers—

imagining the day when she could afford to make such
simple purchases without a thought.

She could remember times like that, when she and
her mother would visit York and her father would give
her a few coins, telling her to buy some pretty fripperies.

Pretty fripperies.

What a lovely thought.

She hovered in front of a haberdashery, tempted by
blue ribbon that would match the embroidered edging
on her gown. It would vastly improve her plain straw
hat. She turned away, but only for now. She *would* be
restored to her proper place in life, and soon. Even the
clouds were moving on, carrying away the lingering threat
of rain. When the sun broke through, Prudence saw it
as a sign that it would be just as Hetty said—when confronted, Aaron would do the right thing.

At a quarter to the hour, she stationed herself near her
brother's employment, trying not to look conspicuous.

A portly gentleman emerged in company with another of his age and they strolled away. Two lads came
out, laughing, and hurried away.

An aproned lad went in with a big basket covered
with cloth. Someone in the narrow building was having
dinner brought to them. Aaron? No, surely fate could
not be so cruel.

When the church clock struck a quarter past the hour,
however, Prudence fought tears. She'd built up her courage for this, but now she'd have to return to White Rose
Yard defeated.

No. She touched the silver pin in her bodice. She'd
brought it for courage, and as a reminder of Catesby
Burgoyne.

Don't dither. Charge in with weapon and battle cry.

She didn't have any weapons, but she wouldn't give
up so easily.

If Aaron wasn't at home, she'd tackle his wife. Yes. Walking briskly on, Prudence resolved that Susan Youlgrave must see reason when confronted with it.

The house looked just as it had before, but now seemed more daunting. Prudence again touched the pin for courage and walked across the street to use the brass knocker. After a few moments, the door was cautiously opened by a young maid. "Yes, mum?"

"Is Mistress Youlgrave in?"

The girl, clearly inexperienced, blinked. "Yes, mum. Who shall I say?"

Why hadn't she prepared for this moment?

Courage!

"Miss Youlgrave, Mr. Youlgrave's sister."

The maid gaped, but then she dipped a curtsy and hurried into a nearby room. Prudence walked into the narrow hall and closed the door, feeling very satisfied with this moment, at least. She was inside, and her resolution was strengthened by everything around. Clearly her brother and his wife enjoyed comfort and elegance, and so would she.

A young woman came out of the room, wide-eyed maid close behind.

"Prudence? What are you doing here?"

Aaron's wife was plain—completely and irredeemably plain, with a sallow, blotched complexion, doughy features, and overlarge front teeth. Perhaps that was why she and her family had favored a quite lowly match.

Prudence might feel sorry for her except that she seemed very sure of herself and her own importance. Her cream-striped gown was simple enough for a respectable young wife at home, but had probably cost many times Prudence's annual allowance. She was also showing no trace of welcome or kindness.

"I had reason to visit Darlington," Prudence said,

taking off her gloves, grateful for Hetty's mother's hand cream, "so of course I came to call. Will you not offer me tea, sister?"

A mulish expression suggested that there was nothing Susan wanted less, but she must see she couldn't throw Prudence out. The Burgoyne approach was working.

"I'm dining," she said.

"How kind. I'd be delighted to join you."

Susan's eyes narrowed, but with calculation, not animosity. She was not at all stupid, and proved it.

"How kind, sister," she said, even managing a toothy smile. "Anne, bring another cover."

Savoring her first victory, Prudence followed into a dining room. It was small, as it would have to be in this small house, but well furnished and with a table that, extended, could seat eight at a pinch. Suitable for the rising young solicitor to entertain his colleagues and other worthies of the town.

"How lovely," Prudence said. "Did you and Aaron choose the furnishings together?"

"My father and I. Aaron is too busy for such matters."

"Is my brother not at home?" Prudence asked as she sat. "I did hope to see him."

"He's away today," Susan Youlgrave said with a glint of satisfaction. "In Durham in connection with some marriage settlements."

An hour ago Prudence would have thought that a tragedy, but now she was sensing this might work to her advantage. Her sister-in-law was probably as selfish as she'd thought, and certainly wished Prudence back in Northallerton, but she was clever enough to grasp the situation. And, Prudence hoped, to understand a subtle threat.

"What a shame," Prudence said as the maid hurried

back with dishes and cutlery. "I hope to be more fortunate next time I visit Darlington."

Pay heed, sister. I'm not lurking in obscurity anymore.

Lips closed over teeth, but then Susan said, "Would you like soup? I've already had it removed."

It had doubtless been excellent soup, if Prudence were to judge from the dishes before her, which were in danger of making her stomach rumble, but she said, "I'll join you in the main courses, sister."

Susan's lips curled up in a smile. Her eyes remained calculating.

Struggling not to show her eagerness, Prudence helped herself to the fish dish. She recognized collared eels, and the first mouthful was so delicious that it firmed her already hard resolve. Such excellent, well-prepared food was part of her rightful place in the world.

"You have a good cook."

"You're too kind, sister. She's only a plain cook-housekeeper. We'll soon require someone more skilled as Aaron rises in his profession. So what brings you to Darlington?"

"Some minor purchases," Prudence lied. "Thank you for your letter describing the wedding. I wish I'd been able to attend."

Susan's eyes narrowed again. She was accepting the essentials of the situation and the implied threat, but cannily waiting for Prudence to make the moves.

Let her wait.

Susan uncovered three more dishes. Cutlets in sauce, cooked spinach, and—wonder of wonders—peas. How long was it since she'd eaten fresh peas?

They both served themselves, and then Susan bluntly asked, "What do you want?"

Prudence decided on truth. She and her sister-in-law were unlikely to ever be on good terms, but perhaps they could deal on honest ones. Susan wanted her out of her life, and Prudence would be only too happy to be so, as long as she moved into her own home.

"I want to marry."

"You have a suitor?"

"I find Northallerton lacking in that respect."

"How odd. Please take wine, sister."

Prudence hesitated, for she'd never drunk real wine. In better days, she'd been too young, and since her father's death there'd been no indulgences. She'd had a little of Hetty's mother's sweet country wines, and, of course, brandy.

With Cate, as she sometimes weakly let herself think of him. She felt a familiar squeeze of foolish longing, but pushed it down and poured pale wine into her glass. Catesby Burgoyne could be at the far end of the earth by now. His only part here was as inspiration—to be bold, to be fearless. To win.

She sipped the wine. Less sweet than the brew made by Hetty's mother, less magical than brandy.

"There is the matter of a marriage portion," she said.

"You have none?"

"You must know that I do not."

Susan concentrated on her food. "It's not my husband's duty to provide you with that which your father neglected."

"Is it not?"

"Aaron can't afford it," Susan said, and put food in her mouth as if something had been settled.

"Oh, dear. I hoped to hear better of his fortunes." Prudence savored tender cutlets and sweet peas. "However, if he's struggling to become established, it's surely even more important that his reputation, and that of his family, be unquestionable."

Susan shot her a narrow look. "Your reputation is tarnished?"

"Not yet, but people might be surprised to hear that I must keep a dame school to survive."

"Aaron sends you an allowance and you seem to be doing well enough on it."

"This is my only decent gown, sister. It's hard to remain decent on three guineas a month."

"Three guineas a month?" Susan quickly hid her shock, but clearly she hadn't known the amount. Now she was thinking even more intensely. It certainly wouldn't enhance her husband's reputation for it to be known that his sister lived in such poverty.

She ate another mouthful and then asked, "What sort of husband do you require?"

Prudence managed not to smile, but she silently toasted Cate Burgoyne as she sipped her wine.

"I don't aspire too high, sister. Merely a prosperous gentleman of good social standing who will provide me with a home to manage and children to raise and love."

"High enough for a lady without a dowry," Susan said dryly. "And though Aaron is doing well in his profession, he isn't yet in a position to be generous."

Prudence ate and waited.

"It is possible my father might be persuaded to provide a modest sum," Susan said at last. "Seeing as you are, in a way, now connected to him. My father is a very rich man."

Prudence smiled, just enough, she hoped. "That would be most kind of him."

She drank a little more wine and decided she liked it very much. Wine would soon be part of her daily fare, along with pretty china, rich carpets, and all the ribbons she could desire.

She and her sister-in-law would deal well together, completely based on their own selfish interests. All that was needed now was courage and resolution to complete the journey.

As she put down the wine, she mentally stroked the silver pin.

All she needed was to remember Cate Burgoyne's bold courage.

And forget nearly everything else about him.

Chapter 4

London
June

"'Struth, Cate, I fear I shall have to cut your acquaintance."

Cate turned in surprise. "Perry? What the deuce are you doing here?"

"Seeking you," said the honorable Peregrine Perriam, surveying the room, brows raised. "Bagnigge Wells? My poor, poor friend."

Cate knew what his friend saw—people of the middling sort along with a few ragged fringes of nobility drinking tea or the medicinal waters, or strolling about exchanging greetings and gossip.

He supposed he was a ragged fringe, except that he'd invested in fine new clothes. His suit of blue braided in bronze might seem finer than Perry's one of plain green cloth, but those who knew would see court grandeur in every line and detail of the green.

Damn him to Hades. Had he come here for amusement or to meddle?

"I'm assured the waters are delightfully salubrious," Cate said coolly.

"Feeling bilious?"

There was no hiding it. "Feeling amorous. Behold, Georgiana Rumford—in pink with blond lace, eighteen years old and only daughter of the very wealthy Mr. Samuel Rumford, oil merchant."

Georgiana stood in conversation with her mother and a number of other women, but she looked across at Cate and blushed. Though rather round and rosy, she was pretty enough. Unfortunate that Georgiana chose that moment to wiggle her fingers at Cate in a coy greeting, and even more so that she then turned to giggle with her companions.

"My dear friend . . ." Perry murmured.

"Her portion is large, and it's been hinted it'll be increased for the heir assumptive to an earldom."

"Your brother could sire a son anytime in the next ten years or more. He has girls already."

"I assume Rumford sees it as a worthwhile gamble for the chance to see his daughter a countess. As for me, I must marry money. You know that."

"Have I advised against it?"

"Then why come here to interfere?"

"Even my devotion to your welfare would not bring me to Bagnigge Wells. A messenger arrived from Keynings. Wouldn't state his business, but stressed its urgency. He'd had some difficulty in locating you," Perry added in mild reproof.

"I hadn't found time to tell the family that I'd moved in with you."

He hadn't communicated with Keynings at all since his explosive departure. They were doubtless content with that. So why the messenger?

"Drastic news, I suppose, so it must be Mother. Merely ill, or dead?"

He should feel more, but they'd never been close,

despite his bearing her family name. Perhaps because he bore the family name. He resented it, and she didn't think he lived up to the Catesby standards.

"You could have directed the messenger here," Cate pointed out.

"I thought to spare a Yorkshire lad becoming lost amid the wilderness of Islington, so I made the sacrifice. Bagnigge Wells," Perry repeated, and shuddered.

It was largely humorous affectation, but Cate felt sure his friend had not previously visited this area. He was a creature of Mayfair and St. James's.

"Did I mention urgent?" Perry said.

"I'll take my farewells."

As Cate crossed the room to Georgiana and her mother, he couldn't help feeling grateful of an excuse to leave. If only the Rumfords were fond of music, art, or antiquities rather than gossipy gatherings of their own sort.

He and Perry were soon in a hackney and heading toward the distant smoke that marked London. Zeus, how he longed for the country.

Perry regarded his perfectly buffed fingernails. "You know I don't interfere, my friend, but are you quite sure about La Rumford?"

"Yes."

Perry sighed. "Where will you buy your estate?"

Cate had shared his plan with his friend, so he had no reason to feel irritated. "Rumford favors somewhere near London, but larger properties come cheaper farther north."

"As far north as Yorkshire, perhaps?"

"Why not?"

"It might be possible to be too fond of your family home," Perry suggested delicately.

"Do you feel no pining for Herne?"

"Never been any point. Fourth son, and now Pranks has a couple of his own."

Pranks was Perry's oldest brother, born with the heir's title of Viscount Pranksworth and destined one day to be the Earl of Hernescroft.

"In any case," Perry said, "the country bores me, whilst Town and court do not."

"You can afford Town and court."

"The charm of sinecures. Perhaps your brother would purchase a couple for you."

"My brother and I parted on less than amiable terms."

"Will it be difficult to return? You had, as you described it, a flaming row."

Cate hadn't thought of that. "Plague take it. If Mother's seriously ill or worse I'll have to go north, won't I?"

Be required by filial duty to go north.

Have an excuse to return to Keynings, where he might be able to mend fences with Roe.

His brother, Sebastian, Lord Malzard, was known in the family as Roe from the heir's title he'd been born to—Viscount Roecliff. Roe was six years Cate's senior, so they'd never been close, but Cate regretted being at odds, and, in particular, being an exile from the home he loved.

He'd been away in the army for years, able to return on furlough only once, but he'd always known Keynings was there, waiting with tolerably open arms. . . .

"You never did say why you quarreled," Perry said.

They were leaving the small fields behind and traveling between cottages.

"Mostly it arose from my pride," Cate said. "After the debacle, I was allowed to sell my army commission in the normal way, but the story behind it spread. I'd been chronically insubordinate, come close to mutiny, and caused a riotous brawl in which three men had died."

"Not exactly true."

"Three men did die," Cate said flatly, "but even without that it wasn't an interpretation easy to contest, especially as no one spoke of it openly."

"A few spoke of it openly to me."

"Ah, so that's why you called Willoughby out."

"Dammed coward retracted his words."

"But it silenced open comment. Thank you."

"How did all that lead to your being alienated from your family? They couldn't have believed—"

Cate laughed. "They certainly could. They showed it by being intolerably understanding. Roe assured me that Keynings was my home—without meaning it for a moment. We're flint and steel at the best of times. He's so damned righteous, and feels that as head of the family he takes Father's place in our relationship."

Cate made himself stop that line of complaint. If Roe despaired of him, he had reason. Even now, courting Georgiana, Cate knew he'd be marrying to disoblige his family. They would not find it pleasant to have to mingle with the Rumfords. Would his mother be able to bring herself to embrace Georgiana and call her daughter?

He took up his account. "Artemis, my sister-in-law, raised the possibility of future professions or business enterprises—fretfully, as if doubting I could find one. Mother . . . Ah, Mother was openly peeved that I was back to bother her again."

"'Struth!"

"We've never been close. The army had offered me one other choice—a regiment about to set sail for India. She couldn't see why I hadn't taken that opportunity, as fighting seemed to be the only situation in which I could bring credit to her family name."

"She said that?"

"Crisply and clearly."

"Why didn't you?" Perry asked. "You did gain admiration in the war."

"My dear friend," Cate said in imitation of Perry's drawl, "India is my Islington, far, far from all I value and enjoy."

"All the same, not surprising if your family didn't understand."

Cate's teeth clenched. Beneath his family's "understanding" he'd recognized the lifelong conviction that he was destined to make a pig's dinner of anything he turned his hand to. They had some reason. He knew that.

There'd been his brief attempt at studying for the Church, ended by too strong a taste for pretty women, strong drink, and action. He'd followed that path only with the dream of becoming rector of St. Wilfred's, the closest parish to Keynings.

After that, his father had found him a place with the East India Company, which was newly expanding into power and wealth. The possibility for adventure had appealed, but when he'd faced the fact that he'd be sent to the far side of the world, he'd found a way to get thrown out. There'd been true reason to protest the company's greed, but he'd picked that fight to escape exile.

Only later had he discovered that exile had been his father's intent.

He'd been twenty-one then, and he'd reencountered Perry in London, so he'd settled into enjoying life—without the means for it. When the debts threatened to drown him he'd been at his father's mercy.

That was when his father had spoken bluntly. He didn't believe in second sons hanging around the family home as if they had a right to it. It was unhealthy for them, and led to discord. The older son and heir was already married and father of one healthy child—a girl, but a boy would follow. Cate must make a life for himself, one in no way connected to Keynings.

He'd been ordered into the army.

His father had hoped his regiment would be sent to the Americas—he'd said as much—but in a twist of fate and army politics, it had taken Cate only as far as Hanover to begin with, and kept him in Europe for the rest of the war. It had seemed far enough at the time, though once he'd become accustomed to the army he'd discovered a talent for leadership and fighting.

And, alas, a strong disinclination to follow the rules.

Perhaps he'd have been better off across the Atlantic, where the army had had to embrace irregular procedures to fight in an untamed land. He'd showed a natural talent for irregular procedures. What was more, the end of war hadn't ended all action. Disgruntled colonists seemed likely to create trouble soon, and the native tribes were objecting to invasion of their lands. Even if there wasn't another war, the Americas presented a land to conquer and estates to be carved out.

But it wouldn't be England, and any estate, no matter how large, wouldn't be Keynings. Perhaps it was insane to be marrying money in order to create a pale imitation of paradise, but it was the best he could do.

The hackney disgorged them outside the building just off St. James's Square, where Perry had rooms. The location was admirably situated for court, clubs, parks, and all London's pleasures, and "rooms" didn't do justice to the extent of his residence. His home was staffed by his valet, a footman, a man-cook, and a lad of all work, and furnished in the height of elegance.

As he'd said, the wonders of sinecures, three of which brought him a handsome income.

The messenger from Keynings was sitting upright in the tiny reception room, his three-cornered hat clutched in big hands. He rose instantly.

"Jeb," Cate said, trying not to show inappropriate pleasure, for it was clear the news wasn't good.

Jeb Littlefair came as close to a friend as possible between a groom and a son of the house. They were of an age, had played together as boys and ridden together as youths. Two months ago, during the fateful visit, Jeb had always accompanied Cate on his long morning rides, relaxing into first names and informality.

"Sir!" Jeb swallowed. Yes, the news was bad. And then he said, "Milord . . ."

Cate stared, wanting to say all sorts of idiotic things about silly mistakes, its not being true, or even that Jeb was speaking wicked lies, but he knew. If Jeb had addressed him as "my lord," his brother was dead.

At only thirty-two, Roe was dead—leaving three daughters and no sons.

Which meant that Cate was Earl of Malzard, owner of all the earldom contained.

Including Keynings . . .

"Sit down." A hard hand on his arm pushed him into a seat and he heard Perry call for brandy.

Cate managed one word. "How?"

"Not exactly sure, sir . . . milord. Sent me off immediately, they did, to ride 'ere with all speed. But as I heard it, the earl just collapsed and died."

A glass in his hand.

He drank and the spirits broke the shock a little.

"When?" he asked hoarsely, and took another drink.

Jeb rubbed his head as if needing to think. "Sunday it was, so . . ."

"Four days ago, and I didn't know."

"I rode as fast as I could, sir."

"I'm sure you did. Horses can't fly." Cate drained the glass, trying to think. One thing was clear. "I must set off immediately. I'll be too late for the funeral, but I must make all speed."

"I'll order a chaise," Perry said. He topped up Cate's glass and left.

Cate turned back to Jeb, trying to make sense of the unbelievable. "He just collapsed? How could he just collapse?"

"I dunno, sir. His lordship did say as he'd 'ad 'eadaches. When he came to the stables that very morning he said something about cursed 'eadaches and perhaps riding'd cure them."

Cate surged to his feet. "No one dies of *headaches*!" He reined himself in. "I'm sorry. I won't take it out on the messenger. How much sleep have you had?"

"I had to stop for a few hours every night, sir."

"I'm sure you did. Get a good rest now."

Cate took out some coins. They were most of what he had to hand. Except now he was rich. Very, very rich. Unless Artemis was with child . . . Damnable that the thought caused a sense of loss.

"Go to the Star," he said, giving Jeb the money. "It's just around the corner and a decent place. Rest well; then take a coach home."

"I'd rather travel with you, sir. I mean . . . begging your pardon, sir, but you shouldn't travel alone."

"You think me incapable?" Cate asked angrily.

"No, milord. But—"

"Don't use that title. It's not settled yet."

Jeb stared at him.

"It's possible my brother's wife might be with child."

Perry had returned. "I'll accompany him north. Take your rest, man. You've earned it."

Jeb left and Cate turned on Perry. "Travel to Yorkshire with me? Don't be foolish."

"You won't dissuade me, so don't try."

Cate wanted to, but his mind felt misty.

"Eat."

He looked at the object presented. "A jam tart?"

"My cook insists sweets are better for shock than brandy. Eat it."

Cate obeyed, and the mist did seem to clear a little.

He sat again, sinking his head into his hands. "I can't believe it. I didn't just dream that?" He flinched at his words and looked up. "I didn't want this. You know that, don't you?"

"Of course I do. It's a damned shame. But—"

"Artemis could be with child."

"Yes, that's possible. Whatever the situation, your family needs you."

"I wonder."

"Don't be a damned fool."

It wasn't something to be spoken, not even to Perry, but Cate was sure his family—his mother and sister-in-law in particular—were appalled at the thought of him in control of the earldom. They were probably right to worry. What did he know of the business?

He'd always been carefree—or careless, depending on one's point of view. Impulsive. More suited to action than measured reaction. He'd always known Keynings was better off in his brother's steady, wise hands.

"Better than Cousin Fred, at least."

He hadn't meant to speak that aloud.

"Cousin Fred?" Perry asked.

"My father's cousin. Next in line."

"Bad lot?"

"Not at all. Solid, good-hearted family man. But he'd move into Keynings with his brood and expect Mother and Artemis to move out. Mother in particular would hate that. It's her home."

"Then it's good you're around to take over. If necessary."

That "if necessary" hurt. He truly had never wished his brother dead, but now he feared he might resent a baby boy.

No, he'd make sure not to commit that sin.

And even then . . . If there was an infant Earl of Malzard, Cate would be the natural guardian, with the excuse, almost the requirement, to live at Keynings and supervise its management.

"What of La Rumford?" Perry asked.

Cate almost said, "Who?" He was ashamed of his rush of relief that Georgiana and her family would have no further part in his life, but there it was. He'd wooed her for her ability to give him what he wanted—a country estate as a substitute for Keynings. He didn't need that anymore, and so he didn't need her.

He was certain she didn't yet love him, though she was definitely in love with the idea of being wife to the brother of an earl. She would probably weep and wail over how closely she'd missed becoming a countess.

Even if she did love him, he knew he'd take the same course.

If he was Earl of Malzard, the one thing he could do right would be to marry a perfect countess. A woman of his own station, one trained in all the duties and responsibilities of high rank, one ready to be mistress of gracious households. She would have dignity and elegance, and be comfortably part of the web of noble families. Even better, she'd be able to help him take his place in that web of social complexities and share the burdens of his new responsibilities.

And, of course, as best as could be judged, she must be likely to produce sons.

Chapter 5

"You need food," Perry said, climbing out of the coach.

They'd stopped at yet another inn for yet another change of horses. Pray God the ones available here were better than the last lot of spavined nags, and the road ahead better than the road behind.

"It can't be far now," Cate said. "We'll press on."

"And you'll tuck into dinner as soon as you arrive? Have sense. Better to face your family with food in your belly."

Even with four horses and a light chaise, they'd been five days on the road. They should have ridden, but he'd thought he'd be able to sleep in the carriage. That hadn't proved true, so they'd had to sleep a few hours every night. Short sleep and hurried meals perhaps hadn't been wise, but he'd been unable to do anything else.

Too late, too late, too late.

But it had already been too late when Jeb set out for London.

Cate was definitely light-headed, so Perry, damn him, was right.

He climbed down, noting that Perry was still in perfect order. His dark gray suit was hardly wrinkled, his linen white, his hair within the confines of its ribbon and bag. Even his nails were buffed to a shine. Cate had always assumed his elegance was the work of his valet, but in a great sacrifice, Perry had left Auguste to follow with Jeb and the extra luggage so he and Cate could travel at best speed.

Perry's clothing was also suitable for mourning, which Cate's was not. For bride hunting, he'd laid out his limited funds on fashionable finery. Perry would have lent Cate anything in his wardrobe, but unfortunately he was half a head shorter than Cate and of a more slender build.

Cate was wearing the soberest clothes he had—his riding clothes. Leather breeches, brown jacket, plain buff waistcoat, and boots were acceptable country wear, but hardly funereal, even with a black band on his arm and black gloves. Perhaps he should attempt to buy some other clothes here, wherever it was. He looked up at the inn sign. The Golden Lion.

He was in Northallerton.

Memory stopped him in his tracks. He turned, and there, surely, was the narrow lane on which Hera lived. Or had lived. If all had gone well with her, she'd be in Darlington now with her brother.

How long had it been? Six weeks . . . No, more . . .

"Cate?" Perry asked.

"Order a meal. I've remembered a matter to take care of."

He had to know. He crossed the wide road between passing coaches. He had money, now. Apart from the earldom's wealth, he had about twenty guineas about his person, all he'd had left, before. If she was still here, still in difficulties, perhaps she'd accept some of it.

The narrow lane looked both better and worse by

daylight. Children played under the eyes of women working and gossiping in their open doorways, but daylight revealed the meanness of the houses.

Which house was hers? His memory wasn't clear and he was attracting attention. The chatter had stopped and wary eyes watched him.

Her house had been on the right and just a few doors in. He chose a door and knocked.

"No one's there, sir."

He turned to a thin, homely young woman who'd come to the open door of the house alongside. "She's away from home, ma'am?"

Now the neighbor was interested, but still uncommunicative. He knew why. A gentleman inquiring for anyone here, but especially a woman who lived alone, could be up to no good. He wished he knew Hera's name.

"Would it be possible for us to talk in private, ma'am?"

Her eyes widened, but then she grinned. "Come on in, then, but we'll leave the door open, and people'll 'ear if there's trouble."

"Warning taken. I mean no offense."

Her door led straight into a small front room, as Hera's had, and in the same way, the kitchen lay to the back, but in every other way this house was an improvement.

The front room was furnished, in simple style but in comfort. There was even a covering on the floor. Some sort of rough carpet made of rags, but better than nothing. The room was clean and dusted and there were even flowers in a jug at the small window. Whatever was cooking in the kitchen smelled good.

Hera's house had felt dismal, but the people who lived here had hope.

He'd long since learned that some of the poor were as clever and quick as others. This young wife was no fool.

"My name is Burgoyne, ma'am, and I'm seeking news of the lady who lives next door."

He hoped she'd supply the name, but she folded her arms and said, "Why?"

"When last I heard from her she was in somewhat difficult circumstances."

"You a friend of 'ers, sir?"

"To an extent."

"She didn't seem to have any friends, sir."

That might be a subtle accusation of neglect, but he'd noted the past tense.

"Has something happened to her?"

"Something always 'appens, dunnit, sir? But yes, she's left. Gone to her brother's in Darlington."

"Ah, then all is well."

Cate acknowledged some disappointment. Hera had sent her letter, her brother had repented of his carelessness, and she was now comfortably situated. He'd wanted to be her benefactor. Wanted her appreciation and gratitude. Now he wasn't needed and had no excuse to linger. Perry would be worrying.

Yet something in the woman's face held him in place.

"I hope her brother's well."

"You a friend of *'is*?"

The emphasis was clear guidance. "'Struth, no! In truth, I have no great opinion of Aaron."

His use of a name changed everything.

The arms unfolded. "Begging yer pardon, sir, but who are you? Prudence never mentioned any gentleman to me."

Prudence. The name didn't suit her at all. Not surprising if Prudence-Hera had concealed their encounter, but he was surprised by the suggestion of conversations, even friendship, between her and this young woman.

"I've been in the army until recently."

That seemed to satisfy her, but she still considered carefully before saying, "She wrote me a letter, sir. From Darlington. The vicar read it to me."

"May I see it?"

Again, he was weighed, measured, and dissected, but she turned and opened a pretty wooden box to take out the obviously precious letter, neatly returned to its original folds. She passed it over reluctantly, so he handled it with care.

The paper was of good quality. Another excellent sign. He glanced at the address on the outside. Hesther Larn, White Rose Yard, Northallerton. The handwriting was neat and without flourishes, but conveyed a distinct impression of the strength he remembered. He unfolded the sheet and suppressed a smile of satisfaction. At the top, as he'd hoped, was her direction.

Prospect Place, Darlington.

An auspicious address.

My dear Hetty . . .

You will share my satisfaction that I am now comfortably settled in my brother's house and already, by his kindness, acquiring a new wardrobe, as fine as could be. I have gone with my brother and sister-in-law to a musical evening, and with my sister-in-law alone to the shops and to stroll in the parks.

I thank you for your many kindnesses.

                              Your friend,
                              Prudence Youlgrave

Prudence Youlgrave.

He had all the details he needed, but they were of no moment. She was miles from here and content, and he had pressing business elsewhere.

He refolded the letter and passed it back. "She does seem well settled. I'm glad of it."

"She was a while in 'ardship, sir," Hetty Larn pointed out.

"I was in the army," Cate reminded her.

"Ma! Ma!" Two small children ran in, excited about something in the lad's hand, a small dog at their heels.

Children and dog halted to stare at the stranger, but then Toby came forward, tail wagging.

"Looks like 'e knows ye," Mistress Larn said.

"We met once. He has no discrimination." She clearly didn't understand. "He doesn't know friend from foe."

She chuckled. "That's the truth, sir. But does that mean you're a foe?"

"No, on my honor. But Toby has no reason to know that. Thank you for your assistance, Mistress Larn." He took out some coins, deliberately choosing two shillings. "May I give you these for your children?"

She studied him a moment and then took the coins. "Thank you, sir. Would you happen to be traveling to Darlington, sir?"

"No, but if you see Miss Youlgrave, kindly give her my regards. The name's Burgoyne," he reminded her.

"Right, sir, I'll do that."

Cate walked back down the yard and crossed the wide high street to the Golden Lion, putting away his irrational disappointment.

Only ten miles to Keynings, his heaven and his hell.

Prudence studied her hands—her smooth, soft, lady's hands—and maintained an impassive face. "Mr. Draydale, Susan? He is a little old."

And fleshy, and robust, which were not in themselves faults, but not really to her taste. Cate Burgoyne was to her taste—lean muscled and strong, and gentle at times. Henry Draydale didn't strike her as gentle.

"He's only in his forties, Prudence, and more than fits your requirements. He rivals my father in wealth and is of higher birth. His brother is a baronet."

But the brother had the manor house, not Mr. Draydale, merchant of Darlington.

They were taking tea in the small room Susan called her boudoir. Prudence had been living in Darlington for six weeks now, and had to admit that Susan had kept their unspoken bargain. Her place in the house was that of sister, not some indigent relative. She had new gowns, hats, footwear, and everything else necessary for her presentation as a lady.

As far as the merchants were concerned, Aaron was paying the bills, but the money came from Susan. In a marriage everything should be his, but by some legal device her brother had only an allowance. The rest of Susan's marriage portion was secured to her and the children of the marriage. Trustees oversaw it, but her father held ultimate command.

Prudence felt for her brother, but didn't blame Susan. In this unfair world, a woman had to seize every chance to control her destiny. As Prudence herself had done.

Henry Draydale, however, was not quite what she'd had in mind.

"He's twice a widower," she said, "and has four children."

"A blessing to have a family from the first, and evidence that you'll soon add your own babies in the nursery. More tea?"

Prudence realized that she'd neglected her cup and sipped. It was cold. True, she wanted children, but Draydale . . .

"I fear he could be a difficult husband, Susan."

"Difficult? Not if you are a good wife."

Good probably meant obedient. Prudence knew she wasn't a submissive woman.

"What did his first two wives die of?"

"Lud, sister, are you imagining a Bluebeard! His first died in childbirth, which is a danger we all must face. His second of some fading disease. An odd, nervous creature, as I remember, though she came from a good family and was well dowered. No wonder he's willing to forgo a handsome portion in favor of robust health."

Perhaps, Prudence thought, she should have resisted the excellent food here.

"Don't tell me you think to reject such a flattering offer!" Susan exclaimed. "In truth, sister, Draydale is better than I hoped for you. Good birth and connections, thriving business interests, and considerable wealth." When Prudence didn't respond, she added, "He currently lives in town, but perhaps, if you wished, he might buy a country estate nearby."

Clearly she'd let slip her wistful memories of Blytheby Manor. Perhaps Susan had already dropped hints to the suitor, for Prudence remembered Draydale mentioning a vague plan to buy a country property when last they'd talked.

That was a consideration, a serious consideration. She'd enjoyed town life, but her sweetest memories were still of Blytheby. Perhaps if she and the children were installed in the country she would rarely see her husband, who did seem to have a finger in every business pie in the town.

"I don't understand you, Prudence," Susan said. "Does he not offer you the respectable status of a well-married woman?"

"Yes."

"A prominent position in local society?"

"Yes."

"A home under your governance, and a family to cherish?"

"Yes."

"And the likelihood of a country estate?"

"Yes . . ."

"Then why do you hesitate?"

Prudence knew why. Because Cate Burgoyne shimmered in her mind, dazzling her to reality and good sense.

What a fool she was! Even if they were to meet again he'd have no interest in her. And if he did, she wouldn't want to marry him—a wild, penniless drunkard. Henry Draydale was sober, rich, and steady.

And, she must accept, no other suitor had come forward.

She'd attended tea parties, soirees, dances, and the theater. She'd met a number of eligible men and some had seemed to enjoy her company, but none had approached Aaron with an offer of marriage. She understood why. Even well fed and groomed, she was no beauty, and her height was off-putting to shorter men. Draydale topped her by an inch or two.

Cate Burgoyne by—

No, she would not think of him, though she did wish there were another suitor.

The portion Aaron—or rather Mr. Tallbridge—had provided was small. She'd thought that perhaps the connection to Tallbridge would attract some merchants, but that seemed not to be the case. Perhaps the sister of a son-in-law—an impecunious and dependent son-in-law—was not of value.

She'd been paraded in the Darlington marriage market and there had been only one bid. If she refused, her

.options were not attractive. Susan and Aaron would have to continue to house her, but they'd have no obligation to be so generous. She'd dwindle into being the sort of poor relation she'd resolved not to be.

Mr. Draydale did seem to be attracted to her, which had to weigh in the balance. It showed in the way he looked at her, and even in things he said. His attention and words sometimes embarrassed her, but she was just being missish there. She knew what marriage involved and would do her part.

Yes, as Susan said, Henry Draydale, esquire, of a respectable Yorkshire family and wealthy through his own endeavors, was precisely the sort of husband she'd bargained for.

"Very well," she said. "If Mr. Draydale offers for me, I will accept."

And I will never let Cate Burgoyne invade my mind again.

Chapter 6

"The old stone cross," Cate said. "When I was returning from school, that was always the marker. Keynings would soon be in sight."

"And a blessing be upon us all," Perry said. "Civilization, a decent bed, and an end to this incessant banging about."

"You insisted on coming."

"I never imagined the roads could be so atrocious, even in the north."

Cate was still looking outside. "Ah, there it is."

On this southern approach, Keynings showed itself on its rise unveiled by trees. When one was traveling from the north, it appeared slowly, as if the trees drew back bit by bit.

"A handsome house," Perry said, "though plain. A modern hand would add pillars and Palladian villas."

Roe had spoken of such things. Cate had hated the idea.

He let down the window so he could see more clearly. It looked well with the lake visible and wildflowers around. The complexity of birdsong made him smile, for it was the music of Keynings.

But then he remembered. How dared he smile? How dared nature celebrate life in the midst of death?

Tears stung his eyes, and not for the first time. He forced them back. Tears might serve him well, persuading others that he grieved rather than gloated, but he'd be damned if he'd weep to meet expectations. In any case, his tears would be over a week too late. The earth must already be settling over Roe's grave.

Perhaps his rush to get here had been a mistake. Given that he could never have made the funeral, he could have lingered a day or two in Town and found some sort of mourning clothes. He could have slept longer on the journey so that his thinking wasn't so fuzzy. He could have eaten with more leisure so that his innards weren't in such turmoil.

All for what?

In an attempt to balance a lack that was no fault of his.

"A pleasant park," Perry said. "Though I dislike the taste for dark trees."

Cate knew he was referring to the dark beech, with its purple-black leaves—one of Roe's prize additions. He, too, thought it jarred with the natural foliage, but he couldn't say that now.

"Suitably funereal. Roe has—had—an interest in exotic trees. We're about to pass some of his more successful imports. Gingko trees, from Japan."

"Charming," Perry said, but perhaps without enthusiasm. Did he, like Cate, think the foreign foliage just a little too bright? While people like his brother imported and pampered gingkoes, good old English oak, necessary for shipbuilding, was in short supply.

Unpatriotic. He remembered saying that to Roe when he'd been here last, but now the thought seemed a betrayal.

But he didn't like the unnatural darkness of that damned mournful beech.

Cate looked the other way, but that showed him the lake and the willow tree, weeping. *Salix babylonica*. He remembered that name because Roe had quoted from the Bible. *By the waters of Babylon, we sat down and wept. . . .*

Damnation. He blinked back tears.

The willow was struggling to live, not being well suited to the northern climate. *I'll keep it alive for you, Roe. Somehow.*

That was his responsibility, now, either as owner or guardian, to care for all of this—for the lake, the trees both native and imported, the grazing deer, the carefully planned gardens, and every damn blade of grass.

And Keynings, a long dun-brown stone building of simplicity and dignity set amid gardens in full spring charm. For the first time Cate realized that the sun shone in a clear blue sky. Nature never mourned, a fact made brutally clear in war, but he wished for rain.

"How old?" Perry asked.

Yes, he did need to talk of ordinary things. "Most of it, seventy years. The fountain garden was constructed to celebrate Roe's birth."

Perhaps that was why no water flowed. Might it not have been more suitable for Neptune and his twining fish to weep?

The fountain was surrounded by a circular knot garden, and the graveled drive curved around it. The coach followed that route and drew up at the base of the wide steps that led up to the tall front doors, upon each of which hung the Earl of Malzard's escutcheon, draped with black.

He'd not seen those before. He'd been too far away and too engaged in action to return when his father died.

With precise timing, the doors opened and four footmen marched out in the green Malzard livery, all with black armbands and wearing black gloves and stockings. Too many footmen for the simple tasks of opening the chaise door and receiving Cate's and Perry's valises, or dealing with the two small trunks in the boot.

Did that mean he was considered the earl? Or was everything in abeyance, awaiting Artemis's word? As he'd hastily packed in London, Perry's footman had taken a letter to the House of Lords. It had informed the officials there of the death, and asked for clarification of inheritance law. The answer had come that it was for the peer's widow to declare that she was, or might be, with child. Barring that, the title and all appertaining to it passed to the heir assumptive.

So what had Artemis said or not said?

One footman opened the door. Another pulled down the steps. Cate felt a shameful temptation to huddle inside, almost as if he faced the gallows. Noblesse obliged, however, with the relentless force of a millstone driven by a river in flood. He climbed down.

Immediately, a gentleman in sober dress stepped forward to bow. "Welcome home, sir."

So all was still uncertain.

The speaker was the house steward, ruler of the domain, but what the devil was the man's name? Not Threaves, the one Cate had known as a boy, and who now lived in comfortable retirement in rooms in the north wing. This brisk, fortyish man had been here during his visit two months ago, but now he couldn't remember the name.

Grief should excuse the lapse.

"Thank you," Cate said. "My friend Mr. Perriam accompanies me."

He made himself walk up the steps without a backward look. No need to pay the postilions. The steward would take care of that. No need to carry his possessions. More than enough willing footmen.

No need to worry about Perry, who could always take care of himself.

Relieved of all burdens except the most onerous, he need only walk and talk and be . . . what? How did he balance the possibilities that he was the earl, or guardian to a future baby earl?

He passed through the hatchmented doors and into the entrance hall. It might have been comforting if it reminded him of his boyhood. He'd been happy then. During Roe's reign, however, he'd refurbished this space in the modern style. The oak paneling had been stripped out and replaced with pale gray walls, faux-marble pillars, and reproductions of Grecian statues in blue niches.

That and other changes had come as a shock two months ago, though Cate hoped he'd hidden it. He'd been able to honestly say that all was elegant and the equal of anywhere, but he'd mourned the old Keynings. During his years away the idea of cozy, old-fashioned Keynings, dark with paneling and alive with his father's dogs, had been a comfort in a chaotic world.

His mother wasn't here to greet him, but he hadn't expected that. No unseemly displays in front of the domestics. She'd be in the drawing room upstairs. Cate turned to Perry and the steward, whose name still eluded him. That seemed an ominous beginning.

"I'll leave you in good hands, Perry. Kindly see to everything," he added vaguely to the steward, and set off up the solid right-angled stairs, savagely pleased that Roe hadn't had time to rip them out and put in a lighter curved design that he'd spoken of.

In fact, nothing had changed in the two months since he'd been here last.

Except everything.

If only he hadn't left in anger.

The drawing room door was closed, but a footman stood nearby and moved to open it. Cate went through and heard it close behind him.

This room, too, had been brought into modern style, but here it was a happier result. Pale walls and bright upholstery caught the light of the three long windows hung with ivory curtains. The lighter wood of modern furniture suited the new design.

His mother sat on one yellow-upholstered settee near the central window, a book in her hands. Roe's widow, Artemis, sat on another at a right angle to it; she was engaged in stitchery, the piece of white cloth stark against black. Both were in deep mourning clothes, their faces etched by their recent loss.

He was etched, too. Did it show as clearly?

On the journey he'd struggled to find the right words for this impossible situation. To offer condolences would imply that he didn't feel the same degree of grief. To express his regret at the possibility of inheriting the earldom would put them in an awkward situation. How could they respond? To ask whether Artemis might be with child was impossible.

He bowed. "Mother, Artemis, this is a sorry matter."

His plump mother responded with a sad smile—and perhaps a wince at his garb—and extended a hand. "Indeed it is, Catesby, but we both know you will do your best."

If only she didn't sound as if his best could not possibly be good enough.

He took her hand. "I've come with all speed, Mother." *Dammit, apologizing already?*

"It happened without warning," Artemis said quietly. "I, too, could have been away. I took the children to Galgarth Hall last month. . . ."

He turned to her gratefully. "There truly was no warning?" Devil take it, tears swelled in her eyes. "My apologies. I'm sure you don't want to speak of it."

"No, it's all right," she said, and blew her nose with a black-edged handkerchief. "But please sit, Catesby. You're so tall. Just like . . ."

"Malzard" hovered in the air. Artemis had always called her husband Malzard in public. He and Roe had been close in height, though Roe had always been less broad. In truth, he'd been thin despite a healthy appetite.

Cate moved a chair and sat between them, perhaps hit hardest by Artemis's deep, quiet grief. Whatever trials she might have expected in life, her husband's death so young could not have been one of them.

Roe had chosen the perfect wife—not a beauty, but a woman of pleasing appearance and kind heart who possessed all the grace and poise necessary for her position. She was a Howard, from that powerful Yorkshire family, though quite far on the family tree from the Earl of Carlisle.

She was also—or had been—a good-humored woman, perfect foil to Roe's sober side. That glow had been extinguished. Though she seemed calm she was drained of lightness, and despite her assurances it seemed she couldn't speak of the death.

"Something in his head," said his mother harshly. "We should have sent for the doctor sooner, but it was only headaches."

"There was nothing to be done." Artemis looked at Cate. "He complained of the headaches only in the last days, though I suspect he'd suffered in silence for a while. They grew in intensity, defying even opium, which is when we grew alarmed. But by the time Dr. Selby arrived . . ." She inhaled and controlled herself. "A blood vessel burst in his brain. There was nothing anyone could have done."

"I wish it had been me."

Cate regretted the words immediately. They must agree, but could hardly say so.

"It was God's will," Artemis said, setting another stitch, "and He will support you in your new burdens. We sent word to you immediately."

Was she apologizing?

"I came as speedily as possible, but we're prisoners of reality. No will in the world can shorten distances or make roads smooth."

As he spoke, he was wondering whether his sister-in-law's words could be taken as a declaration that no child was possible. How did he ask?

As if she picked up his thoughts, she said, "I'm not with child." Staring somewhere beyond him, uncomfortable to be speaking of such things, she added, "I had my courses last week, and . . . I am not with child," she repeated firmly. "You should assume the title and responsibilities of earl immediately."

Cate had no idea whether a woman could be mistaken about such things, but if Artemis didn't want this hanging in uncertainty, he understood. She would very much dislike everyone paying close attention to her intimate affairs.

"Very well. Some announcement must be made, for the household and the neighborhood."

"I'll attend to that," his mother said. She reached into her right pocket and took something out. "You will want these."

He rose to take the two rings—the earldom's signet ring, and a black ring with a design etched through to silver. Roe's mourning ring. Any gentleman who'd attended the funeral would have received one.

Cate didn't want to put them on, but he did, feeling Artemis in particular grow more tense. How hard this must be for her. She'd even stopped setting stitches. His mother's mouth was tight.

Cate thought that came from gloom over his capabilities, but then he realized it might be because fate had given him power over both women's lives. He could, in theory, order them out of the house to live in the long-unused dower house. Or even send them away from Keynings entirely.

"Everything shall be just as you wish," he said.

His mother looked pained. Lord save him.

"I mean nothing else need change unless you wish."

Artemis said, "Thank you. Keynings still feels like my home, and of course it's the only home my daughters have ever known."

"It is your home, their home. Permanently."

"You're very kind, but your wife's feelings must be taken into account." It sounded like an explanation to a simpleton.

"I'm not married."

"But you will be," his mother said.

"Yes, but . . . I assure you, I won't marry anyone who would distress my family."

This conversation was worse than slogging through marshes under sniper fire.

"And then, in time," Artemis said, finally stabbing her needle into her cloth, "I may wish to live elsewhere."

Remarry. Of course she would. She was not yet thirty.

"You will marry, Catesby?" His mother managed to make a question an order.

"That's not—"

She reared up. "Can you not bring yourself to do even *that*?"

"May I at least sleep alone for one night?"

"Don't be crude!" she snapped. "Everyone will appreciate the necessity for haste with evidence of fate's cruelty so bitterly clear."

"Everyone will expect a decent interval, dammit." He controlled himself. "My apologies, Mother, but truly . . ."

She glared, but then exhaled. "You have the right of it, my dear. I too apologize. It's only . . ." Her lips wobbled and she covered them with her handkerchief.

She was trying so hard. So was he. So was Artemis. They were all straining for a modus vivendi in this impossible situation. The best action now was retreat.

He rose. "Is there anything that needs my immediate attention?"

His mother managed a smile. "No, my dear boy. Everyone here knows their duty. Sleep if you wish. You must be exhausted."

More so now than when he'd arrived.

"A friend accompanied me. The honorable Peregrine Perriam. He won't intrude."

"Perriam?" his mother asked with a spark of interest. "The Worstershire Perriams?"

"His father's Lord Hernescroft, yes."

"Ah."

Cate didn't appreciate finding approval only for his companion. He was tempted to say, "We met in a whorehouse," which would, in a way, be true.

He contented himself with bowing and leaving. The outwardly impassive footman still stood nearby, so Cate allowed himself no twitch. He walked briskly away toward his room.

Then stopped.

Which room?

He'd been going toward the room he'd used as a youth, the room that had still been ready for him on his return, months ago. It would be a refuge, but if he was earl, was he expected to use the earl's bedchamber?

It took only a second to know.

Yes.

The whole point was to have the great change over and done with. He was sure Artemis had already moved out of the countess's adjoining rooms.

With heavy reluctance he turned toward the suite of rooms he still thought of as his father's. He opened the door to the bedchamber feeling as if a great alarm might sound to declare, *Intruder! Intruder!* The door did not so much as squeak, but inside he found a servant—a very proper upper servant in soberly elegant clothing.

Roe's valet.

Hell's guts. Had he misjudged? But if he was the earl, he'd tolerate no petty exceptions. They weren't going to be allowed to preserve these rooms as a mausoleum.

Cate continued his entry and shut the door. "Your name?"

The man bowed. "Ransom, my lord. Your brother's valet."

So this servant had already been informed. Shame. He'd have liked a fight. A rip-roaring fight with a noble cause. Like that aborted vengeance in Northallerton, when he'd been raw from events here. At least Hera had triumphed.

Prudence Youlgrave.

His weary mind was wandering and the valet was waiting, blank faced, for a response. He wasn't sure whether he could endure Roe's valet for long, but he needed someone now. Someone able to turn him out in proper style. When he had suitable clothing.

"Washing water, if you please."

The valet bowed and left and Cate allowed himself to slump.

He rubbed his hands over his face—finding that his hair was already half loose. A fine, bedraggled sight he must be. He pulled off the ribbon entirely as he walked over to the windows to look out at the rolling green landscape. So green nearby, but a patchwork of many shades farther away, showing the different uses of the land and the different crops growing there.

Roe would have known exactly which crop and when it would come to harvest. He'd know which fields were part of the home farm and which were worked by tenant farmers. He'd know the tenants' names and details. He'd been trained for the job from the nursery, and spent decades shadowing his father in the work.

Cate could see the roof of the home farm, and the spire of St. Wilfred's, where he'd once foolishly dreamed of being rector. He glimpsed the roofs of Holmewell village and the scattered farmhouses farther away. All paying rent to the earldom. To him. Would some people feel joy at such possessions? He couldn't. Even if he'd hated his brother, he couldn't, and he hadn't hated Roe. He'd never wanted this.

Liar!

He'd certainly never wished for his brother to die. That, thank God, was true.

He turned to focus on the room. He'd visited here only rarely, and only in his father's time. Strange to think of the number of rooms in this house he'd hardly ever entered. The administrative rooms, for example, which lurked on the ground floor, like a beasts' lair awaiting him. Terra incognita.

Focus on here and now.

The hangings were new since his father's day—blue damask instead of some old, worn, gold-embroidered stuff. His father had cared little about the style of the house and had probably gone along with the place pretty well as he'd inherited it back in 1731. The heavy oak bed looked to be from the seventeenth century, perhaps even from before the civil war, as did the carved chest at its foot.

Those old pieces anchored him. He would never change them.

He walked toward the door that led to the earl's library, as it was called, with its matching oak and shabby grandeur. The "earl's retreat" would be more accurate, for no one intruded without invitation. Cate remembered being "invited" there for what he'd always thought of as audiences with his father.

He opened the door and paused, shocked. . . .

"Ah, there you are. Survived the family?"

Cate froze for a moment, fighting fury at Perry's intrusion.

"As well as can be expected," he said, turning toward the other door, the one to the corridor, which Perry had used. "I'm apparently to assume the honors, my sister-in-law being certain no son will arrive to change anything."

Perry executed a flourishing bow. "My lord earl, then." But he winced. "My apologies. Not the right tone."

"No. I'm accustoming myself to changes of many sorts. I remember this room as smaller. In my father's day the paneling was unpainted and covered the ceiling too."

Perry surveyed it all. "Fine plasterwork up there, and pale green's à la mode for walls. But I don't care for painting fine old wood myself."

"I wonder if such changes can be reversed."

Cate immediately regretted saying that. It was as if he wished to obliterate Roe's time here. As well as take down the paintings his brother had brought back from his grand tour. They looked particularly well against the dusky pale green.

"It looks as if my brother truly studied art and culture in Italy."

"Instead of frivolity and whores, as I did."

"Doubtless what I would have done, but younger sons didn't get such treats in this family."

He idly picked up one of two books lying on the desk, but immediately put it down again. The books must be ones Roe had been reading in the days before his death, perhaps seeking distraction from the pain, but with no suspicion that the pain heralded his doom.

"Have you been taken care of?" he asked Perry, leading the way back into the bedchamber.

"Excellently. What of you?"

"This is my domain, where all is mine to command."

"What, then, have you commanded?"

"Don't busy yourself about my affairs," Cate said brusquely.

"This is not a lair to be explored alone."

"This is my home."

"Then what's through here?" Perry opened the opposite door. "Ah, your lordship's dressing room, and an excellent one."

Perry disappeared into it and Cate followed. He couldn't remember ever venturing into this private chamber, but Perry was impossible to suppress or deter, and yes, if Cate was honest, he was glad not to be undertaking this navigation alone.

He stopped, looking around with genuine appreciation. "This must all be Roe's work. Father would never have indulged in such a huge bath, or had walls painted with scenes of gods and goddesses. Roe liked his comforts."

"Nothing wrong with that." Perry strolled around the bath, which sat on a dais in the center of the room. "And he's left you a bath suited to your length. Now, where does that go?" He hunkered down to inspect something. "A tap for easy emptying, feeding into some room below. Excellent design! May I make use of this during my stay?"

"If you don't mind being eaten. The inside is decorated with a painting of some sort of sea monster."

Cate considered the other furnishings—a chest of drawers, shaving stand, and magnificent clothespress with doors decorated with fine marquetry hunting scenes.

He idly opened the doors and then froze. The press was full of clothes. Full of Roe's clothes. God alone knew what made a person's smell distinctive quite apart from any perfumes they might wear, but it was so, and here it lingered.

"Your washing water, sir."

Cate turned to see Ransom ushering in a footman bearing a large, steaming jug. Both had halted at sight of Perry.

"My friend Mr. Perriam will want refreshment. Perry, why don't you request what you want and await me in the earl's library."

Perry's brows rose at the tone, but he went. After putting down the water jug, the footman followed him. Ransom poured the steaming water into the china basin.

Cate asked, "Why are my brother's clothes still here?"

The valet put down the jug. "The dowager thought that you might have use for them, sir, you and your brother being of similar height."

"But not of similar build. My shoulders would burst the seams."

"I fear your mother didn't realize that, my lord."

What to do with the damned things?

"Have everything packed away and consult with my sister-in-law as to her wishes. Leave me now."

Ransom would be used to attending Roe here at all

times, but Cate needed to be alone and he was well used to taking care of himself, even to darning his own stockings and sewing on his own buttons.

Once he was alone, he stripped off his coat, waistcoat, and shirt and washed, only then wondering why he was being so thorough. Perhaps it was some instinctive baptism. Wasn't there something in the service about entering into a new life? Babies generally howled at the font.

Without hope, he hunted through his valise and trunk for a clean shirt, but found only the three he'd already worn on the journey. By tomorrow they would be perfectly laundered and ironed, any defects repaired so skillfully that they'd disappear.

He could soon have new shirts. Footwear, too, replacing his thin-soled shoes and scarred and scuffed boots. New clothes of all kinds, sober in hue but in the latest style and made from the finest materials.

Like all Roe's clothes in that damned press.

He turned toward it. There'd be pristine shirts in there, and shirts were loosely cut. There was probably unscuffed footwear.

No.

He might have to step into his brother's shoes, but he would not do it literally. In any case, his brother's shoes would pinch. He grimaced at the unintended metaphor and put on the cleanest of his own shirts and neckcloths.

He re-dressed in front of the mirror, attempting the most respectable appearance possible. He used a damp corner of the towel to rub away a mark on his coat and another on his breeches, but there the dampness only made the leather look worse.

He should wear shoes, so he took off his muddy boots, but then noticed the state of his stockings—rubbed dark in places by his boots and with darns obvious. Why hadn't he thought to bring his finer, courting stockings? They, alas, followed with Jeb and Auguste.

There'd be stockings in the clothespress, and Roe's knitted stockings would fit. He considered the scene on the doors of the clothespress, in which dogs were bringing down a stag, and weighed the implications.

He wasn't his brother and never would be.

He was, however, the Earl of Malzard, owner of everything here, including any spotless stockings. What point in denying destiny?

He opened the marquetry doors and explored the drawers until he found stockings from fine to practical, neatly in pairs, spotless as rows of saintly souls. He peeled off his own and put on a pair of his brother's everyday ones, having to struggle a bit to stretch them over his more muscular calves.

A first step, but whether toward defeat or victory, he had no idea.

Chapter 7

He crossed the bedchamber to the earl's library, but found it empty. Perry, tactful fellow, had taken himself elsewhere. He'd ordered food, but for Cate rather than himself, because it was just what Cate would have chosen—fresh bread, slices of ham, local cheese, and a flagon of ale.

He had no appetite, however.

Roe's room, Roe's books, Roe's carefully selected paintings, all shouted "interloper." He had no doubt that if his brother was looking down from heaven, he was either weeping or gnashing his teeth. That might not have been the case before the argument, before they'd both said things to be regretted, perhaps especially because they carried truth.

Roe had sought him out to advise him on his future prospects and behavior.

Cate had resented that—resented his brother's assumption that he had a duty, a right even, to advise him, and that Cate needed it. He'd not intended an argument, however, but it had all spun out of control.

Roe's true opinion of him had spilled out. Feckless. Selfish. Care-for-nothing. Insubordinate. Oh, yes, the army gossips had done their work.

He'd counterattacked—that his brother was spineless, petty, and incapable of achieving anything not handed him on a plate by his being the firstborn.

"You think you could do better?" Roe had snapped. "You must delight in my lack of sons, then." Cate had protested that, but Roe had hardly seemed to hear. "I suppose you held a feast when the one died."

Cate had been stunned, for news of a newborn son's death had never reached him. He'd said that, apologizing, offering condolences, but he'd not been believed. His silence had been taken as satisfaction, and that wound had festered to the point that his brother was deaf to all argument. If he'd tried harder to persuade Roe of the truth could the grand explosion have been avoided?

As it was, their words had grown more bitter and he'd stormed out of the house in a rage. He'd taken a horse from the stables and ridden to Northallerton with only the coins in his pocket, and never spoken to his brother again.

The door opened and his mother walked in.

Shocking rage swelled. Plague take it, this was the earl's sanctum, the place where no one intruded except by invitation. If he had to be the damned earl, he would have that respect, at least.

His mother's suddenly wide eyes stopped him. As if she saw danger. He stoppered up the fury, forcing down the bung, but knowing that if he spoke, only vitriol would pour out.

His mother licked her lips, and perhaps words were hard for her, too. "Your brides," she said, thrusting some sheets of paper at him.

He took them, saved by the oddness of the moment. The first sheet held six annotated names, the second twelve, and the third four.

"A harem?" he asked.

"Don't be ridiculous," she snapped, perhaps as relieved as he to reach familiar sparring ground. "Choice, Catesby. Choice. You've been out of the country for years and I doubt your recent adventures have taken you into circles where you'd meet eligible young ladies."

How surprised you'd be, Mother. As long as eligible included the widows and daughters of rich cits.

"Thus, I have listed the candidates." Despite her plumpness and lack of height, her deportment always suggested someone taller. Now she could have had a ramrod up her spine. "On the first page you will find suitable young ladies in this area. I know each and her family, her qualities, her character, and even the family—"

"Breeding records?" Cate supplied.

She inhaled.

"Why be mealymouthed?" he asked. "The matter at hand is the succession."

"Very well, it is. And I expect you to do your duty."

"I assure you, Mother, I intend to do my duty as Earl of Malzard in every *conceivable* way, but to bring the wrong countess to Keynings would distress you even more than it would distress me."

"Hence the lists. There is no one on there I could not tolerate."

So, you intend to live out your life here, Cate thought. *No dower house for you.* He'd promised her that, but it settled on him grimly. They'd always rubbed each other the wrong way.

"The second sheet is of great heiresses throughout the land," she continued. "The estate isn't in want, but an additional fortune is never unwelcome. However, few of them are known to me. Such a shame you weren't home before Diana Arradale was snapped up."

"The Countess of Arradale?" he said, scanning the

lists, recognizing family names but no individuals. "She'd hardly have been interested in a second son. Who snapped up her and a large chunk of Yorkshire?"

"A southerner. The Marquess of Rothgar." A sniff announced her opinion of that. "I've sent out discreet inquiries about the others. The third sheet is of ladies from families of great political influence. There is, of course, some overlap. I assume you intend to play your part in the House of Lords?"

"I suppose I must, though I'd be happy never to see London again."

She frowned. "You were always a mystery to me, Catesby."

"You're a mystery to me, Mother. You must have begun this work within hours of Roe's death."

Her round face twitched. "Not within hours, but soon. I see the urgency, even if you do not."

Cate remembered how his father had made clear his situation as second son. In this room. Direct, practical, and ruthless.

"You and Father must have been well suited."

"We were. And it was a match arranged by our parents, just as Sebastian's was to Artemis. If you wish . . ."

"No! I'll choose my own bride, Mother, but I thank you for your assistance. I'll look over the lists most carefully and decide how best to proceed."

Her features pinched with exasperation. "Promise me you will choose well, Catesby."

"What, precisely, do you mean by 'well'?"

"A suitable Countess of Malzard."

"Then I have every intention of doing so."

"Good," she said, but still doubtfully. With a final sigh, she left.

Cate looked at the neatly written sheets, realizing he didn't know whether the writing was his mother's or a clerk's. There'd been no occasion for her to ever write to him. The letter bringing news of Roe's death had been written by Roe's secretary, Mount.

Had he inherited Mount too? Probably. It would be like the quiet, middle-aged man to hold back until summoned.

If the neat, firm writing was his mother's, he found it repellent, given that it had been written when her beloved older son was hardly cold.

Cate made himself see the other side. As well as suffering shock and grief over the unexpected death, his mother must have seen herself as clinging to a crumbling edge with only Cate—impulsive, reckless, care-for-nothing Cate, as she saw it—between her and exile from her home of forty years.

If the right marriage made his mother's world safe again, it was little enough to ask, but he found himself strangely reluctant to choose a bride from one of these carefully considered lists.

The next morning Cate woke in the earl's large and very comfortable bed. He rolled onto his back, looking up at the complex pleated sunburst radiating out of a gilded boss on the underside of the bed canopy. He couldn't imagine why his brother had bothered with a decoration that no one but he would see.

And Artemis, perhaps. That summoned depressing thoughts about the names on his mother's list. If there were a way to turn back the clock and restore reality, he'd do it without hesitation. Alas, there was not.

He'd visited Roe's grave and read the carved inscription added to the great stone plinth, trying to come to terms with the change. But he still expected his brother to storm in, furious at this usurpation of his place.

He rolled out of bed and went to the window to raise

the curtains. The sun was only just rising. In London, fashionable life went on well into the night, sometimes till dawn, and the day began again after noon. Last night, however, early to bed had been his only escape, one Perry had also taken. Cate had been exhausted enough to sleep, but for only so long.

A folly to miss so many sunrises.

The sun was still below the horizon, but the sky was bright with the pearly shades of dawn. A hint of mist softened the ground and veiled the more distant trees, creating a scene suited for a fairy dream.

To hell with fairies. He wanted a ride.

He dressed, but carried his boots as he went down-stairs so as not to wake anyone.

Of course people were awake—the lesser servants hurrying to prepare the house before the family stirred. He was accustomed to these lowly minions, having often encountered them on his last visit when heading out for an early ride. Back then he'd been given good-mornings and even cheeky grins, but now they bowed or curtsied, averting their eyes and muttering, "Your lordship," be-fore hurrying on their way.

He owned everything here, but was excluded from the Keynings he'd recently enjoyed. For the first time he realized that applied to the greater world as well. He'd be treated differently everywhere he went. He'd never enter a room without being noticed. Might always sus-pect that people smiled at him in hope of some favor.

Thank God the stables were the same, welcoming him with the tang of horse and hay. One bay horse whinnied in welcome and he went to rub the nose of the horse he'd ridden daily on his last visit. Oakapple was a steady goer with an even pace, a mount kept mostly for use by guests. He could have ridden any of his brother's prime horses, but he'd taken to Oakapple.

A groom came out, but unfortunately not Jeb, who was still en route from London. This one bobbed nervously with too many "your lordships." Cate would have preferred to saddle Oakapple himself, but he let the servant do his job and then escaped into the misty beauty of the new day, alone.

For a while he simply rode, luxuriating in the pleasure of it. Riding in the parks wasn't like riding in the country. The estate was completely familiar to him, for this had been his world as a boy, open for endless exploration. Once he was away from the house it was mostly unchanged. The lake still lapped unchanged at its reed-rimmed banks, and there would still be a secret world on the small treed island if he took a boat from the boathouse and rowed there. The old oak on the hill presented the same branches to climb. The long slope down toward the home farm would be as splendid for sliding on if there were snow.

He was pulled out of memories by a "Halloo!" and turned to see Perry cantering toward him on a showy black Arab.

"I see you chose the best horse in the stable," Cate remarked when his friend arrived at his side.

"If you can't see his quality . . ." Perry replied without offense, for none had been intended.

"I see it perfectly, but Oakapple is better suited to my weight. He and I are comfortable friends."

"Othello and you are enemies?"

"He has too high an opinion of himself." As if to show it, the horse sidled a little and preened.

"Up for sale?"

"I . . ." Cate had been about to say that he'd have to ask Artemis, but that was ridiculous. She would have her widow's jointure, but no other interest in anything here except her paraphernalia, her personal possessions, and those of her daughters.

"I don't see why not. He was Roe's Town horse, for display in the parks and such, so he'll be more at home there."

"I knew we were suited," Perry said, slapping the horse's neck. "An excellent estate."

"Mostly my father's work. He did the major landscaping—he and an army of gardeners."

"That the home farm?" Perry asked.

"Yes. We used to sledge down this slope when there was snow."

"Pity it's June."

"There's an oak to climb. . . ."

"That I can forgo. Rejoice—your sons will enjoy oak and hill just as much as you and your brother did."

"Roe and I were six years apart. We didn't play together."

"Ah, I hadn't realized that. Perhaps you'll plan things better."

"No one can plan the sex of their children, or I'd not be earl. You're close in age to your brothers, aren't you?"

"Less than two years between each of us, which meant we formed a small tribe in our youth."

Cate allowed the vision of lads playing here, closer in age and nature than he and Roe, good friends and a joy to their father.

To him.

He hadn't realized how much that would appeal to him, but children required his countess.

"My mother's prepared a list of brides for me."

"A harem?"

"My remark. It wasn't appreciated. No, merely candidates. The first sheet lists six local ladies. Girls, in fact. One's a mere sixteen."

"Too young."

"Yes, but I'm sure in mother's eyes that means more childbearing years."

Perry grimaced in sympathy. "Know any of 'em?"

"Until the last visit I'd been away for years, and there wasn't time to throw an entertainment before the great rift. I know the families a little, but no, none of the candidates."

"Awkward, isn't it? In normal circumstances your mother would arrange a ball and you'd have the opportunity to assess them all without showing particular attention."

"A ball within weeks of my brother's death would be appalling."

"You need to return to Town. Anyone of importance is there at the moment, along with their nubile daughters. And you have an excuse to be mingling. You need to be presented as the new earl, take your seat in the House and all that."

It made sense, but he had Keynings. Why would he want to be anywhere else?

"I couldn't go immediately. I need new clothes."

"Get 'em in London. Provincial tailors." Perry shuddered.

"I promise to put myself in your hands, but I have urgent need of sober clothing now."

"Oh, very well. Summon the local excuse for a tailor and I'll advise and supervise."

Cate laughed, shocking himself, but then realizing that it was healthy. Life must go on.

However, talk of London had reminded him of something else.

"Another problem?" Perry asked.

"Georgiana. No promises were made, but news of my becoming earl will start a furor among the Rumfords."

"Let them explode."

"Preferably with the length of England between us."

"Perhaps you should choose a bride quickly. That'll spike their guns."

"A definite consideration," Cate said as they rode on.

Chapter 8

Cate had been back at Keynings for a week, and was doing his best.

He'd put himself in the hands of Flamborough—having discovered the house steward's name—and familiarized himself with the whole house and its running, thanking heaven that it would soon be his countess's responsibility. If, that was, his countess could wrest control out of the hands of his mother and Artemis, who continued to run the place like a well-matched team.

He'd met his three black-clad nieces, aged from eight down to three, and received only solemn curtsies. Heaven alone knew where they played, for he never heard a sound from them.

He'd turned himself over to various other senior officers of the earldom and was beginning to grasp the complexities of his possessions, which included lead and coal mines, ships, and urban properties. At times, he felt as if his head would burst.

He knew everyone would be happy if he simply signed as directed, but that wasn't his way. Ill prepared though he was, he needed to understand what was going on.

His real lack was a secretary, someone knowledgeable about more personal correspondence and Roe's political and business dealings. Soon after arriving, he'd learned that Mount had left after the funeral. Flamborough had not wished to comment, but Cate had pressed him.

"Mr. Mount was devoted to your brother, sir."

"It would seem Ransom was devoted to my brother too, but he's still here."

"Mr. Mount had the offer of a position elsewhere, sir."

"You're saying Ransom stays only because no one else would have him? I doubt that. Mount didn't want to be my secretary."

Flamborough looked into the distance. "He seemed to think that you were sufficiently dissimilar to your brother, sir, that you would not suit."

In other words, Cate translated, the secretary had disliked him. Secretary and employer was a close relationship, for a secretary would often accompany his employer, even to social occasions. He would also be privy to his intimate affairs.

Had Mount shared Roe's belief that Cate had been pleased by the baby boy's death?

It hurt that he'd never be able to put that right, but there was no point dwelling on it. At least Artemis seemed unaware. He'd thought of raising the subject and offering his sympathies to her, but had not seen any suitable way to do so.

As for a secretary, Perry had stepped into the breach, enjoying the game of it. He was particularly useful when knowledge of court and London was necessary, but also had a general knowledge of politics and international affairs. They were going over some correspondence to do with the colonial taxation issue when a footman arrived to request Cate's presence in the drawing room.

"What now?" Cate muttered. In general, his mother and sister-in-law didn't seek his company, which suited everyone.

When he entered the drawing room he halted. It was full of women.

Impatient after only a week, his mother had summoned some of the potential brides, and as she introduced them, she looked as smug as a hen who'd laid a clutch of golden eggs.

Perhaps she'd been inspired to this because he had his first suit of respectable clothing—a sober black suit with jet buttons and only fine silver embroidery to lighten the waistcoat.

Suppressing irritation, he bowed to Mrs. Wycliffe and her daughter, Julia. Beside this name on the list his mother had noted "well behaved." The only word that came to Cate's mind was "bland." Bland fawn gown, bland brown hair, and a bland, almost vacant smile.

Next, Lady Moregate and Lady Corinna Shafto—"vivacious." Terrifyingly unbland, especially as she was the sixteen-year-old. Glossy dark curls, sparkling dark eyes, a perfectly formed Cupid's-bow mouth, along with an aura of energy. She didn't actually sizzle, but perhaps only out of respect for mourning.

He knew before the introduction that the third young lady had to be Miss Armstrong, aged twenty-two, because his mother had noted "awkward, but kind" beside her name. Even sitting still on a settee, she was awkward. No part of her fit well with another, she carried her head slightly crooked, and her eyes moved anxiously, traveling everywhere except to look at him. She must have come with one of the other parties, as no mother was in evidence.

If he were forced to pick among the three, it would

be Miss Wycliffe, because it would be easy to entirely forget she was around.

He was obliged to accept tea and attempt to take part in trivial conversation. Soon Lady Corinna's true nature escaped and she commenced a stream of suggestions of perfectly delightful events that should be organized to welcome him back to the area.

"Mourning, dear," her mother murmured, but with a doting smile.

"Oh, yes." But the young beauty was undaunted and sent him a blinding smile. "As soon as may be, Lord Malzard."

Cate was amused, but not at all attracted. A man wouldn't know a moment's peace.

"As soon as may be," he agreed, and deliberately turned to the awkward one. "What form of entertainment do you most like, Miss Armstrong?"

She blinked. Her eyes shifted. "Something musical," she muttered.

"You play?"

"Me? Oh, no, my lord. A foolish suggestion. Of a musical event, I mean . . ."

"On the contrary. An excellent suggestion. A musical evening is a much different matter to a ball, is it not, Mother?"

"Very different, Malzard."

"Then we will have one soon."

"How wonderful!" Lady Corinna declared, clapping her hands. She ran off again about when it should be, how it should be arranged, and who should play. She, of course, was skilled on the harp.

Cate seized on a break in the torrent to address the third would-be countess. "Will you enjoy a musical evening, Miss Wycliffe?"

"I'm sure it will be very pleasant, my lord."

"Will you play?"

"I lack the skill, my lord."

"But she sings beautifully," insisted her mother.

"Then I look forward to that," Cate said, but the thought of encountering the rest of the candidates made him ready to put a bullet in his brain.

When the guests took their leave, his mother said, "Well?"

"That gathering was inappropriate, Mother."

"If I do nothing, nothing will happen!"

"Will you hover over the marriage bed, advising and prodding?"

"Catesby!"

"I apologize. But please allow me more time before contriving more meetings."

Her lips tightened with frustration. "Very well. But this has done no harm. You've met three of the local ladies, and all would be suitable."

"You would be comfortable living under the same roof as any of them?"

Her eyes shifted, but she rallied. "I will be comfortable once there's a son in the cradle here."

"Then you'll have an uncomfortable year or more, ma'am, no matter how assiduously I apply myself."

He stalked out of the room, regretting the words and the exit, but at the end of his patience. He had to get away from here.

He went to his room and, without summoning Ransom, changed into his old, familiar riding clothes. Replacing them had not been a priority, and putting them on released some of the tension inside him. He'd be better after a ride. Better able to return to the yoke.

He slipped out of his room like a truant schoolboy.

He thought of inviting Perry to ride with him, but he needed to be alone for a while. Somehow these days he was never alone except in bed.

He fully understood Hera now.

Prudence Youlgrave.

She'd gone foolishly into the night because she'd felt as if she might suffocate inside. She'd fled a small house, while Keynings offered space and air enough for anyone, but the inhabitants oppressed his spirits.

Hera was in Darlington, with her brother. Who had at best been careless of her welfare.

How did she fare there? Was she well fed and well dressed? Had she made the good marriage that had been her dearest desire? Was she happy?

He'd like to see that.

He entered the stables, and one of the dogs came to greet him. They'd become friends and he was beginning to think about bringing a couple inside. Roe hadn't liked dogs in the house, and perhaps Artemis and his mother didn't either, but he liked the idea, and he was the earl.

Suddenly he remembered Prudence's dog.

Why hadn't she taken Toby with her to Darlington?

There were any number of reasons, not least that she didn't want the charity case anymore, but it jangled in his mind.

Darlington was only ten miles. He could ride there and settle his mind about her welfare. He didn't have a single coin in his pocket, so he slipped back into the house. This time, Ransom was in the bedchamber, but he couldn't question his master's actions.

Cate sent him on an errand and then opened the hidden safe. He took a few guineas in case Oakapple went lame or such, and some small coins to pay for refreshment. Before he left, he remembered one more thing. He unlocked the box where he kept private papers and some valuables, and took out a bottle.

It was a pretty thing he'd purchased in London, made of blue glass in a cleverly wrought silver mesh. It was too large to be a perfume bottle, so he'd asked the shopkeeper its purpose.

"It's a flask for a lady who likes to keep some medicinal brandy on her person, sir. Fits in a lady's pocket, you see, and flat so it don't show."

"What does it hold? An eighth of a pint?"

"Thereabouts, sir. A lady wouldn't want more."

"Some might," Cate had said, and bought it.

He'd been thinking of Hera, but with no expectation of giving it to her. Later, he'd wondered what to do with the thing. Georgiana would have been shocked by such a gift, medicinal or not.

Had fate known this moment would come?

That thought made him hesitate, but he put the flask in his pocket and returned to the stables, having to hide a kind of glee at this adventure.

Jeb had Oakapple ready. "You want me to ride with you, sir?"

"No. But I might be a while." Hades, he was the earl. He couldn't disappear without a word.

Yes, he could. For a little while.

"I'm riding to Darlington," he said as he mounted. "On business. Personal business."

"Ah," said Jeb with a suppressed grin, assuming it was a woman.

It was, too, but not like that.

"A pleasant journey, sir."

"I hope so."

Cate rode away, and when he left the estate, he

couldn't stop a grin of pure pleasure. He still loved Keynings, but he needed escape too.

He took off the earl's signet ring, immediately feeling unshackled.

He was free. For a short, blessed while, he was simply Cate Burgoyne again, and free.

Chapter 9

He arrived in Darlington in the late afternoon, but with the long June day he had plenty of time to find out about Prudence Youlgrave and return to confinement. The ride, mostly cross-country, had been wonderful, and he reveled in the ordinary world around him.

Here, he wasn't the Earl of Malzard, but simply Cate Burgoyne, made even less of note because of his shabby riding clothes. Amusingly, when he dismounted at the Talbot Inn on High Row, the ostler looked as if he doubted his ability to pay his shot.

"I'm not staying the night," he told the man. "But I'll leave my horse here."

He sweetened the man's mood with a sixpence, and set off for Prospect Place.

In the past, it had probably held rough cottages, but now it was lined with neat new buildings with fresh paint and sparkling windows. They all opened directly onto the road, but each had a short rise of stairs to front doors enhanced by pillars and portico.

He found the house, and it matched the others in respectability.

He considered knocking and asking to speak to Miss

Youlgrave, but a visit late in the day would only raise questions in her brother's mind. She clearly was not in difficulties and had no need of him.

He strolled back to the inn, smiling wryly at being disappointed yet again. He'd hoped to see her in her triumph, but that wasn't to be.

He could stay overnight and seek a meeting tomorrow. That would be a different matter to calling late. He could pay his respects, claiming some slight acquaintance in Northallerton, which would be close to the truth. Probably Prudence Youlgrave, happily restored to her natural state as prim sister of Mr. Aaron Youlgrave, solicitor, would explode any lingering fascination.

The town clock struck six.

He had time to eat, and Oakapple deserved his rest. There'd be recriminations when he returned and they'd be worse the later he was, but nothing would be improved by his being tired and hungry. He ate in the dining room at a common table, enjoying a tasty soup and the company of ordinary people. When the next courses were slow to appear he muttered a complaint.

"They'll be along soon," said a cheerfully round gentleman who'd introduced himself as Stimpson, a candle merchant. "Got a big do here tomorrow, and the kitchens are in a fuss."

"No cause to stint us," said a younger man with a square, ruddy face, who'd grudgingly admitted to the name Brough and to working in mining. "Our money's as good as anyone's."

The only other person at the table was an elderly woman who was keeping to herself, as if she feared that being at a table with males would be her ruin.

"Not as good as Tallbridge's," Stimpson said. "It's his daughter as is marrying."

"Tallbridge?" said Brough. "I wish I were marrying his daughter."

"Not his daughter, sirs," said their waiter, at last spreading dishes on the table. "His son-in-law's sister."

Cate managed to catch him before he rushed away, and ordered two bottles of wine. Pleasant to be able to afford generosity.

The two gentlemen took a glass with pleasure, but the silent lady shook her head. She enjoyed the food, however, as Cate did.

"So they're having a wedding breakfast here," he remarked, to get the conversation going again.

"That's it, sir," said Stimpson. "Tallbridge has a fine house on Houndgate, but he's a very private man, Tallbridge is. It's a rare few who are invited into his house."

"Born in a farm cottage," muttered Brough. "For all his airs and graces."

"To be praised for rising by his own endeavors, then," said Cate. "And he hosts the reception for the couple. That's well-done of him."

"Indeed it is," said Stimpson.

"Currying favor with Draydale," said the disagreeable young Brough. "Mr. Draydale, you see, sir, comes from a *good* family. His brother's a sir."

"So the lady's marrying a gentleman. Let's toast the bride!"

The men raised their glasses, but Brough said, "Draydale's only a merchant, when all's said and done. And that Youlgrave, he'd be nothing if he hadn't charmed Tallbridge's pudding-faced daughter."

Cate hid sudden, sharp interest.

"Sir, I find your comments disrespectful to any lady."

The young man glared at him, red faced, but then

pushed back from the table. "I'll find better company elsewhere."

Cate shook his head. "Is he an unlucky suitor?"

"I doubt it," said Stimpson. "More the sort who can't bear to see anyone rise in the world while he's stuck in his place."

"And stuck there by his own disagreeable nature," Cate said, filling the other man's wineglass again.

So, Prudence truly had triumphed. Tomorrow she would wed an excellent husband—a man born to a good family and now prosperous by his own endeavors. After the service, she'd be feted in style at the best inn in town.

"To the bride," he said again, and Stimpson joined him in the toast.

Talk turned to the American colonists, who were making unreasonable objections to paying their share of the recent war, but Cate's mind was playing with temptation.

He'd like to see Hera triumphant. He'd like to give her the brandy flask, but it certainly wasn't a suitable wedding present. He could watch her arrive at church, however, a happy bride. It would be truancy indeed, but he couldn't resist.

He discovered that the wedding would be at the fashionable hour of eleven, and asked the best way to send a message to Richmond, the closest town to Keynings. A coach would go that way in an hour, so he wrote a letter explaining that he was staying in Darlington for the night and would return tomorrow, and made all the arrangements for its dispatch.

"Keynings," said the innkeeper, when Cate handed over the letter and the money. "Why, you'll be connected to the family, sir, being a Burgoyne."

"Yes."

"Sad business, the earl dying so suddenly, sir, and him a young man still."

"Yes."

Cate's tone shut the man up and he went away.

It shouldn't surprise him that such news was all around the area, but would anyone yet know the details of the succession? He hoped not. He wanted to remain in pleasant anonymity.

He took a room for the night and settled to a game of whist with Stimpson and a couple of local men. As the stakes were low and the company amiable, he went to bed well pleased.

After breakfast, he paid his bill, but left Oakapple at the inn for a while and wandered the town until it was time for the wedding.

St. Cuthbert's was an ancient church well surrounded by trees, so he could mingle with others gathered to see the bride arrive and not be too obvious. He stationed himself close to a clutch of women, pretending to have come upon the moment by accident.

"A wedding?" he asked.

"Aye, sir," one woman said. "The bride's coming from Mr. Tallbridge's 'ouse."

That obviously gave the event cachet.

"The bride is his daughter?"

"Nay, sir. His son-in-law's sister."

"And the groom?"

"Mr. Draydale, sir."

Had he imagined something odd in the woman's tone?

"A young man?"

"Nay, sir, gone forty and buried two wives."

"Poor man."

The women gave him a look, and indeed, perhaps

there should be some sympathy for the wives. There was something else in the look, however. Did they have doubts about Mr. Draydale, gentleman, who had become prosperous through his own endeavors? He was certainly older than Cate had expected.

"What sort of man is this Draydale?" he asked.

"A gentleman, sir. His brother's Sir William Draydale, of Draydale Manor."

So by fortune of death Prudence could even become Lady Draydale one day. Doubts churned in him, however.

Cate, the woman's no fool. She'll have made this choice with clear eyes. Even if this Draydale's not an ideal husband, she'll have all the things she wanted, and her life will be much preferable to scrimping by in White Rose Yard.

A coach came jingling up from the street to the church door, the two horses bedecked with bells, ribbons, and flowers. When it stopped, a footman got down from the back to open the door, and a distinguished older gentleman with powdered hair stepped down and turned to assist someone.

The bride.

Cate blinked, needing a moment to adjust his image of Hera.

Her gown was a splendidly fashionable sacque in buttercup yellow embroidered with spring flowers. Her pale hair was swept up beneath a frivolously pretty flat straw hat circled with more blossoms. She'd filled out, and only a filmy fichu covered the swell of generous breasts above a low, embroidered stomacher. Her profile was still strikingly classical, but with the extra flesh she could almost be called beautiful.

And she looked like a marble statue.

She or someone else had attempted to rectify pallor

with rouge on lips and cheeks, but the contrast merely emphasized it. Bridal nerves? They said all brides had them, but Cate wanted to rush forward, to take her by the shoulders and ask, *Are you sure you want to do this?*

What if she said no?

Why should that be? This wasn't the Middle Ages.

But what was this Draydale really like? The man who'd buried two wives.

That could happen to any man. It meant nothing....

All the same, Cate had to act.

The bridegroom would be waiting by the altar.

He stepped back and went to the side of the church, hoping for an alternate door.

There it was. Unlocked, as well. It took him into the side aisle, which was separated from the main one by large, old pillars. The pews in the center of the church held perhaps thirty people, all finely dressed. All notables of Darlington. Another sign of how well Hera had done for herself.

But she'd looked as if she were going to the gallows.

He kept to the side aisle and made his way forward to where he could see the groom. At first he could see only Draydale's back—a heavyset man of moderate height, finely dressed in maroon velvet. His suit was cut in the latest style and his bold stance fit it. It declared to all that he was a prosperous man, sure of his place and his power.

When Cate moved farther he saw the glint of gold braid at the front, and also the man's profile. He had a strong, fleshy face with a big nose and rather heavy lips. Nothing wrong with that. He looked fit, prosperous, and commanding.

Four quiet children sat in a nearby pew, in age from about twelve to a toddler in the arms of a maidservant.

So, Draydale had been looking for a mother for his children. Nothing wrong with that, either.

His groomsman somewhat resembled him, in softer and perhaps weaker form. Probably Sir William Draydale, knight or baronet, comfortably ensconced in a country manor.

Sir William suddenly elbowed Draydale and murmured, "You lucky dog, Harry."

Nothing wrong with that, either, for Prudence Youlgrave had just entered the nave on the arm of a young man who must be her brother. There was a resemblance, though Aaron Youlgrave was brown-haired. On him, the classical features were unquestionably handsome.

Cate looked back at the groom—and caught a disturbing smile. It wasn't loving, or even admiring, but closer to a leer. It seemed almost salivating—like a dog seeing a joint of beef left unattended.

No, Cate.

But the bride had her eyes firmly turned down.

Maidenly modesty.

Or fear.

She'd been completely dependent on her brother's miserly allowance. Was she now under his thumb because of poverty? Would he benefit from the marriage? He, or his born-in-a-cottage, but high-and-mighty father-in-law, Tallbridge? Such slave trading wasn't unknown, where a family persuaded or compelled a woman to marry to their advantage and profit.

In coming to Darlington, had Hera walked into a lion's den? No, "lion" sounded too noble. Had she fallen into a dog pit?

As she reached the altar Draydale bowed to her brother, and seemed to include Tallbridge nearby. To Cate it shouted, *Thank you, sirs. Bargain made.*

The service began. Cate assumed it was the age-old one, but he'd attended few weddings. Apart from some rough-and-ready army ones, he could remember only his sister Arabella's, and Roe's, and in both cases he'd been a bored lad in his teens.

"... if any man knows ..."

Ah.

Cate's heart suddenly pounded, just as it had in battle when he'd seen an opportunity to strike, an opportunity beyond his orders.

No, no ...

But he must do something to stop this travesty.

He was watching Hera, trying to resist rash impulse, when she looked up toward the altar with a desperate plea.

"... of any impediment ..."

It was the right thing to do. He'd never been able to deny that knowledge. He stepped into view of the wedding party.

"... or forever hold thy peace."

"I do," he said, tempted to burst into laughter at the use of the wedding vows.

The vicar stared at him. "I beg your pardon, sir?"

"Who the devil are you?" demanded Draydale, red flushing his cheeks.

"Catesby Burgoyne, sir." Cate bowed, calm now that the moment was on him. It was always so. Wryly, he added, "Not entirely at your service."

"Well, take yourself off! You have no business here."

"Mr. Draydale, Mr. Draydale," soothed the vicar, "the gentleman has raised an objection and must be heard. What is your cause for concern, sir? I'm sure it can be smoothed away."

Cate turned to the bride. She'd been sheet white before, but now color had surged into her cheeks, and her blank eyes were alive with some emotion.

He wished he knew whether it was hope or fury.

Watching her, he said, "I apologize for the inconvenience, Reverend, but I must remind the lady that she is already pledged to me."

Chapter 10

Gasps rose in the church like a flock of starlings, and Prudence's cheeks flamed.

"Miss Youlgrave," the vicar said. "Is this true?"

She opened her mouth and shut it again.

And again.

Dammit, had he gotten it all wrong?

You've only to deny it, he thought at her. *Deny it, please, and I won't be in a devil of a mess.*

But then she found her voice. "Yes," she said, and then repeated it clearly. "Yes, it's true."

Now chatter flew around the church.

"What?" Draydale roared. "You promised yourself to me! You *gave* yourself to me. That trumps any mealy-mouthed promises made in the past."

Her jaw dropped, and then she screamed, *"You lie! You lie!"*

Draydale backhanded her into a nearby pew.

Cate had flattened the man with a blow before he even knew it, and was trying to bash Draydale's brains out on the altar steps when others grabbed him and struggled to drag him off. Someone hit him over the head with something. It did nothing but hurt, but was enough to break the red haze of rage. He let go and allowed rough hands to pull him away. But he snarled, "Get up and fight, you scum."

Alas, the dastard only moaned, half-conscious.

And Hera . . .

Cate tore free and turned to where she was collapsed weeping in a pew, her hand to her face, fussed over by a number of women.

One stood apart. "Really, Prudence," she said in a strident voice. "How could you bring such embarrassment upon our family?"

This pudding-faced woman must be the sister-in-law. And heartless to boot.

Her husband—the brother—chimed in. "Indeed, Prudence. This is a terrible thing."

"It certainly is," Cate said, longing to pummel him as well.

However, the wedding guests were avidly watching and listening, and Prudence Youlgrave could end up ruined by all this.

"Prudence probably thought me dead," he said, going to kneel before her. "My love, I'm sorry I didn't return sooner."

She looked at him, eyes as wide, shocked, and frightened as on the night they'd first met. She let him take her chilly hand, but a close observer would have trouble seeing a lovers' reunion in her face. On top of the shock and horror of the last few minutes, she hardly knew him. He'd just beaten a man bloody. And, devil take it, there was blood on his knuckles.

Plunging in again, Cate. But he could never have allowed the marriage to proceed without protest, and Draydale's brutal action had proved his instincts correct. He rose, pulling her up and into his arms to offer comfort, but also to hide her blank, panicked expression.

"Sir!" protested the brother.

Cate ignored him and murmured in Prudence's ear, "Trust me."

The devil only knew what that meant, but some of her tension left her, despite heaving breaths. He recalled that night and their embrace, which had been strangely sweet and had never entirely left his mind.

"Sir," repeated the brother firmly, "I must ask how you came to be betrothed to my sister without my knowledge or consent, especially as she has lived very quietly for many years."

Cate looked at him over her silly hat. "Aren't you interested in the scurrilous lies that cur just laid upon her?"

Youlgrave flushed. "I'm sure Mr. Draydale didn't mean . . . But your claim was clear."

And must be nailed down with details, Cate realized. What details would hold together, and would Prudence support them? She struggled to be free, so he had to let her go, but what in Hades would happen next?

She turned to face her brother, chin firm and raised. "Mother knew and consented, Aaron."

"What?" the brother exclaimed. "She never mentioned it to me."

"You visited so rarely," she said, a dagger in every word.

'Struth! But the courage of her, the magnificent, resolute courage, but Cate could see the strain all this placed on her. He put an arm around her to help. "Prudence feared you might disapprove, sir."

"Would he have had *reason* to disapprove?" the plain wife demanded, eyes narrowed.

"Perhaps, ma'am. I was a soldier and without much substance."

She took in his clothes. "And haven't improved with time. You have just destroyed a very advantageous marriage. Father, do something!"

Her father's features were unreadable. "I believe we should retire to somewhere more private to discuss this, my dear."

A coolheaded man, Tallbridge. Cate wondered if that would work to Prudence's advantage or not.

The vicar hastily shepherded them into the vestry. Cate kept an arm around Prudence, both to comfort and to compel. She'd stepped in to support his lie, but still trembled with shock. She might collapse, but judging from their last meeting, she could just as easily become as rash and impulsive as he.

The wrong move here could ruin her for life.

When he settled her into a chair he gently touched her cheek. "I'm sorry I allowed this, but your disappointed bridegroom is in much worse shape."

"Then I'm glad of it," she said fiercely.

"At your service, as always."

The vicar murmured something and went out, leaving Cate and Prudence with her handsome, weak-mouthed brother; the brother's acid-tongued wife; and cool, keen-eyed Mr. Tallbridge.

Tallbridge was a merchant, but a different type from both Draydale and Rumford. Perhaps he had been born in a cottage, but by good fortune or effort he had the slenderness admired at court, and the fine features to go with it, all enhanced by impeccably elegant clothing. He even had the speech—almost. The effect must impress the worthies of Darlington greatly, but it didn't impress Cate.

"You must be Mr. Tallbridge, sir," he said. "I must hold you partly responsible for this state of affairs."

"How dare you!"

"Be silent, Susan." Steady eyes met Cate's. "I wished to do well by my son-in-law's sister, Mr. Burgoyne. I still wish the same. You admit to being lacking as a suitor before. Are you in a better state now?"

Cate dearly wanted to declare that he was now Earl of Malzard, but he'd never be believed. Even if these people knew the Earl of Malzard had died recently and been succeeded by a scapegrace younger brother, why believe this man in shabby clothing and worn riding boots was him?

Make a claim like that and Tallbridge could use it as excuse to throw him into jail for impersonating a peer. Then Cate would have to summon someone from Keynings to vouch for him, which would reveal to all there that he'd created another shambles. He'd give himself to the devil first.

But he might have done that anyway.

He'd vowed to marry the perfect countess. He'd promised his mother not to marry to disoblige her. Now, if he didn't find a way out, he was going to have to marry Prudence Youlgrave, the most unlikely countess imaginable.

His silence wasn't giving a good impression.

"I recently came into a property and can now provide for a wife. I sought out Prudence as soon as possible, but arrived almost too late. I wish I'd arrived sooner and spared everyone this debacle."

"As do we all, sir. Is this truly what you wish, Prudence?"

She simply stared. Cate could understand why. She'd supported his lie in the church, but now she'd had time to think, to see all the traps before her.

"Prudence?" Tallbridge prompted. "I must remind

you that Draydale made certain claims. If true, they carry weight."

She blinked, eyes suddenly afire. "They are *not* true, Mr. Tallbridge. They are not." She looked once at Cate and then away. "Of course I wish to marry Mr. Burgoyne. I too regret the disruption our situation has caused, and apologize for it."

"So I should think!" protested the strident daughter. "Did you not come to me petitioning—demanding, even!—that I find you a husband? A man with a good position in society, able to provide you with a home and children. At considerable effort and expense I provided such a husband, and as thanks, you have made me a laughingstock!" She turned weeping into her husband's arms.

Tallbridge sighed. "You'd best take her away, Aaron. There must be some back way."

"But what of my sister, sir? After this drama, she must marry this man, but we know nothing about him."

Perhaps he had some decent feelings after all.

"If you will permit, I'll deal with this. I'll discover his credentials and report to you later. Susan!" At his sharp voice, his daughter turned her tear-blotched face to him. "Think on this. You will be better served by presenting this situation to the world as a romance—lovers reunited, et cetera—rather than as a blow to your plans and pride."

"But Mr. Draydale . . ."

"Draydale has proved unworthy. We have Prudence's word that his claims were untrue, and his own crude action speaks against him. Aaron, I will take your sister back to my house for the night and make arrangements for her wedding to Burgoyne tomorrow."

Tomorrow? Cate shot a look at Prudence and saw the same alarm in her eyes. That left no space for maneuvering.

Aaron said, "Yes, sir," and took his resentful wife away.

Tallbridge offered Cate snuff, but Cate declined, trying to see a path out of this mire.

Tallbridge took a pinch himself, enjoyed the effect, and then blew his nose. "Any connection to the Burgoynes of Keynings, sir?"

"Yes." Had he underestimated such a man's knowledge of greater affairs?

All Tallbridge said was, "Are you quite sure, with your august lineage, that you wish to ally yourself in this way?"

"I hope that doesn't imply any lack in Prudence, Tallbridge."

A brow rose, but Tallbridge said, "Of course not, sir. Of course not. But the expectations of society cannot be ignored."

"Society will expect me to carry Prudence away from here immediately."

If he could get her away, he could look after her without marriage. Establish her with a respectable lady. Discreetly provide a dowry that would buy her the worthy husband she desired.

"Society will expect you to *marry* her, and speedily, especially in light of Draydale's insinuation."

"He did more than insinuate."

"You did more than protest."

"Prudence needs time to recover from the shock and brutality."

"Mr. Burgoyne," Tallbridge said, "you are a stranger to us. Am I, or her brother, to allow you to carry her away unwed?"

It was, damn him, an excellent point.

"Prudence should decide these things. She is of age."

"Women are easily duped, or led astray by their hearts. It is for men to guide them."

Cate turned to Prudence Youlgrave, hoping she'd approve his suggestion, but she didn't seem to even be listening. She was staring into space, cradling her bruised face. In shock, or simply overwhelmed.

"Look at her, Tallbridge. She's in no state."

"She'll be restored by marriage. In every way. Any delay, sir, could lead some to think that you have reason to believe Draydale's accusation. Gossip and scandal will fly and grow."

"I don't give a fig for the gossip of Darlington."

Tallbridge's lips turned up slightly in a humorless smile. "This is not the Middle Ages. Coaches leave here four times a week carrying people and letters. Darlington's gossip reaches York in a day, London within a week, and spreads outward from both."

"A hasty marriage will only add to the talk."

"A hasty marriage fits your story. People will thrill to a romance worthy of the troubadours."

"Should I attempt a ballad on the theme?" Cate snapped, feeling the noose tightening around him. It wasn't only a noose of Tallbridge's imagination. It was woven out of facts.

Drama and violence at the altar made just the sort of story to race around the land, with names attached, and it wouldn't take long for it to be known to be a scandal involving the aristocracy. Even if the newspapers disguised them as B——e and Y——e, they'd add telling details such as "recently raised to a high title by the shocking death of his brother."

He wouldn't suffer from it, except in having his reputation for rash folly enhanced. Without marriage, Prudence Youlgrave would be ruined. With it, she could indeed be portrayed as the heroine of a grand romance.

But Hades, the reaction of his family, the disappointed hopefuls and their families, the county, the country, king, court, and all!

"You agree?" Tallbridge prompted, in a manner of one who held all the cards.

Without a doubt he was trying to seal a link to a noble family, but was he aware of the richer one? His daughter being closely connected to an earl? Whichever, he was clearly set on it, but more than that, he was right. By his intervention, Cate had declared his intent to wed Prudence Youlgrave, and so for her sake and his own, he must.

"I agree," Cate said. "But we'll need a license."

"The Bishop of Durham is little more than twenty miles away, but we can discuss that more once Prudence is in my cousin's care."

"Your cousin?"

"A Mistress Pollock who keeps house for me. A kind-hearted woman."

Cate didn't want Prudence under Tallbridge's roof, for the man would always put his own interests first, but there was nowhere else where she'd be safe from Draydale. There was a man who'd want revenge for being revealed as a cur.

Her brother's house would not be as safe, and there she'd be at the mercy of the ranting sister.

He could hardly take her back to his inn.

He glanced at Prudence again, but she was still far away.

Tallbridge was right. They must put as fine, as romantic a gloss on this as possible, but also, everything must be completely beyond reproach. From now on, there must be no hint of scandal. In the not-too-distant future, the whole world would be avid for details about the unlikely new Countess of Malzard. Her life would be difficult enough without shadows and shame.

Chapter 11

"It's time to go."

Prudence looked up at Catesby Burgoyne, the man who'd arrived in her life again to rescue her, but also to create mayhem and bloody disaster. Tallbridge had left. They were alone together.

He raised her gently from her chair, frowning at her throbbing cheek. "He'll pay for that in full one day," he said.

The concern stirred life in her again. He was wild, he was rash, he was violent, but he cared for her.

"Hold me," she said.

He did, enclosing her in strong, warm arms, as he had once before, when her distress had been much less. She'd never forgotten that. She rested there, taking comfort from the smells of his clothes. They weren't the sort of smells to normally entrance a woman—old wool and leather that carried traces of past smoke and other adventures—but they were the same smells that had lingered in her memory from last time.

From the house in White Rose Yard.

From a brandy-fueled conversation between two people with nothing in common, but who had understood each other very well. He was the only person she'd ever felt such a bond with. That bond had allowed her to ask for a kiss. A dangerous kiss that had led to the tender, unforgettable embrace.

Like this one. But this one followed on disaster.

She made herself move away slightly and look at him. "What's to happen now?"

"I'm to accompany you back to Tallbridge's house."

From where she'd traveled here like a prisoner being taken to the gallows.

"He has bars on all his lower windows," she said.

"Then you'll be safe there. Come."

He'd misunderstood her comment. Last night, last sleepless night, she'd thought of running away, but she'd seen no way to escape from an upper window, and the lower ones were covered by ornamental but very solid grilles. She'd been told that the front and back doors were set with alarms that would alert the house if they were opened in the night, from inside or out. By intent or not, she'd been imprisoned as securely as anyone in jail.

And now she was to be returned, and she still didn't know her fate. There'd been talk of a marriage, but that had been a ploy. Cate Burgoyne didn't want to marry her, and she didn't want to marry him.

Not really.

He was a stranger, and a wild, violent, irresponsible stranger.

But what, oh, what was to become of her? Draydale had ruined her; Aaron would wash his hands of her. . . .

She saw that she still wore Draydale's diamond ring on her second finger. She slipped it off, wanting to throw it away, but she put it in a pocket.

Cate Burgoyne led her out of the vestry and into a small room next door, which had an outside door. Fresh air and the sight of grass and trees brought her back to earth, but that was no improvement. People stood in groups nearby, hungry for more of the drama.

"Smile," he said.

She did her best.

Tallbridge's coach rolled up, quickly stripped of its bridal decorations. Cate opened the door and handed her in. Tallbridge was already there, graciously taking the backward seat. When they turned onto the street, the watchers pushed closer, eyes sharp like birds looking for worms.

"Do you want me to lower the blinds?" Cate Burgoyne asked.

"No. It might imply that we're guilty or ashamed."

"Brava." He took her hand and kissed it.

Tallbridge was watching in that falcon-eyed way he had. It was probably important that he believe their romantic story for now. She tried to play her part, but she felt apart from everything, as if this weren't happening to her, or she weren't here. She looked down at the hand Cate held. There was a speck of blood on the ruffle of his shirt cuff.

Despite the violence and drink, she'd cherished memories of Cate Burgoyne, but he could have no such poignant memories of her. Whatever had brought him to Darlington, to the church, to his foolish intervention in her affairs, it hadn't been romantic thoughts about her.

What was to become of her?

Draydale had said that vile thing, branding her a harlot.

He'd certainly pawed at her and tried to do more, but she hadn't allowed him to. Why would anyone believe her chastity, however, especially when her supposed returned beloved rejected her?

No one in Darlington would receive her, and soon word would spread throughout the gentry of the north.

If Aaron allowed her to remain under his roof, it would be as a shamed, poor relation scarcely able to leave the house.

Perhaps running a dame school in White Rose Yard would be her only hope.

She moved her hand slightly, so it brushed over her garter, where a knife was attached. It was the knife she'd threatened Cate with so long ago. She'd made a sheath so she could wear it to her wedding.

It had largely been symbolic, but it had also represented her desperate last resort. She'd dreaded her wedding night, and instinct had made her dread the daytime too. She'd gleaned what she could about Draydale's second wife, the weak and sickly one. She'd not been weak and sickly when she'd married him.

If things became too vile, she would kill herself.

Perhaps that was the way out now.

"We're here, my dear."

He was right. The carriage had arrived at Tallbridge House, a handsome three-story house on Houndgate.

Tallbridge left first, going into the house.

Cate climbed out and turned to help her down.

She stepped out, but saw that there were people in the street here too, staring and whispering. Were they just wondering, or had the dreadful story already reached here?

She put her hand in his.

He kissed it, smiling into her eyes.

Lovers worthy of the troubadours, reunited against all hope. For a moment, it provided a shield. She gave him the widest smile she could, but hurried into the house and breathed only when the door closed behind her.

Mistress Pollock immediately embraced her. "Oh, you poor dear! Such a terrible scene. So *violent*!"

Tallbridge said, "You can set out for Durham now, Burgoyne. I can provide a horse."

"Durham?" Prudence asked, freeing herself. He was to flee her side so soon?

"To the bishop for a license," Cate said.

"License?" She looked between the men. "We can't actually marry."

"On the contrary," Tallbridge said, "you must."

"I'm anxious to have you under my protection," Cate said.

"But . . ."

He kissed her hand again. "Trust me. All will be well." He turned to Tallbridge. "I have my own horse, thank you, sir. At the Talbot."

Where her wedding breakfast awaited. What would become of that? There was something in Shakespeare about baked meats. That was the funeral baked meats making the wedding breakfast, though. Could it work the other way around?

Alack, here, in ordinary circumstances again, she couldn't imagine slitting her own throat, or whatever one did with a small knife to end life.

Catesby Burgoyne looked at her and frowned slightly. "If I send for my horse to be brought here, we'll have a little more time together, my dear. We have much to say to each other."

Yes, indeed they did. She didn't understand anything.

Tallbridge sent a footman to the Talbot and then indicated a reception room. "Would you like refreshments sent to you there?"

Prudence wanted brandy, but she could hardly ask for it, so she declined anything. She found herself alone with Cate, feeling slightly sick. She sat on the settee because her legs felt weak.

He sat beside her. "Would you have preferred the marriage to go ahead?"

She stared at him. "To Draydale. Never!"

"Then why commit yourself to it?"

She heard the question, the doubt. "He *lied*. We did *not* anticipate the wedding."

"Then why go through with it?"

"You sound like an inquisitor. Because I saw no choice! Not then, at least. Earlier, yes, but how easy is it to see the end when we set our feet upon a path?"

"Not easy at all," he agreed. "But there must have been other suitors."

"None."

"I find that hard to believe."

She glared into his cool eyes. "Should I appreciate the flattery, or take umbrage at the implication that I'm lying? No other man offered for me. I had no choice but a return to poverty. I should have chosen that."

"Your brother would have been so cruel?"

"No." She sighed. "But he has little money of his own, and Susan would have seen no reason to support me in comfort. I'd have been a poor relation, dependent for everything, obliged to be eternally *grateful*." She shook her head. "I am justly served, but we'll have no more talk of marriage. Nothing requires you to sacrifice yourself on the altar of my pride."

"Except my honor."

"Your honor?"

"I'm your devoted lover, remember, declared so before witnesses? If I ride away, that brands me the lowest sort of dastard."

"Then why *do* this? Why rush in to rescue me again?"

"Are you claiming to regret it? That you'd rather be Mistress Draydale now?"

"Yes! No." She rose to her feet, hands to her face. "But I wish I were back in White Rose Yard."

"Truly?"

She turned to see him standing, smiling. "Oh! You ... you *man*! I'm sure all's easy for you. You've even fallen into some property without a twitch of work."

"True. But I'm willing to share it with you."

"No, no. There's no need for pretense here. We hardly know each other."

"We've spent little time together, but I feel I know you remarkably well. I can understand that you don't want to marry me, but I think you must."

"Nonsense," she said, but somewhere inside a foolish part whimpered a protest. It wasn't only protection from scandal and Draydale—it was that connection again, that sense of closeness that defied the logic of time spent in each other's company.

He went to the window. "My horse has arrived. My journey to Durham and back will take the best part of the day. Perhaps one of us will find an escape, but in case not I need the date of your birth and, I think, the full names of your parents."

In the midst of great problems, she was suddenly uncomfortable with admitting her age. "I was born on the twenty-sixth day of September, 1739. My father was Aaron Youlgrave, and my mother Joan Wright."

"It's only fair to share the same information. I was born on the fourth day of February, 1739. My father was Sebastian Burgoyne, and my mother Flavia Catesby."

The very names spoke of different worlds. He should marry a Flavia, a Lydia, an Augusta, rather than a Prudence.

"Will you be safe here?" he asked.

"Bars on all the windows," she reminded him.

"But danger could come in through the doors. I doubt your disappointed groom is in a state to invade, but he might use others to seek revenge."

She suddenly saw Draydale's face just before he'd hit her, purple with rage, fury in his eyes. The air turned thin and darkness crept in from the edges of her vision.

His arm came around her. "Prudence!"

He swept her up into his arms and carried her out of the room, calling for directions.

She tried to protest. "Truly, there's no need. . . ."

But Mistress Pollock twittered instructions and he carried her like a child up the stairs into the room she'd used last night, the room she'd paced last night. She was settled on the bed, up against pillows fussed into place by Mistress Pollock, who was uttering an endless string of, "Oh, dear, oh, dear, oh, dear. . . ."

"I'm sorry," she said. "I'm not usually so feeble."

"It's been a day to test Boadicea."

"*You're* not in a half faint."

He seemed to find that amusing. "My sincere apologies, but my ordeal wasn't as great. Prudence, if you truly want me to stay . . ."

"Stay here!" Mistress Pollock gasped. "Sir, there will be no more scandal."

She harried him out of the room, calling, "Carrie! Carrie!" as if for reinforcements.

Prudence collapsed back against the pillows, but a scrunch warned her of her hat. She fumbled for the pins, pulled them out, and spun the thing across the room to hit the wall. Flowers fell off.

Disaster, disaster, disaster!

If Cate Burgoyne took the opportunity to ride away, never to return, she wouldn't blame him. But what then would become of her?

Mistress Pollock bustled back, her elderly maid at her side. "Oh, your hat! Never you mind, dear, stop those tears. . . ."

She was crying?

"We'll soon have you comfortable and then you can rest. Such a day, such a day, and it hardly past noon!"

Cate returned downstairs and asked to speak to Tallbridge again in the reception room. When the man came, Cate shut the door. "You will not allow Draydale in this house while I'm away."

"I dislike your tone, sir, but I'm sure he's in no state for visits."

"There's also your daughter. I don't want Prudence harangued."

"You wish me to forbid my daughter to visit her home? Really, sir . . . But if you insist, she will not come here today."

Cate softened his manner, because unfortunately he'd realized he'd have to ask a favor of the man.

"I'm obliged to you, sir, and regret any inconvenience. I'm naturally anxious for my bride's comfort."

"Of course, of course. Completely understandable."

There was no choice for it. "There is the matter of transportation."

"Transportation?" Tallbridge raised a brow, and there might even have been the hint of a smirk on his lips. It was probably a skill of a merchant to know when someone needed something.

"I'll need a coach to take Prudence and her luggage to my home. I'm not short of funds, but I am short of cash. I began my journey yesterday with no expectation of such complexities."

"Do you go far?" Tallbridge asked.

It was a reasonable question, and Cate had prepared for it with a half-truth. "I thought to take my wife first to my family home."

"To Keynings? A famously handsome house. I'm sure Prudence will enjoy it. Pray allow me to lend you my coach and servants, Burgoyne. It will be an honor."

Oh, yes, Tallbridge was definitely eager for connection to an earl. Cate had hoped for money, however. If he used Tallbridge's coach, the driver and groom would learn the truth when they arrived at Keynings.

So be it. It couldn't be concealed for long.

But 'struth, he hadn't told his bride! How would she react to the knowledge that marriage to him would make her a countess? Some would think it a prize, but he knew better. His sudden elevation to earl was proving to be hell, and he was accustomed to that world.

No need to tell her yet. Some way out might occur to him.

Cate thanked Tallbridge for his generosity and went out to where Oakapple waited. He mounted, seeking any other matter that needed immediate attention. He should send a message to Keynings to prepare everyone, but he wouldn't. There might be time for someone to hotfoot it here to raise objections at the wedding. Twice in two days would definitely be too much.

He set out on the twenty-mile journey, deciding it would be best not to give his family any warning at all. With her new gowns and excellent manners, Prudence would make a good first impression. Let her settle at Keynings on her own merits before the inevitable revelations arrived about scandalous events and her unfortunate background.

He realized he was thinking of the marriage as a fait accompli, and that the thought didn't distress him. Despite the many problems, he'd rather marry his Hera than Bland, Bumble, or Fizz.

Prudence let Mistress Pollock and the maid strip her out of her grand wedding gown and her silk-covered, embroidered stays, but then she remembered.

She pushed away hands and insisted on going behind the screen to take off her petticoat. Then she raised her shift and undid her right garter, the one with the knife attached in a sheath she'd made specially. She'd worn the knife with a morbid purpose, but also for courage, just as she'd worn Cate Burgoyne's silver pin fixed in her flower-trimmed stomacher, where it could hardly be seen.

Courage for what?

She admitted the truth. Even when she'd gone to church full of dread, a part of her had wanted the courage to hold to her purpose—to marry well, and accept Henry Draydale as the price.

Was courage always stupid?

Blessed be the meek, the Bible said. *Turn the other cheek.*

"Here's your nightgown, miss."

A fine lawn-and-lace garment was gently draped over the screen—the nightgown Susan had insisted on for her wedding night.

"Give me one of my ordinary ones," Prudence said.

For lack of a better hiding place, she tucked the sheathed knife behind the washstand and then took off the rest of her clothes. She put on her plain nightgown, came out of hiding, and allowed the fussing women to put her to bed. She drank something bitter that Mistress Pollock pressed on her.

When she muttered, "I'd rather have brandy," the

woman tut-tutted and whispered to the maid that she hoped poor Miss Youlgrave's mind hadn't been turned by the terrible events.

Terrible.

Yes, indeed.

The curtains were lowered and she was alone at last, except for memories.

She remembered the morning, preparing for her wedding in this room, sick with nerves and doubts, but carried along to some extent by Susan's and Mistress Pollock's chatter. They'd gone on so cheerfully about marital joys, the delights of being mistress of one's own home, and of children.

Susan had lent her a brooch, reciting, "'Something old, something new, something borrowed, something blue. And a silver sixpence for her shoe.'"

The elaborate flower brooch had looked well on the richly ornamented stomacher.

Prudence had claimed that the silver pin had been her father's, and thus the old. The new had been nearly everything she wore, and for the blue she'd tucked a length of blue ribbon in one pocket. It was the ribbon she'd wanted on that first day in Darlington. Her hat had been too old to refurbish, but she'd still bought the ribbon.

The silver sixpence had been left from Cate Burgoyne's two shillings.

The knife, the pin, the sixpence. Had she perhaps summoned him, by some ancient spell?

The sleeping draft of poppy juice was playing games with her mind, making the Cate in her mind glow with saintly fervor, while her memory of Henry Draydale burned with a dark, demonic light.

But when Cate had taken her hands in church, there'd been blood on his knuckles, and behind him,

Henry Draydale had been a beaten mess. Who was the demon, then?

She huddled down under the covers, praying that somehow everything would turn out to be a bad dream.

That she had it all to do again, differently.

Chapter 12

Darkness was settling when Cate rode back into Darlington, and he returned without a solution to the problem. The riding time, plus hours spent hanging around in the bishop's palace, had given him time for thought, but he saw no choice but to marry Prudence Youlgrave.

He'd considered and put aside the reactions of family and others to the marriage. There was nothing to be done about it. It would all go better, however, if everyone believed the fiction of long-separated lovers. Then it would seem a love match rooted in years of waiting, not a chaotic mess.

He'd pieced together a story that would work. He'd come north three years earlier on furlough, so they'd met then. In reality there'd been little time for courtship in Northallerton, but probably no one would remember that.

There should have been letters, but they could fabricate some if necessary. Clearly some had gone astray, leaving Prudence to believe him dead. Letters did go astray, especially in wartime, as with Roe's letter informing him of the death of his son. A letter to a soldier could wander around after him for months and come to grief in all sorts of ways.

He hadn't come up with a story to explain lack of contact during his weeks at Keynings in March. Perhaps Prudence had moved. He didn't think she could have lived in White Rose Yard for years.

So he had a story.

Did he have a marriage?

Prudence could balk for any number of reasons, and she had the temperament to do so, even though it would put her on a rough path. A proud, determined, courageous woman, his Hera. Often to her own harm, but he'd harmed himself a time or two with the same qualities. He still wanted to marry her.

Her looks wouldn't please all, but they pleased him, and had from the first. She was tall and robust, which was definitely a consideration. He always felt the need to be careful in lovemaking with dainty women. He thought she'd be lusty once she became accustomed. He very much liked a lusty lover, and to have one as a wife would be an unexpected prize.

She might take time to become accustomed, however, when hastily married to a stranger. Unless Draydale had accustomed her.

He'd butted up against that time and again during the day. He'd tried to eradicate Draydale's accusation but not quite succeeded. Was the man foul enough to fling such a lie at a woman at the altar? Possibly yes, but he couldn't quite be sure. Betrothed couples did sometimes anticipate the wedding.

Prudence could have been overpersuaded, or even forced by Draydale. It would hardly be surprising if she denied such a thing, especially in church, in front of respectable members of the community who would be her neighbors.

If that was the way it had been, he didn't blame her, but he couldn't risk the possibility that she carried Draydale's child into their marriage. If a son, it would be his heir.

There was another side to it too. Even if he were completely sure, Damnable Draydale's words would spread, especially when the world heard that the accused woman was the Countess of Malzard. Everyone would watch a pregnancy, counting the days. His first child had better be born a generous nine months after the wedding or a shadow could hang over him or her forever.

By the time he dismounted at the Talbot, he'd found a solution. He wouldn't consummate the marriage immediately. Once Prudence had had her courses, he'd be sure and enough time would have passed.

If she was with child . . . He'd deal with that if it happened.

By the time he'd seen to Oakapple and sat to a late meal, only one problem remained: telling his bride she'd be marrying the Earl of Malzard. Would she even believe him? He could show her the signet ring, but one crest looked much like another, and he could even have stolen it.

Lack of plausibility and proof allowed him to put off any action.

However, he couldn't let her marry in ignorance.

He drank claret and realized his soup was getting cold.

He drank some, thinking of her modest dreams—a decent husband, a cozy home, enough income to keep her and her family in comfort and security, a respectable place in society.

Instead he offered her a scapegrace husband, houses too grand to be the sort of home she imagined, riches beyond most people's belief, and a place in the upper reaches of society to which she hadn't been trained. As Countess of Malzard she'd be one of grand ladies of the north. Even in London, amid the gathering of the great, she would be important. His mother had spent time as a lady-in-waiting to the queen.

Fried ham came with his soup but was hardly touched, though he'd half emptied the claret.

There was nothing for it. He must tell her and let her decide.

He abandoned his meal, requested a torch to light his way, and set out to walk to Tallbridge's house. It was only partway there that he remembered that Draydale might want to harm him.

Plague take the lot of 'em. Let fate take its course.

He arrived at the house without incident, but found it dark. That gave an excuse to abandon his mission, but he couldn't take it. He didn't believe that Prudence would be in a peaceful sleep after such a day, but if she was, he'd have to wake her. She must know the truth.

Tallbridge's house, however, was as secure as she'd said. The four front windows had those solid ornamental grilles, and apparently the door had some alarm. Probably a small explosive device that made a loud bang when triggered.

In any case, he had no skill with lock picking.

He progressed around to the back of the terrace, attempting the manner of a man returning to his home with no illicit purpose, but contemplating the prospect of being dragged off to court for housebreaking. Peers were protected from some prosecutions, but he wasn't sure the privilege covered simple felonies.

He turned into a lane and extinguished the torch in some dirt, then made his way in darkness toward the back of the houses. Pity there wasn't much moon, but darkness was concealing his criminal activities.

His eyes adjusted, but when he reached the lane behind the houses, he still had to trace the rear walls and step carefully. The lane was rutted, probably by carts making deliveries. At one point a smell told him there were stables to his right. Tallbridge could have stabling back here. That meant grooms, some of whom might still be awake. He heard no voices, but went forward even more carefully.

He could tell Tallbridge's house because the wall was higher and the pale light picked out shards of glass set into the top. A thorough man, Mr. Tallbridge.

Did he also have a guard dog patrolling his rear garden? Cate wished he'd brought pistol or sword.

He made his way carefully to the gate, but of course it was locked.

He had a challenge, then, and he'd always enjoyed a challenge. How did he conquer the glass-topped wall? He was wearing leather gloves, but their protection would be minimal.

He was coming up with schemes when he thought of something simpler. Perhaps Tallbridge didn't guard the sidewalls as thoroughly as this outer one. His neighbors might not like glass shards between them.

He found the next gate and tried it. Locked. The one after was locked, too, but the wood felt rotten. A boot burst the latch from the wood, and with only a dull thud. He waited in case of alarm, but then went into the backyard.

Flagstones beneath his feet, and some garden around. Perhaps vegetables. He found a place where he could get to the wall, which stood only eight feet or so. And no glass. He was over it easily, letting himself down carefully in case of obstacles below.

He smiled. Ahead, Tallbridge's wall was higher, but free of glass.

What was more, his careful hands found odd objects. A pile of bricks, some planks of wood, some tall canes. Nothing very useful, but indications that this house-holder was either a hoarder or in the middle of a construction project.

There might even be a ladder.

Alas, no, but a board on a pair of trestles was almost as good. He carefully removed the board and carried a trestle to the wall. With that extra height, it was easy to get up on the wall.

He paused a moment, listening for a dog.

He also surveyed the garden, which was interlaced with paths of white stone. The effect was doubtless pleasing by day. It was very convenient now, for the little bit of moonlight shone off the stone.

Cate let himself down and followed the path to the back of the house.

As expected, the ground-floor windows were also secured by iron bars, though this time simple rectangles. He hadn't truly expected some conveniently sturdy trellis or vine, and would hesitate to trust one anyway. Prudence was going to have to come down to him.

Alas, she wasn't conveniently looking out declaiming, "Catesby, Catesby, wherefore art thou, Catesby?"

He recalled his route when he'd carried Prudence to her room.

That window.

On the left.

He gathered some of the pale gravel, took careful aim, and tossed.

Direct hit.

But no response.

He was preparing a second throw when the curtains moved and she peered out. Cate gestured for her to come down.

The window went up and Prudence Youlgrave looked out at him, making a frantic shooing motion.

He could only smile. In a prim, pale nightgown, with a nightcap tied beneath her chin, she looked delicious.

He beckoned again.

She shook her head, frowning fiercely.

Enjoying the absurdity of their mute play, he went to one knee, clasped his hands, and implored.

Prudence stared down.

What was the madman doing now?

Why was he here at such an hour? It was gone ten o'clock!

Was he drunk?

Then she remembered. He'd said they should try to find a way to escape the marriage. A sick feeling rose to choke her.

Perhaps it had been the sleeping draft, but she'd woken in the afternoon in a lethargic state, plagued by a dull headache and unhappiness. She'd taken her dinner in her room, and her supper too, the weight of her situation becoming more and more oppressive. She was embroiled in a dreadful scandal. If she didn't marry tomorrow, she'd be a shamed woman for the rest of her life.

Worse than that, perhaps, she'd made a powerful enemy. She knew Henry Draydale well enough to know he'd need his revenge. She'd heard tales of things he'd done to those who crossed him in business matters, and they'd been part of the reasons she'd begun to doubt her course.

If Cate Burgoyne abandoned her, who would protect her? Not Aaron, for sure. Tallbridge? Why should he bother?

And Cate Burgoyne was here, cheerfully ready to explain how they could escape marriage.

If she closed the window and hid under the covers, he'd have to leave, and then surely he'd have to turn up at the church tomorrow. It was a matter of his honor, he'd said. Hiding wasn't her way, however. She had to know the worst now.

She grabbed her robe, put it on over her nightgown, and left her room. The house was pitch dark. She went back and struggled with the tinderbox until she could light a candle, then carried it with her, praying Tallbridge and his cousin were not light sleepers.

She realized that if she was caught, the candle would act in her favor. She could say she was unable to sleep and was looking for a book. She hurried downstairs, realizing that she couldn't go out to him. Those alarm-set doors. It would have to be a window.

The dining room looked toward the back, so she went in there. The curtains were drawn up, so she could see him, on his feet now, looking up at her window, frowning.

She rapped on the window, and he looked her way.

Then smiled.

Surely he couldn't smile like that if he'd come to say he was abandoning her.

He might, if drunk.

She put the candle on the windowsill and struggled with the clasp through the bars. She finally managed to unlock the window and raise it. Thank heaven and good housekeeping, it made hardly a sound. He quickly came to her, his face a little lower than hers, which added to the strangeness of the moment.

"Why are you here?" she asked, trying to only breathe it, alert for sounds in the house.

"Don't fret," he said—softly, but not softly enough for her comfort. "If we are caught, a moonlit tryst is in keeping with a romance worthy of the troubadours."

"Is that why you've dragged me from my bed? You're mad."

"No. We need to talk, remember?"

Only too well. She swallowed and managed to say, "About escaping marriage."

"Do you still want to?"

She tried to make out a face distorted by flickering candlelight. "Do you?"

"Are we playing guessing games? Prudence, I'm willing to marry you if it's what you want. But you don't know enough about me."

I know enough to prefer you to the alternatives, she thought, but knew she had to ask questions. "You truly can support a wife?"

"Yes."

"I will have a decent home?"

He said, "Yes," but had he hesitated before doing so?

"Are you a gamester?" she asked. "Will you lose it all and leave me, and perhaps children, in a place like White Rose Yard?"

"On my honor, no. Nor am I a drunkard, though I do, as you know, enjoy drink."

"So do I," she said wistfully, for some brandy would be nectar at the moment.

"How wondrous then that I have a gift for you."

Moonlight glinted off metal and glass. It was a small, flat bottle of some sort, covered in coils of silver, too large to be a perfume bottle, but no bigger than the palm of his hand.

"It's pretty," she said, taking it through the bars, "but what's in it?"

"Spirituous encouragement."

"Gin?" she asked.

"I've come up in the world, remember. I return your gift of brandy. The cap unscrews to make a small cup."

Bewildered and dazzled by the odd moment, she unscrewed the cap, poured, and sipped, welcoming the tang of spirits. But then the brandy seemed to turn to vapor, diffusing into her mind.

"That's remarkable," she said.

"The miraculous spirit of Cognac, where the best brandy's made."

Prudence considered the bottle. "It's too precious."

"Devil a bit. I can afford cognac, and the flask's a pretty curiosity, no more. I bought it in London, thinking of you."

"In London?" she echoed. "When?"

"Weeks ago."

Could she believe such a thing? That weeks ago and far away he'd been thinking of a woman he'd met only once in poverty in Northallerton? No, she couldn't. He was a kind man, so he was pretending she meant more to him than she could.

But he had stepped in to save her from marrying Draydale.

She sipped again. "How did you come to be in the church?"

"I rode to Darlington to see how you were."

That, too, sounded like caring. "How did you know I was here?"

"A week or so ago, I was passing through Northallerton and visited your house. I spoke to your neighbor."

"Hetty. But why . . . ?"

"Why come to Darlington? I hoped to see Hera victorious."

"Instead you find her in dire straits, and are compelled to rush to the rescue."

"I chose my own path, and am not unhappy with it."

She peered at him again. "Truly?"

"Truly."

She leaned against the bars. "Oh, thank God. Thank you, Cate. I've been so frightened that you'd not want to. Terrified of the consequences. Of poverty, but worse than that. Of being cast onto the streets, known by all as a fallen woman. Of Draydale . . . I know it's weak, but I'm terrified of him."

He covered her hand, which clutched an iron bar. "You're mine now, Prudence, and I can protect you from all your demons."

"Draydale's powerful and ruthless. He takes revenge on those who cross him, and no one's crossed him as we have."

"I don't fear Draydale," he said steadily, "and nor need you. Try to believe that, Prudence. Give me your hand. I have a ring for you. A ring is a sign of allegiance and protection."

Prudence tensed, remembering when Draydale had pushed the diamond betrothal ring onto her finger. The stone had been large, but it had symbolized possession, not protection, and she'd known it.

If only she'd paid attention to those feelings—but then, it had already been too late. She'd encouraged his suit. Others had noted his courtship. If she'd rejected him at that point he would have become her enemy.

This conversation with Cate had been strange. She felt things unsaid, doubts unvoiced, but he was willing, he was willing. She thrust her left hand through the bars. He took it and kissed her palm.

A simple act to cause so deep a shudder.

"I have little money with me on this journey, so I couldn't buy you the rings you deserve, but I found this in Durham, if it fits."

He slid a ring on her finger, and her reactions were so very different from when Henry Draydale had put his ring there. Uncertainty, yes, but hope too.

The delicate ring was too big, but she found that endearing. It was silver set with a small stone, perhaps a
garnet. A simple thing, but she knew it would always be
precious to her.

"Thank you. It's lovely."

"I'll do better soon. What is your favorite stone?"

"I like this one."

"Topaz, perhaps. Or emerald."

She shook her head at him. "There's no need of
extravagance."

"Nagging me already?" he teased. "The wedding
ring's equally paltry. Will you be willing to exchange it
for better? I know some women think the ring they're
wed with is sacred."

"I'll be content with it. There'll be better use for your
money."

"No more of that. I'll beg a loan from Tallbridge to
purchase something better."

"No," she said, suddenly serious. "Beg nothing from
Tallbridge. He'll collect the debt."

"Wise woman, but I've already agreed to use his traveling carriage and horses to take us home tomorrow."

She'd rather have a clean break, but the word "home"
gently washed away all other cares.

"Will I really have a home? Tomorrow?"

"You will, and freedom from fear." But again, she
sensed something unsaid, something that sat uneasily
on him.

"What?" she demanded. "What is it?"

She saw him grimace.

"Do you understand that my family is aristocratic?"

"The Burgoyne family? Yes, I suppose so. And your
mother's family, the Catesbys."

"It will be a change for you, and might be difficult at
times."

He feared she would embarrass him. Knowing she was about to give a false impression, she said, "It won't be so very strange. I was raised in a manor house."

"You were?" he said, as pleased as she'd expected. "I suppose your father lost his fortune."

"Yes," she said, telling herself that was more or less true.

"That's why you wanted so much to return to an elegant way of life. You're a courageous woman, Prudence."

"Courage can lead to peril."

"So can cowardice, and more often." He hesitated, and then said, "We might have to go to London. Even to court."

"Court? Why?"

"One should pay one's respects when in Town."

"Then I'd rather not go to Town."

"I expect to take a seat in Parliament."

"Oh." He seemed unlikely for that role, but if he wanted to take a seat in the Commons, she wouldn't stand in his way. "I could stay at home, though, couldn't I?"

"You could, if you truly wanted to."

There was something odd about the conversation, but perhaps that was brandy on top of poppy juice.

"If it's a pleasant home, I'll not want to wander." She wanted to cut through the mistiness and so she refilled the cap with brandy. "We should drink to our future." She sipped, and passed it through to him.

He drank. "To our spirited future."

"Spirited?"

"I doubt tranquillity is in either of our natures."

"But I want tranquillity, Cate. Truly I do."

"Then I'll do my best to provide it." He passed the cap back to her. "Drink to happiness, Prudence, in whatever form it takes."

"To happiness," she said, and drained the cup.

"I hate these bars between us. It's as if you're in a prison cell. But only for tonight. Tomorrow you'll be free."

"A woman is never free."

"I won't rule you."

"Yes, you will," she said, screwing on the cap. "You have a very commanding nature."

"It must be the officer in me." He moved closer against the bars. "Obey me, then, and come to be kissed."

Prudence eyed him, but she remembered his kiss. It had been sweet. And tomorrow night he would want to do more. She pressed close to the bars and their lips met with warmth, and almost with sparkles.

"Enforced separation is proving unexpectedly exciting," he murmured. "Perhaps I should build a nun's cell in the corner of our bedroom, with just a small grille through which to touch and kiss."

Something shuddered inside her. "It would shock the servants."

"We won't care about the servants. Obey me yet more. Part your lips for me."

She did so, gripping a bar to steady herself. Their warm breath mingled, brandy spiced. His tongue touched hers. She pressed closer, bars hard against her flesh. His hand brushed a breast covered only by two thin layers of linen.

She started backward, then wondered if she'd offended.

"I didn't . . . You startled me."

"I hope to startle you more," he said, smiling, "but in all the best ways. Until tomorrow, my bride."

Until their wedding night.

She still clutched a bar, and he kissed her fingers there. "I promise to do my best to make your life carefree and wondrous, Prudence Youlgrave."

She reached out to touch his face. "I promise the same, Catesby Burgoyne."

"Then together we'll be lovers worthy of the troubadours, and none shall prevail against us."

Cate watched Prudence close the window and disappear.

He'd not told her, but how could he when she so clearly wanted and needed the marriage? He knew her courage. She'd be capable of refusing the marriage if she thought herself unworthy.

She'd been born and bred in a manor house, however, so her family wasn't as modest as he'd thought. Such origins would smooth her path, and she would already understand some of the world into which she'd marry.

And quite simply, he wanted to marry her. After their love play between bars, he wanted to marry her very much indeed.

His greatest disappointment was that he'd have to keep to his plan and not consummate the marriage immediately, but he owed their first child that.

Chapter 13

Prudence found it peculiar to be repeating her preparations of the day before. She began with a bath and insisted on her hair being freed of its elaborate arrangement and washed.

"But it's so pretty, miss," Carrie said. "It'll last another day."

"I don't like it," Prudence said, and perhaps the woman understood her revulsion for all things Draydale.

Carrie began to pull out the pins. "Ooh, it's all stiff, miss. The coiffeur must have put something on to hold it in place. True enough, your husband'll like it better soft and silky come the night."

Prudence blushed pink all over, but not with discomfort. She'd thought often of Cate brushing her breast through the bars, and of the sensation it had brought. Her night had been plagued by deep, hungry yearnings.

Only imagine.

Tonight!

It seemed sinful that she anticipate such pleasures after her foolish ambitions had created disaster, but she did.

After the bath, Prudence sat before the small fire, fingering her hair to catch the heat, turning around to dry all sides.

Mistress Pollock came in to fuss. "Time's flying dear. Why, oh, why have your hair washed when it was done only yesterday?"

"Because I want today to be completely different."

The woman beamed. "Ah, yes, today you wed your own true love."

The romance worthy of the troubadours.

"Yes," Prudence said, smiling.

She wasn't wearing her wedding dress. She'd already told Mistress Pollock to dispose of it. Instead she'd chosen her second-best dress, a sage green silk designed to be worn without hoops, and so suitable for traveling.

She put on a fresh shift and a plainer pair of stays and then sat so the maid could do her hair. "Just pin it up, Carrie. There's little time, and I'll wear the villager hat."

That was wide brimmed and would hide the dark bruise on her face. She'd already attempted to cover it with paint, but the effect seemed ridiculous, and in any case, the world should remember what Draydale had done.

The petticoat was quilted ivory silk embroidered in a green that matched the gown, and the gown was embroidered with dark ivory blossoms in a shade to match the petticoat. It was a pretty effect, but quiet. Would Cate think it too sober?

She had nothing else suitable.

The gown had a closed bodice fastened down the front with tiny bows of ivory ribbon, so it needed no stomacher. The bodice was a little low, however, so she filled it in with a silken fichu.

"That color does suit you," Mistress Pollock said, "though it's all a little plain. Here's Susan's brooch. It will go very well between your breasts and brighten it up."

Prudence stopped her from fixing it in place and put it in her left pocket. "I'll still have it with me," she said, touching the other thing in there. The knife.

She wasn't wearing it on her garter today, or out of fear, but only because it was part of Cate. It and the silver pin in the other pocket beside the blue brandy flask. And the sixpence in her shoe.

Talismans.

She'd thought of the knife and pin like that yesterday out of fear. Today she needed them even more, because she had to make this marriage work for the man who had done so much for her.

She pinned on the wide straw hat, which Mistress Pollock had hastily trimmed with ivory ribbons, and stepped into the delicate heeled shoes made of the same jade green silk. They'd been intended for the dance floor, but they'd survive coach to church and back again.

Everything else was in her trunk, which had already been taken down to the boot of the coach.

It was time to go.

She moved the garnet ring to her middle finger, where it fit much better, and she smiled with memory.

When she left her room, however, when she descended the stairs and took Tallbridge's arm to go out to the coach, she felt too close to yesterday. Henry Draydale would have to do something—something to show what happened to those who crossed him—and Cate had done more than cross him.

He'd want to kill Cate. She knew it.

She entered the coach warily, alert for danger, praying Draydale's injuries would prevent his striking today.

She wouldn't feel at ease until she was well away

from Darlington, and even then she could only pray that Cate was right in believing he could protect them both from Henry Draydale's vengeance.

This ceremony was taking place at nine o'clock, and she'd hoped the early hour would mean few people around to watch. When they arrived at St. Cuthbert's, however, even more people stood around. Why not? She represented a scandal among the best families of Darlington, and a romance worthy of the troubadours.

She didn't want to face them, however. Tallbridge stood outside, hand outstretched, but all her muscles seemed to have frozen at once.

To balk at the altar a second time, however, was unthinkable. She touched the talismans in her pockets and forced her muscles into action. She left the carriage, head high, smile in place, took Tallbridge's arm, and walked toward the church.

Murmurs and whispers made her shiver, but then a woman cried, "Blessings on the bride!" and others echoed it.

Prudence's smile became more natural, and she dared to look to the side, to smile at people.

But then a man shouted, "Curses on the whore!" and a few others joined in with, "Shame! Shame!"

To Prudence's horror, scuffles broke out as blessings and curses fought for attention.

"Come," Tallbridge said, and hurried her into the church.

Once inside, she collapsed against the wall. "Why? Why?"

"Draydale's work, I assume. Pull yourself together. If that's the worst he can do, you'll get off lightly."

She glared at him resentfully, but he was right. Moreover, if the disruption was Draydale's work, he mustn't be allowed victory.

Aaron hurried into the porch from the church. "What's the commotion?"

"Of no matter," Tallbridge said. "I have men out there who'll take care of it."

He'd expected trouble like that? Prudence wished he'd warned her.

Tallbridge shot her a stern look and went into the church, leaving her with her brother.

"More shame on our name," he said.

That stiffened her spine. "Not of my making, Aaron."

"If you didn't want Draydale, you shouldn't have accepted him."

She clenched her teeth. "Let's progress," she said, taking his arm.

But as they went toward the doors into the nave, he said, "It was most ungracious of you to forbid Susan her own home."

"Did I?"

"Burgoyne did, which amounts to the same thing. You've caused a great deal of trouble, Prudence, especially for me."

She stopped. "None of this would have happened if you'd behaved with decency, brother. None of it. I would have been content with a sister's place in your home."

"You don't understand my situation. You should have waited. I'd have found a way."

Perhaps he believed that, but someone was opening the door. "Let's not argue now, Aaron. I hope in future we can find better accord."

Something showed in his eyes, something of the younger brother she'd cherished and scolded into doing his schoolwork.

"You are sure about this man?" he asked. "Once you're married, there'll be nothing I can do to help you."·

"Would you have been able to help me once I was

married to Draydale?" He flushed, and she knew there was no point to this. "I'm sure, Aaron. He's a good man."

He pulled a face, but led her through the doors.

Only a handful of people waited near the altar—the vicar, the verger, Tallbridge, Susan. And Catesby Burgoyne.

He was the shabbiest person present. Perhaps her old blue dress would have been a better match. But as she walked down the aisle, she had the strange impression that he was a fine bird among dull ones. Didn't they call the very grand the *haute volée*? The highfliers?

It was something in the way he stood, in the tilt of his head and his calm-eyed self-assurance.

Highborn.

A member of the aristocracy, as he'd said. She'd known that, but their chaotic encounters hadn't shown it as this moment did. She was hit by another flash of panic, but reminded herself that a member of the aristocracy, a member of Parliament, could still live a simple, earthbound life. She walked onward, focusing on a silver pin, a brandy flask, a ring, and last night's kisses.

But please be sure, she silently implored his smiling face. *Please have no regrets about this. You can see I'm past my prime and lacking beauty. You know I'm penniless and not of your rank in society. If you're doing this out of pity, please stop this now.*

But how could he? For him to jilt her at the altar would be even more heinous than her doing it to him.

Her hand was placed in his. Hers was chilly, but his was warm and strong.

He kissed her knuckles, smiling into her eyes, then turned them both toward the vicar.

Prudence managed to say her vows clearly, and had to fight tears over the ones Cate said to her. A form of words only, used as much for the most unpleasant marriage as for one of true love, but all the same, so beautiful, so comforting.

He put the wedding ring on her finger. As he'd warned, it was a thin, trumpery thing, perhaps not gold at all, but it served its purpose. They were married. Like the simple silver ring, it was a little large, so she curled her fingers, holding it to her to be sure it didn't slip off and break the charm.

It was done.

It was done.

And now they could leave.

Not quite yet. Cate stepped aside to give money to the vicar and the verger.

Susan sniffed. "I hope you're satisfied now, Prudence, with a husband who owns only one suit of clothes."

"Very satisfied, sister. Thank you for all you've done for me."

Susan looked thwarted, but managed a toothy smile. "I'm sure it's all been worthwhile if you're happy."

Determined to create as much harmony as possible, Prudence turned to Susan's father. "Mr. Tallbridge, thank you for your hospitality and assistance. You've been very generous."

Tallbridge inclined his head in that cool way he had, but something sparked in his eyes. It might even be approval.

"Where will your home be?" Aaron demanded. "I should have discovered that before I permitted this."

Prudence didn't want to admit she didn't know. For once, Susan's interfering nature was a benefit. "Wherever it is," she said, "you'll find it a deal less comfortable than Mr. Draydale's house."

"I truly doubt that, Susan."

Susan frowned, puzzled, and then Cate was at her side again, kissing her hand by the wedding ring. "You've made me the happiest of men, my love."

All for show, all for show, but his words created a glow inside her that made it easy to smile back at him.

He too thanked everyone for their assistance, and then said, "I dislike taking you away from your family, my love, but we must be away."

Aaron tried again. "Where exactly will you be living, Burgoyne?"

"Today we travel to Keynings, my family home. A message there will always find us."

Before Aaron could persist, Cate led Prudence down the aisle and out to where the coach waited. Any ill-wishers had been removed, and the small crowd called good wishes and threw grain and flowers.

Cate had pennies in his pocket and tossed them into the crowd, where children scrabbled for them. Prudence found herself laughing as if she were a real bride on a real, happy wedding day.

May it be so, she prayed. *May it be so.*

The coach awaited, but the coachman sat alone on the box. The groom was riding a horse.

"An outrider?" she asked, dismayed. Only the grandest people traveled that way.

"Merely a means of taking my horse with us."

That changed everything. The bay horse was as plebian as Cate's clothes. He might be part of a grand family, but he was an ordinary man, thank God, who might be satisfied with a very ordinary wife.

He handed her into the carriage, joined her, and the horses moved forward. Prudence waved to the onlookers, truly happy. She was leaving Darlington and Draydale forever.

Cate took her hand, looking at the ring. "A tinsel piece and too large. I'll do better soon."

"I rather like the silver one, and it fits my middle finger."

"Then I'm glad, but you'll soon have more. I've inherited some jewels, but I'll choose others especially for you."

"Cate, there's no need."

"Still worried about the workhouse?" he teased.

It wasn't a teasing matter. "I have reason to, having come so close."

"I promise you this, my wife—you will never end up in the workhouse, or in any other form of dire poverty. There will be shelter, food, warmth, and decent clothing all your days."

"How can you be sure? Life can play cruel tricks."

He studied her. "What cruel tricks has it played on you? Tell me about your manor house."

Prudence swallowed. She'd implied more than was true, and couldn't bring herself to reveal that yet. She told him about the end of Blytheby Manor, but let it seem that her father had overspent. The rest still fit—her father's brokenhearted death, and her mother's desperate plan to return them to decency.

"You loved your home."

"Yes, but sometimes I think it exists only in my mind. That if I were to return I would find it much more ordinary than I imagine."

"It could be so. Or not. I loved my childhood home, and thought of it fondly when I was away. When I returned it was all I'd remembered and more, despite some changes."

"But no longer yours."

He blinked at her as if startled. "That's not the problem. Your hat is."

He tugged free the ribbon and tossed the hat on the opposite seat, and then he kissed her.

It was a gentle kiss, but she appreciated that. She would like other kisses, but at this moment gentle was perfect. As was nestling in his arms afterward as she watched the last houses of Darlington give way to fields.

"It's over," she said. The most difficult part of her life was over.

"No, it's begun."

She smiled at him, for indeed, the future lay ahead, promising more than she dared hope. Perhaps later she'd truly understand how this had all come about, but she felt at ease and free now because of this man.

This man she loved.

She'd thought love came slowly, but she suspected the seeds had been sown that night in Northallerton. She'd certainly never forgotten him.

Yesterday had been too tumultuous for gentle emotions, but he'd rescued and avenged her. She might disapprove of impulsiveness and violence, but somehow those characteristics seemed to have helped the old seeds grow.

Then there'd been last night. That strange encounter warmed by brandy, and by gifts, and spiced with hot kisses between cold bars. This love had come swiftly, fiercely, and had created a shivering vulnerability. She mustn't let him know. Not yet, or he might feel he must pretend to feel the same way. When it came, if it came, it must be honest. Kindness and fondness were enough—for now.

She straightened, fussing with her clothes. "How long is our journey?"

"Twelve miles or so, but using the same horses and with the state of the roads, it could take us four hours or more. Better to take our time than to break a wheel or axle." He tugged at an ivory bow on her bodice. "I can't say I mind a slow passage."

She slapped his hand away, but then felt guilty.

"Unless you want to go to Northallerton?" he said, tugging again.

She pushed his fingers away again, but it was a game, a delightful game.

"No, why?"

"I wondered if you wanted the three-legged dog."

"Oh, Toby! I do miss him, but Susan believes a deformed animal will lead to a deformed child, so I left him with Hetty and the children. He's probably content there now."

He had one bow undone. "We can collect him if you want."

"I thought you didn't like him."

"I misjudged him."

"I can't arrive at this grand Keynings with a dog like Toby."

"You're my wife. You may have any dog you want."

"I'm a penniless nobody, Cate, and will need all the dignity and trimmings I can find. And an intact bodice!"

He disappointed her by saying, "True enough," and abandoning the bows. He let down the window and called out, "We'll stop at the next decent inn, coachman."

"Aye-aye, sir."

"I don't want to stop this close to Darlington," Prudence protested as he closed the window. "And what good will it do? Do you not like my gown? I've nothing finer."

"I adore your gown, especially the bows, but you need a better wedding ring."

"You think to find one at an inn?"

"I think to find pen and paper so I can send a message to a friend."

Prudence was remembering all too well his rash impetuosity. "He can produce a wedding ring on demand?"

"I don't see why not, but I'll ask for money."

"Cate, don't go into debt over this."

"I'm already in debt to Tallbridge for this and that."

"I loathe debt. *Please*, I'd much rather live simply."

"Prudence, Prudence, desist. I'm not impoverished. Tallbridge will have his money in days, and Perry will only be sending me my own funds. For some reason, country inns and shops aren't keen to accept promissory notes from passing strangers."

"Perry?"

"Mr. Peregrine Perriam, a very good friend. He'll adore you."

"I doubt that."

He simply shook his head, but she deeply distrusted this mad manner.

"Do you promise you're not going into debt?"

"On my honor. You can apologize for doubting me with a kiss."

"You want me to kiss you?"

"That would be utterly delightful." He was teasing but challenging at the same time.

Very well.

Trying not to show any trepidation, she leaned toward him until she could press her lips to his. He remained as he was for a moment, but then his hand slid behind her head and he took charge, kissing her as she remembered, but then more than she remembered.

She was pressed to his body as she'd pressed to iron bars, but his hardness was warm, and his mouth was hot. A part of her was shocked again at open mouths and touching tongues, but most of her was wildly enthusiastic. This . . . this was the substance of half-remembered dreams. An excited heat rippled through her like a fever, making her press closer, taste more deeply.

She moved, seeking even deeper connection, but he

drew away, ending the kiss, cooling the passion. Lord, they were in a coach, not a curtained bed!

As before, he gathered her into his arms.

And that, for now, was dream enough.

The rest would come later, but now, to be in his arms was heaven. His strength, his warmth, melted her, softening the lingering hard edges in her mind, and all those places calloused by years of hardship and recent battles.

Chapter 14

Cate enjoyed having his wife so close, a shapely arm-ful in pretty silk, delicately scented, his forever, without urgency or danger. His blood still seethed with the passion that had flared between them, but he could bear it. It was a red-hot promise for the future. For now, they had many hours in which to grow used to each other, to learn and teach, to simply enjoy.

Many hours in which to find just the right moment to tell his wife that she was now the Countess of Malzard.

Not yet, not yet. She needed this time of peace and so did he.

He put a kiss on her simply pinned hair. "You have lovely hair."

"It's a dull color."

"It's honey on a sunlit morning."

She stirred to look at him. "Poetry? I didn't expect that."

"You'll find I'm full of surprises." That came too close to the truth. He stroked a loose tendril at her temple. "Perhaps it's the color of pale satiny wood on a sun-lit morning. My mother has an escritoire of much this shade."

"Are you calling me a wooden-head, sir?"

He chuckled. "Sometimes you're stubborn enough."

She looked at him again. "Your mother. She's still alive?"

"Yes, and in excellent health."

"When will I have to meet her?"

Was the moment upon him? He made a sudden resolution not to lie.

"Today. She's at Keynings."

She straightened, putting a hand up to tidy her hair. "Lord save me. What will she think of me?"

He pulled her hand down. "She won't be concerned with your hair. My arriving with a wife will be a shock, of course, but she does very much want me to marry."

"Thank heavens. A resentful mother-in-law could be disastrous. Will we see much of her?"

Another deadly question. "She lives in my house."

"Lives in . . ." She sagged back against the squabs. "Oh, lord."

"I'm sorry I didn't tell you."

"It wouldn't have made me back out of the wedding, and it stands in your favor. You're a good son."

"If only she agreed."

"She doesn't approve of you?"

"Your astonishment is balm to my soul. It's only that she compares me unfavorably with my brother."

"Ah, I remember. The perfect son. My mother preferred Aaron to me. He was the male, the hope for the future. His charm and looks might have played a part too."

"Begging for compliments? You are lovely."

"And charming?" she challenged.

"No, but much more interesting. You're worth ten of him."

She looked away as if uncomfortable with praise. Had she received so little?

"You have a delightful profile," he said. "No, don't move. I'm enjoying it. I recognized from the first that you had the features of a Roman matron."

"The sort who was in the habit of telling sons to return with their shields or on them?"

"That was the Spartans, I believe."

She turned to face him. "Some of the Roman matrons shared the sentiment. Agrippina, for example."

"On the contrary. She was excessively indulgent of her darling son, Nero. You're well versed in the classics."

She colored. "I was obliged to share some of Aaron's lessons. To help him."

"That's nothing to be ashamed of."

"You don't mind?"

"Why should I?"

"Draydale forbade me to mention it."

"If you are to compare me with that specimen, we might come to blows."

"Oh. I never meant—"

"Prudence, I'm teasing. But forget Draydale. He's in your past."

The coach changed directions and Cate looked out. "Ah, an inn. We are about to be embraced by the Monk's Arms."

"Do you want to stop here long, sir?" bellowed the coachman.

Cate opened the door and jumped down. "Not long at all. I merely need to write a letter. Unless," he said, turning back, "you need a pause here, my dear?"

She assured him she was all right, so Cate told the groom to find out the details of their route from the coachman and went into the inn. One of his remaining shillings purchased writing materials and a desk to write at. He didn't attempt an explanation, but simply asked Perry to send back funds with the groom, and to tell everyone that he was safe and would be at Keynings by nightfall. He didn't use the signet ring in his pocket, but simply dripped the sealing wax into a blob.

He went back outside and gave the letter to the groom. "Ride ahead to Keynings with all speed and give this to Mr. Perriam, who's a guest there. Give it into no one else's hands, and don't say who it's from."

"Very well, sir." But the man's look suggested that he thought him up to no good. "Should I await you there, sir?"

"No. Command a fresh horse and retrace the route with what Mr. Perriam gives you."

"As you wish, sir," the groom said with the same doubt, and set off down the road.

"Where's he going, then?" the coachman demanded with bad grace. "What if I need him?"

"If you need help on the way, I believe I'm able." Cate climbed back into the coach and settled into his seat. "A surly creature."

"He drove me to church both times and probably doesn't approve."

"If he's discourteous to you, let me know."

She smiled quizzically at him. "You can be very lordly sometimes."

Cate hoped he'd hidden his reaction. "Perhaps it's officerly."

"Ah, yes, the army. Where did you serve?"

That was a safe subject, so he told her about Brunswick and Hanover, keeping the army talk light, and not mentioning the irregular activities that had created his chaotic reputation. After another hour Cate called a halt for people and horses to take refreshments. Prudence amused him with the great fuss she made of getting her hat back on straight and of being in perfect order.

As if she'd never been kissed.

"What would you like?" he asked as they settled in an adequate private parlor.

"Tea," she said. "It was an impossible luxury for so long, I'm addicted to it now. And to chocolate in the morning."

"You shall have all the tea in China, and the richest, sweetest chocolate."

"Extravagance again," she said, but with laughter.

At ease, she was naturally gracious. She would need to learn a little more hauteur as a countess, but her manners were so excellent that she'd make the transition well. Perhaps more easily than he, who resented all the confinements and obligations of his position after living free.

Was this the moment to tell her?

Their refreshments came then, however, and he decided that it would be best to confess in the coach. He'd not be able to escape her anger, but she wouldn't be able to storm off in a rage, possibly into trouble. He was aware of Draydale all the time. It was hard to imagine that the man would send people to attack the coach, but he might have people shadowing it, alert for a chance to strike.

Once they were on their way again, however, he still put off his confession. He'd never been such a coward in his life. But she was relaxing mile by mile and becoming more delightful with every moment. Then the coach turned off onto a lesser road and the coach jolted down into a deep rut.

"'Struth," Cate said, bracing Prudence. "We're like to break something."

"A leg?" she asked, hat askew.

"I hope only a wheel, but that would be bad enough." He opened the window and yelled for the coachman to be careful. "We're in no hurry, man!"

"I'm doing me best, sir! If you want to get to Keyn-ings, this is your only route."

Cate settled back, shaking his head. "Would you have minded riding pillion? It would have been smoother and no slower."

"I never have, and I confess, I'd rather not arrive at your family's grand home with only the soiled and dusty clothes on my back."

"I'd have hired a packhorse, but yes, you'd be travel-worn. So we'll endure this torture box. Where was I? Ah, yes, my brief time in Portugal . . ."

Prudence enjoyed his stories, but the jolting of the coach jarred her teeth, and her back ached from trying to resist the movement. When they stopped again to water the horses, she declined refreshment in favor of a walk.

"It's a small inn anyway," he said, handing her down. "I doubt it offers more than ale. I apologize for your wedding journey. It's the lack of rain recently. It's left the roads rock-hard."

"Not for long," she said, considering some distant heavy clouds that were already pouring down rain somewhere.

He looked and laughed. "Guaranteed to turn rock into muddy soup. Let's pray it holds off until we reach Keynings."

They strolled down the road, but she soon had to sug-gest they turn back. "These shoes were never intended for country walks."

The coach was ready to go on. "The torture box," she muttered.

"Rethinking pillion?"

She was. She'd only ever ridden a donkey, and never pillion, but it had to be more comfortable. "My posses-sions?"

"The coach will follow with your trunk, and we'll go slowly, so you won't be without them long."

She thought again of dust and dirt, but decided she didn't care. "Then yes, let's."

But the innkeeper had only one very sorry horse and no pillion saddle.

"I'm right sorry, sir, for the road's rough, and no mistake. I've heard of many a coach broken down these past days, even on the toll roads."

"Where's the next place where we're likely to find a pillion saddle?" Cate asked.

"Cawthorne, I reckon, sir. But I tell you, it's like to rain. Your lady would be better in a coach."

Prudence sighed. "I think he's right. I'd rather arrive bruised than drenched."

"The torture box it is, then."

As they climbed back into the coach, Cate wished he could smooth the road for his lady. Alas, an earl's powers stopped far short of that.

When it lurched forward, Prudence groaned. "I can't imagine why anyone thinks travel pleasurable."

"Some think the pains and hazards worthwhile in order to see new places."

"What's wrong with home?" she demanded.

"Nothing at all," he said, "nothing at all. Those of us who've lost a home realize that very well."

"You lost your home?" she asked.

It was time to tell her. "Paradise lost, paradise regained. Prudence—"

But just then the coach tilted so sharply he was almost tossed on top of her. He slammed his hand on the coach wall to prevent it, but her lips ended up too close to ignore.

So he didn't.

Her hat had to go again so he could do the job properly, and then the coach made a sharp sway to the right, which landed her on top of him. He held her there, between his spread legs, and explored her hot, sweet mouth. And her round, firm behind.

Tonight.

No, not tonight, he remembered, breaking the kiss and trying to cool his blood. *Damnation*.

Her eyes were so bright, her cheeks so prettily flushed that it was going to be difficult to hold back here, never mind in the private chambers at Keynings.

"Cate?" she asked, color fading, looking worried.

He smiled and kissed her again, quickly. "You were ravishing me, my wife."

Her eyes widened and she scrambled off him, but he pulled her back. "That wasn't a complaint. You're delightful, but we have to restrain ourselves a little. For now."

She blushed again, looking away, but smiling.

The coach juddered again and some part of it squealed a protest. Cate took the excuse to help her back to her side of the seat so he could open the window and call a complaint to the coachman.

"I'm doing me best, sir!"

A man riding by in the opposite direction called, "Dreadful road, sir!"

"Damnable," Cate replied before closing the window on the dust. "I'm sorry if that expression offends you, my dear."

"I'm not so delicate a bloom. I'd trump 'damnable' with 'hellish.'"

He laughed. "Heavenly woman. We'd not lose much time by walking, you know."

"My shoes," she reminded him, extending a foot to

show green silk shoes that matched her gown and had a delicate, curved heel.

"Very fine," he said, deliberately admiring her ankles.

She quickly tucked her foot back. "I have sturdier shoes in my luggage. And plainer clothing."

"Then you must change at the next stop. Even if we only walk now and then, it'll be a relief." He grabbed the strap as the coach lurched again. "Damn that man! I apologize again, but ..."

"But it's entirely understandable. Is he perhaps drunk?"

"I should have thought of that. He could be slugging from a bottle up there all the time."

At another jolt, protesting wood squealed.

"We could join him," she said, digging in her pocket. "I have brandy."

Right then, a loud *crack!* coincided with a violent lurch that threw her against him. He clutched her to him, trying to protect her.

Something had broken, and broken badly.

The coachman was bellowing, the horses struggling, but the tilt was getting steeper. A wheel had gone and they were too close to the ditch. The coach could go over completely.

Cate could only wrap his wife tightly in his arms and try to take the damage himself as the carriage crashed onto its side, glass shattering amid a hellish cacophony of noise.

He came to rest on a bruised back against the shattered door and window, Prudence sprawled over him. The panicked horses were rocking the torture box in which he and Prudence were trapped, sending stabbing pains in two places.

Wood or glass?

Pray God neither was of a length to do serious damage.

Then the coach jolted forward, sending new spears of pain. "Hold the horses still!" he bellowed, but they must be injured from such a disaster.

"Coachman!"

No reply, but the coach now tossed like a ship in a gale. Hades, had the man been thrown from the box, leaving the wounded horses masterless?

They had to get out of here.

"Prudence?"

"Yes."

"Thank God. Are you all right?"

"I think so. . . ." Not surprising that her voice was breathy. "Are you?" She moved and he gasped in pain. "What is it?"

"Glass, I think," he hissed. "Stay still."

"But we have to get out!" she said with a gasp, clinging to the strap above her.

"Hush, hush," he soothed, trying to ignore the pain, trying to think. "All will be well, though not, I fear, your hat."

"My hat?"

"I've landed on it."

"You're worried about my *hat*? Did you hit your head?"

"Only teasing, my dear. You're going to have to try to get out first."

Then a voice from outside called, "Is anyone alive in there?" A young man's voice with a local accent.

"Thank God," Cate said, and called, "Aye! Myself and my wife. Can you cut free the horses?"

"The coachman's doing it, sir. I'll climb up."

The coach rocked in a different direction. Cate could only grit his teeth.

Then the storm-tossing stopped.

"Thank God," he said. "Though I fear the poor nags must be in a bad way."

"Thank God indeed," she said, relaxing. "I'm sorry for falling into a panic."

"You had reason. Have you any hurt at all?"

"Only some bruises. You protected me." It was as if she'd seen a miracle.

"It's a husband's honor. You haven't been adequately cherished, my wife. That has all now changed."

She kissed him then, a gentle kiss, but fervent. And, thank God, without pressing down on him.

Perhaps he flinched anyway, for she drew back. "Where are you hurt?"

"My back and hip, but there's nothing to it."

"All the same, we won't be able to reach Keynings today, will we?"

"Does the thought distress you so much?"

"I suppose I must face your grand family sometime, but I'd rather it were later, when we've had time to settle into our own home."

What a damnable mess.

"Almost there, sir!" the young man called, amid scrabblings on the door of the carriage, which was now a sloping ceiling.

"Can you stand up without standing on me?" Cate asked.

She shifted carefully. "I think so."

He admired the way she managed it, bracing herself on one seat and the coach wall. At one point, she was propped over him in a very odd position, but it presented her generous breasts to his view, veiled only by a fichu that was coming interestingly loose. In the peculiar way of such things, desire suddenly stirred. . . .

"You are remarkable, you know," he said.

"I am?"

"Three tests of courage you've endured so far, and kept a steady head and a bold heart." But then he hissed as the coach shook again.

"Take care up there!" Prudence shouted, with all the sternness of a drill sergeant. "My husband's wounded."

Their rescuer went still. "Beg pardon, ma'am. Badly?"

"No," Cate called. "Do what you must."

The coach shifted and swayed again; then the door was wrenched open.

A square, amiable face looked down at them. "You're bleeding, sir."

"Very likely. Can you assist my wife to climb out?"

She shifted her legs and hands until she could stand with her head slightly outside. The young man was there to help, but getting any farther wouldn't be easy, especially for a woman.

Cate flexed his arms and tested his back. He seemed to have full use of both, but many places were going to hate this. He sat up, ignoring new stabs of pain. "Put a foot into my hands and I'll boost you."

She twisted her head to frown down in concern.

"Do it."

"If you're sure . . ."

"One, two, three, up!"

Their rescuer must have done his part, for she ended up with only her legs still inside. Despite pain, Cate enjoyed the view of shapely calves and fine ankles, covered in silk stockings clocked with roses.

"I've got you, ma'am!" called the young man, and she kicked with her effort to get out completely.

Cate hastily guarded his head with his arm, but the view was even more interesting. Then, with one wild, painful jolting she was gone and the torture box went still again.

Cate took a moment to mentally check his hurts. He heard noises and quickly called, "Don't come up to help me. I'll manage."

"Right you are, sir!"

The worst pain was from something, probably a shard of glass, that had pierced high on his right thigh. It could be worse. A lot worse. His leather breeches would have protected him, and if it had cut lower, he could be dead. There was a place in the thigh that gushed blood if slashed, and killed in moments. All the same, his hand found sticky blood enough. There was a wound in his side too, but less worrisome.

He got his feet under himself, seeking solid places around the shattered doorframe, then pushed up straight, ignoring the protest from his thigh. His head rose completely out of the carriage and he saw Prudence on the road, looking up anxiously, clothes awry, hair tumbling down. She looked magnificent.

At sight of him, her face cleared into a joyous smile. He reflected it and meant it. Damned stupid time to feel joyful, but then, perhaps not. They'd survived.

He still had to get out and down, and it was going to hurt. He reached back and found the edge of the shard of glass. It was a couple of inches wide, so it must be short or it'd have done worse damage. There was the chance that removing it would cause a gush of blood, but be damned if he'd climb out with it in situ.

It was slippery with blood, but he got a grip and yanked, choking back the pain. He felt new, hot blood, but no great spurt of it.

He'd do.

Prudence wasn't smiling now. "What's the matter?" she called.

"Nothing of importance."

He felt for the glass in his side, but the layers of coat,

waistcoat, and shirt muffled it. He couldn't get at it to pull it out. So be it.

He grabbed the upper doorjamb and muscled himself up and onto the top, cursing as quietly as he could. From there it was easy enough to slide down the coach to the ground. Once there, however, he swayed and found he had to lean against an undamaged wheel to let the world settle around him.

Chapter 15

Prudence ran over to him, touching him, patting him. "How badly are you hurt? Your breeches are dark with blood."

He suddenly felt a great deal better. He looked over at their young rescuer, who was mounting his cob. "I can't stay, sir. I'm on an errand for my master."

"I understand. Thank you for your assistance. Can you leave word at the next place that we need transportation?"

"I'll do that, sir," he said, and rode off back the way they'd come.

"It's been a while since we passed anywhere likely to have decent horses, never mind a carriage," Cate said.

"And it's going to rain. Look at those clouds. I think we're cursed!"

Cate pulled her into his arms. "Never. Merely challenged, and we always triumph. We've just survived an accident that could have proved fatal."

She pushed back to frown at him. "Are you an eternal optimist?"

"Why not? I have you."

It clearly perplexed and pleased her at the same time. "You must have banged your head," she protested. "I've been nothing but trouble. Are you sure you're all right? You've scraped your hand...."

She rattled on, still patting him, seeking damage, or simply caring. Being fussed over was remarkably pleasant.

"I'm sorry," she said. "This is all my fault."

"Nonsense, but I tell you the honest truth, my dear. I've enjoyed today a great deal more than most recent ones. And your legs are delightful."

"My *legs*?"

"As you scrambled out of the coach."

Her jaw dropped, and then she swatted his shoulder. "You shouldn't have looked!"

That made him laugh, perhaps a little wildly, which caused new concern.

"No, no," he assured her. "No head wound. I'm not mad. Merely insanely happy. I was speared by some glass, but I pulled it out."

"Where? Oh ..." Her anxious hands hovered, but she couldn't quite find the courage to touch him there.

Time to take charge and see what needed to be done. He straightened and limped toward the horses.

"You're dripping blood!" she exclaimed. "Stay still. That wound must be bandaged before you move another step."

"Truly, it's nothing, and I promised to help the coachman if he needed it."

The man had the two horses calm, but blood ran from the side of one, and another held a leg off the ground. Even so, they'd come off better than could be hoped.

"Broken legs?" he called to the man.

"No, thank the Lord, but nasty, the poor beasts. They need care."

"Where's the next place ahead?"

"I don't rightly know, sir, and me maps are who knows where in that mess."

"Can the horses walk?"

"I think so, sir." The man took the reins and urged the animals forward. They went reluctantly, but even the one favoring a leg could use it.

"Then you'd best walk them slowly on to the next place and get them attention. Send some sort of transportation back if you can. If we end up with two extra coaches, so be it."

"Right you are, sir. Come on, come on, me beauties. Oats and rest just a little way away."

Cate watched as the horses limped off down the road, hoping their injuries were slight. He then turned to survey the wreck. The broken wheel was in pieces, and that side of the coach shattered. The pole had twisted in some way, which would have spared the horses a bit, but the coachman must have been thrown off.

"We could have died," Prudence said.

He turned to find her hugging herself as if chilly. He felt the same.

"Shock," he said. "You mentioned brandy?"

"Oh, yes." She reached into a pocket and pulled out the dainty flask. As she unscrewed the cap, she said, "It seemed right to take it to our wedding as something both new and blue."

"Do you have the lucky sixpence in your shoe?"

"Yes." She passed him the cap. "Here."

He drank the mouthful it contained. "We might need your sixpence. I'm down to my last coins."

"Penniless, as I suspected," she said, refilling the cap. He couldn't tell if she was joking or not. She, too, drained the cap, and then gave him the bottle. "Time to bandage your wound."

So, she'd found her courage. "Know anything about doctoring?" he asked.

"I nursed my mother."

"Did she often get stabbed in the posterior?"

She blushed, but didn't quail. "No, but I'm the best doctor you have at the moment, so don't quibble." She reached up to untie his neckcloth. "We can use this as a pad." She rolled it up and gave it to him. "Press it on the wound to slow the bleeding."

He did as he was told, admiring her briskness. "Now what?"

"I need to bandage it in place. I suppose that means sacrificing some of my shift."

She reached into her pocket and produced a knife in a crude linen sheath.

"I think I remember that knife."

She shot him a quick look. "Yes."

It was the one she'd threatened him with, and then driven deep into the table. The one he'd pulled free of the table for her. He'd forgotten that violent expression of her fury and frustration.

Did she carry the weapon with her at all times?

That could make life interesting.

"Better to use my shirt," he said. "It's threadbare anyway."

"And probably your only one."

"No, I promise." He gave her back the pad, which was already bright with blood, then took off his jacket and waistcoat. "Perhaps you'll be able to remove whatever's in my side."

"There's more damage?"

"Only a splinter or some such." But it hurt to pull the shirt up over his head. "Dratted small wounds. Often more annoying than large ones. In the short term, at least."

"Have you often been wounded?" she asked.

"I was a soldier, Prudence. Nothing serious, by the grace of God. Here." He handed her the shirt, but she was staring at his bare chest.

Why did he keep forgetting things like that with her? It was as if they were old comrades. Or old lovers. She licked her lips, still staring, which was almost the undoing of him.

"Something in my side?" he prompted.

She jumped. "Oh, of course." She gave him back the pad but hesitated to touch him.

"There's no need. . . ."

"If it's hurting you, there is." She was brisk then. "Raise your arm so I can see properly." After a moment, she said, "It's rather more than a splinter."

She pressed the flesh on either side of the invader, but he could feel her embarrassment. If this were a game, he'd feel guilty, but he needed to be able to move freely.

"It's quite a large piece of wood and there's nothing to get a grip on. It needs to be cut out."

"I'll live with it for a while," he said.

"No, you won't. I'll try not to hurt you too much."

He hadn't been concerned about the pain, only about her being required to perform surgery on him.

She was tentative with the knife at first, but then he felt the quick sear of a cut, and hissed at the pain that followed a moment later.

"Now I can get it," she said with a surgeon's brutal cheerfulness.

Her probing hurt, but by God, the magnificent courage of the woman.

"There." She pulled out the wood and pressed his shirt against it. "I think it will stop bleeding soon. It wasn't very deep. I'm sorry if I hurt you."

"The patient always appreciates speed. Your knife must be sharp."

"What use is a blunt one?" She raised the shirt. "There. It's not bleeding much. Hold the pad there while I look at your leg." She touched his thigh without a flinch that he could detect. "Your breeches are badly stained, so you've bled quite a bit. I doubt the cut in them can be repaired. Do you have other riding leathers?"

"No, but I do have other breeches. I won't need to go naked in the streets."

"To the great regret of the women of Yorkshire, I'm sure."

He laughed and kissed her quickly. "Many other women would be in the vapors by now."

"Most women are remarkably resilient when tested. Let me have the shirt. Ah, yes, the bleeding in your side's mostly stopped."

She considered his shirt, doubtless seeing all the wear and mends. He wanted to assure her again that he had other clothes. That he wasn't the poor man he seemed. But now was definitely not the time to tell her he was an earl. Not when she had a knife in her hand.

She slashed the cuff off a sleeve, and then the whole sleeve from the body. She folded the rectangle of linen into a tight pad. "There. Your neckcloth will hold it in place."

"On top of my breeches?" he said, and undid them.

"Stop that! This is the open road!"

"Perhaps a woman of Yorkshire will pass by to be delighted."

"You can't undress—"

"There's no one to be scandalized, Prudence. Except you, of course. But you are my wife."

She stared at him wide-eyed, but then said, "Very well. You're right. Lower them."

He had to warn her. "I've nothing on underneath, and with no shirt . . ."

"There's no one to see but me," she tossed at him, "and I'm your wife."

"And a woman of Yorkshire," he said, grinning. "A magnificent one."

He turned his back, however, before lowering the breeches, which proved wise when he sensed her come closer, then felt silk brushing him. He heard the rustle of it when she knelt to study the wound, and her pretty flower perfume rose above the stench of blood.

She gently touched the wound, then put a hand on the front of his thigh to brace herself. His cock shot to attention and he shuddered.

"Did I hurt you? I'm sorry, but there's a bit more glass in there. You see—it's a good thing I can check thoroughly."

"Yes, ma'am," he said meekly, then hissed when she pressed and the glass jabbed.

"There's not much to get a grip on," she apologized, pressing again ruthlessly.

"Are you sure you're not a sawbones?" he said through gritted teeth.

"Don't fuss. If I use the tip of the knife. Almost . . . Ah!"

He felt it come out, and he released a breath. At least the pain had rendered him limp again.

"Any other damage?" he asked.

"I don't think so. Any pain when I do this?" She pressed the pad hard against him.

He flinched, but said, "Only soreness. Bind it up."

"Wot's going on 'ere, then?" asked a man.

Cate turned his head and saw a smocked yokel staring at them, pitchfork in hands. A sturdy lad stood behind, a billhook in his hands.

"Stand still!" Prudence snapped at Cate. To the man, she said, "I'm bandaging my husband's wound, sir. As you see, we've suffered an accident."

The yokel seemed deflated by her tone. "Sorry to hear it, ma'am." He was only in his twenties and not as sure of his authority as he'd tried to appear.

"Perhaps you can help us," Cate said. "Bind it up quickly, my dear."

She didn't. She did nothing. After a moment, he understood. The thought of passing cloth through his legs was her Rubicon.

"A fine time to become missish," he muttered. "Pass the neckcloth to me and you hold the pad."

She did so, and he bound the bloody cloth around his upper thigh, pushing his genitals to one side as she surely would have fainted to do. He pulled up his breeches and fastened them as he turned to the men.

"Where be yer 'orses?" the man demanded.

Did he think they'd flown here?

"They were wounded, so the coachman is walking them to the next place."

"Next place is Worsall," the man said. "Not much use, Worsall."

"Then he'll take them on. But he or another will send a cart or carriage for us."

"Rain's coming," the man said.

"So we see. Is there somewhere nearby where we can find shelter as we wait?"

This was greeted by a suspicious silence.

"We're not brigands, sir," Prudence said. "Only travelers who've suffered a misfortune."

Cate added, "My name's Burgoyne, and this is my wife. We come from near Richmond."

Neither of their statements was proof of anything, but they seemed to ease away doubt.

"My farm's down yon lane," the man conceded. "You can rest there awhile if you want."

Cate gave him a slight bow. "Our thanks to you."

"We'll be back there, then. Come on, Lolly."

The two turned and walked off down the road, then turned left into a lane or road and disappeared.

"I'd better dress," he said, "even though you've destroyed my shirt."

"*I've* destroyed . . . ?"

"Pax!" he cried, raising a hand. "I'm teasing you. You're delightful to tease. I'll put on what's left. With my waistcoat and jacket on top, the lack will hardly be noticeable."

She passed him the items, but then turned away. He spun her to him and stole a quick kiss.

She protested, but her sparkling eyes told him she was enjoying it. She was a world away from the frozen woman who'd arrived at the church to marry Henry Draydale, and he intended to progress from here. To the stars.

Except they were progressing to Keynings, and all that implied.

He put on his waistcoat. "Perhaps we should elope."

"We're married."

He began to put on his jacket but must have winced. She hurried to help him.

"Elope from life," he said. "Run away to a place where nobody knows us, and be impetuous lunatics forever."

"I'd like that," she said, straightening his coat, patting him again, perhaps without realizing it. "But you've inherited a property, Cate. You must take care of it."

And you've taken possession of far more than you realize.

"Prudence, I need to tell you something."

Chapter 16

"Not now," Prudence said, looking at the sky. "It could pour at any moment. Let's find this farm."

It was an instinctive interruption. His suddenly serious tone warned that he had something unpleasant to say—some reluctant confession. Probably that his property was far less than he'd implied, or that he really was penniless, despite his protestations to the contrary.

She didn't want to hear it. Not here. Not now, with her best gown smeared with blood, her hat ruined, her hair astraggle, and her feet sore from the rough road. Later, when they were comfortable, when the world seemed on the right tilt again, she'd be able to cope with the problem, whatever it was, and find ways to manage.

After a few steps on the rough road, however, she turned back to the coach. "I need my sturdy shoes."

They went to the boot, but the whole carriage had been twisted in the accident. Cate tried to wrench open the boot lid, but couldn't do it.

"Stop," she said when he was about to try harder. "You'll open your wound."

"You'll twist your ankle in those."

She linked arms with him. "We can limp along together, supporting each other."

"Through life," he said, smiling at her.

She smiled back. "Come on, then. It's going to pour soon."

The rain was speckling the dry earth now, so they hurried toward the path as best they could. Cate was favoring his leg, and her shoes protested. As they turned off the road onto the downward-sloping lane, Prudence felt the right heel loosen.

"I keep thinking matters can't get worse, yet they do, like a wheel rolling down a hill. I'll soon be shoeless, my gown is ruined, your clothes are in shreds. . . ."

"We're heading for warmth, food, and rest," he said. "As soon as the rain passes, we'll force open the boot and you, at least, will be in fine form again."

"Optimist," she said, but with a laugh.

Life was promising. She could be on the first day of the rest of her life as Henry Draydale's wife. Instead, she was Mistress Catesby Burgoyne, and the farm at the end of the rutted track offered shelter from the elements.

It was a long, narrow building of gray stone, but pleasantly situated by a stream. There was a stone-walled yard facing them where poultry pecked and some piglets ran around. Behind, she could see the roofs of some outbuildings and fields of sheep. Smoke drifted from the chimney.

"It looks pleasant and cozy," she said.

"Wistful to be a farmer's wife?"

"Wistful for shelter. This place looks picturesque, but it must be harsh in the winter."

As they reached the stone wall, a young woman came to the door, her apron swollen with pregnancy. She waved. "Come in, sir, ma'am. Come in. The rain'll be sheeting down soon."

They obeyed willingly, though Cate had to duck to get through the doorway.

The farmhouse was as small as her cottage in White Rose Yard, but they entered into the kitchen. It was only just large enough for a table, a settle near the fire, and a low cupboard with shelves above, but the room took up the full depth of the house. The floor was flagstoned but the ceiling low. Cate could only just stand straight under a beam.

There must be more rooms to the right, beyond the hearth wall, where a pot hung over the fire, giving off a tasty smell. The fire almost made the room too warm, but at the moment that was welcome.

"Sit you down, sir, ma'am. I'm Mistress Stonehouse, and Green Hollow is me man's farm," she said with pride. She was a pretty young woman with a complexion any fine lady would envy and soft brown hair tucked into a mobcap. "A coach accident, you say. What a terrible thing. Can I draw you some ale?"

Prudence longed for tea, but there'd be no such luxury here. Brandy would do, but pulling a flask from her pocket might make them suspect.

She sank onto the settle, slipping off her shoes, feeling at home, perhaps because this room reminded her of Hetty's kitchen. Hetty, like this farmwife, knew how to make a comfortable home out of a bleak structure. Prudence and her mother had never been able to do that.

Why blame it on the house?

She rubbed her feet, sighing at her soiled stocking, accepting that she might lack the ability to create a comfortable home in a bleak structure, and that something like this might be all Cate had to offer. Everyone had been skeptical of his claims to property and money and they'd doubtless been right. His shirt was threadbare and mended in a number of places. Why wear it if he had better?

She'd still choose him over Draydale a hundred

times, but why could her life never be smooth? In truth, she asked little of it. She was suddenly teary and pulled out her handkerchief, but when she raised it, she saw blood on her hands.

"Are you hurt, ma'am?"

The farmer's wife stood there with two pots of ale.

"No. My husband was. By glass when the carriage tipped over. Can I wash my hands?" The rain was coming down now, but she said, "Perhaps in the stream?"

"No need for that," said Mistress Stonehouse. She put down the ale and went to dip water out of a cask into a basin. "We always keep water inside." Again she spoke with pride, but she apologized when she put a wooden bowl of flaked soap on the table. "It's not fine stuff, ma'am, such as you'll be used to."

It was harsh soap, probably made of sheep's fat and lye, but a few weeks ago it had been the sort she'd used.

"It'll clean my hands, which is all that matters."

As she washed her hands Prudence resolved to give their hostess a gift. She had a pot of sweet soap in her trunk.

"That's a nasty bruise you 'ave on yer face, ma'am. Come up fast, that 'as."

Prudence dried her hands, wondering if the woman was suspicious. She might know the look of a blow a day old. "It happened earlier," she said, and went to Cate smiling, hoping to remove any suspicion that he'd hit her.

Cate toasted her with his ale, but he was standing, not sitting.

"Uncomfortable?" she asked.

"I'm not going to try it. Sooner or later I'll have to sit again, in carriage or on horseback, but no need to rush it. How are your bruises? The new ones, I mean."

"Minor."

But then Mistress Stonehouse cried, "The rain's here full pelt. Quick, the shutters!"

The four small windows didn't have glass and they all hurried to slam shutters closed; then Mistress Stonehouse ran through a door by the hearth and they heard more shutters slam. Her smocked toddler stood in the midst of the flurry, thumb in mouth, staring at Prudence.

"Good day to you," Prudence said.

The thumb came out; the child said, "Day," and shoved it back in again.

His mother came back. "There's a good lad, Jackity."

"A very clever boy," Prudence agreed, making the mother beam.

All mothers loved praise of their children. Except that she didn't remember hers showing pride in her, and it seemed Cate's mother didn't appreciate his qualities. His unappreciative mother was at Keynings and wouldn't approve of him any the more for a bride who turned up bloodstained and dirty, her hair a bird's nest.

A carriage accident was excuse for her tattered condition, but all the same she wanted to present herself to her mother-in-law in as respectable a state as possible. Before they left here she'd change into something else, though she had nothing else as fine.

Farmer Stonehouse came in then, sacks over his head. "We need the rain," he said, as if daring anyone to criticize anything here.

His son toddled over to him and was lifted proudly. "There's my grand lad!"

"Sit you down and rest a moment, me love," said his wife. "I'll make the griddle cakes and we can eat."

"And you'll eat well," the farmer said. "A fine housekeeper, my Peg is."

"I can see that, sir." Cate raised his ale. "You're a fortunate man."

"I am, sir, I am," said the young farmer, sitting down, and simmering down as well.

"Do you have good land here?" Cate asked, and that led to a conversation about rich land and poor, and the uses it could be put to. Talking of such matters, the men seemed almost equal, but Cate seemed well-informed for a soldier. Perhaps he'd inherited a farm and was learning about it.

Perhaps that was what he'd been about to confess—that he couldn't take her to a manor house, but only to a farmhouse. She didn't mind too much, apart from the fact that she lacked all the skills. A farmer's wife had to know about pigs and poultry, and about making butter and cheese. She might have to help at harvesttime, and then there were the other skills, such as making wine, cordials, and cream for the hands.

She considered her clean hands, so smooth and lady-like. She'd better see if she could get the recipe from Hetty's mother. She might also need to know how to make bread on an iron griddle, for a small farm like this one wouldn't have an oven.

Then she remembered that Cate had promised her servants. He wouldn't have lied to her, and good servants would know how to make bread, oven or not. She could do this. She could be Catesby Burgoyne's good-wife and make him comfortable, even on little money.

But first she had to survive their visit to Keynings.

She didn't understand why they had to go there so quickly. Perhaps it was some sort of obligation in the aristocracy that a bride must be presented to the head of the family. Perhaps he was even expected to ask permission. She'd heard officers in the army had to have permission of their general before marrying.

She picked at the bloodstains on her green silk skirt, as if they could be scratched off. Her next-finest outfit was stylish, with braid and frogging, but of sturdy cloth intended for travel. She'd have put it on this morning except that it had seemed too military for a wedding dress.

There were three day dresses in her trunk, one of white with a yellow stripe, one of cream with small printed flowers, and one of a bright chintz. All were lightweight, however, and odd garments to wear on a journey. The only other gown was her blue, which she hadn't been willing to discard after doing so much work on it. It was definitely unsuitable.

"Dinner's ready," Mistress Stonehouse said. "Call the lad, Jonny."

The farmhand soon raced in and they all sat down. Farmer Stonehouse said grace, and his wife then ladled a thick stew into wooden bowls. It was mostly vegetables but very tasty, and the griddle bread spread with butter was delicious. There was even a dessert of stewed pears, probably from fruit dried the autumn before. A provident housewife could do so much with so little.

She would learn to be a provident housewife.

She'd felt differently in White Rose Yard, and in the places they'd lived before. She'd had no heart for learning such skills and looked only toward the day when she would return to her rightful place. Now she'd cast her lot in with Cate Burgoyne, and she certainly had the heart to try to make their home comfortable.

She offered to help with the cleaning up after the meal, but Mistress Stonehouse said, "Sit y'self down, ma'am. I'll scrub the dishes in the stream later. It'll be a pretty afternoon when the rain's passed."

Cate went to crack open a shutter. "There is some clearing in the distance."

Prudence went to look for herself. There was a hint of brightness, but she realized how tucked away this farm was. She couldn't see road or carriage.

"What if my trunk is stolen?"

Cate looked at her. "Then it's stolen, but it's unlikely on such a quiet road. And someone would have to force open the boot."

"The rain might get in."

He shook his head at her. "Then it gets in."

"But I'd have to travel on in this gown." She turned. "Mistress Stonehouse, do you have salt to spare to try to remove the bloodstains on my gown?"

"Aye, but is that silk? Salt could damage silk."

"If the stains won't come out the gown's ruined, so I'd best try."

The farmer's wife provided water again, a box of salt, and a rag to clean with. Prudence dabbed salt on the worst stain.

"You'd do better out of it," Mistress Stonehouse said. "I've spare clothes in t'other room if you want."

"Are you sure you don't mind?"

"Nay, get on with you. My things'll be a bit short, mind."

"It's only for a little while. Thank you."

Prudence was truly impressed by such easy generosity. When had she known the like? From Hetty, she supposed. As she went to the small door alongside the hearth, she remembered Hetty saying something about people being best off in their place. Perhaps it was easier to be born to a simple life and be content to stay in it all one's days. She'd been raised up, cast down, raised up again, and now she didn't know quite where she belonged.

There wasn't even firelight in the bedchamber, so Prudence opened the shutters a crack. The rain had perhaps slackened, and there might be brightness in the distance, but at the moment its steady fall suggested that it liked it here and intended to stay.

She turned to consider the room, which was clearly the only other one. Beyond the end wall must be part of the farm buildings, perhaps a barn of some sort.

This room held a big bed, a small one, and a cradle in a corner, waiting for the new arrival. The bed was crudely made, probably by the farmer himself, but covered with a patchwork coverlet in bright colors. A similar one covered the child's small bed, and a third lay in the cradle. Despite poverty and sometimes hardship, the babe would arrive into a loving, pretty world.

She would manage to create the same for her children.

There was no clothespress here, only hooks on the wall and a couple of wooden chests. Two hooks held clothing covered with unbleached cloth. Curious, she raised one cloth and saw a man's suit. It was made of rough brown wool, but would be Farmer Stonehouse's finery, reserved for church and other special occasions.

Beneath the other cloth she found a yellow gown embroidered with colored flowers made of simple hook work, perhaps done by Mistress Stonehouse herself. It would be the woman's wedding gown, again reserved for church and special occasions, but strangely similar to the dress Prudence had worn to marry Draydale. It was a world apart in elegance and price, but this one was more valuable by far. It had been made with love for a loving marriage and spoke of shining hope of future happiness.

She dropped the protective cloth back over the gown. Her marriage to Draydale had carried no such hopes, but what of her marriage to Cate? She did hope for happiness, desperately.

She looked at her wedding ring. It was a tawdry thing, but she might want to wear it all her days. It symbolized forever, which was a treasure beyond price if only she could be worthy of him.

And if only, if only, he came to love her too.

She quickly chose the simplest clothing available—a skirt of pale blue linen and a bodice in a deeper shade. She took off her stained gown and checked her petticoat. No stains had penetrated. Her stays were also unblemished. She stepped into the skirt, pulled it up, and tied the laces at her waist. When she looked down, she saw inches of ankle. It must have already been short for working wear, and now it was too short. She might not have minded, except that it exposed dirty stocking and battered shoes.

She felt like a slattern, but this was only for a little while. If she could restore her green to some sort of decency, she'd be ready for Keynings. If not, she hoped her trunk was still in the coach and undamaged by the rain. She'd be able to change into clean stockings, sturdy shoes, and the rust-red traveling gown.

Chapter 17

Cate leaned on the wall by the slightly open shutter, watching the weather not improve to any appreciable degree. He knew Yorkshire rain. It could sweep by quickly, or settle in for days.

The rain would have put off any coach or cart coming to rescue them, so what to do when it cleared? Wait or walk? He'd walk if he had to, but the wound in his leg didn't make it a pleasant prospect.

If a vehicle did turn up, how was he going to pay for it? The few coins in his pocket wouldn't be enough, and he doubted Prudence had much more. He had the earl's signet ring and Roe's mourning ring, but couldn't consider trading either for transportation. A ridiculous situation, all in all, but his wife was worth the price.

Impulse had served him well for once. He'd recognized Prudence Youlgrave's qualities from the first, and the past days' events had confirmed them. She might not have been born to be a countess, but she'd make a wonderful one.

What would Artemis, or his mother, or Bland, Bumble, and Fizz have done if faced with today's events? Been uselessly terrified during the action and thrown a fit of the vapors afterward, ending up good for nothing but a bed with people fussing over them. Instead, his wife had fussed over him. He didn't remember anyone doing quite the same.

She was quick, clever, and in all ways admirable.

Then she came out of the other room, the green silk gown over her arm, looking like a peasant.

"Was there nothing better to wear?" he asked.

She frowned, shooting a meaningful glance at their hostess. "This will suit very well."

She spread the skirt of the gown over the end of the table and set to dabbing at it with water and salt. The child toddled over to touch the embroidered silk, batting at it, chuckling. Prudence smiled and teased, but Mistress Stonehouse came over to chide her child.

Prudence said, "Let the child play. He'll do no harm."

"He'll make dirty marks."

"Of the sort easy to remove. I'm not so sure about the blood. I'm only spreading the stain."

"It should be washed, but can silk be washed?" The farmer's wife stroked a sleeve. "Such lovely stuff."

The child ran under the table, laughing when he went through the curtain of silk and back again, and the women laughed with him.

It was a charming picture, but Prudence fit it too comfortably. His wife would have a maid to take stains out of silk, and her children would have their own servants and be housed in the nurseries. That was where he'd been raised, seeing his parents only on occasion, and he'd enjoyed it that way. His children would be happy with that situation too, but how would Prudence feel?

She seemed so at ease here, where his mother and Artemis would be uncomfortable, but how would she cope with Keynings? It would not only be a foreign land to her; it would be a hostile one. No one would approve of this marriage, and her fine qualities of courage, resilience, and honesty could be seen as unwomanly.

One thing was sure—she must arrive at Keynings armored in fine clothes and full dignity, but he could tell that her efforts to clean the blood were making the silk gown worse rather than better.

"Abandon hope of that," he said. "As soon as the rain stops, we'll get you something else from your trunk."

She dropped the cloth into the basin. "It's such a waste, though. It was very expensive. Peg, would you like it? There's yards of material in the skirt and you might be able to make something out of the good parts."

Damnation. His countess was already on first-name terms with the farmer's wife, just as she'd been with her neighbor in White Rose Yard. She might have been born in a manor, but she'd traveled a long way from there and become a different person, one at ease here, but who would be very ill at ease in aristocratic circles.

It was done, however, and he must help her survive.

His first obligation was to confess the truth, but he'd need a moment in private. That explosion wasn't for public fare.

Prudence became aware of something shadowed in Cate's mood. Perhaps it was the bothersome weather, or perhaps the ruination of her fine gown. He would prefer that she present herself to his grand relations in silk, she was sure.

She, too, regretted the ruined dress, but in a way she was happier at the moment than she'd been in an age. She was enjoying Peg Stonehouse's company and the antics of her charming child. In this firelit room, shutters drawn, Green Hollow Farm was a cozy burrow.

Peg was putting a pot full of poppy flowers into a basin.

"What are you doing with those? Potpourri?"

"Nay, there's no pretty smell to them. I'll steep them in my rose-hip wine to make a fine cordial. Do you not make poppy water?"

Prudence smiled at the universal nature of wines and spirits, and none of it from France. "No. Show me how."

"There's not much to see now. I'll just put 'em to steep and set 'em aside for a few days. But then I'll add some dried blackberries from last year and set it in the sun awhile. Add some crushed snails, strain, and there it is."

"Snails?"

"Powerful good, snails are. Don't ye know that?"

"No," said Prudence faintly, wondering what was in Hetty's mother's cordial. Perhaps she could make the poppy water without the snails.

"What's it good for?"

"Most things. The cold, stomach upsets, fever, pain. For stomach, the best thing's chalk in goat's milk, but there's not much chalk around here."

Prudence encouraged Peg to share her knowledge, wishing she had paper and pen.

"How do you make your own wine?" she asked.

"All ye'll need is some very sweet fruit and yeast from the ale. Let it stand long enough, lightly covered, and 'tis done. Blackberry's a fine wine and makes good cordials."

All drunk for health, but enjoyed anyway.

Farmer Stonehouse poked his head in the back door. "The rain's stopping, sir. Do ye want to try to open t'boot?"

Cate said, "Assuredly. Do you have a likely tool?"

"The spike on me 'ammer'll likely do it." He brandished it.

Prudence had seen Cate wince as he moved. If his wound was healing it would burn to be stretched.

"I'll go," she said.

"On no account."

"Cate, it's a long climb, and your wound—"

"Is nothing."

Stonehouse said, "I'll be coming t'elp, sir."

"Thank you, but there's no need," Cate said tersely. "I'm sure you have more work than hours in the day."

"That's true, sir. If ye're sure." The farmer handed over his hammer and went back to his work.

Cate headed for the door, but Prudence followed. "I'm coming with you."

"Nonsense."

"Don't argue over this!" When he turned on her, she stood her ground. "It would be foolish to carry the whole trunk down here, but how will you know what to bring me?"

"I believe I can choose a suitable outfit."

"But not the one I'd choose."

"Prudence . . ."

She suddenly realized she was haranguing him as she'd once harangued her brother, and he was outraged. Though it was an effort, she changed her tactic. "Please," she asked. "I'll only worry about you. Let me come."

She thought he'd refuse even that, but then he said, "Very well. But when your shoes are in shreds, don't complain to me."

"I have sturdy shoes in my trunk," she pointed out.

When he rolled his eyes, she realized she'd fallen back into a starchy tone. Being a meek wife was going to be challenging.

When they opened the front door, she did hesitate. Because the farmhouse sat in a hollow, a mire of mud had formed beyond the step. Having made such a point of it, she couldn't turn back now.

She took his arm and sloshed into the mud. "These shoes are already past prayers, but at least my skirts won't trail in the mud. I can't imagine why we ever wear them down around our shoes."

"Why not skirts up to the knee?" he teased. "We gentlemen would appreciate that."

A mad impulse took her. Once they were on firm ground, she raised her skirt that high.

The look in his eye rewarded her. Suddenly hot, she dropped the skirt to set off up the long, slippery lane.

He caught up and hooked arms with her again.

When they turned onto the road, the coach lay just as they'd left it, shattered and on its side, and there was no sign that anyone had come by.

Birds trilled and chirped among wet hedge and grass, and sunshine was forming a rainbow.

"We could seek our fortune at the end of the rainbow," Prudence said, wanting to wander into the fields and away. Just away, with Cate.

"We have riches enough, wife. Let's restore your dignity."

Prudence followed him to the coach, dismayed by how much he seemed to care about her appearance. She could never look aristocratic.

The hammer had a long iron spike opposite the round head and he used it to lever open the boot. Wood shattered and splintered, but amid so much damage, that hardly mattered.

"Hold the boot lid while I pull out your trunk a bit," he said. "I think I can straighten it without having to put it on the wet ground."

She did, and he manhandled the trunk more or less straight.

"Your key?"

"Thank heavens I didn't take off my pockets," she said, putting her hand through the slit in her skirt and finding the key.

But then she heard hoofbeats.

"Someone's coming at last!" Cate said.

She stepped out, but it wasn't a coach. "Only two riders. One gentleman, one groom."

Cate came up behind her, then limped past. "Perry! How the devil did you get here?"

Perry? His friend?

The cloaked gentleman smiled. "With great difficulty, you madman. Is that your carriage?"

"What's left of it, which makes you an angel from heaven."

"I shall be Raphael, I think," the man called Perry replied. "'Raphael, the sociable spirit, that deigned to travel with Tobias, and secured his marriage with the seven-times-married maid.'" He smiled across at Prudence and bowed. "Has your wife been married seven times before?"

She felt obliged to curtsy, though his manner was ridiculously airy, and her clothes weren't suited to elegance. Here was her first encounter with someone from Keynings, and she must look like a peasant, a very grubby one.

"Prudence has only been married once," Cate said as his friend dismounted. "Where does that quote come from?"

"*Paradise Lost*. But referring to the Bible, in which Raphael did assist Tobias to free the beauteous Sara from a demon."

"How suitable, then."

"You have a demon?"

"No more. Except for demon poverty, which I hope you're about to exorcise."

"Yours, as always, to command." Perry tossed over a fat purse.

The weight of it was startling, unless it contained shillings. She was sure it did not.

If one could judge a man by his friends, what was she supposed to make of this one? Despite plain clothes and a heavy riding cape, he seemed all air and spirit, both in manner and build. He was shorter than Cate and much more slender, but in some way he didn't seem *lesser*.

Prudence caught the other rider staring at her, and realized that the groom was Tallbridge's man, who'd been sent with the message and must now be completely bewildered.

"Wot 'appened 'ere?" the groom demanded. "Where're the horses, and Mr. Banbury?"

Cate went over to explain, and the fanciful fribble approached her. Prudence dearly wished she were in silk and good order. He gave her an elaborate bow in which his right hand must have inscribed four full circles in the air. "My Lady Malzard, I assume. *Enchanté*, dear lady!"

"Who?" The man was addle-witted as well. "I'm Cate's wife, Mistress Burgoyne."

He blinked at her, smile fixed. "Ah . . . of course. A thousand apologies! But that only increases my delight to make your acquaintance, which has not formally occurred, as my friend has so neglected his duties. Let us correct his error. Peregrine Perriam, ma'am"—he bowed again—"very much your devoted chevalier. You may command anything of me. Absolutely anything!"

Prudence curtsied again, thanking him, but having to fight laughter at such a stream of nonsense. Until she realized something.

Mr. Perriam was acutely embarrassed.

He'd expected Cate to be with someone else.

With a Lady Malzard.

He was saying something about the weather and Yorkshire. She responded with something along the same lines, striving not to show her distress.

Cate and another woman, traveling together? That could only mean a mistress. Cate had a mistress and Mr. Perriam had expected Cate to be traveling with her.

A Lady Malzard had to be a married woman.

An adulteress.

Or a widow.

That was worse. A widow was available for marriage. Lord save her, had Cate begun his journey in pursuit of his one true love and then been snared by her misfortunes?

She'd been silent too long. "My apologies, Mr. Perriam. As you can imagine, events have been distressing."

But none so distressing as this.

Cate joined them then. "I see you've made each other's acquaintance. My apologies for not performing the introductions. We're about to find decent clothes for Prudence. At present she's in something borrowed from the farmer's wife."

He was apologizing for her. Lady Malzard, she was sure, always dressed to perfection.

Prudence wanted to crawl into a hole, but instead she turned back toward the trunk. "Let's be about it."

She heard Mr. Perriam say, "Cate," behind her, as if to attract his attention, but then, "Gads, are you wounded?"

"Nothing dramatic. The trunk is the first priority."

Getting his unwanted wife into something decent was the priority.

Dress a pig in silk . . .

Lady Malzard had to be highborn and elegant. She was probably petite and soft of feature, always charming and sweet, never haranguing her lover, not even for his own good.

Prudence unlocked the trunk. When Cate raised the lid for her, she said, "I can manage." She wanted him to go away so she could pull herself together. So she could fight the tears that wanted to spill.

"You'll need another pair of hands. You can't put things down in the mud."

He was right, which upset her even more.

Her rust outfit lay on top and was very suitable for travel. Lady Malzard, however, doubtless always dressed in frills and flounces, so she dug deeper and pulled out her yellow stripe.

"That's too delicate for travel," he said. "You must have something plainer."

Plainer? Very well, sir, I'll give you plain.

She took out the blue.

But then she came to her senses. No one would be hurt by that but herself. She tucked it away and passed him the skirt and bodice that made up the rust-colored outfit, then added a pair of plain stockings.

"I just need the bag with my black shoes."

She dug deep for that. When she straightened with it and turned to him, he asked, "What's the matter?"

She wanted to tell him exactly what the matter was—she wanted to swing the shoe bag at his thick, thoughtless head—but what was the point? What was done was done.

"Just the effects of the day."

"Or Perry. It's unfortunate that he arrived when you were in those clothes, but he can be trusted."

Trusted not to spread the story of how inferior and unsuitable she was.

"We should get back to the farm," he said.

"I need to get some gifts for Peg Stonehouse."

She was glad to turn away to find the soap in its pretty china pot and one of her new, lace-trimmed shifts. Whatever he truly wished, Cate was married to *her*, not Lady Malzard. He was hers, and it was better so. That fine lady wouldn't have been able to tolerate his poverty. She wouldn't know how to make bread and hand creams.

Well, nor did Prudence yet, but she could learn. She'd learn everything necessary to make a comfortable home so he would come to love her. Her, not another woman.

If Lady Malzard was married, however, and Cate's beautiful, elegant, sweet mistress, Prudence had no weapons at all.

She closed the lid, turned the key, and announced, "Now I'm ready."

She set off back to the farm, hearing the angry thump as Cate closed the boot. A fine way to begin making the marriage work, radiating ill usage, but how did a person extinguish such a fire of anger and pain?

What stupid dreams she'd built, only because he was kind and sometimes lustful. Men didn't need to feel anything for a woman to lust after her, but men like Cate didn't fall in love with women like her.

She was more like her sister-in-law than she thought.

She continued toward the farm without waiting for the men, fighting for calm, trying not to care, hurt and anger building with every step.

If he loved another, he shouldn't have married her, no matter what straits he found her in.

He should have left her to her fate.

At least Draydale would never have broken her heart.

Chapter 18

Cate turned to see Prudence marching back down to the farm, her posture declaring that she was still in a tiff over something. He left Perry and the groom to bring down the horses and set off after her.

"Let me carry all that."

"I'm no delicate lady. Spare your leg."

"A few bits of clothing won't strain me."

She glared, but then dumped it all in his arms and marched on.

"Prudence, Perry won't make anything of your appearance."

She turned on him. "My appearance! My appearance! I apologize for embarrassing you, husband."

"I'm not embarrassed by you." It came out between his teeth. Both his wounds were pestering him and he had no patience for megrims at the moment.

"No? Then you'll have told him all about White Rose Yard, I assume, and my penniless state."

"There's no need for anyone to know about White Rose Yard."

She smiled in a very humorless way. "Quite. *I* won't tell anyone," she said, continuing on her way. "After all, I promised to obey you, and *I* will keep my vows."

What the devil was that supposed to mean?

He tried again. "What's amiss?"

She turned an artificially wide-eyed look on him. "What could possibly be amiss, such a placid time I've had of it?"

"Don't blame your recent adventures on me, ma'am!"

He saw the flash of hurt before she turned forward and walked faster.

"Prudence!"

But then he realized this must be one of those times when a wise husband held his tongue. Perhaps she was even starting her courses. That was said to turn reasonable women into termagants, and would certainly add to the distress of the day for her. It would improve his, though. No risk of a Draydale cuckoo in the nest. No need to put off consummation once her bleeding was over.

He followed her in silence, rather inclined to whistle.

The mire had subsided to mud, but as soon as he entered the kitchen, she snapped, "Take off your boots. You won't want to tramp mud on Peg's floor."

She'd discarded her ruined shoes and stood in her dirty stockings, her hair straggling again, with muddy streaks on her face. Was she going to be so ill-humored every month? To add to his problems, with his wound he couldn't get his boots off unaided.

"Go and change. You'll feel more the thing." It came out more curtly than he intended.

She grabbed her clothes and stalked away.

He slumped against the doorjamb, watching his wife give her gifts to Mistress Stonehouse. The farmer's wife was in heaven over the shift and pot of soap. She insisted on instantly washing her hands with it, and then her child's hands.

"There, Jackity, don't that smell pretty? All flowery it is."

Prudence was watching and even smiling. But then she looked at him and annoyance lowered her brows before she turned and went into the other room.

Devil take the woman.

The others were arriving at the door. Perry, for some reason, was carrying a stick of some sort.

"Take your boots off," Cate growled at Perry; then he turned to Mistress Stonehouse. "As you see, ma'am, a friend has arrived, and a groom. May they come in?"

She was still fondling the shift. "Of course, sir."

Cate told the groom to settle the horses so they could graze. "Don't unsaddle them. We'll probably be setting off again soon. Boots, Perry."

Perry's brows were high at his tone. "You'll have to assist me. Glove-tight, as boots should be."

"You'll have to wait for the groom. What would you do if stranded without help?"

"It doesn't bear thinking of. Allow me to remove yours. I'm sure I may step just inside the door."

Cate's boots slid off easily. Perry shook his head. "I'll take you to my boot maker as soon as we return to London."

"I prefer to be able to get into and out of my boots alone, thank you."

"Barbarian."

"I'm astonished you made the sacrifice of riding through Yorkshire in the rain, though the sweet, fresh air will have done you good. In London, that's rarer than diamonds."

"Whereas here, anything other than sheep is more precious than rubies."

"Sheep are damned valuable," Cate countered. "England's wealth is built on the woolpack."

"You're becoming distressingly provincial. Ah, the trusty groom."

It took the man some minutes to ease off the boots, and Perry's expensive clocked stockings had probably never touched such a lowly floor before, but he was all amiability about it. He went to thank his hostess as if she were a duchess, executing a bow that made her jaw drop.

In a moment, he was flirting, just as he might with a young duchess at court. She turned pink, and once she slapped his arm in mild reproof, giggling. Pray heaven her husband didn't come in, billhook in hand.

Had Perry flirted with Prudence? Was that the problem? Had she been offended? Or had she liked it too much, and now found Cate coarse by comparison?

The groom had shed his own boots and was accepting ale from Mistress Stonehouse. Perry accepted his ale as if it were nectar.

Farmer Stonehouse did come in then, but was pleased to hear his wife's ale praised. Her excited pleasure over her gifts mellowed him even more.

"This is right good of you, sir."

Cate smiled. "It's my wife's generosity, but the thanks are from us both." He took out the purse Perry had brought and found some shillings among the guineas. If people like the Stonehouses suddenly had a golden guinea it would cause talk, especially now, with gold coins in short supply.

"I'd offer this too, sir, if you will, for your kindness and trouble."

The young man took the silver. "That's right kind of you, sir. Wasn't nothing but simple Christian charity."

"Which sometimes is rare."

Stonehouse clearly thought that odd, the blessed man, but he went back to his work. The groom and Mistress Stonehouse were chatting. Prudence hadn't emerged.

Cate realized that Perry could reveal at any moment that he was Lord Malzard. He had to be the one to tell her, but should he invade the other room and risk catching her in her undergarments? She was in a dashed odd mood.

Perry came over, ale in hand. "What are you tangled up in now?"

"Nothing unusual. Wheel came off."

"Why?"

"Because the roads are atrocious."

Perry glanced toward the other two and said quietly, "Ill luck or foul play? That wheel had been tampered with." He went to get the piece of wood that he'd leaned near the door and gave it to Cate. It was one of the spokes.

"Sawed through in places," Perry said, "then the cuts hidden with packed sawdust."

Cate looked at the spoke. There was no denying it. "Draydale."

"Is that a novel curse?"

"It's a foul demon. A Mr. Draydale of Darlington has reason to dislike Prudence and me. I've expected something in due course, but this . . . this seems petty."

"Petty? I've known people killed or maimed in accidents like that."

"Devil take it." He fingered the wood. "That's cooked his goose."

"I'm glad to hear it. Do please remember that angels are efficacious against demons."

Cate smiled at him. "Would I deprive you of the pleasure?"

"And what of your wife?"

"Be careful, Perry. Yes, she's an unlikely countess, but she's better suited than she appears."

"I'm not criticizing her. I mean—"

Prudence came out of the other room, in truth looking more her part. The outfit was smart and new, with a military touch to it in the braid and frogging down the front of the bodice. Her hair, however, was still a mess, and she knew it.

"I forgot to get my comb," she said, not looking at anyone. "I've pinned up my hair as best I could."

There probably was no mirror here.

"You can use mine," Cate said, taking his comb out of a pocket.

Her lips pursed as if she'd object, reminding him that she had some grievance. If she was in a pet over some little thing, how would she react to his great deception? He should try to get that knife off her before confessing.

She took out all the pins, putting them on the table, and ran her fingers through her hair. It was longer than he'd thought, and . . . How had he described it? Sunlight on pale honey? Then she began to work his comb through it, her back to him. Deliberately? All the same, it seemed so intimate a matter that he wanted to order Perry and the groom out of the room, especially as the gown fit so neatly to her curves.

She turned to look outside, her head tilted as she combed in one direction. He enjoyed the clean line of her neck, and the beginning of the dip of her spine above the narrow band of white shift that showed above her gown. He let his imagination follow the line of her spine to the curving buttocks concealed beneath skirt and petticoat. She was a fine, proud, passionate woman, and he appreciated even her anger.

His heart began to thump, and he wanted to lead her into that other room and strip off every stitch until she lay naked on the sheets. He wanted to kiss her and pleasure her, and experience to the full the lusty enthusiasm he'd already tasted.

But would she even let him touch her when she knew? She might demand a divorce, which would be a

fine scandal to smear on his family. Or an annulment.
Would anyone believe him impotent? In France they
had a court for that, with matrons appointed to prove or
disprove a man's virility. *'Struth!*

In any case, he didn't want to end this marriage. She'd
be hurt, she'd be angry, but he'd find a way to heal her
wounds and make her his countess in all meanings of
the word.

He was suddenly aware of Perry watching him and
looked away, but it would be too late.

Well, there was no sin in a man admiring his wife.

Prudence coiled her hair and pinned it up again. Time
had allowed her to regroup. Petty anger would only
make matters worse.

She turned to Cate with a smile. "Is that tidy?"

"Almost," he said, and came over to take the comb.
He took out a pin, combed, and reset it. "There."

The touch of his fingers in her hair sent shivers
through her and brought heat to her cheeks. She hated
to be so revealing, but surely what she revealed should
please him?

"We need to get to Keynings," he said, "but no coach
has arrived, so we're going to have to ride a little."

Oh, lord. Lady Malzard probably rode with skill and
elegance, but there was no point in hiding the truth. "I've
never ridden. In any case, there are only two horses."

"You'll ride pillion. We'll take it slowly; don't worry."

"Do we have to go to Keynings today?" she asked.
"Why can't we go to your home?"

He looked away, tight-lipped. "Yes, we must."

How had she offended him now?

Mr. Perriam said, "You and your wife take the horses,
Cate. The groom and I will shift for ourselves."

"I can't abandon you here."

"You abandoned me at Keynings."

"My apologies. I never meant to be gone so long."

"So I should hope. You created a stew of anxiety and speculation. I took the first opportunity to run for my life."

Cate laughed. "I truly do apologize."

"Your return will hardly calm the waters," Perriam said with particular meaning.

He was referring to her. To Cate's returning with his inadequate wife.

Returning? She hadn't put it together before. He'd been visiting Keynings with his friend and his mother. He'd ridden off to Northallerton, but not returned. Hence the anxiety and speculation. And now he was going to return newly wed, with no prior announcement, bringing a wife with nothing to recommend her. Hardly surprising if Cate seemed at a loss.

"We must be on our way," he said, and gave the groom some money. "You'll have to walk a way, but if you retrace the route to Darlington you might come up with the coachman. If not, take a coach from the first place you come to. Give my apologies to Mr. Tallbridge and tell him I'll send a full account of matters as soon as possible."

"As you will, sir."

When the man had left, Cate turned to the farmer's wife. "You have our profound gratitude, Mistress Stonehouse."

"I'm sorry for your troubles, sir, but it's been a treat for me to have visitors, and these lovely things your lady's given me. I'll always remember this as a bright day."

He smiled, and Prudence saw true sweetness in it. "I hope you're right, ma'am, and it's a bright day for us all."

Prudence took her own farewell of the woman, feeling almost teary at having to leave. She felt safe here. Once away, she suspected many troubles lurked.

Cate and Mr. Perriam led the horses up to the road. Once there, Cate said, "There's something I have to tell you, Prudence."

He was going to confess his mistress. She'd much rather he not, but she asked, "What?"

"The accident wasn't. The wheel had been tampered with. Draydale's work, I assume."

It was so different from what she'd expected that her mind went blank for a moment. "*Draydale?* Why would he do such a thing?"

"In hopes of harming us. A die cast, only, but he had little time to plan a first strike whilst nursing his wounds. He's the sort of man to have to strike, however, and to try again, which is why we must get you safe in Keynings."

"I've put you in danger."

"*I* put me in danger, and you too, perhaps—"

"No."

"But don't worry. You're well protected. Both Perry and I have pistols on our saddles, and I'll get my sword."

He wrenched open the boot again, and dug deep inside. When he straightened he had a scabbarded sword on its belt and he buckled it on.

Prudence hated all this preparation for violence, but the very idea of Henry Draydale plotting to harm her weakened her knees. She could imagine the sort of revenge he'd like to take on her. If her riding would help keep them all safe she'd do it, but when Cate told her to mount up behind Mr. Perriam, she protested.

"It's a matter of weight. You two are the lightest." He helped her get a foot into a stirrup and Mr. Perriam hoisted her up to sit sideways behind him.

"Put your arm around me, ma'am," Perriam said. "You'll feel more secure."

She did, but when Cate mounted she saw his mouth tighten with pain, and how carefully he settled into the saddle. She wished there were something she could do to help him, but he was right. The great house, Keynings, had ceased being a threat and become a sanctuary.

It was only after they'd turned a bend in the road that she realized that she lacked gloves and hat.

That wouldn't add to her dignity, but she no longer cared.

Chapter 19

At walking place, the countryside seemed endless. Prudence saw nothing more threatening than a bull in a field and there was no hint that it would rain, but the threat of Henry Draydale hung over her. Cate was right: Draydale was the sort of man who'd have to take his revenge for such blows to his pride.

She told herself that his attempts would be concealed or indirect, as with the carriage accident. If she and Cate were openly attacked, he'd be the first suspect. But if their party were set upon by vicious footpads? Who could draw the line from that directly back to Henry Draydale, who was doubtless still nursing his wounds in Darlington?

Cate had pistols and a sword, she reminded herself. The effete Mr. Perriam had a gun in a holster on his saddle, but it was Cate she put her faith in, even wounded. She'd seen him in action.

When they finally rode into a modest town called Storborough, however, it was as if she breathed properly for the first time. Here were tidy houses and bounteous gardens, and streets busy with normal people going about their normal days. They soon realized why it was busy—it was market day, with the extra life, noise, and bustle that brought.

"Civilization!" Perriam declared. "I was beginning to think it had ceased to be."

"You must be in a dire state," Cate said with a grin, "if you're comparing this place to London."

"Don't, please. I could fall into a decline on the spot. I demand a pause here. I must wash and recover."

"We could all do with that. Which inn takes your fancy?"

"The Bull. It has a modern air to it."

They stopped outside the porticoed door to the modern stuccoed building and ostlers ran forward. Cate eased off his horse and limped over to Prudence. Before she could protest, he grasped her at the waist and lowered her.

"Idiot! Your wounds."

"Are naught compared to the pain of a cross word from you." She touched his head again, but he laughed. "I'm not fevered."

"Then you are, as I always expected, mad."

"Insane from birth," said Perriam. "You two can stand out here in a dream if you wish. I'm for food, drink, and hot water."

He walked away, but neither Prudence nor Cate watched him go.

"Prudence, what did I do to upset you so?"

"Nothing," she said, terrified that he'd confess his mistress.

If he never spoke of Lady Malzard, if he was so discreet that she never had to hear about the woman, and certainly never had to meet her, she thought she could bury the beautiful shameless hussy deep in her mind.

Perhaps.

"Is it still Keynings?" he asked.

She seized onto that. "Of course it is. Look at me. I have no hat!"

"No hat?" he repeated. "Nor have I. I assume it's broken and battered in the carriage, along with yours."

"It's different for a man. I could perhaps buy a hat here. And gloves. No, I see a better way. We can rest here and send for my trunk. Then I will arrive in decency in due course."

"No," he said, then grimaced. "Prudence, I have something I need to tell you. Come into the inn. They'll have tea."

Tea. He thought this could be solved by *tea*?

"I would rather buy a hat," she tried, but in the face of his grim mouth, it was a faint effort. He was determined to confess, and she must try to make the best of it.

When they entered the inn, they found Perriam was already being led upstairs, demanding hot water immediately.

"Do you want hot water?" Cate asked her.

"Oh, yes, please." Prudence toyed with asking for a bath, but could see that wouldn't do.

They were soon in a private parlor with bedchamber attached, tea and washing water ordered. There was a mirror on the wall facing the door, and her reflection made her want to cry.

"Why didn't you tell me I had smudges on my face? And my hair's a disaster!"

"You look well enough to me."

Well enough? She was sure he never told Lady Malzard she looked "well enough." She shot him an angry glance. "You're no image of perfection, you know, especially with bloodstained breeches."

"Letting you down, am I?" He wasn't smiling.

That terrified her. Perhaps it was worse. Perhaps he

needed to tell her that he'd realized he'd made a dreadful mistake. That he was going to abandon her and go off with his one true love.

It had been Peg Stonehouse's clothes. And probably Prudence's manner there. Peg had reminded her a little of Hetty, but she was a gentleman's wife now. More than that. An aristocrat's wife. He'd probably decided he couldn't bear to take her to meet his grand relations, including his mother. How could she bear it?

With the briefest knock, a maidservant came in with a jug of steaming water.

"I'll let you wash first," he said, and went into the parlor.

Prudence looked at the closed door, biting her lip on tears. Truly, she didn't feel she demanded too much from life, but comfort kept being snatched away from her. She should always have known, however, that Cate Burgoyne was beyond her reach. She almost lacked the heart to try, but she made herself wash and tidy her hair, feeling as if she prepared for the gallows.

Then she realized that she was waiting for him to return, when he must be waiting for her to join him. She gathered all her strength, straightened her spine, and went into the parlor.

He was looking out at the street, but turned to her. "Just people going about their business."

He'd been on the watch for Draydale's agents?

Hesitantly, she joined him by the window. "It does feel odd to find everything so ordinary after our dramas."

"Life goes on as a river flows, smoothly around obstructions. I remember once riding from a bloody skirmish into a place where people were haggling over the price of vegetables." He turned to look at her then. "Prudence—"

"I think I see a stall selling handkerchiefs," she said desperately. "I don't even have a handkerchief."

"Prudence, I need to make a confession."

"Is it that you're poor?" she asked, still trying to deflect the awful truth. "That there's no home after all? I don't—"

"There's a home, and I'm not poor."

"You're an impostor. Your name isn't Catesby Burgoyne."

"What? No."

She lost all will to fight. "You have a mistress," she said.

He stared at her. "Devil take it. What put *that* idea into your head?"

She suddenly felt dizzy. Such astonishment had to be real. But what could be worse?

"You . . . you're already married? We've committed bigamy?"

"Of course not. Prudence—"

"You're a criminal, on the run from the law!"

"With Perry as my low associate?" He rolled his eyes and leaned against the window frame. "Pray continue. What else can you devise?"

Not poor, not homeless, no mistress or other wife. "You're . . . dying?"

"For heaven's sake. I'm in the peak of health."

"Then what?"

He took a moment to speak—a long moment that said his confession was terrible, so terrible she'd been unable to imagine it.

Finally, he said, "I'm an earl."

"What?" Prudence stared, trying to make sense of nonsense words.

"I'm the fifth Earl of Malzard, and Keynings, to which we travel, is my home. This means," he said, watching her carefully, "that you are now the Countess of Malzard."

It was as if he spoke Greek.

Except that she knew some Greek.

"Countess of Malzard?" she repeated. "Oh, God! Oh, God! *I'm* Lady Malzard!"

"Yes." But he was looking at her with concern, as if she were running mad.

Perhaps because she'd giggled. There was no wicked Lady Malzard to steal Cate from her. *She* was Lady Malzard!

"I should have told you before you married me," he said, still watching her with concern. "I went to Tallbridge's house that night intending to tell you. But in the end, I couldn't risk your refusing to marry me."

Prudence stared at him. "Refusing to marry you?"

"You'd have had every reason, and you're strong enough, resolute enough, to have done it, but the consequences for you . . . All the same, I should have given you that freedom."

She pressed fingers to her temples. *"Refusing to marry you."*

"Hit me if you want."

She did, a strong slap across the head. "You thought I'd rather be left to Draydale's mercies than marry an earl?"

"I could have offered you some alternative. Money . . ."

"You think I'd rather be a kept woman?"

"I don't mean that. I'd have set you up in respectable comfort somewhere."

"After Draydale's accusation? How could that possibly be? But . . ."

She considered his shabby clothes, which were the same ones he'd worn at their first meeting, when he'd assuredly been short of money.

"Are you *sure* you're an earl?"

"All too sure."

"But you have no money."

"I merely never seem to have enough in my pockets when I encounter you."

"The money Mr. Perriam brought. It's yours, not his?"

"Yes."

"Then why are you still wearing those clothes?"

He shook his head. "I became the earl recently. I've been replenishing my wardrobe, but I didn't think my riding clothes had priority. Once we're at Keynings, I can impress you with my elegance, Prudence. I am the Earl of Malzard; I give you my word. See, here's my signet ring."

She only glanced at the heavy gold ring. "My clothes! No wonder you were bothered by them. Even my finest aren't fine enough. And your family! How could you have married without telling them?"

"You know how."

Prudence covered her hand with her mouth. "My fault, my fault. Your mother . . . Is she Lady Malzard, too?"

"Yes. So is my brother's widow."

"Your brother," she said, suddenly understanding. It blanked out all else. "The perfect one. Oh, Cate, I'm so sorry."

Without thought, she went to him and took his hands, but then she pulled him closer to hug him as he had once hugged her.

"I'm so very sorry," she repeated. "When did all this happen?"

"Time's become meaningless. But nearly a month ago. I was in London and it took time to travel north. I missed the funeral."

She held him tighter, and they stayed like that, drawing strength each from the other. That was what it felt like to her, at least, as her mind calmed and she settled into astonished acceptance.

Cate was an earl, and she was his countess.

He never wanted to be the earl, and she'd never have chosen to be a countess. But she would always have chosen to be Cate Burgoyne's wife, no matter what the cost.

"I'm learning," he said, "but I wasn't trained for this. Second son, you know. Firmly directed to make my own way in the world." He separated to smile ruefully at her. "The other day, I ran away from my responsibilities like a truant schoolboy. You were my excuse."

Only an excuse. That hurt.

"You shouldn't have married me."

"I know. I'm sorry."

She backed out of his arms entirely. "For *your* sake. You say you weren't trained to be earl. I certainly wasn't trained to be a countess. I'll be a burden, not a helpmeet."

"It's done, Prudence. There's no escape."

She didn't want to say it, but forced out the word. "Divorce?"

"Slow, messy, and scandalous, and would leave you ruined and me unable to marry again and get an heir. You see why I apologized. I've committed you to this without hope of escape short of death."

Prudence wanted to speak her heart, to tell him that she'd have married him rich, poor, or even criminal. That she loved him. Those words would only add to his burdens, however, so instead she said, "Marriage to you is a great improvement on the alternatives."

"Prudence, this is going to be *difficult.* I want you to understand that."

"More difficult than marriage to Draydale?"

"No, but—"

"More difficult than ruin and shame?"

"No, but—"

"More difficult than White Rose Yard?"

"No."

"Tell me this. Am I ever going to have to fear poverty or homelessness?"

"No."

"Am I going to have to fear Draydale's next attempt at revenge? Lud! No wonder you seemed so careless of his wealth and power."

He grasped her shoulders. "Prudence, listen. It's not going to be an easy road."

"Cate, Cate, when a person has lost a comfortable home and sunk lower and lower until ending in the depths of White Rose Yard; when they've huddled in winter in all the clothes they possess, never able to feel warm, and eaten potatoes and cabbage for weeks, because it's all they could afford; when the cost of repairing shoes is terrifying—when someone has been through all that, 'an easy road' takes on a different meaning."

He was staring at her.

"What?" she demanded. "Are you offended that I'm not falling into a fit of the vapors, as a fine lady should?"

He took her hands into his own. "Don't start ripping up at me again. It's only that you surprise me. Again." Smiling, he drew her closer. "You're magnificent, my Lady Malzard, and I want no other, but don't discount the difficulties ahead. Everyone expected me to marry a highborn lady, and there were already contenders in the neighborhood. They could be spiteful in their disappointment. Tales of events in Darlington will reach Keynings, and despite our romantic gloss, my marriage within weeks of my brother's death will be seen as shameful."

Prudence hadn't thought of that. "My fault again, and people will be watching my waistline, won't they? When I have a child, they'll be counting the months."

"That and many other problems. I'm struggling in deep waters, and now I've dragged you into them."

"You snatched me from the jaws of a demon."

He smiled. "Like Saint George, or the archangel Michael? But believe this," he said, stroking her cheek. "I'm not at all displeased with my wife."

"Truly?"

"Truly."

He drew her closer for a kiss, and relief stirred something wild. She grabbed his head to hold him closer and lost herself in passion with her mouth, with her body pressed to his. It was as if they tried to fuse, and she wanted that. Never to part, even an inch.

Never, ever to be alone again.

A knock on the door. By the time they'd sprung apart a flustered maid was already in the room, tea tray in hands.

"Beggin' yer pardon, sir, ma'am. Shall I come back?"

Prudence whirled away, hands to flaming cheeks.

"No," Cate said. "Lay out the tea. Thank you."

After a moment, the door closed, and he said, "Tea, my lady?"

She turned, and then she broke into laughter. "What must she *think*?"

"That we are loving and desirous, but as we're married, it's no shame."

Loving and desirous. Prudence shivered with pleasure at those words, but he was holding a chair for her. She sat at the small table, trying to calm herself back into sanity.

It was hard when it was all sinking in. No mistress, only herself.

Unbelievable—the Countess of Malzard.

With a shocked and disapproving world to face.

But Cate was hers. And he claimed not to mind. She checked the tea in the pot and gave it a stir, but then she said, "No wonder Mr. Perriam was in a fluster when he called me Lady Malzard!"

"He did? When?"

"At first meeting. I corrected him and told him I was Mistress Burgoyne, and he embroidered the air with convoluted sentences."

He chuckled. "He would. You didn't guess?"

"Guess that Lady Malzard was me? How could I?" She poured tea into his cup, then glanced at him. "I thought you had a mistress. A very elegant, highborn lady who'd never get into the sort of disasters I contrive."

"Ah, now I understand the tiff." He put a large number of sugar lumps in his cup. "I have no mistress, I promise."

"Good, but I see sugar will be a major expense in our household."

"I enjoy sweet things."

He somehow made that sound scandalous, but Prudence was blushing for other reasons too. How shabby to mention household expenses when he was a rich man who lived in a mansion.

He sipped his tea. "How pleasant this is. No secrets between us."

"Man and wife and a pot of tea."

It sobered him. "Prudence, Keynings isn't like this."

"I don't suppose it is, but will we not be able to take tea together in some modest room now and then?"

It brought back his smile. "Yes, we will. You'll have a boudoir. That will serve as our tea parlor."

"There, see. All can be arranged. Do you have other homes?"

"*We* have a house in Town. There are other estates, but all let to tenants."

"How many?"

"Eight, I think."

Eight! She clung to her light manner. "We could

throw the tenants out and live in a constant progress, as your medieval ancestors did."

"Beds, furniture, and windows trundling after us in carts? Your imagination delights me, but only think of the roads. It would be torture."

She wanted to cling to rainbow silliness, but "torture" triggered thoughts of challenges ahead. "Cate, don't you think we should delay our arrival just a bit? If I'm to turn up as your countess, I want my luggage. I don't have even a change of shift or stockings. Or my hairbrush. Or a nightgown. If we delay for a few days, you could warn your family."

"You tempt me mightily, but I have duties, and Draydale still worries me. I want you at Keynings, where I can command all the authority of the earldom. We won't hide the carriage accident, and that explains any shortcomings."

"True. Perhaps someone will have run away with all my possessions, and that could be for the best. I'm sure none of them are up to countess standards. Draydale worries me too, but what can you do about him? You'll never prove he ordered the damage to the wheel."

"I'd like to thrash him more thoroughly, but I'll have to use more subtle means. Wouldn't you think that his business dealings are crooked?"

"Yes," she said, alert now. "In fact, I heard Tallbridge imply as much."

"Indeed? I'm surprised Tallbridge associates with him."

"All's fair in business?" she suggested. "There was much about that world I didn't like."

"I doubt you'll find court and politics any cleaner."

Court and politics? "More tea?" Prudence asked, and refilled their cups.

"I'm sure Draydale has his fingers in irregular or even illegal activities," he said, again dropping many lumps of sugar in his cup. "I seem to employ a great many people ideally suited to ferreting out such things." He sipped his sweet tea. "I intend to ruin him."

Prudence stared, and then she smiled. "That will be the best punishment, won't it? To render him poor and powerless."

He toasted her with tea. "I see we're in accord, as always."

"As always?"

"More accord than discord. We still have much to learn about each other, which I find delightful, especially as some of the learning will take place in bed." He picked a jam tart from the plate and offered it to her. "Very efficacious against shock, I understand."

"I'm not shocked," she said, taking it. "I am, I think, desirous."

She took a bite, then hastily swept pastry crumbs off her lips with her tongue.

His smile deepened. He captured the tart and took a bite from the same place. "Lick your lips again."

"No, you."

He flicked a crumb of pastry away. Slowly.

Prudence suddenly felt very hot. "I think I'm shocked."

"Or desirous."

There was a bedchamber next door, and they were a married couple. . . .

He put the remaining bit of tart in his mouth and rose. "Come. We should find you a better ring."

"What . . . ?"

"Wedding ring." He pulled her to her feet. "We must return to Keynings, my dear, and our accident doesn't explain a shoddy wedding ring."

"But what of Mr. Perriam?" she asked as he led her to the door.

"He's the soul of tact and amiability."

"Danger?" she reminded him.

"I have a sword, and know how to use it."

She laughed at the memory as he swept her down and out into the street.

Chapter 20

Prudence felt giddy with delight, and the bustle of the market only made her more lighthearted. Everything pleased her—the stallholders' cries, the ballad singers hawking their music, the piles of greens, and the punnets of early strawberries, perfuming the air.

He bought some of the small sweet fruit and popped one into her mouth.

She did the same for him.

They paused, smiling into each other's eyes.

"Ring," he said. "No time for dalliance, wench."

She pouted, feeling like a girl again. Like the girl she'd never been.

He inquired about a goldsmith, and they left the stalls for the regular shops.

The shop was mostly a clockmaker's, but it did have a small selection of rings. Only one wedding ring fit, but it was of bright gold. Cate slid it onto her finger as he had at the wedding, and Prudence felt as if this were their true bonding, in joy and honesty and hope for the future rather than amid tension and doubt.

He turned to look at the other jewelry on display.

"Your colors, I think," he said, picking up a ring with

a pale yellow stone surrounded by pearls. "And this brooch. With a dagger through it."

"Stop! That's enough."

"I've hardly begun. I finally see a use for my wealth." But he only added a silver cross on a chain before paying an alarming number of guineas.

He pinned the dagger brooch in the center of her bodice—"You should be armed"—and put the cross and chain around her neck, telling her it would be "useful for warding off demons."

"Where's your cross, then?" she asked as they left the shop.

"The hilt of my sword."

Prudence looked around. "I wish I could buy you a gift."

He promptly took out his purse and poured some coins into her hand.

"That's too much," she protested.

"Nonsense. As soon as we're home I'll arrange pin money, settlements, and all that."

Pin money and settlements should thrill her, but it was the word "home" that she dwelled on. Keynings wasn't her home, but it was his, so she'd make it theirs. For all its challenges and problems, she'd make it their true home.

For now, she must find him a gift, but she was distracted.

"Hats!" she said, spying a shop with ladies' hats in the window and dragging him over.

"I like that one with feathers," he said.

"For travel? And with this gown?"

"Spoilsport. Very well, have something dull if you insist."

They went into the small shop and a woman hurried

forward to serve them. Cate explained about the carriage accident and the loss of his wife's hat.

"A straw, madam? I can trim it with ribbon to match your gown."

Prudence wrinkled her brow. "Straw doesn't go well with a military style."

"I wore a straw hat at one point," Cate said. "Portugal could get hot as hell. What about this one?" He picked up a flat brown disk with silk frills along the edge.

"I see you're not a good adviser on fashion," Prudence said.

"No, you need Perry for that."

"Perhaps this, ma'am?" The milliner held out a hat with a slight crown, all covered with black silk, and with knots of black ribbon. "It matches the black braid on your bodice, madam, and I could add some ribbon to match your gown."

As the woman hurried away Prudence said, "I'm sure that's the most expensive one she has."

"Do you think so? I doubt I look like a wealthy customer."

"You have that lordly air about you."

The woman returned with three rust-colored ribbons and found the one that matched. With clever fingers she added some to the hat.

"There, madam, but you'll need a hatpin." She chose a plain one, but Cate picked another, gold-headed one.

How long had it been since anyone had lavished gifts upon her with a generous heart? Perhaps never, for even in the best times, her parents had not believed in extravagance.

When the hat was fixed in place, she agreed it was exactly right, and tried not to think of the cost. Cate was a wealthy earl—she believed that. She simply couldn't get over years of scrimping. To pay a lot of money for jewelry was one thing, because jewelry had value. To pay an extortionate amount for some silk fashioned into a hat seemed wicked.

"Back to the inn," he said as they left the shop and wove back into the market crowd.

Prudence halted by a linen stall. "I'll need a nightgown, in case my trunk doesn't reach Keynings today."

There were simpler ones laid out in front of her, but four finer nightgowns hung at the back of the stall, away from dirty fingers and thieves. They weren't as fine as the ones in her trunk, but Prudence thought she might value more the one she chose with Cate. As the woman wrapped it, she thought of the night ahead and bit her lip on wicked thoughts.

She remembered she wanted to buy a gift for him and saw some neckcloths. None of the lace was fine, but she chose the best and paid for it with one of the coins he'd given her.

"I knew you were ashamed of my appearance," he said.

She reached up to drape it around his neck and then cross it and bring it back to the front, where she tied a loose knot. Then she produced the silver tiepin from her pocket and fixed it in place.

"I gave you that to turn into money to keep you warm and fed," he said.

"I kept it for the darkest moment, which happily did not arrive. There. Apart from the breeches and lack of hat, you're almost respectable, my lord earl."

"And in that hat, you're quite delightful, my lady countess." He dropped a quick kiss on her lips, right there in the marketplace.

"Don't forget shift and stockings," Cate reminded her, when she was still dazzled.

She quickly made her selection, hardly caring about the details, but as they walked on toward the Bull, she said, "Not long ago, a new shift was a dream."

"'With all my worldly goods . . .'" he quoted. "What else would you like? A bucket. Firedogs. A goose in a basket?"

"Madman!" She laughed. "We mustn't dally."

"You're going to nag me about my duties," he said. "How delightful. Let's find Perry."

They found Mr. Perriam comfortably settled in a parlor, having, he declared, restored civility by bathing and changing his linen for stuff bought at the market.

"I see you've been similarly engaged," he said. "A charming hat, ma'am, and you've covered his shameful neck. As reward, I have cold pie and wine, and settings for three."

"Ah, real food," Cate said, but he smiled at Prudence. "Delightful though tarts were in the circumstances."

"You're looking very pleased with yourself," Perriam said.

"And you're wondering how much longer you're going to have to countenance deceit. Thank you, but I've told Prudence all."

"And you still have your head." Perriam turned to her. "*Enchanté*, Lady Malzard."

"Thank you, Mr. Perriam. And for your discretion."

"One of my many skills, ma'am."

Cate took another piece of pie. "I've tried to impress upon Prudence how challenging the future will be."

"He's correct," Perriam said seriously. "You will be disliked for snatching the golden prize." Cate snorted, but Perry turned to him. "You could be bandy-legged and warty and still be a prize."

"Being an earl is no prize."

Perriam waved a hand. "Enough of your nonsense. Have you considered how to smooth your wife's path?"

"Get her to Keynings quickly and let her own fine qualities speak for her before stories circulate."

"Adequate, but if you can get your mother and Artemis on her side, it will help."

"Mother . . ." Cate shrugged. "She might decide to be pleased I'm married, or cross over the manner of it."

"And over the bride," Prudence pointed out.

"You are my choice," he said. "Anyone who insults you will rue it. I hope Artemis will support you. She's kindhearted." He finished his pie and rose. "Come, let us acquire our carriage and six."

"My packages," Prudence said, absorbing the flat arrogance of his statement: *You are my choice.* That showed a different side of him, making him seem somewhat a stranger. And rather more the earl.

Cate knew his manner was awry, but he was suddenly sensitive to everything that might disturb his wife. Prudence was like a tree in bud that was beginning to unfurl at first touch of summer sun. Frost could still kill the buds, however, and he wanted her to flower.

Perry rose and scooped up her packages. "I'm able to play both your secretary and your angelic messenger, my lord earl. I'm sure footman isn't beyond me, my lady."

Prudence looked bewildered. "Will you have to call me 'my lady' all the time, Mr. Perriam? It seems very distant, and we have shared something of an adventure."

He smiled at her. "From this moment you are Prudence and I am Perry—if your lord and master permits."

Cate wasn't sure he did. "In private only," he said.

"You will permit me to be private with your wife?" Perry asked, all mischief.

"Your angelic halo is slipping. But yes, within reason, I will trust you."

"I am definitely *aux anges*!" But Perry turned to Prudence. "You must not relax formality in public. My reputation is far too delicate."

She laughed at his nonsense, and Cate ground his teeth.

As they went out to the coach yard, Prudence asked Perry, "What do I call Cate in public? Husband?"

"Déclassé," Perry said firmly. "You aren't shopkeepers."

"Watch your tongue," Cate snapped, before remembering that Perry didn't know about Prudence's lowest times. "My apologies. I'm on edge. Let's complete this journey."

Cate knew he should tell his friend everything, but he hoped to keep White Rose Yard, at least, secret from all.

The chaise stood ready but he hesistated, unwilling to begin the journey that would lead to the inevitable troubles at Keynings.

"I see I am condemned to ride again," Perry said with an injured air.

"Ignore him, Prudence. He wins steeplechases, and he'll be more comfortable than we will."

"Torture box," she said with a sigh. "But I don't much like riding, and I don't want to damage my hat. You could ride, however."

"I prefer to be with you."

Cate handed her into the carriage, but then he circled the vehicle, thoroughly checking it for tampering.

"You're being very careful," Perry said.

"I have much to cherish."

"She's a remarkable woman."

"Yes."

But that didn't mean that the next little while wasn't going to be hell.

Chapter 21

They traveled in silence for a while, and Prudence couldn't think how to break it. She still stung a little from Mr. Perriam's careless comment. She'd never been a shopkeeper, but the women of White Rose Yard often used "husband" instead of a name. So had her mother, if it came to that.

How many other things that seemed normal to her were déclassé or simply old-fashioned? A deep weariness swept over her, drowning the exhilaration and joy she'd briefly felt. She was married and would remain so, and she loved her husband, but she was completely unsuited to her new position, and Cate, though kind and appreciative, didn't love her.

If she was exhausted, it was hardly surprising. This morning she'd said her vows, but that had been the culmination of days of turmoil and sleepless nights.

She glanced at Cate and saw tiredness stamped on him, too. He'd ridden to Darlington, and then yesterday to Durham and back. Today he'd been wounded and bled quite a lot. He limped only a little, but his wounds must still bother him.

She was bruised from the accident, and her face still

ached a little at times. She supposed that mark could be put down to the carriage accident, so Draydale's menace had served one good purpose.

She looked outside, wondering whether Draydale would try some open attack. Surely not. They traveled with three postilions and two armed gentlemen, and Cate had checked the vehicle for tampering. She'd seen that. They were probably safe from Draydale, but not from the terrors that lay ahead.

Cate's home, Cate's family, Cate's mother.

Even if that went well, how on earth did she become a true countess?

She'd once seen the Countess of Arradale on the street in Northallerton, pausing on her way to or from London and her estate in the dales. Though she'd been dressed plainly for travel, it had been obvious that every stitch was of the finest, and she'd worn it with such an air, like a creature from another world.

She choked back a laugh.

"What's the matter?" he asked, rousing out of his own thoughts, or even a doze.

"I was thinking of a countess I once saw."

"I sometimes think of other earls. Which countess?"

"The Countess of Arradale."

"'Struth, don't measure yourself against her. She holds the title in her own right. She was born to the splendor and has married even higher—a marquess."

"So I won't be expected to be like her?"

"No."

"Thank heavens for that. But you'd better start teaching me some of what I need to know. The order of rank is duke, marquess, and earl, isn't it?"

"Then viscount and baron."

"Then you outrank Lord Lolingford."

"Who's he?"

"The grandest personage in the neighborhood of Blytheby. He was a baron. We were all in awe."

"And now you find he's the lowest of the low," he said with a smile. "If you ever meet him, you can look down on him from your lofty height."

He was teasing, but it made her uncomfortable. "I won't be expected to, will I? I'd hate that."

"No, but people have expectations and they seem upset if we don't conform to them. Servants at Keynings who were at ease with me as simple Cate Burgoyne now keep their distance from the earl. It's not fear. It's their sense of what's right. At least Jeb's still the same—when we're alone, at least. He's one of the grooms, but we're the same age. We played together as boys."

"I used to play with the gardener's daughters, but Mother never really approved. When they turned twelve, they went into service."

"Have there been any friends since your father's death?" he asked.

Prudence thought about that. "No. There's Hetty, but I can't count her as a friend, though I think in other circumstances we could be. Does that make sense?"

"Perfectly. I met a few men in the army like that. But their rank was too low for true friendship. It would fracture the stability of the universe. Let's attempt to prepare you so that doesn't happen."

Prudence paid attention, but she struggled to truly grasp the nature of Keynings, house and estate. She'd never been inside a house larger than Blytheby Manor, and clearly Keynings was of a different order.

"How many rooms are there?" she asked.

"I've no idea. Perhaps fifty."

"Fifty!"

"That's a mere guess. Why does it matter?"

"They all have to be taken care of. Why so many? You can't use all of them."

"Not day to day, but we need many bedchambers for a house party, and a series of saloons that open into a ballroom when required. As for the others, I was surprised to realize that there were a number I'd never entered."

"I'll get lost."

"The house is quite regularly laid out, so I doubt it, but if necessary, there are plenty of servants to rescue you."

"Very well," she said. "Tell me about the servants."

"They are as orderly as the army. We'll start with the general—the house steward, Flamborough. . . ."

They paused briefly for a change of horses, and as they rolled onward, the lessons continued. By the time they stopped for another change, Prudence's head was pounding with information, most of it undigested. She accepted the offer of tea with relief, and tried to pay attention as Cate and Perry discussed niceties of etiquette, in particular how to distinguish between the three Lady Malzards.

"You're Lady Malzard," Perry said. "Cate's brother's wife is Artemis, Lady Malzard. Only his mother is the dowager countess."

"I can't call her Artemis, Lady Malzard, day to day."

"You don't have to. If you ask where Lady Malzard is, it clearly isn't you, and it's not the dowager. However, it would certainly be simplest if you could settle on 'sister' between you."

"I'd like to have a sister," she said.

"Then I hope it becomes so," Cate said, "but she'll likely leave Keynings soon. It can't be comfortable for her."

His mother, however, would remain Flavia, Dowager

Countess of Malzard. When they returned to the chaise for the last stage to Keynings, she asked, "How will your mother react to our arrival?"

"With shock, I'd think."

"Don't say it as if it doesn't matter! You should have sent warning."

"It wouldn't have made any difference."

"She'd have had time to prepare."

"To load the guns, you mean."

"Cate!"

"I'm sorry, but she's not going to like it, if only because I've married without a word to her."

"It's reasonable that she feel that way. I was hurt not to be invited to my brother's wedding."

"You weren't invited?"

"No, but stick to the immediate. Your mother will be hurt."

"Perhaps," he said. "But I told you the truth. She wants me married. If you prove fertile, and especially with male children, she'll forgive all."

Prudence shivered under that announcement. "And if I don't?"

"We'll all live with the disappointment. It won't be disastrous as long as I outlive her. You see, if I die without a male heir, the next earl will expect her to leave Keynings. Which would break her heart."

Prudence understood how having to leave a home could hurt, but he painted an ominous future.

"How old is she?"

"Fifty-five, I think."

The Dowager Countess of Malzard could live another thirty years. Thirty or more years, during which she'd disapprove of her son's wife even if there were children. If there weren't, she'd watch Prudence's waistline until all hope was gone.

All the same, she said, "I do understand. Leaving Blytheby broke my father's heart."

He took her hand. "And yours, perhaps."

"Yes, though I didn't realize it at the time. My father felt it most. He'd been there fourteen years, and built the collections of antiquities from nothing. When . . ."

Prudence had been about to speak the truth—that the owner had died and Blytheby had been sold to pay Sir Joshua's debts—but she remembered her deception. She'd let Cate think her a daughter of the manor and it had pleased him.

"When we had to leave," she said, "Mother and I tried to adjust, but my father wanted only one thing—to return. When he accepted that would never happen, he died. Shattered dreams can break hearts. But so can dreams clung to for no reason."

He drew her hand to his mouth and kissed her palm. "We'll keep our dreams modest, and nothing will shatter them. We will be good companions, and we'll do our duties well."

That intimate kiss jarred with his words. She didn't want to be only a companion, or only attend to her duties, but it was probably all she could dream of. Cate was good and kind and he didn't love another, but he didn't love her.

She would cause him as little trouble as possible. "Tell me about the local families."

But he said, "There you need Mother. I can give you only the slightest sketch." He began to list gentry families and their houses.

Eventually she said, "You'll have to repeat all this when I have pen and paper. My head's full."

"Mother will probably write it all out for you anyway." She thought he was going to say something else on that, but instead, he touched her forehead. "Does your stuffed head make you feel more at ease?"

"No."

He drew her into his arms. "It will be difficult, Prudence, but not hellish."

"No? I've never given an order to a servant. Well, to our maids-of-all-work when we had them, but that's not the same."

"At heart it is. Your hat's in the way again."

Smiling, she tilted her head and was kissed. "Don't scramble it off, though, sir. I will arrive in the best condition possible."

"If you insist. As for servants, simply make your wishes reasonable and clear and don't tolerate impudence or shirking."

"I suspect that sounds easier than it is. They'll soon learn all about me. The Darlington scandal. My background. White Rose Yard, even."

"They'll know none of that when we arrive. That's why the right first impression is crucial."

"Thank heavens for the hat."

He laughed. "A magnificent piece of armor." He tilted her head and kissed her again. His fingers slid into her hair above her ear.

She moved back. "Be careful."

"Kissing without disturbing a lady's hat and hair is a necessary skill."

"*Your* hair's escaping its ribbon," she pointed out.

"It always does. I'm sure you could tie it more firmly." He shifted to present his back.

Why a broad back and loosely tied hair should be so alarming Prudence couldn't think, until she tugged the ribbon off. A man's loose hair was somehow . . . loose. It reminded her of his naked back when she'd tended his wound, his wide shoulders, long spine, strong buttocks. . . . Even though it was all covered now, she wanted to stroke down his jacket, thinking of all that lay beneath.

She swallowed. "Your comb?"

He took it out of his pocket and passed it back to her.

She combed his dark hair, feeling the springiness that must fight to be free of restraint. As did he.

"I'm sorry you had to become an earl," she said, drawing the comb down through his hair.

"You'd rather have been an ordinary wife, I know."

His hair was combed enough, but she didn't stop. "Not for me, for you. You didn't want such a burden of responsibilities."

"I was an officer in the army."

He didn't sound offended, and she knew through his back and the tilt of his head that he wasn't.

"An earldom is different. It's relentless, and for life."

"Wise woman. I was forced in an instant to be a different person. As you were." After a moment he said, "I did want Keynings, however. Very, very much. I've not admitted that to anyone else."

Prudence's breath caught, but she continued to comb in long, slow strokes.

He added, "Sometimes we love 'not wisely but too well.'"

"*Othello*," she said. Then, still combing steadily, she risked the question that came to mind. "You were jealous of your brother?"

"Not that he'd become earl. But when I came to an age to realize that Roe would stay at Keynings all his life and I would have to leave, then I thought it unfair. I tried to become a parson."

She couldn't stop the laugh. "You?"

"I've known a few as unsuited, but it was solely in hopes of having the living near Keynings. Of staying at home."

She gathered his hair together, her fingers brushing his warm neck. "So you lost your home too."

"Yes. But I never wished Roe dead. I'd bring him back to life now if I could, even if I had to remove entirely to the Americas or Indies."

"I know you would," she said, and tied the ribbon as tightly as possible. Then she couldn't resist kissing the little bit of skin between his hair and his neckcloth.

He turned and kissed her lips. "Now you know all my secrets."

"And not a thing to your discredit."

"I hope not, but there is one other thing."

The coach changed directions and he looked out. "We're getting close. It's a complicated story. I'll tell you later, but I have made mistakes. It doesn't concern you in any way, except that you've married a man with a shadowed reputation in some circles."

"Whatever it is, I know you did no wrong."

"Such faith in me?"

"Yes."

"Our acquaintance is very short, you know."

"But deep."

"Wise again," he said. "I've been closely acquainted with some people for years and not known them as I know you, Prudence Malzard."

She frowned at him. "Not Prudence Burgoyne?"

"A peer's wife uses his title as her surname."

"Lord. Something as simple as that and I didn't know. How will I manage?"

"You will. You're the strongest, bravest, and most resourceful woman I've ever known, and kind as well. You'll triumph, my warrior queen."

"Remember Boadicea."

"Think instead of Elizabeth, emboldening her troops before the armada."

"'I know I have the body of a weak and feeble woman, but I have the heart and stomach of a king.' I always liked that."

"I'm sure you did. I'll buy you a new knife, I think. An Italian dagger, with a hilt of gold and set with pearls, for you are all steel, and gold, and pearls."

"Extravagance, sir!" Prudence protested, but she was melting at such praise.

"You vowed to obey me, and I command you to appreciate all my gifts without protest."

"Thank you, then, for the cross and brooch."

"You have many grander jewels, if Mother and Artemis don't cling to them."

That burst her rainbow bubble. She was approaching a house already ruled by two women, each of whom had training and lineage far beyond hers.

Then Cate took out two rings and slid them onto his fingers—the heavy gold signet ring and a circle of gold and black. A mourning ring.

There'd been mourning rings and black gloves for those attending her father's funeral, even though they'd not been able to afford it. At her mother's simple funeral, there'd been no question of extra expense.

He had a strip of black cloth. "Can you fix this around my arm?"

She did so, but with fumbling fingers. "Why did you take these things off?"

"I was escaping. Perhaps even the reality of Roe's death. Foolish. I won't do such a thing again."

She tied a neat knot underneath his arm, a sick feeling rising in her.

"Cate, we're approaching a house of mourning, and here I am in red!"

She saw him stop some blistering curse. "How could I have neglected that? It's also your wedding day, but . . . Your ribbons. Turn, quickly."

She did, understanding. She felt him cut loose the multicolored knot of ribbons on top of the hat. It would be plain now. Much more suitable.

His large hands were struggling with the ribbons, so she took the knot and quickly untied it all. She discarded the rust ones.

"Take off my cross and chain," she said as she unfastened the brooch he'd bought and put it in her pocket.

The frogging on her jacket was black, and the rust color wasn't quite as bad as a bright red. She took the cross off the chain and managed to thread a length of black ribbon through the ring. She turned. "Tie it on."

He did so. "You're astonishing. A silver cross on a black ribbon. That does make all the difference. Here, I'll wind the rest around your sleeve. It's more usual for men, but will do."

Prudence took off the garnet ring, and the pretty one with pearls and the yellow stone, leaving only her wedding ring. But she rubbed her hands together nervously.

"The best we can do for now," she said, "but what of tomorrow? I have no mourning clothes." She laughed. "Not long ago, that was all I had, for I plunged everything into a dye bath after my mother died. Except the blue. I could dye the blue." She looked at him. "Is a countess allowed to dye a gown black?"

"She can command the laundry to, and we can have mourning made for you speedily."

She put hands to her face. "We arrive with so much to offend, and now this."

"They'll understand. It is also your wedding day. Ah," he said, "Gibbet Cross. The turning into the park is just ahead."

She heard the joy in it, and perhaps familiarity made the gruesome marker commonplace. But Prudence grimaced at the iron cage in which an executed criminal could be hung as a warning to others.

The cage hung empty at the moment, thank heavens, but it seemed a very ill omen.

Chapter 22

The coach turned slowly between pillars and Prudence looked ahead, fearing to see the house directly in front of her. All she saw, however, was a smoothly graveled road that wound between countryside too beautiful to be natural. She was inside a nobleman's carefully tended park, and for some reason, the reality fully hit her then.

Cate was a nobleman.

He owned all this perfection.

And he'd married her.

"You won't see Keynings for a little while. This drive is carefully designed to present beauties in good order. My father's work, mainly, though my brother was very fond of imported trees."

Prudence could hardly hear him over the panicked beating of her heart.

"What are they going to think, Cate? What are they going to say?"

After a moment Cate let down his window and attracted his friend's attention. "Are you willing to go ahead and pave the way? Announce the safe return of the prodigal son?"

"With wife?" Perry asked, riding alongside.

"With wife."

"On your head be it," Perry said with a laugh, and rode off.

"Why did he laugh?" Prudence asked.

"Because the bearers of bad news often get shot."

"Bad news . . ."

He turned. "I didn't mean it that way."

"Don't set to soothing me. I *am* bad news!"

"Only a surprise."

"You said you didn't think warning wise."

"A day's warning, or hours. A few minutes should be safe, and moderate the shock."

No time to load weapons, but perhaps time to get the first angry reactions over so they could all attempt to be polite. If that worked, she'd be thankful.

He looked out again. "Ah, your first glimpse."

She looked, but as one might look toward a prison. The center part of a stone house was elegantly framed by trees. As he'd said, the vista had been carefully planned. It was a very regular, classical three-story house, but clearly extended beyond her view on either side. A pale sculpture of some sort sat in front of the center. As they progressed, the trees seemed to move back like a curtain, showing more and more of the house.

Her first thought was that it was plain.

When the whole was revealed, she knew it was perfect.

So very unlike herself.

"Have you read Milton's *Paradise Lost*?" he asked.

She turned to him, wondering if she'd missed something else he'd said. "Yes."

"Do you remember Pandemonium?"

"It's the principal city. The domain of Lucifer. Cate—"

"Precisely," he interrupted. "The city of demons. A trifle extreme as a description of Keynings, but pandemonium has the other meaning now—disorder and a wild uproar. That's what we face, but we have angels on our side."

Remembering his wounds, she touched his head.

"Stop doing that." He pulled her hand down and kissed it. "Perry has claimed Raphael, the messenger. I will be Michael, conqueror of all demons. You can be Good Queen Bess and urge us on to victory."

"I grant you Draydale as a demon, but not your mother and sister-in-law."

"True enough. But expectations, Prudence. They can be the very devil. Here we are."

Despite his warnings, there was fondness in his voice. He loved his home. He wanted it to be a home. It was for her to make it so.

The chaise followed a curving drive and came to a halt at the base of steps leading up to grand doors that still bore black-draped hatchments.

If only she could magically transform her gown to black.

Four liveried footmen with powdered hair already stood ready. The livery was a dark green with gold braid, and they all wore black stockings, gloves, and stocks, and black bands around one arm. They were better equipped for mourning than she or Cate.

A very dignified man in a suit of black cloth awaited in the open doorway. Guardian of the portal. Could he deny her admittance?

"Who's that?" she whispered as the footmen came forward to attend to them.

"Flamborough, the house steward. I told you about him."

He had, but her brain had sprung leaks. She couldn't remember anything.

One footman opened the door.

Another let down the steps.

Cate climbed out and turned to assist her, but Prudence's heart was racing so fast, she wondered if she'd manage the exit with dignity, and if she did, if she would walk into the house in a straight line. She very much doubted that she could speak coherently. She'd felt the same way when arriving at the church to marry Draydale. *You* have *to*, she told herself, and inhaled a deep breath. *This is Cate's beloved home. For his sake, you have to manage this perfectly.*

And at least Demon Draydale didn't await.

She made herself move, and stepped down, welcoming Cate's firm hand. He tucked her hand into his arm and led her toward the steps. "Welcome to Keynings, my dear." He sounded at ease, but she could sense the tension ruling him.

Pandemonium.

She heard hooves and wheels, and twisted back to see the chaise departing. She felt as if her escape went with it.

"Welcome home, my lord."

She turned back.

Cate said, "My dear, this is Flamborough, our house steward. My countess, Flamborough."

The man bowed to her, expressionless. "My lady."

"Come, let me show you our home."

She knew he phrased it that way for the man's ears.

They progressed into a spacious hall with gray walls and pillars. Along the side walls, blue niches held classical statues, some lacking most of their clothes. A number of servants hovered, but a woman came forward to greet them. She was of moderate height and build, dressed in deepest black, including a black cap on her smooth brown hair. The housekeeper? Mistress Ingleton?

"Welcome home, Malzard." She turned to Prudence.

"I'm Artemis, Lady Malzard." She stared at Prudence's cheek.

"Our carriage overturned," Prudence said. "Thank you for the welcome . . ." There didn't seem anything to say but, "Artemis."

Artemis's eyes slid away. "It's no longer my place to welcome you to Keynings, *sister*, but I do so anyway."

Was that a subtle correction? If so, was it well-meant or not?

Well-meant, surely.

Some of Prudence's tension unwound. Her sister-in-law was cool, but she was willing to be called sister. She might be willing to advise and support, and perhaps even befriend in time. She began to smile, but realized it was inappropriate. "Please accept my condolences on your loss, sister."

"Thank you," Artemis said, but she was looking at Cate's breeches, brows raised.

"I was wounded by glass in the carriage accident. I assume Perriam told you about that?"

"Briefly. Is your wound serious?"

"Not at all. Where's Mother?"

"Lying down. She's a little unwell."

"I see."

So, the Dowager Lady Malzard had heard the news and retreated to her room either in true distress, or simply to avoid having to meet her unwanted, unwelcome new daughter-in-law.

"Come, my dear," Cate said. "I'll take you to your rooms."

"Perhaps," said Artemis Malzard, "the senior servants could meet their new mistress?"

The overly patient tone made Prudence want to slap her, but she reminded herself that the marriage came as a shock to Artemis too, and probably did seem impetuous and irresponsible, especially within weeks of her husband's death.

Prudence went to meet a grizzled-haired, dignified woman, who was the real housekeeper, and an overly plump man called Belshaw, the clerk of the kitchen. The role meant nothing to her, but she assumed he was in overall charge of food for the family and the servants. Ewing was the butler, and though thin, he had a redness to his nose that suggested he might be too fond of the wines he managed.

Ewing gave her a sharp, assessing look, but the others were politely impassive. She was sure they'd have plenty to say as soon as they were away from here, but she didn't think she'd done or said anything to create pandemonium from the very beginning.

That ordeal over, Cate led her up heavy wooden stairs that were magnificent, but went oddly with the light, modern hall. She wouldn't comment on that, but when they reached the turn halfway up, she saw that the stairs matched the paneled upper hallway.

An odd effect.

They walked a little way along the corridor, but then Artemis said, "You must want to change your clothes, Malzard. I'll take your wife to her rooms."

"Thank you," he said, and to Prudence, "Do you mind?"

She suddenly hated the thought of separating from him, but that was childish. "Of course not. You need to have your wound seen to."

"Indeed," said Artemis. "You could have been killed."

"Only by the worst of bad luck."

"You took no hurt?" Artemis asked Prudence.

"Only bruises. And I had opportunity to change my clothes. My trunk follows. I apologize for not being in complete mourning, sister, but . . ." She trailed off because she couldn't think quite how to quickly explain the circumstances.

"Something to be taken care of," Cate said. "But this is also our wedding day." He kissed Prudence's hand and went into the room.

"This way," Artemis said, and walked to the next door, stiff backed. This was a difficult situation for everyone, and Prudence couldn't think how to make it better. Artemis Malzard seemed disposed to be kind, but this marriage could be hurting and offending her. Prudence truly regretted that.

"Your bedchamber," Artemis said, opening it and going in. "With adjoining door, of course, to the earl's bedchamber."

"This is lovely," Prudence said with complete honesty.

The walls were decorated with paintings of delicate branches of blossoms and brilliantly colored birds. It must be the Chinese wallpaper she'd heard of. The ceiling was a blue that suggested the summer sky, and that color was picked up in the draperies, and in parts of the thick carpet on the floor.

She turned to say something else complimentary, and found Artemis's face pinched. *Lord above.* Until recently this must have been her bedchamber, perhaps decorated to her taste, from which a death had evicted her. Prudence wanted to apologize, even offer the room back, but that was impossible.

Instead, she offered condolences again. "I'm very sorry about your husband. . . ."

Stiffness shifted into tight disapproval. "We'll have no lies between us in private, if you please. You must be glad of my husband's death, as it enabled you and Catesby to wed."

"What? No—"

"Don't play me for a fool. He hardly had a penny before."

"I know, but—"

"And he's married you in indecent haste." Artemis began to pace, as if caged. "You must have been pining for years. If, indeed, you waited to satisfy your lust."

Prudence gasped with shock.

Artemis whirled to face her. "He's *always* wanted Keynings. I've known it. I know he rejoiced—*rejoiced!*—at the death of my son."

"I'm sure he didn't."

"We'll have the matter plain. Your husband murdered mine, and if there's any justice in the world, whatever wound he has will fester and kill him."

Prudence's legs failed her and she collapsed onto the bench at the end of the bed. "How can you say such a thing?"

Artemis studied her, still looking unbelievably sane. "Is it possible that he's deceived you?"

"I know him. I know your notions are impossible."

"Notions? Ask him. He can't deny coming here in disgrace, so that my poor husband felt the weight of it crushing our family reputation. . . ."

Disgrace?

"Nor can he deny generating a raging dispute that caused my husband's seizure of the brain."

"Please, Artemis—"

"You do not have permission to use my name!"

Dry mouthed, Prudence tried to speak soothingly. "Lady Malzard, what you think can't be true. If you know Cate at all, you must know he's incapable of such coldhearted wickedness."

The other woman laughed without humor. "It's you who doesn't know him. My husband understood his brother for what he is—shiftless, reckless, a disaster at all he attempts. I fear you'll learn his shortcomings to your own cost. If you haven't already."

She was looking at Prudence's bruised face.

"Cate did not cause this bruise," Prudence said.

Artemis shrugged, and then turned briskly toward a door and opened it. "You have a boudoir through here." She didn't go in. She walked a few steps and opened another. "And a dressing room here. It's unfortunately small. We had talked of enlarging it. . . ." She went stiff and silent, but then collected herself. "Do you have a maid?"

"No."

"I'll send one to attend you." She looked around, still neat to the last inch, then left, closing the door with a quiet, firm *click*.

Chapter 23

Prudence remained where she was, hugging herself as if cold.

Two-faced. Sweet in company, acid in private.

But no, that wasn't quite fair. Artemis had never been sweet, and she was the sort of lady who would never create a disturbance in front of servants. She probably believed everything she'd said about Cate.

She was wrong, however. Wrong.

Cate could never have rejoiced at the death of a child, or plotted to kill his brother. Prudence knew that in her heart, but her brain warned that Artemis was right in one thing—Prudence didn't know her husband well at all. All very well for Cate to say their acquaintance had been deep, but it was still very, very short.

What disgrace had he brought here? He'd said something as they'd drawn close to this place.

Why had he and his brother argued so violently? Perhaps a raging argument could cause a seizure of the brain, but surely no one could design such a thing. Certainly not Cate. His flaw was hot impulse, not cold cunning.

Yet . . . he'd confessed how much he'd always wanted Keynings.

She sighed and rolled her head back, trying to release painful tension.

Pandemonium, indeed. Not only from devilish expectations, but from dark suspicions.

She wanted to run to Cate and put all this before him, but he clearly didn't know of his sister-in-law's hatred. She'd keep it from him if she could. She had to consider, however, whether Artemis was capable of doing him harm.

She didn't think it would go beyond ill wishing. After all, if Artemis had wanted to poison him, she'd had weeks to try. Prudence prayed that she'd leave Keynings now that a new countess was in place.

After a tap, the main door opened and a maidservant came in. She was young, round cheeked, and nervous. She was also poorly dressed in contrast to the smart livery of the footmen. Her gown was a shapeless black, mostly covered by a coarse white apron. Cap and stockings were black, of course, but the stockings sagged around her ankles and the cap looked too large. If her clothes were normal for maidservants at Keynings, that would have to change.

She was carrying a large jug of hot water and almost spilled some as she dipped a nervous curtsy. "I'm Karen, yer ladyship. Sent with water, yer ladyship. And to 'elp you."

What had Artemis said to make the maid so ill at ease? That the new countess would be a harsh mistress?

Prudence smiled as she rose. "Thank you, Karen. That's an unusual name."

"Karenhappuch, yer ladyship. It's in the Bible."

"Truly? Where?" Prudence needed ordinary conversation. The maid was simply standing there, however, so she prompted, "Pour the water, please."

Karen hurried to fill the china bowl. "The Book of

Job, yer ladyship. Karenhappuch was one of 'is daughters, yer ladyship, born after 'is woes were over. The vicar says as it should be Kerenhappuch, yer ladyship, but I've been Karen all me life."

Prudence realized she still wore her hat and unpinned it. Perhaps that would ease her growing headache. The stream of "your ladyships" was adding to it. Was it essential? Even if so, she'd have an end to it here.

"Please address me as milady, Karen," she said, passing the hat to the maid. She went to the washstand, but then looked around. "Is there soap?"

"Oh, yes, yer ladyship! I mean, milady." The maid put the hat on the bed and dug in a pocket. She took out a china pot and hurried to put it by the basin.

Prudence thanked her again, but she was realizing that Karen was unskilled. Doubtless the dowager and Artemis both had highly trained lady's maids, but neither had been sent to assist her.

As she washed her hands, she said, "What are your usual duties, Karen?"

"I'm one of the under housemaids, yer . . . milady."

The young maid was an insult.

As Prudence washed her face she pondered what to do about it. Cate had warned her not to tolerate impudence from the servants. He'd said nothing about malice from his family. She could demand another maid, but this poor girl might then feel that she'd offended. If she did nothing, the whole household would snigger at Prudence as being either too ill-bred to know better, or too cowardly to demand her due. She longed for Cate's advice, but household matters were her responsibility and she must stand on her own feet.

She dried her face and turned. "I shall hire a lady's maid soon, Karen, but you will do very well as my maid for the next little while."

The girl's eyes widened. "Be yer *maid*, milady?"

"Is that not what you are at this moment?"

"I . . . I were just sent with the water, milady, and to 'elp if you wanted anything."

Prudence had a sinking feeling that she'd made a mistake, but she wouldn't retreat now. "That's part of being my maid. Whoever sent you must have thought you capable, so the position is yours pro tem."

"Pro tem, milady?"

"For the moment. Only for the moment, for you don't have the necessary skills, but for a few days you will be my maid." She suddenly realized the implications. No wonder the girl looked dazzled. "And will have the appropriate pay. For the few days when you're filling the post."

"Yes, milady! What do you want now, milady?"

To see Cate! But she couldn't run to him with every little thing.

"Tea," Prudence said, wishing she could demand brandy with it.

The girl curtsied and hurried away.

Prudence rubbed her hands over her face, smelling the sweet perfume of the fine soap. At least that hadn't been skimped, and the linen towels were the finest she'd ever handled.

And she did have brandy.

She took out the pretty flask, suddenly remembering what it meant. Cate had purchased this in London with her in mind. That wasn't love, but it was something. She drank some, but only a little, for there wasn't much left and she thought she'd need it again soon.

Dutch courage, Cate had said of gin. Perhaps brandy was French courage. Whatever it was, it was time to take ownership of these rooms.

She went into the boudoir, finding a pretty room with good light. A delicate Chinese carpet covered the center of the floor, and the pale blue walls were hung with paintings of flowers. A settee and two upholstered chairs faced the fireplace, and a small table had been placed by the window for private meals. An empty bookcase and a writing desk sat against the wall.

Prudence felt a ghostly presence. This had been Artemis's private room, where she'd been at ease. Another place from which death had evicted her. How difficult this all was.

The desk was beautiful. She trailed a finger over the top, which was decorated with marquetry flowers. When she raised the lid, she found a leather writing surface edged in gold. The inside of the lid had been painted with shepherds and shepherdesses in an amorous country scene.

Why hadn't Artemis taken this and anything else she valued to whatever rooms she now used? Would it help to offer them to her? Would it offend if she had it all taken away and replaced with other pieces?

Perhaps Artemis had left these furnishings here because she loved Keynings as much as Cate and didn't want to leave. Perhaps, like Prudence's father, she clung to the hope that reality would change and everything would return to the way it ought to be.

What of Cate's mother? Did she pray that her beloved older son, the good son, would rise from the grave like Lazarus?

Prudence sighed and opened the shallow drawers. They were empty. She'd need writing papers, pens, ink, sealing wax. . . .

A seal, as Cate had?

Too much to know. Too many ways to make errors. Errors Artemis would be hoping for.

She looked longingly toward the door to Cate's bedchamber, but turned and went into the dressing room.

As Artemis had said, it was small. A handsome clothespress was too large for the space. She opened it to find it empty, as expected, but perfumes lingered. She could pick out lavender and rose that whispered of gardens, and laughter, and happy days.

Only weeks ago.

Prudence began to close the doors on those shattered dreams, but instead she opened them wide, and opened the window as well.

What was, was.

A new order was in place.

She heard children laughing.

She leaned out and saw two young girls in the sunny flower garden, accompanied by a maidservant. Their black gowns were stark against green grass and colorful flowers, but they were brightly at play, running around holding canes bearing ribbons that fluttered in the breeze.

Artemis's children. If one had been a boy, how different everything would be.

She heard a noise and went into the boudoir to find a different maid placing a tea tray on the table. This one was in her thirties, at least, and much better dressed.

"Where's Karen?" Prudence asked.

"She's returned to her regular duties, milady. Did you require anything else?"

"Who are you?"

"Rachel, milady. Artemis, Lady Malzard's maid, milady." The maid was perfectly polite. Too perfectly. In some way, she was looking down her rather fat nose.

"Thank you, Rachel, but I wouldn't wish to give you more work. Karen will do well enough until I hire my own lady's maid."

"That would not be suitable, milady."

Prudence fixed her with a look. "I will decide what is suitable. Take that away and have Karen bring it."

The woman's chest expanded, almost as if she might object, but then, stiff spined, she put everything back on the tray and left.

Prudence waited, wound tight in preparation for another battle, but soon Karen returned, struggling with the tray, perhaps because she seemed wide-eyed with fear.

Oh, dear.

"Have I made things difficult for you?" Prudence asked.

"No, milady! I mean," she said, putting the tray on the table, "some of 'em don't like it."

She stepped back, but Prudence said, "Put everything out on the table."

"Oh, sorry, milady. I don't—"

"I don't expect you to know everything, Karen, only to learn."

"Yes, milady." But the maid's hands shook as she spread teapot, water jug, cup and saucer, sugar, cream pot, and cakes on the table. Then she stepped back, tray clutched nervously to her.

Prudence sat, aware of an impulse to befriend the girl. She wasn't much like Hetty—for one thing she was probably less than sixteen—but there were enough similarities for Prudence to care about her. She must keep a suitable distance, however, for both their sakes.

The tea had already been made in the pot, which made her think of something else. Who had control of the precious tea? At Blytheby, her mother had guarded her tea caddy most carefully. Susan did the same in Darlington.

"The tea is excellent," Prudence said, sipping. "Who prepared it?"

"Mistress Ingleton, milady."

Prudence relaxed. She wouldn't have to fight Artemis over that.

"But Lady Malzard ..." Karen said, "I mean the other Lady Malzard, and the Dowager Lady Malzard, milady, they have their own tea boxes."

"My husband's sister-in-law is correctly called Artemis, Lady Malzard," Prudence told her, wondering if she truly had just been given useful and appropriate information. That was why Karen reminded her of Hetty. Just because she was young and inexperienced didn't mean she was stupid.

"I too shall have my own," she said, taking a small cake. It was light, lemony, and delicious. She only just stopped herself from offering one to Karen.

But then, perhaps a lady's maid would normally enjoy such treats. She'd find out. But from whom? She wouldn't trust a word Artemis said, and probably Cate didn't know. Perry might.

For the moment, Karen might have more useful information.

"When you say some won't like it, Karen, I assume you mean the more senior housemaids, who feel they should have been chosen."

"Yes, milady, but really, it's all of 'em." She raised her chin. "I'm above all of 'em now, you see."

"You are? How?"

"In rank, milady! The servants all have their place, milady, but the personal servants, like Mr. Ransom and Miss Gorley, they go by their master or mistress's title. So Mr. Ransom, we call 'im milord, or Lord Malzard. And Miss Gorley, we call 'er milady, or Lady Malzard. I suppose we'll 'ave to refer to 'er as Artemis, Lady Malzard, now. Anyway, you see, milady, now they'll 'ave to call me milady too!"

The girl's eyes shone, but she still clutched the tray.

Prudence drained her cup and refilled it, the lemon cake threatening to return. Sudden elevation to high status was not an undiluted blessing. She knew that, and so did Cate.

"Would you rather not be in that position, Karen?"

The girl bit her lip. "I don't know, milady. It's exciting, and I could giggle at the sour faces on them all. But it doesn't seem right."

Prudence put down the cup, rattling it because of shaking hands. Cate had spoken about how the servants had strict ideas about what was right, and here she'd turned everything upside down. The blame rested on Artemis, but the consequences on herself, and she had no idea how to free herself or this child without creating new problems.

She wanted to send Karen away while she thought, but would the other servants be cruel to her? They'd have ways.

She'd find work for her.

"As you might have heard, the earl and I suffered a carriage accident and were forced to leave my luggage behind, but it should arrive soon. We purchased a few essentials en route."

Where had they gone? One of the footmen would have removed the package from the chaise.

"There's a nightgown and some other items in a package somewhere. Please find it and bring it to the dressing room. Before you put anything away, damp-dust the clothespress and the chest of drawers."

If Artemis Malzard took offense at that, she could choke on it.

"Yes, milady!" Karen said, and hurried away.

Prudence dropped her head into her hands, trying to force back tears, trying to see a way out. But then she pushed away from Artemis's table and fled Artemis's pretty boudoir.

The bedchamber was no better. It must all be Artemis Malzard's creation. Could she even bear to sleep in that bed?

She broke, and ran to fling open the door to the next room. "Cate!"

He turned, clad only in a gray robe, a crow-dark valet frowning behind him. He came quickly to her. "What is it? What's upset you?"

She gripped his hands, but glanced at the disapproving servant.

Without turning, Cate said, "You may go, Ransom."

Prudence watched the man, waiting until the door clicked shut. "I'm sorry. I can't do this. I'm making a disaster each way I turn!" She tried to be dignified, but she collapsed against him.

He hugged her to him, saying things that she couldn't hear because a storm of weeping had burst all her barriers. She tried to stop. She tried because it would be upsetting him. She tried because it hurt, because she feared she might never stop, might cry herself to death.

And then the storm of tears passed, leaving her limp, exhausted, wrung out, and simply lying there.

Lying?

On his bed. In his arms.

His wonderfully strong, comforting arms.

"It has been quite a difficult day, hasn't it?" he said.

She laughed, but stopped before that took her over as the weeping had. They said some mad people laughed incessantly. She could imagine that.

"I really have created a disaster," she mumbled into the wool covering his chest.

"I've done that a time or two myself."

She looked up at him. "What did you do afterward?"

"Got drunk, I believe. I have brandy. . . ."

"I'd better not. I'll become a sozzle-head soon."

He ran a finger gently across her cheek, wiping at

tears. "What you need, what I need, is sleep. Shall we sleep awhile, my wife?"

No. She couldn't face the marriage bed. Not now.

He must have read her expression. "Sleep," he repeated. "Simply sleep."

"Karen . . ."

"Karen?"

"Karenhappuch. Daughter of Job."

"I'm sure that makes perfect sense, but for now"—he sat them up—"I'll help you out of your gown and stays and we'll simply sleep."

"Your valet will come back."

"Not unless summoned."

"Karen . . ."

"If she's your maid, she'll behave the same way. There are some privileges to our rank, you know, and being allowed to go to bed at just past eight of a summer's evening is one of them."

"I have a nightgown."

"Your shift will do."

He unfastened her bodice, but she took it off, and the skirt, and then turned so he could undo her stay laces. Part of her mind trembled at the intimacy, but the rest was a fog of exhaustion.

Heaven knew what people would think.

But they were married. This was allowed.

This was her wedding night!

Once she could, she took off her stays, and then her stockings, her back modestly turned to him. She'd used her shift as nightgown for months in White Rose Yard to avoid the expense of replacing a worn-out one, but now she was aware that it reached only to her calves, and that the neckline rode low. Even when she tightened the strings, it only just covered her uncontained breasts.

Her hair was still pinned up, so she loosened it, glancing behind. Cate wasn't there. Then he returned from his dressing room, now in a nightshirt under his robe. Completely covered, neck to toe. He lowered the brocade curtains at the two windows, shutting out the low sunlight until the room was almost dark. He was favoring his leg.

"How's your wound?"

"Healing. Ransom obtained some of Mistress Ingleton's miraculous healing salve and applied some to my side as well. It certainly worked when we were boys, but both parts will appreciate a peaceful opportunity to heal." He drew back the bedcovers and turned to her. "Come and be peaceful with me, my dear."

A peaceful opportunity to heal. Perhaps that was what she needed—a chance for all her wounds, large and small, but especially those of the past days, to heal.

There were steps on both sides of the bed, so she climbed up and onto the cool, sweet-smelling sheets and then quickly pulled the covers up over herself, watching him shed his robe and join her.

Would he really do nothing?

Parts of her remembered touches and kisses and stirred with desire, but the rest of her said no and hoped she wouldn't have to put the rejection into words.

He walked around drawing the bed curtains, shutting out the remaining light, and suddenly this was a place where she could sleep, could simply sleep. After weeks of worry, fitful nights, and a long, challenging day, here was peacefulness, security, and rest.

She felt him get into bed on his side and perhaps even sensed his heat.

"I've never shared a bed with anyone before," she said. "It's comforting."

"I've never shared a bed like this before," he said. "You're right. It's comforting."

Prudence wanted to move closer, perhaps even into his arms, but he'd said they'd only sleep and that was most of what she wanted. She had something to confess, however, before she could rest.

"I have created a disaster, Cate. Probably a new pandemonium . . ."

He found her hand and held it. "Is it likely to become worse in the next ten hours or so?"

"I don't think so, but . . ."

He rolled closer and kissed her lips. "Then sleep, my wife. We'll face our nest of demons in the morning." He kissed her again, a very tender, comforting kiss, and then rolled away.

Prudence smiled into the dark and then turned in the other direction, sleep flowing over her.

Chapter 24

Cate woke, accustomed enough by now to the grand bed to begin thinking of the routine challenges ahead. But then he remembered the woman by his side.

His wife.

He gently parted the bed curtains a little, letting in muted light. She was lying on her side, facing away from him, pale hair tangled.

He smiled, wanting to touch it, to smooth it, to comfort her, but his urge to kiss the sliver of her nape revealed by parted hair came from baser needs. Her shoulder, exposed by the slipped sleeve of her shift, tempted him, as did the curve of waist and hip beneath the covers. He could smell her, softly earthy and desirable—and forbidden.

He mustn't go where touching her, kissing her neck, stroking her shoulder would lead. There was no sign that she was having her courses, and he never wanted to doubt that their first child was his.

Thank God she wouldn't mind delay. She'd made that clear last night. It wasn't surprising. They were almost strangers. It didn't feel that way, but it was true, and delay would give him the pleasure of wooing her with all the graces and felicities she'd been denied.

He rolled onto his back, looking up at the damn sunburst. It made him think of Louis XIV, the Sun King, and what did that have to do with Keynings—at least the Keynings of his youth?

All the problems were seeping back into his mind and he'd rather like to draw the curtains again and shut out the angry, disapproving world. He couldn't, however. His family must be faced, and his taskmasters would be pawing the ground in their eagerness to put him to his work.

His mother was being outrageous. If she didn't emerge and be gracious, he'd have that to deal with. Thank heaven for Artemis. She was being kind, and she'd provide companionship for Prudence and ease her into the way of things. Artemis would soon leave, however, and then whom would his countess have?

Himself, but he still had so much to learn, and that took most of his days. Moreover, he should go to London soon to make his bow at court and complete the formalities to do with his seat in Parliament. Would it be kinder to take Prudence with him—to an even more frightening world? Or to leave her here alone?

Damnation. He could have acted no differently in the church, and he'd found no other path since. But perhaps he hadn't truly wanted one.

He looked at her again. He'd been attracted to Prudence Youlgrave from the first, and she'd lingered in his mind. He'd purchased her a gift, even when he'd not expected to see her again. He'd thought about her, worried about her. It felt completely right that she be his wife, in his bed.

But then he remembered Squire Trent and the innkeeper's widow. The marriage had been the scandal of the area a decade ago, but he'd been surprised to find it still mentioned and unforgiven now. Mistress Trent still wasn't accepted in the better circles.

Of course, Prudence wasn't the same—she'd been born to a manor. Her recent years would count against her, however, if they came out, and the events in Darlington could turn her too into an unforgotten scandal.

He wouldn't permit it. He was the Earl of Malzard, dammit, and the people of the area would accept and respect his wife or heads would roll.

It was Sunday in three days, and the family at Keynings always went to service at the village church, along with a number of other local families of distinction. That would be the first test, and they'd better all pass.

He eased out of the bed to commence his day, regretting the kiss he didn't place on that creamy spot on his wife's nape.

Prudence awoke slowly in a very comfortable bed, surprised by a sense of well-being that was completely new to her. Comfort, safety, and ease, right down to her soul.

But then she remembered disturbing dreams—and that not all of them had been dreams.

Draydale in the church, face purple with rage.

The shocking, painful blow.

The terrifying carriage accident—which Henry Draydale had caused, hoping to kill or maim.

Perhaps worst of all had been that time when she'd believed Cate loved another—the lovely, perfect Lady Malzard.

She turned to him, but in the dark she couldn't see where he was. Hesitantly, she reached out, seeking his body.

And didn't find it.

She sat up and parted the curtains. She was alone in

the bed. What time was it? She crawled over to part the curtains on the other side to see the clock, and there was Cate, smiling at her, back in his robe. Looking magnificent with his height, his broad shoulders, and his loose dark hair.

"Good morning," he said.

Prudence retreated a little, pulling covers up over her chest, fussing with bird's-nest hair. "What time is it?"

"Not much past eight. I don't suppose I can tempt you to a ride?"

"No. And you shouldn't, with your wound."

His smile widened. "I did hope you'd fuss over me. All the same, it's a shame. I hope you'll learn. I'd find you a dorado."

"Is that a special sort of saddle?" she asked, hoping it was safe and secure.

"It's a breed, or more precisely a color. A pale gold with a cream mane and tail. Like you."

"Are you saying I'm sallow, sir, or horse faced?" But Prudence was smiling too. She loved this playful conversation.

"Along with a wooden top, as I remember." He came forward and leaned down to kiss her. "Your skin is milk, your hair pale, silken gold, and your wits are as sharp as a dagger. Will you invite me to breakfast with you in your boudoir, my wife?"

Prudence knew she was blushing all over. "Of course."

"Order it posthaste. I'm famished."

He left through a side door. Despite his words, Prudence lingered in a daze. Then she shook herself, scrambled off her side of the bed, grabbed her discarded clothing, and ran into her own bedchamber. No need to fuss about what to wear when she had only the one gown.

Washing water. How did she summon washing water?

She wished she had her tooth powder. She'd discovered that in Darlington, and it was a great improvement on the salt she'd always used before. That, of course, was in her trunk. Was it possible her trunk had arrived?

How did she summon Karen? She couldn't put on her stays without help. She'd used to wear ones that laced at the front, country style, but they'd been given to the poor, like all her old clothes, and now she had only fashionable, back-lacing ones.

How did she summon her maid? It seemed an idiotic thing to fail at. At Blytheby, Sir Joshua had simply bellowed, but that house had been much smaller than this. In any case, she couldn't bring herself to do that.

She looked at her skirt and bodice, wondering if she could put them on without stays. They'd look awful. She headed for the dressing room, hoping her trunk might have arrived in the night. She had a pretty robe in it that would do for breakfast.

But then she saw her new nightgown draped over a rack. Did Karen know she'd not used it? Did that announce things . . . ?

Things that hadn't happened, but might have?

She grabbed the nightgown and put it on over the shift, welcoming its cover from neck to wrist to toes. Thus armored, she opened the dressing room door. There was Karen, sitting by the window, sewing.

The girl leapt to her feet. "Washing water, milady? Breakfast?"

She looked much improved in a crisp gray gown, and with a black apron and cap of finer quality. Perhaps she'd had a bath. She certainly looked scrubbed within an inch. Someone in the household had done their best to make the situation more suitable, and that was hopeful.

"Both," Prudence said. "Water immediately, and breakfast in the boudoir for the earl and me." Simply saying that made her blush.

The maid dipped a curtsy and then surprised Prudence by leaving through a door in the corner of the room. When she'd gone, Prudence inspected this feature. The door was as flat as the wall and painted the same color. When she opened it, she saw plain stairs going down. It would enable a personal servant to enter and leave without disturbing the master or mistress.

Karen hadn't used those stairs before, probably because as an under housemaid, accustomed to cleaning grates and scrubbing floors before the family was up, she'd known nothing about them.

Had her trunk arrived in the night? Prudence opened the press. Alas, it held only the few items she'd purchased at the market, but those Artemis smells were gone. The smell now was not particularly pleasant—perhaps something meant to repel moths—but it held no ghosts of the past. She found her clean shift and stockings and took them into the bedchamber.

Karen returned the way she'd gone, and poured the steaming water into the basin.

"Draw the screen around the washstand, please. I prefer to wash in private." Perhaps a fine lady didn't care if her maid saw her unclothed, but she did.

When the maid had done that, Prudence went behind and took off her clothes. "Is someone teaching you how to be my maid?" she asked.

"Yes, milady. The dowager. I mean, Miss 'opkins, milady."

"That's kind of her." Did that augur well for the real dowager?

"It is, milady. And of Mistress Ingleton, who told 'er to."

Ah, yes, the housekeeper. Not so hopeful, but better than antagonism from all.

Prudence began to wash as quickly and thoroughly as possible, wondering how easy it was for a countess to have a bath.

"Is anyone being unkind?" she asked.

"I know as some complained to Mistress Ingleton, milady, but she told 'em off sharpish. Let them say what they like," the girl added saucily. "They all still 'ave to 'milady' me."

Prudence winced. She could feel pandemonium growing.

"My clean shift, please, Karen."

That was passed over, and Prudence put it on. Then she went out to put on her stays, which Karen began to lace up the back.

"These are right pretty, milady," she said. Then, "Sorry, milady. I'm not to chatter."

"I'll tell you when to chatter and not chatter. I'm happy to hear about the house."

The maid didn't take that hint, however.

When the stays were laced, Prudence turned to put on the petticoat, but caught sight of herself in the mirror. Her hair was a mess and she still didn't have a comb! But then she saw a brush and comb on the dressing table.

"Whose are these?" she asked. If they belonged to Artemis, she wouldn't touch them.

"Yours, milady. Mistress Ingleton provided 'em. She keeps such for guests. And I'm to brush yer hair, milady."

Prudence was a bit nervous about that, but if anything the young maid was too gentle. Prudence eventually took over herself. She brushed it vigorously, working out a few knots, wincing not at the pain, but at the sight Cate had woken to.

Karen gasped. "Yer lordship!"

Prudence twisted to see that Cate had come in.

Despite last night, Prudence put a hand across her chest, aware of the low-cut stays pushing her breasts up, of her bare legs showing beneath the calf-length shift.

He smiled. "A charming sight."

He was dressed in another robe, this time of green, but clearly over shirt and breeches.

"You may go," he said to Karen, who dipped a curtsy almost to the ground and fled. He took the brush from Prudence. "Allow me."

"You shouldn't. . . ."

"It's forbidden?" He drew the brush gently through her hair, which in truth was almost smooth by now.

"I watched you tend your hair in the farmhouse and was charmed."

"By me combing my hair?" Something shivered deep inside.

"By you combing your hair," he agreed. "The nape of your neck is exceedingly fine." He dropped a kiss just there. "You were cross with me then."

A tremor had run all the way down her spine.

"Because of my devotion to the ravishing Lady Malzard," he said. "She pleases me very much, and I am hers to command."

Prudence turned, taking the brush from him. "And she vowed to obey Lord Malzard. How agreeable we are."

He smiled with her. "Or indeterminate. I can determine, however, that a lady's stays are the most entrancing garment she owns." He ran a finger lightly across the exposed frill of her shift, his touch so close to her breasts. "Stays restrain but expose, invite but challenge." He stroked the swell of her breasts.

Prudence inhaled.

"You permit?" he asked.

"I vowed to obey...." She could speak no louder than a whisper.

Last night ... last night had been for sleep. Was it possible that now was the time?

He leaned to kiss her shoulder, sending a new shudder through her and causing a strange clenching deep inside. Oh, yes, now was the time. She reached up to draw his head down, inviting his kisses to her lips.

It was daylight.

Karen might return.

She didn't care.

He sat beside her on the bench, turned the opposite way, which seemed an ideal position for a deep kiss, for his arm holding her close, his other hand on the bare skin of her shoulder, her neck, her cheek.

Skin-to-skin, so hot and connected, as if they were one. She shifted to press closer, resenting now that only their upper bodies touched, and that they wore so many clothes.

His hand threaded into her loose hair, cradling her skull. She did the same to him, breaking the kiss to move to a better position....

But then he rose, trailing fingers down from shoulder to hand in slow farewell. "Breakfast awaits?"

She clung to his hand, wanting to draw him back down, but breakfast did await, and it was probably indecent for them to behave so in the bright morning.

She released him. "Go through to the boudoir," she said as calmly as she could. "I'll join you in a moment."

"As always, I obey my mistress." He blew her a kiss and left.

If I truly could command you, we'd not part at all.

Prudence inhaled, cooling herself. She could wait. It would only be until tonight. Tonight would be their true wedding night.

She dearly wished it weren't close to the longest day of the year.

Chapter 25

Cate found breakfast laid out on the small table. The kitchens knew what he liked, so there was beef and ale. They couldn't know Prudence's tastes, so they'd sent both coffee and chocolate, an assortment of breads and a plate of cheeses, finely sliced ham, and boiled eggs.

It was well-done. He must remember to send thanks and appreciation.

He sat to eat, for he'd eaten little during the extraordinary yesterday, but his mind was full of the present and future.

What had possessed him to play such seductive games? He'd almost broken his intent right there. And Prudence would not have been unwilling. Her glowing willingness had almost pushed him over the edge.

Hell and damnation.

He put down his knife and fork and drank ale.

She came in fully dressed, her hair simply pinned up. "Eat. There was no need to wait." She sat, smiled, and poured chocolate, as brisk as a stranger, but he wanted her even now.

She sipped, then said, "Oh, my. This is the best chocolate I've ever tasted."

"I must reward my chocolate maker," he said, but the flick of her tongue to clear chocolate from her upper lip almost destroyed him.

"You'll beggar yourself," she said, "for I'm sure everything at Keynings is of the best."

"I would pay every penny for your delight."

She smiled, but clearly took it as a joke. It wasn't.

She'd been so deprived that she was easily delighted. He wanted to delight her to death.

"Even two days ago I couldn't have believed all this," she said, buttering a bun. "It still doesn't seem real."

"Breakfast?"

She shot him a look. "Breakfast with you."

Those heavy-lidded eyes, a smoky blue-gray . . .

"Two days ago you were preparing for your wedding to Draydale," he reminded her. "No, I'm sorry. Don't even think of it."

She had frozen, but she smiled again. "I intend not to. Ever. What were you doing two days ago?"

"Having breakfast at the Talbot and planning to go to the church to see my gallant Hera triumph . . ." Another unfortunate subject. "Tell me about your little pandemonium."

"Oh." She put her bun down. "The demons' dance around Karen. My maid," she explained.

"Karenhappuch, daughter of Job. I do remember. She does seem young for the post."

"And inexperienced."

"Then why is she your maid?"

It was a simple question, but it struck Prudence dumb. She'd carelessly forgotten that the situation wouldn't make sense without mention of Artemis's hatred. She still didn't want to tell him of his sister-in-law's accusations, but she'd have to involve her.

"Artemis sent her," she said. "I think she resents me.

It's understandable. I've replaced her here, even taking her rooms."

"She vacated them as soon as Roe died, so that makes no sense. It must have been some confusion in the servants' hall."

Prudence could argue, but it would serve no purpose.

"Choose another maid," he said.

"Karen's quick and can learn."

He frowned slightly, obviously puzzled. "But you need a skilled maid now, just as I need a skilled valet. One who can turn you out in style to meet local society."

Local society. Lord, she'd forgotten there was a world beyond these rooms.

"Until my trunk arrives . . ." she said.

"Which should be today."

"Even then, I have nothing suitable for mourning, so I can't meet local society."

"Some might invade. You need to look the part. A trained maid could attend to your hands."

"You have broken nails too," she pointed out.

He spread his hands and she saw trimmed, buffed nails. "One of the first things Ransom insisted on."

"Very well, but I can't acquire a skilled maid instantly."

"Mother's will assist you."

"Your mother is avoiding me."

He sighed. "I'll speak to her."

They were squabbling, but she'd succeeded in deflecting him from Karen. It was weak of her, but at the moment she felt the young maid was her only friend at Keynings—apart from Cate and Perry.

"Your wounds must be healing well," she said, picking up her bun again. "You aren't limping much, but do please summon the doctor to look at them. Wounds can fester. I knew a man who died from a gashed leg."

He smiled. "Neither wound festers, but I love being fussed over."

Then I'll fuss over you morning, noon, and night, my love.

"Promise me you won't go riding for a while."

"You impose a penance, but I fear I'll be so tied to a desk for the next day or two, my only hurts will be from another part of my arse." He refilled his tankard. "I still don't entirely understand your pandemonium. So, your maid is young and unskilled."

"It seemed more dreadful yesterday," she said, "but it's still complicated. I told Karen she could be my maid for a while, but I gather that means she ranks high among the servants."

He whistled. "Countess of Malzard in the servants' hall. No wonder Ransom looked as if he were chewing lemons this morning."

"But if I return her to her under housemaid duties now, I suspect the other servants will be cruel."

"You have a kind heart, Prudence, but you can't keep her as lady's maid. She's completely unsuitable."

"*I'm* completely unsuitable."

"Which means you need an eminently suitable maid to balance that."

Unreasonable to have expected him to protest her unsuitability. "Very well. But why can't I keep Karen too, to run errands and such?"

"No reason at all. There have to be some benefits to our rank, and one is commanding what we wish. She'll need some official designation or rank. Ask Artemis. She'll know."

Prudence managed not to react. "I don't like to bother her. This must be a terrible time for her."

"You're right. I don't know how she manages to remain so calm."

By eating bile, morning, noon, and night. It was going to be torture not to tell him the truth.

"What plans do you have for today?" he asked.

Prudence realized she hadn't made any, but she couldn't skulk in her rooms as if afraid.

"I intend to ask the housekeeper to take me around the house."

"Have her show you the kitchens and such, but I want to show you the family part of the house. It'll have to be later, however. I was presented with extremely urgent matters as soon as I arrived, and I gather the merely urgent await."

"I'm sorry you're plagued, but I look forward to the tour of the house."

He drained his ale and rose. "Don't forget to order mourning clothes."

"I won't, and when my trunk arrives I'll order my old blue dyed black. Do you have people here able to make simple gowns?"

"I believe they make the servants' clothes, and mother and Artemis would have had sudden need of blacks. Ask Artemis."

That phrase was going to choke her soon.

"I thought of visiting your mother." She might be no better, but she, unlike Artemis, was here for life.

"I could order her to visit you," he said.

"No. That would be awful."

"She's behaving badly."

"She's had a shock on top of grief. Be gentle with her, Cate."

He grimaced in a way that told her he and his mother truly were at odds. Was that something she could amend?

"I must to my travails. Remember, command anything you like. Including Perry. He's a treasure house of social wisdom. You can't have him all the time, however. He's playing at being my secretary."

"Playing?"

"To him, everything is play. But summon him anytime you wish. He's your man for finer etiquette."

Prudence remembered the conversation about names and being alone with Perry. "I don't want to do anything even slightly irregular."

"Keep your maid with you. It's fashionable for a married lady to have a gallant attendant for the times when her husband neglects her."

"I'd rather not be neglected."

"And I'd rather not neglect, but duty calls." He came to kiss her cheek. "Don't distress yourself over my mother. She's not a delicate bloom, and she has sharp spines when upset."

"She's grieving, Cate."

"Yes, but for what?"

It was an odd thing to say.

"I go to face my demons," he said lightly, "and start a demon torment of my own."

"What?"

"Draydale, remember. Once I know the full extent of his sins, I'll send him where he belongs."

She rose. "Kill him? Cate, even a lord can hang! One did, not that long ago."

"I'm not going to kill him, even in a duel. For a man like Draydale, poverty and powerlessness are a finer hell."

"Oh, yes. I'd like to see it."

"You will. His destruction shouldn't take long, but be a little careful for now. Don't go wandering."

"Wandering?"

"Escaping wildly into the night? Or day."

She suddenly felt cold. "You think Draydale would come *here*?"

"Or send a lesser demon. He's the sort of bully who'll not rest until he's had his revenge."

"But once he knows who you are, he won't dare."

"He hit you in front of the town worthies," he reminded her, "so when enraged he loses all restraint. But, yes, I expect an indirect attack. I'll write to your brother and Tallbridge to warn them to be on guard too."

"You'll tell them who you are?"

"It's not a secret."

"No, but . . . I think I should write the letter to Aaron. He'll be guided by Tallbridge, anyway."

"Will he, nill he," he murmured. "He'll pay a heavy price for that marriage."

"I was willing to pay a heavier one, remember. The difference is that Susan is clever enough not to make him feel it too much."

As you will try to do, but I'll always know.

"You're looking sad. On your paltry brother's account?"

"No. But fair warning—Susan will boast of her connection to you all over Yorkshire, and she'll expect to visit here."

"If you can bear with my family all the time, I can bear with yours on occasions."

He left, and Prudence could sigh. This breakfast had been sweet pleasure, but beyond these rooms lurked a kind of hell. She'd like to stay tucked away here until Cate was free to take her around Keynings, but will she, nill she, this house was now hers to command. To shirk would be to give victory to Artemis and the dowager, and she would not do that.

May all the angels of heaven be on her side.

Chapter 26

The tour of the house passed easily. Mistress Ingleton was calmly courteous and extremely efficient. Prudence didn't try to claim experience she didn't have, but her memories of Blytheby helped her to show some understanding. She knew that would be noted, and put to her credit.

First impressions, first impressions, she reminded herself as she met various servants.

Cate might not have been joking when he'd said he'd reward the person who made the chocolate. He employed a baker and a confectioner in addition to the plain cook. All inquired as to her favorite foods, so they seemed eager to please.

She gathered that the dowager was skilled in the still-room, but there was a maid especially for that area, and another with particular responsibility for the jams and preserves. Keynings was supplied from the home farm dairy, but had its own brewhouse and, of course, linen and laundry areas.

The laundry mistress was appropriately called Mistress Waters, and assured her it would be easy to dye a gown black. "Though not all colors and cloth take dyes well, your ladyship. The only way is to try and see."

"It's an old gown, Mistress Waters, so if it's ruined, it will be no great loss."

She would feel a pang, however, about the long, eye-straining work she'd done on it to prepare for her brother's wedding. That seemed another world, but she reminded herself she must write again to Hetty, and perhaps include a gift.

She bit her lip on laughter at the thought of Hetty's reaction to her becoming a countess. There'd be lawks-a-mercys by the bucketload.

The linen room was impressively lined with shelves upon which cloth-covered bundles contained everything from towels to curtains. Two maids sat at a long table in good light, making almost invisible mends to white sheets and garments. Three more were making clothes.

"We make the simpler garments, milady," said the seamstress, Mistress Sawley, "especially for the servants."

"Could you make me a simple black gown?" Prudence asked. "My trunk will arrive, but it contains no mourning wear."

Let the servants speculate as they would.

"Certainly, your ladyship, and in a day, if very simple. Betty, get down the crape." One of the maids hurried to climb a stepladder and take down a roll of cloth. "We always have crape to hand," the seamstress said, "in case of . . ." But then she bit her lip.

"It was a terrible thing," Prudence said, hoping to be believed. "So sudden."

"Shocking it was, milady. Shocking."

She unwrapped the roll and flung out some of the densely black material along the table. Crape was woven to be without any sheen and had the quality of seeming to suck away light. Prudence remembered that from her mourning gowns for her father.

"Please make one gown as quickly as possible. And a cap."

The seamstress measured her and assured her she would have everything by the next day. If the blue took the dye, she'd have two black gowns, at least.

Prudence went on her way, dutifully inspecting a range of storage areas, noting that those containing the most expensive items were kept locked. Mistress Ingleton had keys for everything among the big bunch dangling from her belt.

"How many sets of keys are there, Mistress Ingleton?"

"I have a set, milady, and Mr. Flamborough, though he's rarely called upon to use them. I believe a set is held by his lordship, but I've never known that set used. Of course, some people have some keys, such as the butler having keys to the wine cellars. . . ."

"Does either of the other Lady Malzards have a set?" Prudence asked.

"Oh, yes, of course, milady! That's only right." But then she turned slightly glassy-eyed at the implications.

Prudence supposed that in a more normal situation Artemis's keys would have been passed on to her, though notably the dowager hadn't handed over her keys when Artemis came here.

"I assume a set is being prepared for me?" she said.

"Right speedily, milady. The locksmith will get to it immediately."

Of course, Keynings would have its own locksmith. And clock winder, she realized, as clocks struck eleven.

"I would like tea," she said, feeling desperate for it, and the break it would require.

"Would you honor me by taking tea in my parlor, milady? It would give an opportunity for you to look through the account books."

Prudence longed for escape, but how could she decline?

It was another hour before she collapsed in the sanctuary of her own rooms, her head aching with all she'd been told, and with the pressure of everything now resting on her shoulders. Cate bore the weight of the earldom, but the house—the houses—were hers.

She could entrust Keynings to Mistress Ingleton, but though she seemed an excellent housekeeper that would be to shirk her duties. She could probably leave it in the hands of Artemis and the dowager, but she'd eat glass first. She'd not realized she had such a fierce need to prove herself their equal in all this. She could only hope she wasn't driven into disaster again by imprudent courage.

"Oh, there you are, milady. Do you need anything?"

Karen had come out of the dressing room. Prudence realized she'd forgotten about the girl. When she said, "No," she saw disappointment.

"Have you simply been waiting all this time with nothing to do?"

"It's my place to wait, milady," Karen said with dignity. "I'm like a lady-in-waiting, Mistress Ingleton said. And I have a basket of plain mending to do."

Prudence wondered if the girl would like to spend some time in the more familiar servants' hall below, or if she valued her place up in the heights. Heaven and hell, she thought wryly, but the servants' hall had looked very comfortable.

"Where are you sleeping, Karen?"

"Right below you, milady! I've a room all to my own." That was clearly heaven. "You can knock on your floor in the night and I'll hear you, but there's also a bell. Here."

She went to the head of the bed and showed Prudence

a cord that disappeared through the floor. The maid gave it a tug, and Prudence heard a little tinkle below.

"That's very clever."

"It is, isn't it? I never knew about such things."

"Can you read, Karen?"

The maid suddenly looked miserable. "Very little, milady. I'm sorry. . . ."

"It's not your fault. What education do the children on the estate get?"

"Old Miss Wright has the little 'uns read a bit from the Bible on a Sunday, milady. She were Lady Arabella's governess, I hear, and, being old, stayed on when Lady Arabella left to marry."

"Lady Arabella?" Prudence asked, not sure if her head had space for another fact.

"His lordship's sister, milady. Five children she has now, and right terrors when they came to visit last year, especially the boys. Oh, sorry, milady. I'm chattering again."

"I'll tell you if your chatter bothers me. How many boys?"

"Three, milady, and nothing but trouble."

Prudence imagined the pain those boys had inflicted on Artemis and her husband, who'd not only lost a precious baby, but the son they needed for the succession.

She pulled her mind back to education. That was a proper matter for a lady to be interested in, and she was. Though she had no calling to it herself, she'd seen the benefits to Hetty's children.

Hetty's children. They'd been without a teacher since she left, which saddened her. Perhaps she could send some simple lessons.

She needed to start writing things down.

"Karen, do you know where to find writing paper, pens, and such?"

"No, milady." The girl was looking anxious again.

"I'm sure it's not part of your duties. Please go and ask Mistress Ingleton, and if possible bring such things to my boudoir."

The maid left and Prudence went to the window to look out at the estate. Was it possible danger lurked out there? She could, alas, imagine Henry Draydale sending one of his unpleasant employees here to attempt something. She'd tried not to pay attention to such matters, but she knew he employed a number of ruthless men to collect debts, evict tenants who couldn't pay their rent, and doubtless do other things to make sure his will was obeyed. She'd seen him speak coldly to his servants and children and had begun to suspect that his poor second wife had been driven to a mental decline. What an escape she'd had—for Prudence strongly suspected she'd have been driven to kill the man. Not herself. Him.

She felt for the knife in her pocket. She'd keep it with her always, just in case.

At the moment, the gardens and park looked the epitome of tranquillity. The only movement was the slow, precise walk of some deer cropping grass, and ripples at the edges of the lake.

"It's there, milady!" Karen declared, bursting in. "The paper. In yer desk. But yer trunk's come! I'll go and arrange for it to be brought up to the dressing room immediately."

She was off and Prudence went to the dressing room to wait. At last. She'd soon have her dyed gown, but more important, she'd have the few precious items that would make this place seem a little bit like a home.

She owned four books. One was Malory's *Morte d'Arthur*, given to her by her father, which she'd never been able to bring herself to sell. The other books were favorites that she'd replaced in Darlington. She also had her mother's favorite vase and the two glasses—the ones she and Cate had used that first night.

Karen opened the hidden door, and a footman backed through holding one handle. Soon another appeared in charge of the other. They put the trunk down, bowed, and left. Prudence had her key ready, and knelt to open it.

"There," she said, and threw back the lid.

"Oooh, milady, that's a pretty nightdress!"

Yesterday, when she'd dug through the trunk to find suitable clothing, she'd disordered the contents, and her finest nightgown was now rumpled on top. It was the one Susan had given her as a wedding present, made of fine lawn, pin-tucked and inset, and trimmed with soft, ruffled lace.

She took it out and passed it to the maid. "I'll wear that tonight."

For her true wedding night.

She passed over shifts, stockings, fichus, and handkerchiefs, but then came to the few items she'd prepared herself. A bride should make linens for her future home. Draydale had told her not to bother, that his house had all the sheets and towels it needed, but she'd done it anyway. Her first, weak rebellion, but what use were they here, especially monogrammed with "P.D."? Prudence Draydale. The thought of it was enough to make her sick. She gave the towels and pillowcases to Karen. "Dispose of these."

The girl looked dubious, but she said, "Very well, milady," and put them aside.

When the trunk was empty Prudence picked up the blue gown—the only piece of clothing left from her days of poverty. Weakness tempted her to preserve it, but for what purpose?

"Take this to the laundry to be dyed black, Karen."

She left the rest of the clothing for the maid to deal with and took her homely items through to the boudoir. She put the books on one bookshelf, the vase and glasses on another. The desk did now contain expensive writing paper, pens, and all else necessary, but she put her few sheets of simpler stationery in there too. Her wooden jewelry box contained little of value, but she added the pretty pieces Cate had given her and locked it in the central door.

All her possessions made hardly a mark here.

She realized that this announced to all how little she brought to this marriage. Everything in this house now belonged to her, but that wasn't the point.

After a knock, Cate came in from the corridor.

Prudence knew she blushed as she smiled. It had been so long. "My trunk arrived," she told him.

"Then all is well. Ah, do I recognize those glasses?" He picked one up, shooting her a wicked glance.

She blushed even more. "I'll never use them, but . . ."

"On the contrary, we'll sip brandy from them by night, and share our problems."

"I hope to keep all problems at bay."

"Optimist."

"Why not," she said, "for my situation is much improved."

He touched her mother's rose-painted vase. "Remember that a bed of roses must by nature have thorns."

Cate immediately regretted his words. Time in the earldom's offices always made him jaundiced, even with Perry's wit to keep the blue devils at bay.

"I do worry about my lack of possessions," Prudence said, seeming anxious. "It looks odd."

"What do you want? More books, glasses, figurines, fans, feathers . . . ?"

She laughed, but said, "Just more. I mean, I *should* have more, if I'd come from a suitable situation. I had little when I moved to Darlington, and I bought only what I needed, because I knew it was all being paid for with Tallbridge money. I didn't want to be in their debt."

"I've endowed you with all my worldly goods," he pointed out.

"I'm not making myself clear. I wish I had more possessions arriving here from my past."

Now he did understand. "I arrived here as earl with little, but no one expected otherwise. You're correct that your possessions are part of your first impression. But it's easily solved. We need Perry. Where's that wench of yours. *Karen!*" he called.

The girl rushed in, eyes wide, looking scared to death.

"I need you to find Mr. Perriam and ask him to join Lady Malzard and myself here."

The girl almost sagged with relief, which unsettled the curtsy she dipped at the same time. She then staggered off.

"She is rather endearing," he said. "Like a puppy."

"I know. Why Perry?"

"I'm hoping he'll undertake a mission."

"Another one? You abuse him terribly."

He smiled. "You have a kind heart, but don't waste it on him. He'll refuse if he wants to. Truly, he loves to ride. That makes London living a challenge, but he rides out on a shocking number of occasions."

"Where do you want to send him?"

"To York, for possessions."

Perry came in then, smiling as he bowed and declared, "Lady Malzard! *Enchanté!* How may I serve you? Do you have a demon for me to slay?"

"Nothing so dramatic," said Cate. "You may, however, ride full-tilt to York and ravage some shops." Cate explained what he meant.

"The possessions of a respectable lady of the middling sort," Perry said. "An interesting challenge. Including clothes?" he asked Prudence.

"If there's mourning to be had."

"Another challenge. Is Othello up for cross-country work, Cate?"

"I'd hope so, or he's not worth his oats."

"Then I fly like an angel on horseback."

Prudence smothered a laugh with a hand, but Cate let his out. "Angels on horseback" was a dish of oysters wrapped in bacon.

Perry laughed with them. "Delicious, but hardly heroic. I simply fly like Raphael on my mission. My dear lady, may I request a gown?"

"You mean to travel in a *gown*?" Prudence asked.

"A thought! Angels are usually represented wearing gowns. . . ."

"Saint Michael is usually in armor," Cate said.

"But not Raphael."

"And never, to my knowledge, on horseback," Prudence pointed out, looking as if she feared Perry might truly make the ride in a gown.

Perry smiled at her. "Your gown will give your size. If you permit, I could leave it with a mantua maker in York so that others could be made from the pattern."

"Oh, how clever you are," she said, beaming, and went herself to get it.

"I would dislike to fall out with you," Cate said.

"Jealous? That's promising."

"She is my wife."

"Not all men are jealous of their wives' attentions. In fact, some are glad to see them happily distracted. . . ."

But Prudence returned then with a yellow dress.

Cate said, "I'm sorry you're not able to wear something so pretty."

"It doesn't matter, truly." She gave it to Perry. "Thank you for doing this."

"I am your angel to command." He bowed again and left.

Cate ground his teeth at his wife's fond smile, wanting to warn her against Perry's charm, but that would be ridiculous. He had enough complications in his marriage without adding that.

He held out a hand. "Let me show you around part of the house as we make our way down to dinner."

Chapter 27

Prudence was astonished by the number of formal and informal rooms, all elegant and awaiting activity. Perhaps Keynings had been livelier before the death, but there were still a great many rooms.

Cate said, "There are apartments in the north end of the house used by some dependent relatives and retired senior servants. We won't intrude there. Those residents largely keep to themselves, but you might meet them around. There's an elderly gentleman who was librarian here when I was a boy, and two spinster cousins of my mother's who like to prune the garden, much to the gardeners' dismay."

He led her into a long gallery, where a number of portraits hung. "We must have your portrait painted soon."

"Heavens, no!" Prudence protested, but when he said, "It is necessary," she sighed.

"Why that should seem more of a challenge than anything else, I don't know."

"Perhaps because a portrait shows us ourselves as others see us. Or how we want others to see us, which could be even more telling. I must face it too. At the moment, there's only this one of Roe and me as boys."

The resemblance was clear, but they were a mismatched pair. The thin boy of about twelve sat in a sober suit, reading a book, while a sturdy child still in a dress held a hoop as if impatiently waiting permission to run off and play.

"I think that artist was skilled," Prudence said.

"Probably. He painted us separately. Roe sat patiently for hours because he was always happy to read, whereas he had to catch me in moments."

"Will you be any better behaved now?" she teased.

"I'm thoroughly cowed by nobility. Perhaps we should have a wedding portrait. They're becoming the style. Out in the grounds, surrounded by our grandeur."

"In mourning?"

"A point. And an excuse to put off the day. Ah, this is my father in his middle years."

Prudence considered the robust man with a firm jaw. "A stern gentleman."

"That must have been how he wanted to be seen by posterity. He could be genial with some. And here's my mother as a new countess."

Prudence was very interested in this one, but she doubted that the dowager today resembled this slightly built young woman.

"She wanted to look like a countess," she said. "Composed and dignified. But nervousness shows. I'm sure it will with me too." She looked to the next one. "Your brother, grown up."

"How did he want to be seen?" he asked.

Prudence didn't want to say anything that would offend. "Composed and dignified, down to his soul. Very sure of himself. Was he?"

"Being born to inherit Keynings ensures that. How do you read Artemis?"

Prudence looked at Artemis Malzard, again surely as a bride, but in this case, not so many years ago. She could weep for that happy young woman. The portrait showed her seated, hands in lap, perhaps attempting to appear dignified, but a smile brightened her eyes.

She'd been happy.

"It's so unfair," she said.

"Life often is."

A bell rang.

"Late for dinner again," he said carelessly. "Come."

He took her through a small door and along a narrow corridor that brought them out near the stairs down to the hall.

"Keynings seems to hold a lot of secrets," Prudence said.

"Let's hope so. It would be pleasant to keep some."

"Who'll be at dinner?" she asked quietly as they went down the main stairs.

"It's established custom that any family at home dine together. A few employees may if they wish. Rathbone, the librarian, does if not lost in a book. Dramcot, the estate steward, rarely does. He prefers to dine with his family. He has a house on the estate. The north-wing residents suit themselves."

There were two footmen in the hall, so Prudence didn't ask any more questions, but was she about to meet the dowager?

"This is the family dining room," Cate said as they went in. "There's a state one for banquets."

The table could comfortably hold ten, she thought, but only four people were present, and none was the dowager or Artemis. The four had all risen—two elderly ladies on the far side of the table, and two elderly gentlemen on the near side, turning in a slightly doddering way to bow.

"My countess," Cate told them. "My dear, I present Miss Catesby and her sister, Miss Cecily Catesby, who are cousins of my mother's."

The slender, silver-haired ladies dipped curtsies. Prudence's mother's old instructions returned to guide her: *No one ever offends by an excess of courtesy.* She only hoped that applied in the highest circles, and returned the curtsies.

Cate went on, "Mr. Coates was our house steward here for thirty years, and Mr. Goode was our librarian for even longer."

Employees—that presented a dilemma, but she curtsied to them too. She noted that both ladies were in black, and the gentlemen in sober clothing with black armbands. Her dark red dress must look garish.

Cate led her to the seat at one end of the table. Once she sat, the others did. He went to the seat at the far end, seeming miles away. A stillness settled. His lips twitched, but the smile reached his eyes like a reassuring kiss as he glanced at the golden bell by her place.

"Are we all here?" she asked brightly, and rang it.

Instantly servants entered to lay out dishes on the table. A great many dishes for six people, but Prudence hoped the etiquette was the same as in Aaron's house.

She turned to the gentleman on her right. "May I help you to some of this fish, Mr. Goode? I believe it is carp."

"It is indeed, Lady Malzard, from the estate's own carp pond, so always very fresh. Thank you, thank you."

As she'd hoped, that was the signal for everyone to serve themselves and others, and for dishes to pass along the table if requested. She put small amounts of various dishes on her own plate, but wasn't sure whether she could swallow any of it.

This was the first occasion when she felt completely a countess, and hopelessly out of her milieu. And this was only an informal meal.

Only the butler had remained to pass around the

table with the wine. She gladly drank some, then ate a little fish.

Cate was talking to the Catesby ladies, so she turned to the gentlemen. "I've not yet explored the library here, Mr. Goode. I'm sure it's a wonderful collection."

"A practical one, my lady," he corrected. "Alas, neither the previous earl nor his father was interested in rarer editions."

"More interested in rare trees," said Mr. Coates in a quavery voice. "Half of which died. I'll have some more of that fricassee, if you'd be so kind, Miss Catesby."

Silence settled, but Miss Cecily Catesby said, "You come from Darlington, I believe, Lady Malzard?"

Prudence agreed, but tensely. Did the ladies know the town well, or, more to the point, know people there?

"We visited once," Miss Cecily said, "when the clock was mounted on the spire. An excellent service to the town."

Relieved, Prudence seized on a topic of conversation. "That would be St. Cuthbert's. An interesting old church."

Mr. Goode took that up. "Ah, yes, St. Cuthbert's. The choir stalls there are very old, and . . ."

Prudence had no objection to his lecturing on the subject at length.

She stole a glance at Cate and found him smiling at her. Perhaps he too was remembering the church. There were dark memories centered there, but it had been where they'd said their vows.

Mr. Coates broke in to say that the local church, St. Wilfred's, had an equal claim to age and dignity. "As you will see, my lady, on Sunday. There's an ancient cross in the churchyard, and a suggestion of a church there dating back to the time of Saint Wilfred himself."

Mr. Goode said, "I find the arguments put forward unconvincing, Coates."

A debate threatened, but Miss Cecily said, "Sunday. An opportunity for the worthies of the area to meet you, dear Lady Malzard. We were saying yesterday—weren't we, sister?—that the situation does present some difficulties. Normally, a new countess would mean a fete or a ball. . . ."

"But at the moment," said her sister, "that would not do. However, Sunday will provide a very suitable occasion." She looked at Prudence with an uncertain smile. "Forgive me for mentioning it, dear lady, but it would be better to appear in black."

Cate responded to that. "I'm at fault there, cousin, for urging a hasty marriage. My wife had no time to prepare for a house of mourning, but she will have blacks by Sunday."

The elderly ladies smiled at her and Miss Catesby said, "The urgency of young love."

They seemed kind, but Prudence suspected that they were gossips who sought out every tidbit and wrote many letters. Today's events at Keynings would be racing to all points by tomorrow. Well enough if they had a positive view, but when the truth began to trickle in here . . .

She rang the bell for the second course, wishing this meal over, but aware it was the first of hundreds. Thousands, even.

Once the new dishes had been attacked, Miss Catesby said, "We heard you suffered a carriage accident, dear Lady Malzard. What happened?"

Cate again stepped in to relate the incident. Of course, he didn't mention the tampering with the wheel.

"How terrifying!" Miss Cecily said. "A miracle that you both survived."

"I avoided hurt through Malzard's gallantry," Prudence said. "He protected me from shattered glass and woodwork at some cost to himself."

"Shocking," said Mr. Goode. "The state of the roads is shocking. Even the new toll roads. I always rode when I traveled. I may be Optimus by name, but I'm a pessimist when it comes to vehicles."

Everyone smiled or laughed, but Prudence's smile was strained. Optimus Goode! That wasn't a name to be forgotten, especially by a girl of twelve. He'd visited Blytheby to see the famous collection. He'd hardly seen her then, and would never recognize her now, but he'd recognize the name Youlgrave.

She wished now she hadn't let Cate assume she was the daughter of Blytheby Manor. She'd wanted to seem a more suitable match, but now her deception could be revealed at any moment.

She should tell Cate the truth as soon as possible.

Her throat was too tight for her to eat any more, so she only sipped wine as the meal dawdled to its end. Oh, lord, she'd be expected to invite the ladies to take tea. Where? She rose. Which would be the correct drawing room?

That was no problem, as the Catesby ladies hurried ahead of her to a pleasant, bright room she'd admired. She was braced for more questions, but the ladies were happy to do all the talking. They went over the recent tragedy, and Prudence learned more details. It did sound harrowing, with the earl in such pain until he died.

"Dear Flavia was so brave. Completely shattered, of course, but strong, as she always is."

"Artemis collapsed and wasn't seen for a whole day, but when she emerged she was the same. An admirable young woman."

"But changed, sister."

"Only to be expected, sister. And it is not so long since her poor baby was born dead."

"Oh, dear, oh, dear, that was a hard time."

"October. All Souls' Night. I remember that."

Less than a year ago, Prudence thought. No wonder the wound was still so raw.

"Then her husband," said Miss Catesby. "So unexpected, and no one quite sure where Catesby was."

"Fortunate he was found so quickly."

"And he *is* applying himself," Miss Catesby said, the emphasis hinting at surprise.

"*Most* worrying when he disappeared," her sister said.

"Not disappeared, dear. Off to Darlington."

"But not back by nightfall."

Miss Catesby tut-tutted. "Gentlemen have their ways, Cecily."

"Oh."

Had they both forgotten she was there? "He came to visit me," Prudence said.

When they both looked at her, mouths in Os of surprise, she realized what they'd heard.

"To visit," she said quickly. "By daylight."

"Oh," they said in unison. "Of course, we heard the story in brief yesterday from Mr. Perriam. So romantic. When did you first meet, my dear?"

Prudence had no idea what story had been told. "Some years ago, when he was on furlough."

"So many years apart," said Miss Catesby.

"But happily reunited." Miss Cecily sighed. "In general I would have recommended that you wait, but it will be good for Malzard to have a helpmeet at such a difficult time."

"He has Mr. Perriam," said her sister. "Such a pity he's left again. Such a breath of Town about him."

"We used to visit Town," said Miss Cecily, "when we lived in the south. We kept house for our father, and then for our brother, but when Jeremy died . . ."

More sighs, and of a different sort.

"We were so fortunate that Flavia offered us a home."

"Oh, yes, so fortunate."

Constance wondered, however, if they, like Perry, preferred Town to country.

More women left in hardship when their men died or neglected them. It wasn't right, but she saw no way to change their unfair world. She had her own struggles in hand—those of being a new wife and a most unlikely countess.

Chapter 28

When Prudence returned to her rooms, she was asked to go for a fitting for her black gown.

On seeing it, she had to hide her disappointment. Black had never suited her—it made her look sallow—and the flat black of the crape was very black indeed. It made Prudence think of soot. The fit of the skirt and bodice was adequate, but there'd been no time for ornamentation. It was simply plain, black, and unbecoming.

"Do you perhaps have braid or beading for it?" she asked.

"I'm afraid not, milady. With the sudden need for mourning we used all we had, and we've not yet replaced it."

So this was all she had to wear to church on Sunday, and she'd be judged by it. She gave thanks and praise, however, for clearly everyone had worked hard to make such progress in a short while.

Might the blue be better? But when she asked about it, Mistress Sawyer pulled a face. "I'm afraid it didn't take the dye well, milady."

She took Prudence to where the gown was hung out to dry.

The blue had become a muddy gray and the new em-

broidery, so carefully color-matched, was now a stark
black that made the gray look worse.

"Never mind," she said. "It's better than nothing for
now."

Prudence returned to her rooms feeling weighed
down by minor problems. None of them would matter
if she were welcome here, but apart from Cate, she felt
friendless. She, too, missed Perry. He had a way of making things seem lighter.

Letters, she thought. That would be contact with the
wider world. Neither Aaron nor Susan was a friend, but
now they almost felt like it. Hetty shouldn't be a friend,
but Prudence might weep to see her cheerful face.

She wished she had Toby with her, but he was definitely not a countess's dog.

She used the fine paper to write to Aaron, trying not
to weave in spines of recrimination or glee. She asked
him to keep the news quiet for now, and to consult Tallbridge about Draydale, for her husband was writing to
him. She kept the tone cool and said nothing of future
meetings. She knew she'd never be able to cut herself
off from her brother, but he and Susan could grind their
teeth over it for a while. She folded the letter and lit the
candle for the wax. There was a metal seal with a crest,
but she didn't use it. Let the contents come as a complete surprise.

It was doubtless unchristian of her, but she wished
she'd be there to see their faces.

She put another sheet on the writing surface, but then
thought such rich stuff might be too much for Hetty. She
chose a sheet of her own paper, and began to write.

She wanted to share the whole story, but if she did the
news would be all around Northallerton in hours. Hetty
could keep secrets, but she'd need someone to read it
to her. Would the reader be able to resist telling the

world that Prudence Youlgrave of White Rose Yard had become a fine milady? And Cate hoped to keep White Rose Yard secret forever.

She still wanted to share some of her good news, so she simply said she was married to the handsome gentleman who'd come to Northallerton in search of her, and was currently living at Keynings, a very grand house. That alone would have White Rose Yard exploding for days.

She realized a little bit of her missed White Rose Yard. Here, she felt so alone. She'd felt lonely in the various places she'd lived with her mother, but she'd had her mother for company and also the knowledge of people around, people to watch. In White Rose Yard she'd been a little more connected to the neighbors by Hetty. In Darlington she'd made acquaintances, but the time had been too short for friendships.

Except that she and Cate had become friends in a day.

Oh, for the modest circumstances she'd expected, and the cozy house where they'd not be apart so much. Oh, for the business of the middle-class wife, supervising a few servants and doing many tasks herself. Here, she felt at a loss. She was mistress of a great house. How could she have nothing to do? She was almost tempted to invade the kitchens, or try to wash blankets.

She probably should prowl the place in case the dowager or Artemis was usurping her authority, but she simply hadn't the spirit for it right now. Instead, she went to the library to stock the shelves in her boudoir.

She hadn't yet met the current librarian, Mr. Rathbone, and she'd imagined him young and bony. When she encountered him in the library, however, he was a portly gentleman in his fifties, unashamed to show his baldness. What was left of his graying hair was tied back, but most of his head shone in the sunlight.

She expected a welcome, but instead he was cool. She had no spirit to fight that, either, but turned to explore the shelves. When she came across a volume she fancied, she put it on a table.

"My lady, what are you doing?"

"Choosing books for my boudoir, Mr. Rathbone."

"For . . . for your boudoir? I must protest."

She turned on him. "Why?"

He flushed at the confrontation. "The collection is my responsibility, my lady."

Prudence wondered if she was in fact committing an outrage, but she couldn't believe it. "The books here are not to be read, Mr. Rathbone?"

"Er . . . yes, my lady, of course."

"Only in here?"

He must have realized he'd walked onto uncertain ground. "The other ladies do not take books from my library."

"Perhaps the other ladies don't like to read. I shall remove what I wish from *the earl's* library, Mr. Rathbone. You may return to your duties."

He turned crimson. She wondered if he'd refuse and what she'd do then, but she would not, could not allow such insufferable insolence.

By the time he turned to stalk away, she was shaking. He left the room entirely, which allowed her to collapse and gather herself. How *dared* he behave like that? If she told Cate, she knew he'd dismiss the man.

Therefore Rathbone didn't believe she would.

Why? What did he know?

She straightened, took her pile of books, and returned to her sanctuary very inclined to take out the brandy bottle and get drunk.

Instead, she picked up the copy of *Candide; or, the Optimist*, by Monsieur Voltaire, pleased to have found a copy in translation. She'd heard much about it, and the title sounded hopeful.

It was quite the opposite. Dr. Pangloss's insistence that everyone lived in the best of all possible worlds hardly fit when Candide was unfairly ejected from his uncle's castle and forced into the Prussian army. She read on, waiting for matters to improve, but they didn't.

She shut the book and put it aside. Clearly Monsieur Voltaire's message was that optimism was folly and life was nothing but misery. She'd have none of that. Instead, she sat at her desk and began to lay out a story of a heroine, Honesty, who was cast out of her home unfairly, but went from triumph to triumph, defeating demons at every step. Demons of cruelty, demons of injustice, demons of malice . . .

"What are you so intent on?"

She turned, guiltily aware of her scribbled pages, to find Cate had come in.

"Have you ever read *Candide*?" she demanded.

"No, what is it?"

"A story by Monsieur Voltaire, containing the most miserable events. I'm writing an antidote."

"With enthusiasm marked by blotches. You can tell me the story as we stroll in the gardens. It's lovely outside."

Prudence realized it was gone five o'clock—and that she had inky fingers. She went to wash them, but of course the ink remained. She pulled on gloves before joining him.

"So, tell me your joyful story," he said as they went downstairs.

"It's only silliness. What's occupied your day?"

"Not silliness, but a lot of it seems pointless."

"Then why must you do it?"

"Because if I don't, the fabric of society will crumble

into dust. Or so I'm told. So much of life is pointless if looked at directly, don't you think?" As they crossed a room toward glass doors open to a terrace, he asked, "Why, for example, do we wear clothes when it's hot?"

"Decency."

"Then why anything other than the simplest? A toga might be sensible. Perhaps I should propose a law."

"You'd have the mantua makers and silk weavers after you with scissors."

He laughed. "I would, wouldn't I? An English silk weaver slashed the gown of a woman wearing French silk. And the jury let him off."

"Excellent. People need work."

"Odd that the end of war brings hard times."

"This isn't a day for gloom," she said as they went down the shallow steps to the lawn. "I shall relate the triumphs of Honesty, vanquisher of demons."

She amused him as they strolled over lawns and through gardens all in a daunting state of perfection. She would like a little more nature and a little less artifice, but didn't mention it.

"Ah," he said. "The swing."

She saw that a wooden board hung on ropes from a branch of the majestic beech tree in the center of this part of the lawn.

"Let me push you," he said.

"Me?"

"Afraid?"

"Yes."

"Trust me."

With that, she had no choice. She sat awkwardly on the plank and clutched the ropes. He pushed her gently from the front, and the swing went back and forth.

She smiled. "This does feel rather nice. A bit like flying might feel."

He pushed her a little harder. "You can fly higher."

She squeaked with alarm, but then laughed, feeling free of burdens as well as the ground. When he pushed her higher still, she looked up at the magnificent tree and the glimpses of sky, wondering what it was like to be a bird, free to go anywhere without sore feet or rough roads. To go only in feathers, as nature designed, unhindered by clothing. As she swung down, she kicked her legs and saw him grin. He must have quite a view.

"Rascal!" she called.

"Temptress!" he called back, and they both laughed. She hoped she was a temptress, however, because he tempted her to the point of insanity.

She swung backward and forward, exhilarated and happy. Yes, this was happiness, unhindered happiness, and she didn't remember feeling this way before.

She looked toward the house, so lovely in its lines, and warmed by the sun. But then she saw a dark figure in an upper window, watching. She had no true way to be sure, but she knew it was Artemis. She also knew that this was Artemis's swing, which her husband had pushed for her so little time ago.

When Cate would have pushed her again, she said, "No, that's enough for now," and let the swing work down to earth.

He lifted her off and pulled her close for a kiss, but she couldn't even enjoy that properly, knowing Artemis was watching, seared by bitter loss.

He didn't say anything about her mood, but she knew he would have noticed. The words escaped: "When will Artemis leave?"

He looked at her in surprise, and perhaps with disappointment. "I've promised her she can stay here as long as she wants."

Prudence looked away to hide her sinking heart. "I

just feel she must be unhappy. Now I'm here, now you're married, it must have opened wounds."

"All the same, it's been her home for ten years. It's been her daughters' home all their lives. If it comforts her to stay, she must."

He was disappointed with her, and she couldn't explain. Probably soon Artemis would drop hints that Prudence was avoiding her, and she wouldn't be able to explain that either. If she told Cate the truth, he might not believe her. If he asked Artemis, she'd deny all malice. Prudence could only hope that either Artemis did leave, or she showed her true colors soon.

They strolled back to the house hand in hand, talking of changes they might make. Without saying it, they agreed that there could be no hasty alterations, but it was pleasant to discuss some less orderly gardens and the possibility of climbing plants to soften the walls of the house, especially as they were talking of their home. This wasn't the home either of them had expected, but it was theirs to shape.

All the time, Prudence was thinking of the approaching night. It was like an anticipated feast. Their true wedding night.

How early could they retire?

Not immediately, for when they entered the house, he said, "I must go and visit Mother. I'd rather let her stew, but I'm at fault for marrying out of hand."

Prudence suppressed her less worthy reactions. "I hope you can ease her mind. I hope to meet her soon." As she returned to her rooms, she realized she could put the time to good use. She asked Karen, "How do I have a bath?"

"There's a tub, milady." The maid went into the dressing room and opened a cupboard in the wall to pull out a small wooden tub. Susan had a larger one made of enameled tin, and Prudence was surprised Artemis had made do with this, but she reminded herself that not long ago such a tub would have been pure luxury, especially with servants to carry up buckets and buckets of hot water.

She was soon sitting in water at just the right temperature, washing herself thoroughly, relaxed even about her nakedness. Karen seemed to make nothing of it, and she was necessary to manage the extra jugs of hot and cold water.

Such delightful luxury. Even when she was clean, Prudence sat back, playing her hands in the water and thinking dreamily of the best parts of the day. Being with Cate. Especially being alone with Cate. And the promise of the night. She wasn't quite clear what it all involved, but she knew she wanted it. Cate's kisses and touches had taught her of delights to come.

"Begging yer pardon, milady, but if you don't get out soon you'll wrinkle."

Prudence stood so Karen could rinse her off, and the rinse water was cool enough to make her shiver. All the same, she felt wonderful.

She dried herself with the large, soft towel; then, as the sun was going down, she put on the lovely nightdress with her woolen robe over it. She sat to comb out her hair again, hoping Cate would come in.

Alas, he didn't. Was his mother keeping him, jealous of his other interests?

What to do with her hair? Normally, she wore it in a plait at night, but she suspected that Cate would like it loose.

She liked his hair loose.

She liked him naked. That was a shameful confession, even in the secret parts of her mind, but she did. She liked what she'd seen of his hard, scarred body and hoped to see more of it, soon.

Last night he'd worn a nightshirt. Was that the way of
it? Instinct said no, as had some pictures Draydale had
shown her. He'd had a way of suggesting things without
going completely beyond the pale. As she'd confessed
her knowledge of classics, a book on classical art had not
seemed outrageous, but some of the illustrations were,
and some of his comments even more so.

They'd spoken of the East India trade, and he'd
brought her a book about India, insisting that they
look through it together. When she'd turned away
from some illustrations of carvings, he'd chided her,
saying they only depicted marital matters that they'd
soon enjoy. The people in the pictures had been naked, and the men had been extraordinarily formed.
Draydale had murmured that she'd soon find he could
compare.

That had been the final straw that had turned her
resolution into dismay, and then despair.

She shook her head and banished all thoughts of that
man. She was married to Cate, and her marriage bed
would be wonderful.

She looked at the clock. Not yet ten. Perhaps Cate
had been summoned to more duties.

She rose and went toward the adjoining door, thinking to knock, but then she paused. She was in her night-
wear. What if his valet answered?

She could send Karen, but with what message? *Milady wishes to know when milord will join her in bed?* In
which bed?

How could it all be so complicated? She'd expected
Cate to join her and arrange everything, but what if she
was supposed to do something? If so, what?

She told herself Cate was no shy violet, and no stick-
ler for the rules. He'd come when he was ready.

She sent Karen away, telling her she was free for the

night, and then tried to concentrate on a book about the court of the previous king. She'd hoped it would educate her, but it all seemed to be gossip, and a great deal of it scandalous. She'd not thought herself a prude, but perhaps in these circles she was.

Another book was a guide to London. She was sure it would be very useful one day to know where the hackney stands were, and the rates to various parts of the city, but it didn't amuse. She looked at the engravings, studying the Queen's House and the Houses of Parliament, St. James's Park and Westminster Abbey, but none of it could hold her attention.

The clock seemed to tick very slowly. What a pity a lady couldn't ring a bell and summon a husband! She chuckled at the thought, but she was restless with impatience and her imagination was building physical need. She might as well await him in bed.

The mattress was rather hard, perhaps overstuffed with wool. Not long ago it would have seemed perfection, so she wouldn't complain. The bolster was also hard, but that was normal. The pillows, however, seemed thin. She put one on top of the other, wondering if this was as Artemis liked it, or if the woman had arranged things for her successor's discomfort.

She wouldn't think of Artemis either.

This night was for her and Cate.

Was Cate's mother keeping him so long out of jealousy of another woman?

No matter.

She couldn't keep him all night.

Cate was in his boyhood bedchamber, looking out of the window, drinking brandy and trying not to drink too much. If he passed out, he'd not be able to make love to his wife, which was as it should be; but if he was found passed out on the floor here, it'd do no one's reputation any good.

Last night she'd rejected consummation. If he could be sure she'd feel the same tonight he'd be with her now. He'd take her to his bed again, be together with her again, and even indulge in the sort of kisses and closeness that wouldn't carry him too far.

If there were any.

This morning, at her dressing table, he'd almost lost control, and she'd not seemed to be rejecting anything. Had foolish, impulsive confidence that morning made lovemaking possible, or had she changed her mind? He couldn't risk sharing a bed with her yet. For his own sanity, he had to be certain that her first child, especially a son, was his.

He screwed the cap back on his brandy flask and made his way down to the earl's bedchamber, turning all thoughts from his delectable, desirous wife.

Chapter 29

Prudence awoke to sunshine, and to the fact that she was alone in her bed and had been alone there all night. She flung an arm over her eyes, fighting tears.

What had she done wrong? Had it been her comment about Artemis?

Or did he not truly desire her? Once, that would have seemed obvious. Why would a glorious man like Cate Burgoyne want too-tall, too-mannish Prudence Youlgrave? He made her feel otherwise, but if it was all deception, she'd rather he be honest.

Then she remembered her reaction the previous night, when she'd been so exhausted. Had he taken her unwillingness as more general than she'd intended? If so, how did she correct the impression? She couldn't imagine saying it directly, but if he kissed her again, flirted with her again, she'd make it clear that she wasn't an unwilling wife.

If he didn't kiss her again?

She wouldn't even contemplate that. In any case they must; he needed an heir.

The thought of being bedded only to get a child made tears threaten again, so she sat up and climbed out of bed. She was going in search of her maid when she remembered the bell. She pulled the cord, hearing the little ring below. Soon Karen hurried in, cheerful as always, already with washing water.

As the girl poured it into the basin, Prudence asked, "Is my black dress ready?"

"Sorry, milady, but they say as the 'em's not quite done. The cap's here, though, milady."

"Ah, well, as long as it's ready for tomorrow. The dyed blue, then."

She sat to work the tangles out of her hair. Another night without a plait, and all for nothing. She pinned it up tightly on the top of her head, and once she was dressed, she fixed the black cap on top. There. No one could accuse her of unsuitably light spirits.

But then Cate walked into her bedchamber and wished her a good morning. Despite her disappointment, the day was suddenly bright again.

"Have you breakfasted?" he asked. "If so, I can eat alone."

"No, no." She rose, flustered, and sent Karen for the meal. A moment ago she'd had no appetite, and now she wasn't sure she could swallow for other reasons, but she'd grasp any time with him she could.

"That's the blue?" he asked with a slight grimace.

It made her smile. "I like that about you."

"What?"

"That you say what you mean. And look what you mean."

"It's pushed me into trouble. I never did tell you that, did I?"

She didn't want a trace of a shadow on this morning, but if he needed to tell her something, she'd listen. "What?"

He leaned against a bedpost. "I was ordered to sell my commission."

"In the army? Why?"

"To get rid of me. I could have been cashiered—that means thrown out in disgrace, and also without rank, so the commission can't be sold. The price is the only money most officers leave with."

"Cashiered? For what cause?"

"Consistently refusing to follow orders and, they claimed, inciting the men to do the same. I do have a strong dislike of idiotic orders and pointless rules. I'm trying to suppress it here, but I can feel it rising."

"Idiotic rules such as . . . ?"

"Here? For example, that the clerks must rise whenever I enter their room. It disturbs their work and sometimes causes inkblots and errors, but it must be so, I am informed. I suspect it's because Flamborough, Dramcot, and the rest enjoy the reverence. It's the same up and down the line."

"Like the servants having their ranks. Does everyone hope to have someone below them who must take orders?"

He smiled ruefully. "Having been born to high rank with many below, I can't comment. Do you value it?"

Prudence thought. "No, but it is delightful to have servants to make life comfortable."

"Isn't it?"

"What idiotic rules did you ignore in the army?"

"A host of them to do with uniforms—not just for me, but for my men. They can be punished for a loose button or an unpolished badge. The good generals let the petty things pass during the fighting, but once we had peace, it was back to every button and bow, and punishment for offenders. Then there were the drills. Coming from action, we were all bored, and endless drills didn't help, so I devised training exercises that could be useful in real fighting. That sowed discord. Some of my men would have preferred boredom, and some other units wanted my regime. Most other officers didn't want any bother or unrest. I'm a restless sort of fellow."

Which took you restlessly to Darlington, and me.

"So you were asked to leave."

"I was given the option of a regiment heading for India, where my restless nature might be appreciated, but I declined. Too far from Keynings, you see." He looked outside, gazing through the window. "Do you wonder if wanting things too much can create chaos in order to provide it?"

If not for last night, she would go to him, touch him. All she had was speech. "You are in no way responsible for your brother's death, Cate."

He looked at her. "We quarreled, furiously."

Had Artemis accused him? Surely not, or he couldn't have such faith in her. It must have preyed on his mind.

"A quarrel doesn't kill anyone," she said.

"I did once know a man to die of rage, but Roe wasn't purple with it. He was pale and cold. It was his way."

"What made him so angry?"

"Me. It's always been me. My very nature offended him, and he had reason. I failed at a number of things, and have a way of disturbing orderly lives."

He was looking at her.

She said, "My life wasn't at all orderly."

"But perhaps I made it worse."

She did go to him then, to at least be closer. "Worse? We've had this debate before. There is nothing about my life that is worse for your actions."

He took her hand. "Thank you for that. I get night demons sometimes. Roe's lack of faith in me galled. I was a good officer in wartime; no one denies that, but it counted for nothing here. He knew I'd been encouraged to go to India and was furious that I couldn't see the blessings of that. He knew all the army stories, of course. Plenty of people happy to report, none of them friends of mine. I resented everything he said and implied. I resented his assumption that as head of the family he could command me. We opened old wounds, both said things we didn't really mean. . . ."

About the baby, she realized. *But your brother did mean that, and you still don't know it.*

"In the end, I slammed out of the room and shook the dust of Keynings off my shoes with only the money I had to hand. I rode with Jeb to Northallerton to catch a coach to London and sent Oakapple back with Jeb. If I'd taken the horse and ridden south, Roe wouldn't have accused me of horse stealing, but I was determined to take nothing that was not mine. Pride and folly. But it brought us together," he said with a smile. "So it wasn't as bad an impulse as it seemed at the time."

She had to say it. "It trapped you."

"If you'd listened to my story, you'd know I never allow myself to be trapped by the rules."

She shook her head at him, longing so much to take him into her arms, but Karen announced that breakfast was ready, and the moment was gone.

They went into the boudoir and sat at the small table. "Did you speak with your mother yesterday? Is she very angry?"

"Peeved," he said, pouring ale. "She's not one for the deeper emotions, but she's easily peeved and gives it teeth. She stated that I'm a fool to have married so unwisely. I countered that if she met you, she'd know differently."

"In this gown?" Prudence asked.

"It's not a matter of dress. She'll get over her spleen. She wants a son and heir in the nursery, and you are the vessel."

Prudence looked up from her tea, wanting to ask the obvious question, but unsure how.

"She's still chewing her bitter cud," he said, "but she's not one to cut off her nose to spite her face."

"You sound bitter too," she pointed out. "She's your mother. She must love you."

"What a pleasant notion, and odd, don't you think? Is there some alchemy to it? If so it failed to work here, and in many other cases. She and I understand each other as little as Roe and I did, and neither of us saw any need to overcome that. I had my nurse and attendants, who were loving enough, and she had the heir to focus on, the one who'd stay here and affect her life."

"That's very odd."

"Is it? As I said, it's not uncommon, perhaps because in a place like Keynings parents see little of their children."

"Oh. Cate, I don't think I'd like that."

Prudence realized too late that her comment brushed against the lack of consummation, but there was no taking it back.

"I suspected as much. I won't try to rule you in that, and I think I might like to spend time with any boys, but we will have other duties that take us away. London, for example."

"I remember your mentioning London, even before you confessed the terrible flaw of being an earl."

"How do you like it now, my lady?" he asked wryly.

"I'd prefer a smaller home and less pandemonium, but . . ." She'd almost said that she'd welcome anything if she had him.

"You will, like the practical woman you are, make a home out of a nest of demons."

"Stop talking like that about your family."

He smiled at her. "Very well. Demons don't go to

church, but my mother will. That will be her way out of the coffin she's put herself into."

"I hope she'll approve of me. I'll only have a very plain black dress."

"Cease this obsession with clothing!"

"You were concerned enough when I was in Peg Stonehouse's clothes."

"Yes, yes, I was, but it was more out of guilt. You seemed comfortable there, and I was bringing you here."

"I have no desire to live in a small farmhouse that lacks even glass in the windows!"

"Practical, always. Mother is too. She's ready to build bridges. I think she's mostly peeved because I didn't choose a bride from her lists."

"Lists?"

"Terrifying lists. Even more terrifying when the names became flesh. Let me tell you all about Bland, Bumble, and Fizz."

Prudence listened with amusement, enjoying chocolate and warm, sweet bread, happy enough to be here, cozily talking of humorous matters. She felt sorry for the unsuccessful candidates, for they did not have him, even though she did not have him in the complete sense.

He finished his meal and rose. "Will you drive out with me later?"

"Drive?"

"In an open chair. We can see more of the grounds."

"I'd like that."

He came to her, reaching into his pocket. "A gift for you, my wife."

It was a pretty brooch of cream and reddish stones that she knew would look well on her rust-colored outfit.

"Not suitable for mourning, alas," she said.

"No, but that time will pass. There are more—all the family jewels, in fact, but I won't fight Mother for the ones she clings to unless you insist. Artemis gave up the family pieces she had, of course. That brooch came from those."

Which meant Prudence certainly couldn't wear it where Artemis might see it. Despite the woman's behavior, she'd not cause her any pain.

"I shall indulge in giving you a minor ornament a day," he said, "but as soon as possible I will buy you something more magnificent."

"Extravagance," she chided.

"Investment. I'm having the settlements drawn up to provide your pin money and jointure, but any gifts I give you will also be yours unless I specify otherwise."

"Mine when you die. I don't want to think about that."

"Nor do I. Let it be decades into the future. But if I leave you a widow, I want you to be comfortable and independent."

"Independent," she echoed. "It hardly seems possible."

"Perhaps you'd like to be a merry widow soon," he teased.

"No, never."

"Not, at least, for fifty years or so." He came to drop a kiss on her lips and then left.

Prudence went over it all in her mind. He wasn't angry with her. He couldn't imagine her unwilling, so why had nothing happened? Everyone placed such importance on the wedding night. The actual night.

She remembered reading one of her father's books and finding reference to the display of bloody sheets. She'd gone to her mother in distress, which had led to her mother scolding her father that some books not be left around the house.

Her mother hadn't explained the blood, but said that she would when the time was right. That time had never come. Prudence understood the blood now, but not this delay.

Perhaps she was supposed to do something, just as she was supposed to ring the dinner bell for the courses. Perhaps she should hunt for the concealed husband-summoning bell.

She chuckled, but just in case, she did go and search.

Alas, no.

She summoned Karen to have the breakfast cleared away, amused to notice that that meant Karen going away to summon lower servants to do the task. Ranks, again. Did some of the lower servants now have to curtsy to the girl?

The situation ceased to be amusing. Karen must not be returned to her lowly station. Prudence knew how she'd feel to be returned to White Rose Yard. Cate had said it would be possible to keep her as some sort of junior lady's maid, but carelessly. From what she knew of the ordered ranks of the servants' hall, it wouldn't be as simple as that.

She put that aside for now, for it would be some time before she hired a proper lady's maid, and her immediate concern was to take up her duties.

She would not skulk again. She had mourning clothes of a sort, and must establish her authority. She summoned the housekeeper and went over the day's menus. She even signed her first document—an approval of a purchase of tea, and was consulted on a problem.

"I'm sorry to say, milady, that the pastry cook has left."

"Left?" Prudence said. "Why?"

"He felt he was not appreciated, my lady."

"By whom?"

The woman pursed her lips, and Prudence knew the

answer was herself. It had to be Artemis's work, and as a result the housekeeper was now distant.

"I found his cakes delicious," she said firmly. "Has he truly left? Can we not persuade him to change his mind?"

"I believe he departed at first light to catch a coach to London. Many have tried to tempt him away, milady."

"Then we must tempt one equally good from somewhere else."

Prudence hid it, but she was furious. Where would her sister-in-law shoot her poisoned darts next? It was bad enough to have skilled servants leave, but ill-humored servants could wreak havoc in all kinds of subtle ways. She'd heard of such things from the servants' side. Will Larn was an ostler at the Crown Inn, and if a traveler didn't tip the servants enough, he'd get cold food and damp sheets.

What she needed to counter Artemis was to make some changes that would be to the servants' benefit.

"I will inspect the servants' bedrooms," she said.

The housekeeper stiffened. "Why, milady?"

Prudence resented the question, but she answered, "To see if I can improve their comfort."

Mistress Ingleton probably saw this as trespassing on her authority, but Prudence wouldn't back down. She knew it was the lady of the house's responsibility to see to the welfare of her servants.

She did find a few improvements to make, such as some windows to be repaired so that they closed snugly and opened smoothly. She knew all about the cold in winter and the heat in summer. She noticed that many of the water jugs and basins were chipped, clearly being ones used in the family part of the house and then passed down. She ordered that they be replaced with plain ones.

Would the servants feel grateful or resentful?

She had no idea.

She then went over the servants' food allowances.

There were separate menus for the upper servants and the lower, so they must eat separately. That meant, she realized, that Karen was now eating in a different place with companions who must resent her.

Having approved the food, she escaped into the flower gardens, but kept near the terrace just in case Draydale had sent minor demons to invade the estate. It seemed impossible, but she knew he must be seething with the need to hit out again, and more effectively. She rubbed her cheek, where the bruise was almost gone, wishing she'd refused to have anything to do with the man.

She decided she could walk as far as the swing, which was within sight of the house. Perhaps she'd sit in it and see if she could swing it herself. When she got there, however, she noticed one rope frayed down to threads.

Draydale's work?

"What a shame. I hoped you'd be foolish enough to attempt it without looking."

Prudence turned to face Artemis. "This is petty. You're wrong to hate Cate, but why attack me? I've done nothing to harm you."

"He loves you," Artemis said.

Prudence almost protested, but that would be to reveal too much. "He's done nothing to harm you or yours, and your bile will choke you."

Artemis turned away, refusing to respond.

"If I have to, I'll force you out," Prudence said.

Artemis turned back. "He's promised I can stay."

"I'm less softhearted than he is. Why stay, Artemis? It can bring you nothing but pain." But then Prudence realized. "It's the memory of paradise, isn't it? But the paradise is gone. Nothing you can do can bring it back."

Artemis flinched as if hit, and then walked away.

Prudence looked sadly at the swing, but then took action. She returned to the house and ordered Flamborough to have it repaired. It probably didn't come under his command, but he could arrange it.

Then she went to the library and removed more books. That might be petty, but she would not be cowed. She'd just ordered a footman to take them up to her boudoir when Cate found her.

"It's nearly dinnertime."

Prudence wanted to plead that they eat at the small table in her boudoir, but she couldn't afford to hide.

"Has your morning had more point today?" she asked.

"In fact, yes. There are some local disputes to do with land. I still don't understand the finer aspects of agriculture, but I can see the importance of water, drainage, and pasture." He explained the situation. She didn't understand it either but she loved talking of such things with him. Such sharing was a great part of a marriage, surely, and it was good.

She told him about her improvements to the servants' rooms. "There's nothing wrong with that, is there? Mistress Ingleton seemed put out."

"Not that I know. You could ask Artemis."

She suppressed a sigh as they entered the dining room, and then halted.

Both Artemis and the dowager were present. At least, the short, plump, disapproving woman in black had to be Cate's mother, no matter how little she resembled the slim young woman in the wedding portrait.

"Mother," Cate said, bowing slightly. "It's good to see your appetite restored. And you, Artemis."

Both women curtsied, smiling with lips only. The dowager's dark eyes were taking in every detail of Prudence. She wished she weren't in the shabby dyed blue and that she'd taken the time to make sure her hair was tidy.

The other diners were the same, but Artemis and the dowager had places opposite each other in the middle of the table, separating the sisters and the old gentlemen.

As Cate escorted Prudence to her place, she was aware of yet again usurping something so recently belonging to her angry sister-in-law. But this was simply the way it was, the wheel of fate. Once Artemis had taken over these duties from the dowager.

She sat, smiled, and rang the golden bell. A soup was brought first today—a white soup with the delicious flavor of almonds.

Prudence looked down the table. "We must compliment the cook, Malzard. This is particularly delicious."

He inclined his head. "Especially for delighting you, my love."

She almost spilled the soup on her spoon, but, of course, he'd said it only for effect. All the same, it showed he was supporting her.

"The Keynings cook is excellent, Lady Malzard," Optimus Goode said, reminding her that she hadn't confessed her untruth to Cate. She'd had the opportunity, but forgotten. Perhaps on purpose.

She asked him if he'd read *Candide*.

He sniffed. "I don't care for modern work, my lady."

"I see. I found it oddly pessimistic."

"I found it true to life," said the dowager. "There are too many people who claim things to be pretty that are not."

"Truly, ma'am?" Prudence said. "I find that often people complain about problems that could easily be corrected."

"That's true," said Miss Catesby, an unexpected ally. "It's usually quite easy to make the best of things."

"Of my son's death?" challenged the dowager.

Prudence just managed to restrain herself from snapping back, *You have a live son, ma'am.* Instead, she rang the bell. The soup plates were removed and the first course set around the table. The butler poured wine. She tried desperately to find something safe to say.

Cate said, "The silk weavers of Spitalfields are in some distress. I hope none of you ladies will buy foreign silk."

"Are we to be dictated to by such people?" the dowager demanded.

"Isn't it wise, Mother, to support our own workers rather than those of our enemy, France?"

Artemis said, "We're not at war anymore, Malzard," as if she spoke to an imbecile.

"But will be again," he replied. "I have no doubt of that. May I pass you the potatoes, Mr. Coates?"

"Thank you, thank you," the old man said. "An interesting food, the potato. Caused some deaths when first brought to this land, for people ate the fruits of the flowers, which are quite poisonous, though related to the tomato, which is not. Though in fact, some still fear to eat the tomato because of the plant's slight resemblance to the potato."

"So easily grown by the poor," said Miss Cecily. "The potato, I mean. Very little effort, I understand. We have received many of God's blessings from abroad, have we not?"

"Like the Black Death?" asked the dowager. "And the plague."

Prudence bit her lip on laughter. This was ridiculous. She saw Cate fighting the same impulse.

"I've received an interesting letter," Artemis said. "From Darlington."

Prudence lost all temptation to laugh. The news had arrived. But how much of it?

"An account of our wedding, I assume," Cate said. "I'm sure it was a minor wonder there."

Artemis's face pinched, as if she would have preferred to draw it out. "My friend Anne Chaloner lives there now. Yes, your wedding was a notable affair, but oddly no one seems to know yet that the groom was the Earl of Malzard. Of course, Anne recognized your name, but she can be relied on to keep the matter secret."

"It's not a secret, Artemis. There simply seemed no point in drawing the attention of hoi polloi."

"If you'd married in a normal manner," his mother said, "there'd have been no need to conceal anything! This has been poorly handled from the start."

"I had the notion, Mother, that if I brought Prudence here as my promised bride, you might attempt to prevent the marriage."

"Well, of course I would."

Prudence knew her cheeks were turning red and wished they weren't, for it might look like guilt. Cate wasn't reddening. She'd be hard put to say what was revealed by his still features—until she realized it was danger.

No wonder the dowager had fallen silent.

"I would take it amiss," he said into the silence, "if anything were said to upset my wife."

"I'm sure no one would wish to do that," said Miss Catesby quickly.

"Of course not," said her sister.

The two elderly gentlemen were very deliberately paying attention to their food.

Prudence knew she had to say something. "Please don't feel distressed, sister. There's no shame in relaying news that must reach here soon anyway."

Artemis stared at her. "Shame? You're the one who should feel shame. How can you claim to love Catesby, when you were at the altar about to marry someone else?"

One or both Catesby cousins gasped.

The dowager simply gaped.

Cate said, "Artemis," in a warning manner, but Prudence was elated that Artemis had finally shown her teeth.

"My first groom was most definitely an error of judgment," she said.

"An *error . . .* !" spluttered the dowager.

"Enough of this," Cate said. "Prudence thought me dead. I arrived in Darlington to find her about to marry another. Once she knew I was alive, there was no question of the wedding going forward. Someone even remarked that it was a romance worthy of the troubadours."

Optimus Goode raised his head as if he might quibble about medieval romances, but addressed himself again to his plate.

Artemis fired another shot. "Did it really come to blows? At the very altar."

"I do not wish to discuss this further here."

The dowager ignored Cate's edict. "Was your marriage *legal*, Malzard?"

"Yes," he said shortly.

Miss Cecily tried to deflect. "Were you born and raised in Darlington, Lady Malzard?"

Prudence was grateful, but didn't want to delve into her history. "No, I moved there recently to live with my brother. He's a solicitor there."

"A Mr. Youlgrave," Artemis said. "Very recently qualified, I understand, and impecunious, but also fortunate in marriage. His bride is the heiress of a city merchant, I understand."

"True," Prudence said, "and yes, I have married above my station. Is that a crime?"

Artemis glared at her, the dowager was looking peevish, and Cate was dangerously still and silent. Could she declare this meal at an end by rising and taking the women away? It would cage her with them, but relieve the pressure here.

She was about to do just that when Optimus Goode spoke.

"Youlgrave? Youlgrave! Aaron and Prudence, Aaron Youlgrave's children." He smiled at her. "You were a very clever girl, my dear. Always asking questions." He turned his smile on the table, but Prudence's heart fell.

"Visited Sir Joshua Jenkins's collection," he explained. "Twelve years or more ago now. Wonderful medieval weaponry and manuscripts. Of course, Sir Joshua was a philistine—came into a lot of money in the East in some fashion—but he'd hired the right man to take care of it all. Aaron Youlgrave was an expert in such things. Shame Jenkins lost everything at the tables and killed himself. Collection broken up, but I acquired a few things for your father, my lord."

Cate was looking at her, blankly unreadable. She hadn't exactly lied, but she'd misled.

"What became of your father, Lady Malzard?" Goode asked her.

"He died not long after Sir Joshua."

"Ah, sad, sad. Can't have been that old. And your mother? Charming lady."

"She died quite recently."

"Pity, pity. But they'd have been happy to see you so well set up in the world."

"Astonished, I should think," said the dowager. "A *librarian*?"

"A scholar, ma'am," said Goode, rather frostily, "like myself."

Prudence rose. "Tea, ladies?"

The ladies all rose, but Artemis said, "You will excuse me, sister." To the dowager, she said, "You will enjoy the letter," and passed over the folded sheet of paper before leaving.

The Catesby cousins looked around uncertainly and Miss Catesby said, "Perhaps we'll take tea in our rooms today, dear Lady Malzard."

Prudence hoped the dowager would return to her hole, even if it was to read the letter, but she said, "Tea, indeed," and headed for the door.

Prudence hesitated, wondering if she dared speak to Cate here and now. No, for a great many reasons, no.

She went upstairs behind the Dowager Lady Malzard, who had a way of standing taller than she was. She'd finally achieved a meeting with her mother-in-law. Would she escape alive?

Chapter 30

In the drawing room, there was no doubt as to who ruled. The dowager commanded the tea and sat first. Prudence almost remained standing like a child summoned for a scolding, but she sat, striving for composure. She completely lacked the courage to compete for supremacy, however.

"I was shocked by Catesby's wedding," the dowager said, "but I thought it mere romantic folly."

"A romance worthy of the troubadours," Prudence said wryly.

"Whatever that means. I will read this letter."

Prudence watched, as she might watch a thrush beat a snail against a stone until the shell cracked and the creature could be consumed—feeling like the snail.

The dowager's eyes widened. Her head moved faster from side to side. She looked up at Prudence just as the tea arrived. Suddenly Prudence had to fight laughter. It was all so peculiar. She took charge of the preparation of the tea, listening to the footman retreat and the door close, then looked up to find the dowager studying her.

"Are you carrying another man's child?"

Ah, she'd forgotten that detail would be in the letter.

"No, ma'am. Do you take milk in your tea?"

"Yes. Are you truthful?"

"That's an old dilemma, ma'am. I am in this. In fact, I'm still a virgin."

The dowager stared at her. "Can that boy do *nothing* right?"

"You're referring to Cate?" It was no effort to show shock.

"He's made a mess of everything he's done, and this marriage is the culmination."

Prudence thought a moment, but only a moment. "You're wrong, ma'am, and I think it a great shame for any mother to speak so of a son or daughter."

"Ha! Wait until you have some. Unlikely as that seems, according to you. Pour me some tea."

That made Prudence laugh, but her hand shook as she poured.

"You're having your courses?" the dowager asked. "You didn't time your wedding very well, did you?"

Was there no matter to be left to discretion?

"No, ma'am, I am not having my courses." She needed to defend Cate, and came up with an explanation. "Because of Henry Draydale's accusation, which will soon be known by all, Cate and I have decided not to consummate the marriage yet. That way, any child will be born more than nine months after the wedding, and no shadow will hang over him or her."

"Humph. That shows more sense than I give him credit for."

"But then, ma'am, you don't seem to know him very well."

The dowager's eyes narrowed. "You're an impudent upstart."

"I'm the Countess of Malzard and your daughter-in-law. We can deal well or badly, ma'am, but we're stuck together for a very long time."

The dowager looked away. "I don't know why fate is so cruel."

Prudence was about to say something sharp, but then she saw that the older lady's lips were unsteady and remembered that she'd so recently lost a son.

"My dear ma'am, I feel for you—truly, I do. It's a terrible sadness to have a child die, even when they're adult. I have no wish to hurt you more, and neither has Cate. Let him be a good son to you."

The dowager still looked away. "Everything was so perfect. We were the happiest of households."

"I'm sure you were."

"Sebastian was the best of sons, and a worthy earl."

"Cate said as much once."

The dowager turned to her. "He did?"

"Yes. He respected his brother very much. I think he described him as a tender son, a devoted husband, and a loving but firm father."

The dowager pulled out a handkerchief and blew her nose. "I always thought he resented him. My husband thought so. That's why he insisted Catesby join the army. He thought he wanted Keynings too much. The first plan was the East India Company, but Catesby created a ridiculous uproar about the treatment of Hindus, and that put an end to that. He promptly tumbled into debts and debauchery, and so it was the army. With a war going on we could rely on his being sent abroad."

Prudence reminded herself that nothing could be gained by berating the woman. She did, however, say, "He was a good officer."

"If foolhardy exploits count as good. We heard all the stories. The army spit him out in the end, and he was fortunate it wasn't worse. So then he was back here, making trouble again."

"Perhaps he simply returned to visit his family."

"Why, when he cared nothing for any of us? When the baby boy was born dead, we heard no word from him. Not the most cursory message of condolence."

"I'm sure he can't have received the letter."

"A convenient excuse. At best he cared nothing. At worst, he celebrated."

"Ma'am, I know that's not true." Prudence leaned forward. "Artemis seems to believe the worst of that. Can you not convince her of the truth?"

"I don't *know* the truth."

"Yes, you do! You have to know your own son better than that. You have to."

The dowager leaned back. "Don't speak to me in such a manner!"

"I will always defend Cate."

"Foolishly. Do you know that he was wooing another woman in London very recently?"

Prudence stared, afraid to speak.

"I see not. The daughter of a rich oil merchant. I didn't interfere. He needed some means of support. I suppose I should be grateful not to have Georgiana Rumford foisted upon me, and merely a librarian's daughter."

Afraid to speak her mind, Prudence rose and curtsied. "Good afternoon, ma'am."

She swept out of the room and stalked back to her rooms in a rage—rage at the heartless mother, and raging hurt at news that there had been another after all. Not an exquisite society lady, but an heiress of no lower birth than herself, who would have brought a fortune to Keynings instead of trouble.

Karen came out of the dressing room. "Is something the matter, milady?"

"No."

"The black dress is finished, milady."

Prudence looked at its grim sootiness spread on the bed and wanted to growl.

Everything was going wrong.

Cate had some idealized vision of Keynings, but all she saw was a house haunted by his dead brother and with malice and discontent seething from every wall. Artemis swam beneath, oozing more poison, with the dowager at her side.

That ridiculous image became vivid in her mind, and she laughed. There was no humor in it, however. Everything was definitely awry, and she had no idea how to put it right.

There was a knock at the boudoir door.

Karen hurried to answer it, and returned to say, "Your other trunks have arrived, milady!"

Other trunks?

But then she remembered Perry. "Oh, yes. Have them brought up."

Bits and pieces of possessions didn't seem important anymore, but she welcomed anything that might ease the situaton.

There really were two trunks, and at the sight of them a little excitement brightened her mood. What would be in them? She opened the first and took out a green gown. It looked exactly like a lady's favorite from a few years past, kept because it was comfortable. There were other similar garments, but none suitable for mourning. Karen put them away in the clothespress, showing how satisfied she was to have the piece of furniture beginning to fill.

Prudence wondered if they'd all fit her, but she suspected that with Peregrine Perriam involved, they would. There were stockings of various sorts, including a silk pair almost as pretty as the ones she'd ruined, and two darned pairs to show her frugality. Shifts, hoops, caps, hats. She ended up chuckling at the ridiculousness of it all, but then Karen wanted to know why.

"It's just lovely to be reunited with my bits and pieces."

At the bottom were books and some carefully wrapped pieces of china and glass. Prudence unwrapped one long shape and found a classical statue of a man.

"Lawks!" Karen exclaimed, but then added, "It's like those shocking ones in the entrance hall."

"Yes, but this one is . . ."

"Oh, milord!"

Prudence looked up quickly. It was Cate.

"Your possessions," he said. "I heard they'd come."

Prudence studied him. He didn't seem angry.

"As you see," she said. "Karen, you may go for a while."

As soon as the maid had left, she rose and said, "Cate, I'm sorry for misleading you about Blytheby."

"I wish you'd been honest, but only because it would smooth your path."

"Whereas now it gets rockier by the moment. Artemis's letter related Draydale's accusation."

"The devil."

"Cate . . . I . . . I had to say something to ease your mother's anxiety. I . . . I said we'd decided to delay consummation."

"What was her response to that?"

She wasn't about to tell him. "I had an explanation. So that our first child wouldn't be suspect in the eyes of the world. And now I think that's right. That we should. Or should not. I'm sorry. . . ."

He pulled her into his arms. "Don't be. That's an excellent reason. Far better than mine."

"Yours?"

"A confession. You made it clear Draydale lied, but I couldn't entirely believe you."

She pushed back. "Cate!"

"Not in that way. But a woman forced might not want to admit it, and I could imagine him forcing his bride-to-be."

"He did try to go too far."

"I'm sure he did. When it comes down to it, my thinking was much like yours. I never wanted to have a moment of doubt. I didn't want that possibility hanging over our first child. That's the only thing that kept me from your bed last night."

"Oh. I thought you didn't want me."

He laughed softly and touched his head to hers. "I want you, my wife. But it seems we must practice restraint."

There was a sweetness to the moment and she didn't want to disturb it with mention of his London lady. What did it matter? He'd married her.

He said, "You're the most comfortable woman I've ever known."

Comfortable wasn't love. That sounded more like a soft chair.

"I wasn't comfortable when I was ungrateful in Northallerton," she pointed out. "Or when I was snarling over pretty, fashionable, elegant Lady Malzard."

He laughed. "No, you weren't, but I don't like feather beds. You speak your mind; you can take care of yourself when necessary. You even have a knife. Have you unpacked all that Perry's sent?"

"What? No . . ."

"Then you must." He took her hand and towed her into her dressing room. He peered into the bottom of the open trunk, then said, "Open the other one."

It seemed like a game, which delighted her. She

raised the trunk lid. On top was another gown, swathed in white cloth. She took it out and pulled off the muslin. "Oh. How clever he is!"

"I'll call the villain out. But no, as he's acting as my secretary, I shall take the credit. That's a splendid piece of mourning finery."

"I shall thank him in particular," she retorted, holding the black gown against herself. "It's long enough, I think."

"Have no doubt of it. Perry never mistakes matters of fashion." He picked up another swathed bundle and revealed more black. "Petticoat, I assume. And here's the stomacher. All costly, but so very, very sober."

Prudence hurried to spread it all together on her bed. "It's lovely."

The material was crape, trimmed with black lace and embroidery, still without a touch of gloss. The only shine was in panels of black damask let into the bodice, and in the stomacher of the same fabric. The ruffles were attached to the long sleeves, and were merely a frill of black.

She'd still look sallow, but like a sallow countess.

"My Storborough hat will go perfectly with this. I won't embarrass you at church tomorrow."

"Come and explore further."

Clearly he wanted her to find something, which made her feel like a child at Christmas. She took out some other garments, only glancing at them. Cate's surprise wouldn't be one of those.

She found a sewing box, prettily covered in embroidered panels. No, that wasn't his gift.

A tea caddy, already stocked with tea, but like everything else, not suspiciously new. "I'm so glad to have this," she said, but it wasn't the special something.

Three large bundles revealed a china water bowl and

jug, decorated with spring flowers. And even a matching chamber pot.

Prudence bit her lip. "Just the sort of thing a lady would cherish."

"More than likely," he agreed. "Perry must have enjoyed this enormously."

A box contained fans of various sorts, and a tube shape was a parasol.

Then she picked up a flat leather-covered box not much longer than her hand. A piece of jewelry? She was a little disappointed that Cate had left such a purchase to his friend.

When she opened it, however, she found a knife. No, not a knife—this must be the Italian dagger Cate had spoken of. The sheath was plain and narrow, but the hilt was only a knob of fine silver set with pearls. The dagger seemed too ornamental to be practical.

"Ah, he found one. I forgive him the excellence of the rest."

She smiled at him. "Thank you, it's lovely. But I hope not to have need of it."

"I hope that too, but you never know."

"The hilt seems insubstantial."

"It's a bodice dagger."

"A bodice dagger?"

He hooked a finger in the front of her bodice and pulled her closer.

"Cate?"

His finger wiggled, causing some alarming sensations. Especially when she'd told the dowager they wouldn't . . .

"You have a busk," he said, looking. "The dagger fits down there and only the top shows." He took the sheathed knife from the box and, with her unsteady and dazed, slid it down the pocket in the center of her stays.

Then he took her to her mirror. "See."

Only the pretty top showed, looking like a brooch.

"Take it out," he said. "Just a little carefully. The sheath's roughly textured, so it should stay behind."

She grasped the top and pulled, watching the action in the mirror, aware of him behind her. "It's not comfortable to hold."

"It's not meant for regular use. It'll serve to skewer a demon if necessary."

She turned to him. "I truly hope that's never necessary. How goes your demon slaughter?"

"In only a couple of days I know most of Draydale's open business and where he's vulnerable there. I have people uncovering the rest. I'm sure there is a rest."

"Tallbridge probably knows a great deal."

"I won't use him unless I must."

Prudence put down the knife and poked into her busk for the sheath.

"Allow me."

She did, liking it altogether too much.

He pulled out the sheath, which did indeed catch on the lining of her busk pocket, and then stroked it up her neck and around to her lips. "I believe we're allowed to kiss," he said.

They did so, slowly and deeply, stirring all those hungers she wouldn't be able to feed for a while.

"When?" she asked.

"A few weeks, at least."

She sighed. "At least now you see that Artemis isn't perfection."

"You had warning of her spite? You should have told me."

"It would have been hard to believe. She's mad with grief, I think. Not just over her husband, but over her stillborn child. She blames you for one and thinks you heartless over the other."

He shook his head. "I never heard anything about the baby. Letters get lost in wartime. As for the other, how would that work? Roe died weeks after I left here."

"Perhaps his headaches started then."

"He wasn't mad with rage. I was more openly angry than he was. I'd never known how little he thought of me. I'd never realized how little I thought of him. Oh, he did his duties well, but there wasn't a scrap of innovation or adventure in his soul."

She took his hands. "Don't relive it. You'll regret it. So, probably, did he, if only the opening of Pandora's box. His seizure, his death, were coincidence."

She kissed him, offering comfort, and he turned it into a hug, which was what both of them needed more than anything else.

"You hugged me in Northallerton. I never forgot that."

"Hugs are as free as the air," he said. "Are we not rich? Let's take that drive."

Chapter 31

Prudence felt less unhappy in her lonely bed that night now that there was a purpose, but she lay awake wishing they could at least share a bed. She longed for that closeness, and she'd feel less worried about tomorrow and church.

Thanks to Perry she'd have the lovely gown to wear, but it would be her first encounter with the neighbors. Perhaps the families of Bland, Bumble, and Fizz would be there, resenting her.

There could be other confrontations too. Artemis seemed to live in seclusion, but she wrote letters and could have dripped poison into a few ears. No, that wasn't right. That killed people, like Hamlet's father.

She hadn't arranged for softer pillows, and the mattress really was too hard. Cate's bed was perfectly to her taste. In all ways. She tossed restlessly, wild thoughts churning until she fell asleep.

Karen nervously woke her. "Begging your pardon, milady, but if you want to go to church, you'd best rise."

Oversleeping might have been pleasant, but duty called.

The news that the earl wished to breakfast with her made the day brighter, and she dressed only as far as her stays and petticoat and put her robe over before joining him. His smile matched hers, but she made him tell her about the local worthies as they ate. The would-be countesses and their families didn't live close enough to attend St. Wilfred's, so she'd be saved that trial.

After breakfast, they separated to complete their dressing. When he returned in a soberly fine suit of somber black she was especially grateful for her elegant mourning wear. He produced another piece of jewelry. "I think this could be worn with mourning." It was a chain of silver set with black beads.

"Thank you," she said, putting it on. "But I'm greedy enough to want to see the whole collection."

"A lust for life. I like that about you. Are your shoes comfortable? In good weather the healthy members of the family walk to church. Don't ask me why, for most ride back in carriages. But it's tradition."

"I don't mind. As long as the path is smooth."

"In reality or metaphorically?" he asked dryly, and she remembered the challenges ahead.

Two of the challenges were waiting in the hall—Artemis and the dowager. Artemis's face pinched at the sight of Prudence. Had she hoped to see her in her shabby dyed blue? Now that Artemis's malice was in the open, Prudence no longer feared her sister-in-law. She only wished she knew a way to help her.

Mr. Flamborough, the house steward, offered Artemis his arm, which doubtless reminded her of when her husband had that duty. Now she must walk behind, when so recently she'd led the little procession.

The dowager walked on Cate's other side, round face dissatisfied. Behind Artemis came her two older daughters in the care of a maid, and behind them the servants who were free at this time, presumably in order of rank.

And there was little Karen, looking terrified to be part-
nered with the valet, Ransom.

Prudence remembered she had to find a solution to
that problem.

It was a silent walk.

They entered the village, and the church came into
view. Many people were walking that way, along with
a few riders and carriages. Everyone made way for the
party from Keynings, bobbing and bowing. Prudence felt
pinned by a hundred pairs of eyes. Had Artemis spread
the Darlington story here?

When they entered the church and went to the front
box pew belonging to the Burgoyne family, Prudence
reminded herself that she had only to make the right
impression to weather this. She knew what to do and
what not to do. All would go well.

Whatever stories circulated, after the service all the
local gentry proved eager to pay their respects. Or to
have a closer look at the surprising countess.

Prudence smiled and nodded, saying all the right
things while assessing who was friend and who was foe.
The dowager and Artemis stood slightly apart, with
their own circle. Were there truly two camps, or was that
an incidental impression?

As people began to disperse to carriages, or to walk
home, Prudence felt it had gone as well as she could
have hoped. One young wife, a Mistress Wrotham,
might even become a friend. She'd hoped Prudence
might be interested in assisting local orphans, and Prudence had said she would. The vicar's wife had also
tried to interest her in charitable works, but with less
warmth.

"Do you want to ride back or walk?" Cate asked.

"Walk," Prudence said, hoping no one would want to
walk with them. She saw Karen leaving with a cheerful

group. She'd given the girl permission to spend the day with her family.

As Karen and her family left the churchyard, they encountered a bedraggled little group of beggars. Karen turned back to indicate the rector, Mr. Loveday, Prudence observed. This could provide an opportunity to see whether the rector and his wife were true Christians.

But as the vagrants came closer, they looked not to the rector but to her, their faces full of anxiety and hope. Their lame dog barked and rushed to Prudence, tongue wagging.

For a horrible moment, Prudence wanted to deny that she knew Hetty and her children. She couldn't do it, but she dearly wished they'd not arrived now, with the local people still around. Heart sinking at how this would appear, she bent down to greet Toby and then walked over to her friend. "Hetty, what's the matter? What's happened?"

"Oh, Pru! They've evicted us and taken Will to jail! I couldn't think who else might be able to save him!"

Prudence put her arm around her, and around the children too. "Of course I'll do what I can." Aware of the interested crowd, and especially the stares from the Keynings carriages, she said, "Come into the church and tell me all about it."

"Who are these people?" the dowager called in a clear, sharp voice.

Not even looking at Cate, Prudence faced her. "Mistress Larn is a friend who helped me when I needed it. I will help her in turn."

"Dinner will be served when we return from church."

"I may be late, ma'am. Please don't wait for me."

"*We* may be late," Cate said, coming to Prudence's side. "Mistress Larn did me a service too." He looked down at the two teary children, who were now leaning against their mother. "You must be very tired. Shall I carry you?"

They both nodded, and he scooped them up, dust and all, and carried them into the church. Prudence followed, her arm around Hetty, loving Cate even more. Let the world think them a shame to their rank. Christ, she hoped, would see love and charity.

They sat in a pew at the back of the church. "Now," Prudence said, "tell me all."

Hetty clutched a well-used handkerchief. "I shouldn't have come, should I, especially here, with you so fine and with your fine friends. Shown you up in front of his family, haven't I?"

"Nonsense. Tell me what's happened to Will. Why has he been arrested?"

"It were like this. Will went off to work as normal, and then 'ours later, there came a hammering on the doors, and bailiffs said we had t' leave 'cause Will 'ad been taken up for thievery and the landlord would 'ave no thieves in his 'ouses." She turned to Cate. "It weren't fair, sir. It weren't. Will's no thief!"

"Of course he's not," Prudence said.

"What work does your husband do?" Cate asked.

"He's an ostler at the Crown, sir, and 'onest as the day is long."

"What's he supposed to have stolen?"

"Some money a man left in a bag on his 'orse. Stealing's a hanging offense, sir. They can't 'ang my Will!"

Tears created new tracks in the dust on the children's faces. Prudence wiped them away with her own handkerchief. "We won't let it come to that."

"What can anyone do, though?" Hetty wailed. "I just thought, with you marrying 'im, and 'im so ... well, lordly, and you living in an earl's house ... I didn't know where else to turn. Me family's no use in this. I didn't even dare leave the little 'uns, because there's something not *right* about it, sir. There isn't."

Prudence had a shocking thought. She looked at Cate and mouthed, *Draydale?*

His eyes widened, but then he nodded, his face turning grim.

He asked, "What makes you think it anything but an unfair accusation?"

"There's been other things, sir. A few nights ago, someone smashed in the windows in yer old 'ouse, Pru, and threw in oily rags aflame. The Armstrongs who live there now stopped the fire, but no one could imagine who'd do such a thing. Then the pump down the yard wouldn't work, and it turned out to have been tampered with."

Draydale. Sending messages—that he'd hurt them through others, and perhaps even that he knew about White Rose Yard and would use it in his revenge.

Petty stuff to begin with, but the tampered coach wheel could have killed or injured them, and this latest move could get Will Larn hanged.

"Where's your husband now?" Cate asked.

"In jail, and that's a nasty, dirty place, sir. I went to see 'im, but had nothing to take 'im because the bailiffs didn't let us. The jailer scarcely let us have a moment together. I told him I were coming to you, sir. You and Pru. Someone said he could go on trial tomorrow!"

"Magistrate only," Cate said. "If they judge him guilty he'll be held until the assize. I'll have taken care of everything by then. Don't worry."

"But what can you *do*?" Hetty wailed. "I thought you could, but the law's the law, and they found three guineas and some other things in his bag, where he hangs it in the stables when he gets to work. There's nothing you can do. Nothing anyone can do."

Prudence said, "Hetty, my husband's the Earl of Malzard. I'm sorry I didn't tell you, but we wanted to keep it quiet for a day or two more."

"An *earl*?" Hetty was reacting with the same disbelief Prudence had shown when he'd confessed it, but he did look more the part now. "Lawks," she said, but in an awed whisper. "But, Pru, that means . . . You're a *milady*?"

"I'm afraid so."

"Lawks!"

"I'm still just Pru to you, but you'll see that my husband does have powers to put matters right."

"Oh." Hetty stared at him, dabbing her eyes. "Oh." Then she broke down in tears on Prudence's chest.

The rector appeared to ask whether help was needed, but he looked reluctant and disapproving. No parish liked to have vagrants expecting help from local funds. Prudence wished she could take Hetty up to Keynings, but where could she fit there? Not in one of the grand bedchambers, for sure. Was there a vacant cottage on the estate?

Cate said, "Mistress Larn and her children are coming up to Keynings with us, Loveday. Have any of the carriages waited?"

"Yes, milord," said the rector, astonished now.

The two children had sunk into a doze and they hardly woke as Cate picked them up. Prudence picked up Toby, and helped Hetty up and out to the carriage.

Hetty held back, as if afraid to enter. "We're too dirty for those fine seats."

"Nonsense. In you go, Hetty. All will be well. We'll find you a place to rest, and there'll be food too. When did you last eat?"

"Before," Hetty said, sitting stiffly on the brocade-covered seat. "I 'ad no money, you see. People aren't kind in the country to weary strangers, are they?"

"Not if they look like vagrants," Prudence admitted.

The Stonehouses had been generous, but they would have been much warier about a ragged group, and with reason. Often such people were flea-ridden pilferers at best and outright thieves at worst.

"My father lamented the destruction of the monasteries," she said, "for at their best they provided charity for all, and they could deal with thievery and other problems."

"Whereas now," Cate said, "the parishes are responsible for such services, which means the ratepayers. They're naturally reluctant to support other people's problems. True Christianity can prove difficult in practice, can't it?"

But you are a true Christian, Prudence thought, *for all your high birth and privilege*. She did still wonder, however, where they were to house Hetty and the children.

At Keynings Cate ordered the carriage to take them to an entrance on the north side. "There's at least one spare suite of rooms there," he said to Prudence. "It will do for now."

He'd provide accommodation at Keynings? That was more than she'd expected, and a part of her shivered at how the other residents would react. How would the Catesby sisters, Optimus Goode, and Mr. Coates respond to such neighbors?

She tried to put aside such fears. Keynings was her home, hers and Cate's, to manage as they wished. She only prayed Hetty wouldn't be overawed to the point of discomfort.

Hetty was astonished by the rooms, and yes, nervous, but the needs of her children overrode that. Cate had been about to put them in the bed, but she said, "Can I find water to wash 'em first, Pru? They're fast asleep, the poor mites, but they'll soil the sheets something terrible."

"Of course," Prudence said, but she saw no bell ropes here.

"I'll send someone," Cate said, putting the children gently on the settee.

When he left, Hetty exclaimed, "That'll be worse to clean than sheets!"

"He won't care. He'll only have thought that the bed will be more comfortable clean."

"Oh, Pru. Such a lovely man, but it don't feel right t'be here."

"Of course it's right. You're my guests."

A maid as young and lowly as Karen came in with a jug of hot water, followed by another with a jug of cold. They were both wide-eyed at events, but showed no insolence.

Prudence thanked them and sent the first one for food. "Something simple and quickly provided, if you please. And a bowl of water for the dog."

Toby was as tired as the rest, and had curled up near the children to go to sleep, but he'd need to come and go. So many details.

Prudence helped wash the dusty children, who hardly stirred, and she almost cried at the blisters on Willie's feet.

"And he never complained," said Hetty, kissing the spots. "The brave little man."

"I suspect you have blisters too," Prudence said.

"Aye, but I understood the necessity. I'm not sure he did."

They tucked the children into the big bed, and then

went to the parlor, where the food was laid out—bread, meat, cheese, and a small jug of beer.

With a dog's instinct, Toby woke to trot after them. He drank from the bowl, then looked urgently at the table. Prudence put some of the cold beef on the floor for him.

"When the children wake, Hetty, send for milk for them, and anything else they need."

"How?" Hetty asked.

"An excellent question. I've hardly sorted out such things myself. I'll arrange for a maid to attend you here, ready to run errands."

"Oh, Pru . . ."

"Don't object. It's the only way. This is a vast place."

"If you think it's best." Hetty took a deep drink of the beer. "I really should call you 'your ladyship,' shouldn't I? You so grand an' all."

"Don't you go doing that," Prudence teased, "or I'll call you Hesther. I'm glad you came to me, Hetty. I think I know the cause of your misery, and it all comes back to me, so it's for me and my husband to put all right, which we will."

"He's that sort of man, isn't he?" Hetty said, biting into a piece of bread. "One who gets things done, like me father."

The comparison made Prudence smile, but it was true—it was a quality that didn't depend on rank.

"Yes, he is. Be at ease here, Hetty, for you are my first guests, and you are very dear to me."

"Me?" Hetty said.

"You." Prudence realized how true that was. Hetty was a dear friend, and she wanted to keep her nearby. Somehow. "You're honest, kind, and strong," she said, "and I've truly missed your haverbread."

Hetty chuckled. "Go on with you. When you have food like this?"

"I enjoy the food here, but sometimes food is more than food."

Prudence left the room feeling strangely liberated. It wasn't only that she had a friend—a friend who meant more to her than she'd realized—but that she'd perforce shed her fretfulness about being a perfect countess. She was herself, and that would have to do. People now knew most of the worst about her, directly or by implication, so nothing hung over her head.

And Cate . . . Cate—his kindness to Hetty and her children had sealed her devotion to him. She was the most fortunate of women. She wanted to go to him immediately, but she must attend to other matters first. She returned to her boudoir and summoned the housekeeper.

"Is it possible for one of the maids who brought water to my guests to be their attendant for a while, Mistress Ingleton?"

"Why, yes, milady." But the woman was startled.

"Will she feel demeaned by it? I'll have no discourtesy to my *friend.*"

The housekeeper's reaction to that was unreadable, but she said, "Clarry will enjoy the lighter work, I'm sure. So long as the guests don't behave badly."

Prudence decided anger at that wouldn't serve. "Mistress Larn and her children were unfairly evicted from their home, Mistress Ingleton, which is why they arrived here in distress. They had to walk here from Northallerton. They are resting now, but when they wake they will need clean clothing. Can we provide such?"

"Yes, milady," the housekeeper said, looking more

sympathetic. Everyone knew their world could be unfair at times.

"They are to have everything and anything they request," Prudence said, then saw another way to appease the housekeeper. "I believe you have a miraculous salve, Mistress Ingleton. The little boy in particular could use some when he wakes. His feet are blistered."

"Oh, the poor child. I'll see Clarry has some, milady."

Prudence thanked the woman warmly, and once she'd left, blew out a breath. That had perhaps gone well. Next she needed to speak to Cate. He'd been kind and hospitable, but how would he react to her desire to keep Hetty here? Not in the house, but nearby. Will worked with horses. There could be a place for him in the stables. They could have a cottage nearby. One could be built if necessary.

She could imagine the problems. She wanted Hetty as a friend, but that would create a new pandemonium if it put the servants' and tenants' noses out of joint. It could even further damage her reputation with the local gentry. She could imagine what Artemis would make of it, probably assisted by the dowager and the Catesby sisters.

What was more, Hetty might not be comfortable in that situation. She was the type to want to be part of her community. If she was seen as a privileged outsider, she'd be miserable. Prudence rubbed her forehead, definitely needing to discuss this with Cate. Or rather, simply needing to be with Cate.

When she sent Karen to inquire, however, she learned that he was closeted with his senior officers. He must have summoned them from their Sunday dinner, so it was urgent, and she knew the topic under discussion.

Draydale. News of his vicious spite made speedy action necessary, and she hoped Cate could make the man suffer as he deserved.

But what should she do now? She had no interest in dinner.

When they woke, the children would appreciate amusements such as books and playthings. She went upward in search of the nurseries and schoolrooms. She remembered passing them on her first tour of the house, but it took some trial and error to find them.

As she approached, she heard voices. Of course. They weren't unused. Artemis's daughters and their attendants were up here. Would Artemis object to this invasion? She entered the nursery parlor with trepidation and winced to find not only the three girls, but Artemis herself, looking frosty.

The room was small and comfortably furnished in a style able to cope with children. Shelves held a number of books, and there were also dolls, a dollhouse, blocks, and other amusements. How wondrous it would seem to Willie and Sarah.

"Forgive my intrusion," Prudence said. "I've brought Mistress Larn and her children back to the house, and settled them in the north wing for now. They're asleep at the moment, but I wondered if there were some playthings or learning materials that could be spared."

The two older girls had risen and curtsied, but they stood like statues. The toddler sitting on the floor with a jumble of blocks smiled. Prudence smiled back before she thought of it. The child scrambled to her feet and ran over to Prudence's skirts, laughing.

Prudence glanced at her sister-in-law, but as Artemis didn't object, she picked up the delightful child and kissed her cheek. "Aren't you a precious, me hinny?" She realized she'd used a fond term from White Rose

Yard but was past caring. She smiled at the two other girls. "A good day to you."

They dipped curtsies again and said good day, but still in that distant way. Clearly Artemis had painted her in dark shades.

Prudence tried to create some warmth. "I'm sorry, but I don't know your names, my dears."

They glanced at their mother, as if names were a secret.

Artemis sighed. "May I present Flavia, my oldest daughter." The tallest one curtsied. "And Julia, my second daughter." Another curtsy. "My youngest child is Maria."

At the sound of her mother's voice, little Maria squirmed to go to her, so Prudence carried her over.

Artemis took the child, who settled against her shoulder. "By all means, take what you wish, sister."

Prudence looked around, wondering which toys were special to her nieces. "Perhaps you could choose some," she said to Flavia and Julia. "Are there any playthings suitable for a boy? And books. They are only just beginning to read."

The girls set to willingly enough, and soon Prudence could leave with a basket of amusements. She'd like to be a loving aunt, but doubted she'd be allowed the chance.

Chapter 32

Prudence delivered the basket, satisfied to have the door opened by the maid set to attending Hetty. All the guests were asleep, the girl whispered, seeming pleased with her new duties.

Prudence realized she was hungry now, but she had no intention of trying to join the table if dinner was still being served. She sent Karen to find Cate and discover whether he'd eaten. The maid returned with an invitation for Prudence to join him in his library, where she found him already dining.

"I've had a place laid for you," he said, "but as you were busy, I didn't wait. I was hungry," he confessed.

Prudence had never been in this room before. It seemed rather more like her boudoir than she'd expected, and as she sat, she said so.

"It used to be paneled and manly."

As she served herself soup, she considered his tone. "Your brother changed it, as he changed the hall."

"And I can't change it back without seeming unfeeling, or even antipathetic. The paintings are ones Roe collected on his Tour."

"Perhaps Artemis might like them?" Prudence suggested, helping herself to soup.

"Wondrous lady! And the furniture too, if she'll take it. Thank you."

Prudence smiled at him. "I've already hoped that she'll take everything from the boudoir too. I don't mean that in a bad way, only that it's her room, not mine, and imbued with her bitterness."

He sighed. "Here, I'm constantly aware that Roe must be gnashing his teeth in the grave."

"He's in heaven," she reminded him. "I'm sure truths are known in heaven."

"In some cases, that's an alarming thought!"

She shook her head at him, and told him about the arrangements for Hetty. Then she confessed to wanting to keep her friend at Keynings. "Will it create a great deal of trouble?"

He grimaced. "That probably depends. If Hetty and her husband are willing, however, we'll attempt it. Would you like some chicken?" As he served roast chicken, he said, "If it creates discord, I can provide for them elsewhere. Perhaps with an inn of their own."

She smiled at him. "You're very generous."

He poured her wine and refilled his own glass. "To give a little when I have so much hardly deserves praise. I know you'd like her here, however."

"But not if she's unhappy. I know all too well how we can be unsuited to our place. Now, tell me what you plan for Draydale."

"I went over what we know about Draydale's misdoings and set people to compiling it in usable form. Nothing outright illegal as yet, unfortunately, but plenty to shame him. I'd like to act now, but too many people would object to mayhem on the Lord's day. I've dispatched people to Northallerton to look after Will Larn, however. To pay for comforts in the jail, and make it clear to the authorities there that someone of importance is taking an interest. Tomorrow they'll retain a lawyer for his case."

"If the complainant realizes the Earl of Malzard is on Will's side, he'll probably flee the area."

"Which will suit in one sense, but my men are instructed not to let that out unless absolutely necessary. An indulgence, but I hope to startle Draydale with that detail. I also hope the complainant doesn't disappear, because it might be possible to persuade him to give witness to Draydale's hand in the matter."

His tone made her shudder slightly, but she did want Draydale punished.

"Then there's the attack on your old home, and on the coach. That fire could have cost lives, as could the tampered wheel. My men will look for those involved. I doubt any of this will be enough to get Draydale transported, never mind sent to the gibbet, but it should shrivel his powers, which will be a start."

"As you said, poor and powerless will be hell for him."

"But I'd still like to strike a more telling blow." He sipped his wine. "My being a very new earl weakens me. People have been given no reason to dread my power."

"They would have dreaded your brother's?" she asked. "That seems almost medieval."

"There's a great deal of the past lingering in the north, and the nobility up here wield more overt power. I'm sure Roe showed the equivalent of the mailed fist when called for. My father certainly did."

She frowned. "I could be a problem there, couldn't I? Aaron Youlgrave's sister, who created such a scandal at the altar, hardly fits with long lineage and established power."

"And I'm the shabby gentleman who assisted her." He toasted her. "We're warriors, at least, and people will have seen that. Are you finished? I want to show you my bath."

"Your bath?"

"Fit for a warrior. Come and see."

She did, and gaped at the monstrous thing on its dais. "A person could almost swim in that!"

"Not quite," he said, "but there could be other games." She saw a wicked smile, but all he added was, "We could swim in the lake."

"Swim? Women don't, do they?"

"You can if you want. I'll teach you."

Prudence was very uncertain about that, and about the bath. "It must take buckets and buckets of water."

"Employing servants is a good deed. It spreads our wealth."

"I feel I should be able to contest that argument. . . ."

"Don't try. Instead, employ. Use this bath whenever you want."

"It must be wonderful. And I have only a very small one." She looked around at the walls. "This is such a lovely room, as well. Are the paintings copies of Roman ones?"

"Some artist's vision of Olympus. You should have a dressing and bathing room as grand as this. Come."

He hurried her to her rooms and inspected the bedchamber beyond. "This. You can design every detail to suit."

"But we'll lose a bedchamber."

"We're not short of them, but if necessary, we'll build another wing."

She laughed, but already such an attitude didn't feel beyond reason.

Prudence woke on Monday to a note from Cate saying that Will Larn was as comfortable as possible in jail and had a lawyer ready to attend to his case.

She dressed in her dyed blue dress and went to tell Hetty the good news. She found her and the children in clean clothes, all thrilled to have had proper baths, with clean water for each of them. The children, who had books and playthings, seemed to be enjoying their new situation without a care. Hetty still seemed anxious, clearly worrying that they'd soil or damage something.

"You mustn't worry about a thing," Prudence said.

"How can I not?" Hetty said. "It'd be a sin to mar such lovely things."

"The children are careful, but why not take them outside so they and Toby can run around?"

"Will that be all right?"

"Yes, certainly."

Prudence took them all into the grounds, where gardeners and groundsmen were busily working. She showed them the swing, and the children took turns, laughing with delight. A swing was a simple thing. Why wasn't there one in a place like White Rose Yard?

She wanted her breakfast, and the practice of eating breakfast with Cate was so fixed now that she couldn't imagine it any other way.

"I have to return to the house," she told Hetty. "Enjoy the gardens." She suddenly remembered Draydale. The morning was so peaceful it was hard to imagine danger, but she said, "Don't go out of sight of the house for now."

Hetty's eyes widened, and she nodded.

"Can we go to the lake, Mam?" Willie asked.

"Not yet," Hetty said.

Prudence hurried inside, irritated that Draydale was causing problems here. The sooner he was done for, the better.

She found Cate already eating breakfast in her boudoir, but he rose to kiss her. "Fully dressed and in full vigor?"

"I went to tell Hetty the good news. They're used to

rising early, so they're outside now." As she sat down, she added, "I warned them not to go far from the house."

"Good. I've ordered all available men to make themselves busy outside, to keep an eye out for danger."

"How thorough you are."

"Long practice trying to keep my men alive. I've always disliked waste. Another thing that put me at odds with some in the army. I won't permit Draydale to harm anyone here."

"Would he really try?"

"He won't put himself in danger of prosecution for murder, but if he can maim or kill in an apparent accident, he'll arrange it. Especially now. He has to be hearing something of what I've set in motion in Darlington."

"Lord, we've increased the danger."

"You'd rather have left Will Larn unaided?"

"No, but I hate all this. Why can't we put an end to him now?"

"Impatient as always," he said with a smile. "As am I. But more information is coming in. Another day might bring us bigger nails for his coffin. Only one day, however. I'm going to Darlington tomorrow to cook his goose. Do you want to come?"

The idea startled her, but she said, "Yes. Especially if I can witness his fall into hell."

"I'll do my best. I promise. At the moment, so many people are vulnerable. He's striking anyone connected to you, even the new tenants in your old house."

Prudence froze, a piece of buttered bun halfway to her mouth. "The Stonehouses! Might Draydale know about them?"

"Damnation, yes, from Tallbridge's groom." He rose and dropped a quick kiss on her lips. "I must send people there—to warn them and keep them safe. Anyone else you can think of?"

Prudence thought hard. "If Aaron and Susan are safe, no, I don't think so. I wasn't close to anyone in White Rose Yard other than Hetty."

He left, and Prudence found her appetite gone. Suddenly anxious about Hetty, she went back outside, but she saw them all safely near the house. The children were playing with a ball, with assistance from Toby. Hetty was sitting on a bench beneath a tree. Prudence wondered if she was enjoying the rest or twitchy for something to do.

She heard children in the other direction and saw Artemis's daughters over near the lake. She'd like to see all the children playing together, but that was reaching too far.

Flavia and Julia ran onto the little Chinese bridge that went over the stream that fed the lake, and Prudence suddenly felt nervous. Water was an obvious danger, and in Draydale's warped, vengeful mind anyone at Keynings might be a target.

There were a remarkable number of men working outside, however, including some clearing bulrushes at the lake's edge. Cate definitely did care, perhaps too much and for too many, but she couldn't fault it.

She couldn't hover, however, seeking danger everywhere. She had duties to perform. She returned to the house, but then, despite feeling a little foolish, she put her old knife in her pocket, and the bodice dagger down her stays.

Everyone in the family turned up for dinner that day. Apart from saying, "Your friends do not dine with us, Prudence?" the dowager created no problems, and Artemis was silent. Mr. Goode seemed to honestly see Prudence as an old acquaintance.

The Catesby sisters were enlivened by the children. "Such a sad case," Miss Catesby said. "Such cruel treatment."

Mr. Coates shared, at length, his opinions on vagrancy laws, and Cate put in some opinions, creating a conversation until the dowager said, "I hope those children will behave themselves. They can't be accustomed to such surroundings."

"They're very well behaved," said Miss Cecily bravely. "We hardly hear a sound, do we, sister? The little dog too. No barking."

"No breeding," said the dowager.

Prudence chose to believe that she meant the dog.

The brittle mood continued over tea, but no outright war was declared and no one seemed inclined to linger. Prudence was surprised to realize that she simply didn't care anymore. The dowager and Artemis could stew in their own bitter juices. She herself had better things to do.

In the immediate, she wanted to see if it would be safe for Willie and Sarah to go out on the lake. Boldly, she invaded Cate's estate offices to ask him, hardly sparing a glance at the clerks in the outer room—though she noticed that they did all stand, and that it was ridiculous. In the inner one, she found Cate alone, reading through some papers.

They kissed as if that were as natural as breathing.

"Is it safe? I'm sure it would be a great treat."

"I had the boats and bridge checked this morning, and men have been working near there ever since, so no one should have been able to damage them. I'll come with you to arrange it."

She eyed his desk. "Don't you have much to attend to, my lord?"

"Nailing me to my duty, my lady? I plan to play truant again. Last time was very rewarding."

Smiling, they kissed again, and went in search of their guests.

They found Hetty and the children back in their rooms, but at mention of a boat, Will was raring to go. Sarah was a little less sure, but she consented to walking to the lake. The boats were kept in a boathouse, and Cate instructed a man to check one again and then take Hetty and the children out.

Prudence watched their pleasure and excitement. "I do hope they stay."

"This is an example of the problems," Cate warned. "At the moment, they're guests, but if Will Larn is working here, the family can't have privileges denied to other servants. However, I don't see any reason not to make the boats available to all now and then. The men are already allowed to fish in the lake when they have time off. No, that's not my doing. It was my father's."

"He was as kind as you, then."

"Say, rather, pragmatic. He wasn't an angler, so he didn't care about the fish in the lake. When he had guests who liked to fish, the servants knew to stay away. Would you like to go out in a boat?" When she hesitated, he teased, "Do you have less courage than Hetty's children?"

"Damn you," she said cordially. "Very well, but if I drown, on your head be it."

He took her to the boathouse and released some constraints on a flat-bottomed boat. Then he held out a hand.

"What if it tips?"

"I won't let it."

"I know, I know. 'Trust me.' I suppose I should be grateful to be in my plainest gown that won't be entirely ruined by drenching. If I drown, however, it will be your fault."

"If you drown, I'll drown with you."

She looked at him, startled, but he was adjusting some cushions in the back of the boat. He turned and held out his hand. She took it and stepped carefully down and sat on the seat, tucking her skirts in. He took off his jacket and tossed it to her, then picked up a pole and, stepping into the other end, used it to push the boat away from the shore. As soon as it wobbled a bit, she clutched the edges.

"Trust me," he said, smiling.

"How much practice in this have you had?"

"Plenty—when I was a lad."

"That's what I feared."

He grinned and sent the boat into the middle of the lake, but away from the laughing children. Prudence had never felt so cut off in her life. It wasn't a very big lake, but all she had to support her was the boat. And Cate. Without the boat and Cate she'd be at the mercy of the water and would drown.

"Don't die," she said.

"Punting? Of course not."

"Ever. I mean, not for a long time. You're all I have in this world."

He looked at her seriously as he smoothly drifted the boat across the water. "You're not quite all I have, Prudence, but you're a great part of it. Don't die."

"I'll try not to. That's all we can do, isn't it? Try."

"We're very good at trying. Let's try for a little privacy."

There were small treed projections from the shore, so it was possible to find places where they seemed alone in the world, and Prudence began to find tranquillity. The sky was largely cloudy, with only patches of blue, but that made it pleasantly cool, and white fluffy clouds could be beautiful.

"I wonder what would happen if I could fly up and touch a cloud."

"They're only mist. I've been in them on mountains."

"You're spoiling the magic," she complained.

"I'll take you to some mountains so you can touch the clouds. Even a high hill would do in the right weather. Have you seen the sea?"

"No."

"We can do that even more easily."

"I'm sorry," she said.

"What for?"

"For having experienced so little."

"It presents me with more opportunities to delight you. Take your glove off and trail your hand in the water."

She did so. "Ah, the movement against my skin. Such a simple thing."

"Many delights are. Like clouds and rainbows. And hugs."

"You're doing all the work here. I feel very lazy."

"I'm enjoying it. The greatest trial to me is lack of activity. I normally ride in the mornings, but I've been trying to favor my wound. I'd ride to Darlington tomorrow if I didn't have to arrive in state. Perhaps I should dig out an old suit of armor and ride in, banners unfurled."

She chuckled, but sobered at a new thought. "Have you thought that people might see your vengeance as rooted in Draydale's supposed violation of me? Supporting it as fact."

"If I thought it a fact," he said flatly, "I'd call him out and kill him."

He still could surprise her with such statements, and the day seemed suddenly darker. "Don't, please."

He watched her. "Are you saying I might have cause?"

"No!"

"I believe you. You seemed to suggest otherwise."

"I didn't. . . . No. But I'm unused to violence. It disturbs me."

"Would you prefer not to come tomorrow?"

"No, I want to be there." She tried to shake her morbid feeling.

"Good. I don't expect violence, anyway, only drama. We'll prove the truth of our cause by our actions. A romance worthy of the troubadours, remember?"

She smiled. "That doesn't seem so fanciful anymore."

"Not fanciful at all." His smile made her blush, and she turned to watch the passing trees near the rush-fringed bank.

She'd worked it out. Her courses should begin in a week, which meant that in two weeks they'd be over. Cate would have no lingering trace of doubt, but would it be too early to risk conceiving a child? Not every wife conceived immediately, but she might, and then it would still be possible, in the eyes of the suspicious, that the child was Draydale's.

Perhaps it was the thought of waiting longer that made her feel as if the clouds had darkened, or perhaps it was other things. "It's growing colder, I think. I hope it doesn't rain."

"Do you want to go back to shore?"

"No. Oh, there are Artemis's girls on the far side, looking wistful. Do they not go out on the lake?"

He turned to look. "I don't know. I've never seen them do so. Shall I arrange it?"

"We could go over and ask them."

He poled the boat out from their little bay, sending it shooting across the water at alarming speed. Prudence clutched the sides, praying, telling herself to have faith.

Flavia and Julia watched, but then they picked their way closer to the edge, coming to meet them.

"Be careful!" Prudence called.

A nursemaid was with them, little Maria in her arms, but she didn't seem to be controlling them. Thank heavens one of Cate's men was nearby. He must have been cutting the bulrushes, but now he'd put down his tool and was hurrying to the girls.

But then the man snatched the toddler from the nursemaid and hurled the little girl into the lake.

"Cate!" Prudence shrieked. The girls and the nursemaid screamed too, crying, "Help!" and "Maria!"

Cate dropped the pole, kicked off his shoes, and dove into the water, sending the boat swaying from side to side. Prudence clutched the sides, wanting to scream herself, but her eyes fixed on where he swam swiftly toward the struggling toddler. The little girl seemed to be buoyed up by her gown, but any moment . . .

Another scream whipped her head toward the shore. The man must have struck the nursemaid, who lay on the grass. He had one girl over his shoulder and was racing away, pursued by the other, who was yelling, *"Stop! Stop! Oh, help, please! Someone help!"*

The other boat, the one carrying Hetty and the children, was speeding their way. Men were running from all around. Cate had the thrashing Maria safe, but couldn't race to the bank.

Prudence's boat had continued on its way and now jolted into the reedy bank. She scrambled out without a thought—to sink thigh-deep in reeds and water. Desperately, she struggled forward, her skirts dragging, her feet slipping in mud, clutching anything that might help to impel her after the villain and the girls, who'd disappeared into some trees and shrubs.

Shouts told her that others were coming, but she was closest.

She scrambled onto firm ground and collapsed on her hands and knees for a moment, but then forced herself up and stumbled into a run, her skirts a deadweight. Gasping, she burst into the trees, following the path of broken branches, having to dodge higher ones. She could hear the girls ahead, still wailing for help.

But then a blow clipped her head. Perhaps she'd thought it a branch, for she'd ducked and missed most of it, but it made her stumble to the ground. She saw him then—a man aiming a thick broken stick at her again. She rolled away, scrabbling for her knife, but her pocket was lost beneath her tangled, sodden skirts.

The girls, the girls . . .

But he must have abandoned them and doubled back. For her.

She grabbed the bodice dagger and yanked it out just as he came at her again. She stabbed at the man's legs, then scrabbled away. His stockings bloomed red and he cursed her.

Somewhere, Cate yelled, "Prudence! Prudence!"

"Here! Here!"

The man raised the branch over her, with vicious intent this time.

A shot fired. His eyes went wide and he collapsed, blood pouring from his mouth.

Prudence rolled away from the terrible sight, sobbing with exhaustion, terror, and relief.

Then Cate had her in his arms. "Are you all right? Are you hurt?"

She looked up at him. "I think so. . . . All right . . . Did you shoot him?"

"No gun and soaking wet," he said on a gasp. "One

of the gamekeepers, I think. Whoever it is will get a rich reward. And Draydale's signed his own warrant to hell."

Despite her protests, he picked her up and carried her out of the woodland, where Artemis was running to be reunited with her children. A man gave her the screaming toddler, and the older girls ran toward her.

"You saved the little one," Prudence said.

"Easy enough, but the child was only a distraction."

"As was the older one. It was me he wanted. Me Draydale wanted. Cate, your wounds! Put me down."

"My wounds are as good as healed," he said, but he did lower her carefully to her feet. "'One shoe off and one shoe on,'" he said, looking at her feet.

Leaning against him, she completed the nursery rhyme. "'Diddle, diddle, dumpling, my son John.' Put an end to this, Cate. I can't bear to have such danger all around."

"Have no fear, I will."

Artemis was hurrying her children back into the safety of the house. Would she see this too as all Cate's fault? By tortuous reasoning, she could. It was certainly all Prudence's fault, rooted in her folly of accepting Henry Draydale.

As soon as they entered the house, Cate shouted for his bath to be filled. He took Prudence to her bedchamber and told her to come to his dressing room as soon as she'd rid herself of her sodden clothing.

"My poor blue dress," she said. "I think this has tolled its final knell."

He pulled her into his arms. "Don't talk of death. I died a thousand times racing after you. Now change and take the bath. I won't lose you to pneumonia."

"What about your valet?" she asked.

"He won't intrude. You and Karen will have the room to yourselves."

Prudence didn't want to part from him, but she could hardly bathe with him around, and she was feeling deeply chilled. When she went nervously into his dressing room, naked beneath her robe, she found the big bath steaming, and on a table nearby a decanter of brandy, a glass, and a spray of pink roses.

Karen was gaping at the bath. "I've never seen the like, milady!"

"I doubt they're common." But when Prudence carefully stepped into it and sat down, able to stretch her legs and even lie back, she sighed happily. "This is wonderful. Pour some brandy into a glass and give it to me."

"Yes, milady." As Karen handed the glass to Prudence, she said, "I 'ave 'eard as brandy is medicinal, milady."

"It is. Very. For soul, mind, and body."

Now, suddenly, the thought of what might have happened hit her and she shuddered.

Henry Draydale must be crushed.

Chapter 33

With the best will in the world, the water couldn't be kept warm, and Prudence had to climb out to be dried and wrapped again in her robe. She returned to her room to dress, this time in the plain crape dress.

She'd washed her hair, so that had to dry. She didn't mind. She needed time to herself. How easily things could have been disastrous, but by prompt action and resolution, they'd all survived.

The Catesby Burgoyne way.

She'd brought the brandy and roses with her, and put the roses in her mother's vase. She sipped the brandy and smiled at them, amazed to find that love could run even deeper in her heart.

Her reverie was cut short by a knock at the boudoir door. Karen returned to say that Artemis, Lady Malzard, wished to speak to her.

To voice her complaints, no doubt, though perhaps she'd have some grudging thanks as well. Prudence decided they'd be best away from the boudoir, and suggested a meeting in the yellow drawing room.

Prudence went there resolved to be tolerant, even of ungrateful abuse, but Artemis was already there, and said, "I will be leaving Keynings as soon as possible. Returning to my father's house."

Prudence was startled but grateful, though she couldn't help looking for a trap. "I'm sure it will be hard to leave, but for the best in the end."

"What's done is done," Artemis said bleakly. "It can't be changed."

"It takes time to accept that."

Artemis looked at her. "You've known loss too."

"My early home, followed by the death of my father. I remember my mother's grief."

"I doubt she persecuted her successor."

"There was none. My father was employed there, as you know, so we had no claim on the place. Blytheby was sold to new owners who had no connection with the past. Mother had no choice but to quickly turn her mind to the future."

Artemis's eyes slid away. "I've never known grief until recently. My parents still live. My brothers and sisters are healthy. But the baby . . . That was hard. Very hard. And it angered me that my husband would rail about losing his son. He was my baby! The child I'd felt moving within me, whom I already knew, whom I'd expected to welcome and love, boy or girl." She turned away, one hand to her mouth. "I don't know when the pain will end. But all he was to Sebastian was his son, his heir, his way to keep Catesby from ruining Keynings."

Prudence longed to take her sister-in-law into her arms, but didn't dare. "I'm sure that's not true. It's so easy to misunderstand when we're in distress. And to misspeak."

Still looking away, Artemis said, "At times I hated him. Then when he died, it all fused together. I grieved for Sebastian, but a part of me was still bitter, and

Catesby was at the heart of all of it. He caused Sebastian such anxiety, but never acknowledged his faults. Never seemed to care! When the baby died and he sent no word of sympathy . . ."

"He never heard."

Artemis turned wearily to her. "I'm sure now that's true. He's not that sort of man."

"No, he isn't."

"I've suspected it for a while, but now . . . Yesterday, when he picked up those dirty children and they settled in his arms, feeling safe, my certainties cracked. Today . . . he saved Maria. You risked your life for Julia. I can't hate you anymore. It's painful in its own way, but better. I think."

"Artemis, would you accept an embrace from me?"

Artemis stared at her, but then nodded. It was a stiff embrace, but as Prudence was about to step back, Artemis held her closer, slumping slightly, perhaps weeping a little. Prudence tightened her arms, remembering that night in Northallerton when Cate had held her just like this.

When they separated Artemis blew her nose on a black-edged handkerchief, moving away, perhaps embarrassed. "It's the touch I miss most. I have the children, but I miss arms to hold me. Is it wrong to already be looking ahead to the day when I might marry again?"

"It's only natural."

"But is natural right?" She looked at Prudence with a frown. "What do those people mean to you and Catesby? Why are they important?"

"Hetty and her children? We believe they're victims of Henry Draydale, the man I was supposed to marry. You know he was behind what happened today?"

"Catesby told me."

"I thought you'd blame me. You could have reason."

"Why did you engage yourself to such a man?" Artemis asked, but apparently in curiosity, not accusation.

"I've asked myself the same thing. I set my heart on something, blindly, as you set your mind on blaming Cate for everything. It took a shock to break me free of that. I escaped, but he's not the sort to take disappointment well. Especially when he hit me in front of the congregation."

"It did sound appalling, in the letter."

"Cate thrashed him thoroughly, right there at the altar."

Artemis bit her lip, but her eyes flashed with something positive for the first time. "Appalling, but satisfying, I'd think."

"I was in no state to appreciate it at the time, but later, yes. And now Cate's going to put an end to him."

"Kill him?" Artemis asked in alarm.

"No, but he'll destroy him in every other way."

"I hope so, but I'd be happy to know he was dead." Artemis moved to the door. She paused there, however, and turned to say, "Your situation won't be easy, Prudence, and not of my doing. The tales from Darlington will become common knowledge and many will believe the worst. Your being the daughter of a librarian and sister of a young solicitor is unfortunate, but the rougher background suggested by the new arrivals will count against you in the neighborhood, and word will spread farther afield. I'd suggest trying to hide that part of your life, but you won't, will you?"

"No, for there's nothing shameful about it. My mother and I lived in poverty so that my brother could train for a profession and support us." She didn't share Aaron's failings here. "When I sank to my lowest, Hetty befriended me, even fed me. I'm not ashamed to call her friend, and I hope she and her family will stay nearby."

"You're braver than I could ever be."

"You'd be surprised, but I hope you never have need of that kind of courage."

"So do I. I'm a very conventional person, afraid of seeming different."

Prudence shrugged. "I have no choice. There's no hiding the truth, and it's simply too difficult to attempt to be anything other than myself. If the world is unkind, so be it."

Artemis put her hand on the doorknob, but hesitated again. "Will I be welcome to visit here?"

"Of course! Whenever you will."

"You're more forgiving than I could be."

Artemis left and Prudence lingered, thinking over the conversation. She prayed that she'd never have to face the death of a young child, though it was common enough. Hetty had lost one at six months.

The thought of losing Cate, however . . .

He came in. "What are you doing here?" Then he said, "What's the matter?"

She went into his arms. "Just hold me."

Chapter 34

When they parted, she shared her talk with Artemis. "Poor woman," he said.

"Yes. Would your brother truly be so unkind?"

"I'm sure he didn't mean to be, but yes, his desperation for a son was obvious. Don't see him too harshly. It was reasonable for him to regard my taking over Keynings with horror. I'm still not sure I can do a good job."

"Yes, you can."

"Such faith in me." He kissed her. "I'm on my way, armed and accompanied by armed men, to inspect the scene of the abduction in case anything can be learned. I wish the man had lived to point the finger at Draydale."

"Has the body been removed?" Prudence asked.

"Yes, of course."

"Then I want to come. It was all such a blur. I want to see it in a calmer state."

"If you're sure."

"Yes. But are you sure it's safe?"

"I refuse to skulk in the house, and I've had every available man beating the park. If he had accomplices, they've fled."

Prudence considered hat and gloves, but didn't bother with them.

When they left the house, six men fell into place around them, alert for anything. It seemed absurd, for the gardens and park appeared to sleep in the warm afternoon, showing no hint of mayhem or death. Prudence felt grateful, however, that she'd replaced both her knives, but her chief emotion wasn't fear but anger—anger that Henry Draydale had sullied this place with his violence.

When they approached the woodland area and Prudence saw the trampled shrubs and broken branches, she hesitated. Cate gave her a concerned glance, and she gathered her courage. "Bold of him to pretend to be one of your men," she said, raising her skirts out of harm's way.

"A possibility I overlooked," he admitted. "I called in workers from nearby farms, which meant not everyone knew everyone else well."

She plucked a piece of dark cloth from a branch. It had torn from her gown as she'd run along this rough path. "He can't have planned the abduction, can he, or he'd have chosen a smoother path."

"He can't have known you'd be on the lake. He simply hovered, pretending to work, looking for a chance to do mischief, or worse."

"Above all, Draydale wants me."

"Yes," he said. "There were horses nearby, kept there for many hours in hope of success. If you'd wandered out on your own . . ."

"Henry Draydale always did assume I was a fool."

He laughed. "A cunning man, but at heart stupid."

They arrived at the bloodstained area.

"I shouldn't have brought you here," he said.

"I needed to see it."

As Cate and the men poked around, looking for anything left behind, Prudence recollected what she could of the event.

"Did this serve your purpose?" he asked as they left the shady, treed area.

"Yes. I know it now, so it won't form nightmares."

He smiled. "I should have known you weren't one to hide from reality. Enough of this. Let's return to the house."

They strolled back, more at ease.

"Is it possible to have instincts of danger?" Prudence asked. "On the lake, I felt it. And not of drowning. Now I feel safe."

"Such things certainly exist. Celebrate it."

"I hope not to have need of it."

"Amen again. I truly hope for a peaceful life here. Ordinary days, making up a tranquil life." But he looked toward the house. "Strange. Someone's arriving."

A large traveling chariot was approaching the front of the house, drawn by six prime horses, and with four outriders as well.

"Someone very grand," Prudence said.

"And here we are with mud on our shoes and leaves in our hair. Shall we run in to make ourselves respectable, or brazen it out?"

"Brazen," she declared.

"That's my Hera. And in any case, that's Perry."

Indeed it was Perry emerging from the grand traveling chariot.

"I thought he liked to ride?" Prudence said as they walked over. "What a tale we have to tell him."

"He'll fume to have missed the drama. There's someone with him."

Perry had turned to hand down a lady. As Prudence and Cate came close, she could see the lady was of about her own age, and brown-haired.

There was something about her, however. A presence.

"My lady," Perry said to the visitor, "may I present the

Earl and Countess of Malzard, your hosts? My friends, this is the Marchioness of Rothgar, Countess of Arradale, and great lady of the north!"

Lady Rothgar laughed at that, smiling at them. "Perriam insisted that you'd welcome me, and also that I could be of use. He also shared your romance worthy of the troubadours. I couldn't resist the latest Yorkshire story to carry south."

Chapter 35

Prudence thought in despair of her drab black and her hair, which was escaping her cap and, yes, probably stuck with leaves. She curtsied and welcomed, wondering how on earth she should treat the marchioness-countess, who owned vast parts of Yorkshire.

But Lady Rothgar had turned to receive a bundle from a servant. A whimpering bundle. She turned back with a rueful expression. "In truth, Perriam offered us refuge. I'm afraid my darling has chosen this moment to cut a tooth and she's so miserable that traveling is torture for all of us. I was arranging to stay some days in York when we met, and he was so bold as to suggest that you'd give me refuge."

Prudence could see the baby now, doubtless a pretty girl, but with her face crumpled in discontent. She was drooling and a rash marred her chin. The baby's whines began to work toward screams. Prudence had no experience with teething, but when the baby let out a yowl of complaint, she said, "Please, my lady, let's go up to the nursery. Perhaps someone there will have something to help."

There was Nurse Cawley, who cared for little Maria. She must have experience.

They hurried in and up, the nursery maid and another maid trailing behind, the crying seeming to echo off the walls.

Nurse Cawley hurried to meet them. "A baby!" she declared happily.

"A teething one," Lady Rothgar said.

"The poor dear. Becky, get the brandy!"

"Brandy?" Prudence protested. "Surely not."

"Just the thing, milady. A little rubbed on the sore gum. And something hard to chew on. Do you have a teething ring, milady?" she asked Lady Rothgar.

"No. We received a few as christening gifts, some of them ridiculously precious, but I don't have one with me."

"And a teething ring!" the ruler of the nurseries called.

Artemis's older daughters came to see what the fuss was about, took one look at the baby, and left again. Clearly they knew what teething meant.

"Come through here, milady," the nurse said, leading the way into another room. "There's a crib here that can quickly be made ready."

"Thank you," said Lady Rothgar, "but I would like it put in my own bedchamber. I keep my daughter with me."

Now, there, Prudence thought, was how one gave an indisputable order in the most pleasant manner possible.

Nurse Cawley was not pleased, but she gave the orders. "Then perhaps we could go to your bedchamber, milady."

Lady Rothgar looked at Prudence, who realized she had no idea which would be most suitable.

"We have many," she said. "I'm very new here."

"So I understand," Lady Rothgar said. "Such a romantic story."

Prudence was beginning to distrust the many nuances of the word "romantic." The Countess of Arradale had probably married her marquess simply for power, wealth, and higher rank.

A maid came in and gave Nurse Cawley a small vial and a carved circle of what looked like bone or ivory. Nurse Cawley applied a little of the brandy on a rag to the baby's lower gums. "There, my little angel, there. Doesn't that seem better? No more tears, no more tears . . ."

The baby's squalls simmered down. Prudence thought it could just be surprise at the new taste, but perhaps brandy did numb the gums. The nurse put the ring in the baby's hand and then guided it to her mouth. The baby chewed a little, and then set to gnawing with a look of powerful intent.

Prudence chuckled, and Lady Rothgar thanked the nurse, but one of her servants was glowering. Probably the baby's own nurse. Nurse Cawley proved her worth by surrendering the baby and offering an understanding, "A first tooth coming early," to explain away lack of preparedness.

Pandemonium banished, harmony restored.

Prudence took a deep breath. "I don't think I properly welcomed you to Keynings, Lady Rothgar. Of course, you are welcome to stay as long as you wish."

"That's very kind of you, but we'll push on south as soon as possible. I'm anxious to return to my husband." It was a simple statement, but something in the tone and eyes told Prudence she'd misjudged the situation. It was a love match. "A minor crisis developed on one of my estates up here, but Lord Rothgar felt unable to leave London with so many matters on the edge, so I came alone. It was too long, in any case, since I'd visited my estates, but traveling with a baby is difficult."

"I'm sure it is. Shall we go down and settle you in your rooms?"

Prudence led the way, still unsure where to establish such an important guest, but when she arrived on the next floor down, she found one of her problems solved. The dowager had emerged to take charge.

She, of course, was well acquainted with Lady Rothgar, and not particularly awed, but still gratified to have her as a guest. Soon the marchioness was installed in an excellent bedchamber with an adjoining door to a room that would serve as a nursery. Footmen were summoned to bring down the crib, and the dowager offered refreshment.

"Thank you, Lady Malzard, but for the moment I must settle my child."

The dowager inclined her head and sailed away, duty done. It wasn't exactly her duty, but Prudence was grateful that her mother-in-law had taken over.

Lady Rothgar smiled at her with some understanding. "In a little while, I would appreciate some tea. It would be kind if you'd share it? I long to hear all about your adventures."

Prudence could only agree, but she hurried in search of Cate, finding him in his library with Perry.

"You survived?" he said. "We have brandy."

"So does the baby."

Perry whistled. "Is that the secret?"

"Just rubbed on the gums." Prudence accepted a glass and sipped. "She wants to know all my adventures!"

"Don't be too awed," Cate said. "She's only a little higher in station than you."

"It doesn't feel like that. I remember seeing her once in Northallerton. It was as if she came from a different sphere. She has such an air."

"Impressively sure of herself and her authority," said Perry. "That's why I brought her here. My angelic gift—her limitless cachet."

"What?" Prudence asked.

"Playing host to the Countess of Arradale—we'll leave aside Lady Rothgar for the moment—covers you with approval here in the north. Even though you can't fete her with a ball, word will spread."

Cate toasted her. "According to Perry, and he would know, her glorious light will eliminate the smallest shadow from your character."

Prudence knocked back some more brandy. "But should I tell her the truth?"

Cate fired a questioning look at Perry.

"Lord Rothgar has the reputation of being omniscient," Perry said. "All a matter of eyes and ears in many places, I suspect, but it's his way to dig out details on anything or anyone that could affect him and his. When his lady returns to his side and tells her stories, he'll turn his attentions on Keynings and the Burgoynes."

"Then why the devil bring her here?" Cate demanded.

"To enhance Prudence's reputation in the north, but also because you both must go to Town. The Marquess and Marchioness of Rothgar can smooth your way there."

"Have you considered that the marquess might not bless us with his favor?" Cate asked. "We could entangle his wife in dangerous matters."

"True enough—if harm comes to her or the child here, you'd best flee to the ends of the earth, but if you have her favor, you'll have his. You might find, Prudence, that you and she have more in common than you think."

"Apart from being women, I can't imagine what that might be."

"You're both countesses," Cate pointed out.

"But she's also a marchioness and born to greatness." Prudence drained her brandy glass and went to order the tea.

Then she hurried to tidy herself, regretting the lack of a lady's maid who would know how to arrange her hair, and probably how to make a plain gown look finer than it was. She was tempted to change into her finer one, but that would look ridiculous.

"Both countesses," she muttered to herself in the mirror. "Ha!"

When she sat to take tea with Lady Rothgar, however, she was put at her ease. Lady Rothgar immediately said, "In the north I prefer to use my own title of Lady Arradale, but I would take it kindly if we could be on first-name terms. I'm Diana."

"Then I'm Prudence," Prudence said, struggling not to add a "my lady." She poured the tea.

"An unfortunate name," Diana said frankly. "Yes, milk, please. Such names are not common in the nobility. Too reminiscent, perhaps, of the Commonwealth period."

"It came down in my father's family, and they were supporters of Cromwell."

Diana took her tea and drank. "Ah, that's very welcome. Now, tell me your story. Perriam would give me only hints, the wretch."

"You know him well, my . . . Diana?"

"Everyone in Town knows Perriam. He's a delightful imp."

"Or the archangel Raphael," said Prudence, and told Diana about that bit of nonsense.

Diana smiled, but said, "The demons interest me more, especially so close to my lands."

My lands. It was said with such confidence. Prudence wondered what it would be like to feel that sort of unconstrained possession of so much. But surely by marriage, all Diana owned was now her husband's.

Diana was looking at her quizzically, doubtless wondering at her silence, so Prudence began her story, leaving nothing out.

"Your brother didn't treat you well," Lady Rothgar said, accepting another cup of tea.

Her tone was so cold that Prudence defended Aaron. "It was more carelessness than malice. He's always been blind to what he doesn't want to see."

"Many are. And his wife? Is she the same?"

"Oh, no. Susan isn't blind to anything. I doubt we'll ever become friends, but I understand and respect her. Her father too. I don't regard him less because he's built his good standing from nothing. People put great importance on birth, but I've learned that the lowborn are as capable of great things as any."

"Or incapable. There are idle, wastrel fools among the poor as well."

That way of putting it made Prudence laugh.

"We're all the same clay? Then shouldn't the poor have more opportunities? Hetty's little boy may prove capable of more than simple labor, but without education, he'll have no opportunity."

She found herself in a spirited discussion of education for the poor, for girls as well as boys, and that moved on to the inequality of women in the eyes of the law.

"Only consider your case, Prudence. If women were able to seek the same employment as men, you would have been able to support your family. I suspect you'd be better suited to that than your brother."

"Become a *lawyer*?"

"Why not? All it requires is study, of which you're capable."

"My head's spinning."

"You see," Diana said cheerfully, "I'm far more outrageous than you. Now, let's summon Lord Malzard. I'm very interested in his plans for Demon Draydale."

She didn't seem to think that summoning an earl in his own house was outrageous. If Cate did, he still came, and Perry too.

"In essence," he told Diana, "I plan to ride to Darlington with attendants, make myself known as the Earl of Malzard, and confront Draydale with his sins. In public."

"If he denies them?"

"As far as his business sins go, I have evidence and witnesses—those who've been afraid to speak out and complain, but will, with my support."

"And mine," Diana said, smiling fiercely. "Darlington isn't in my territory, but all matters in the north interest me. You will permit me to accompany you?"

Cate considered her. "I planned to ride, and there could be risk."

"I am an excellent rider. Also an excellent shot and swordswoman."

"Remember," Prudence said, "I'm going too."

Cate looked at her. "Matters are more serious now. You can't ride, shoot, or wield a sword."

"But this *is* my territory. I sowed the seeds of much of this, and Draydale has attacked me and those close to me. I wish to see his downfall. And I need him to see me seeing it."

His lips tightened as if he'd object, but then he nodded. "It's your right. And, Lady Rothgar, if you wish to come, I won't attempt to stop you."

"As well," she said tartly. "If you please, Malzard, address me as Lady Arradale in this. I am not acting as my husband's deputy."

Prudence had to bite her lips on laughter to see Cate struggling with this unnatural situation, but for her own part, she liked a great deal about it. She hadn't been born to great station as Diana had, but she was now a countess, with powers and authority. She hoped to learn how to use them well.

"Excellent," said Perry, who didn't seem surprised by any of it. "Then let's consider how to make this progress of retribution in grand style."

Chapter 36

The next day they set out for Darlington in force, Prudence riding pillion behind Cate on a substantial horse, wearing her fine black outfit. The pillion was very like a sideways chair, even having a little platform for her feet, but she said, "Surely this will slow you."

"There's no need for speed, and I want people to see us and note us."

"I'm sure they will," she said, looking around. Perry had taken charge of the event, and the result was unforgettable.

They were attended by six armed and mounted retainers—that was to say grooms—wearing a livery from the previous century that had been dug out of the attics. There was a great deal of braid, and they had wide-brimmed hats with plumes.

She hadn't known Cate had a running footman, but he did, and the man paced ahead in his splendid livery, carrying the gold-topped staff that warned a great person approached.

Perry rode a magnificent black horse and wore elegant riding clothes, sword at his side. In contrast, Cate wore his old riding clothes, the ones people in Darlington might remember. His breeches had been skillfully mended, but the mend and the bloodstains showed.

Diana rode astride in a crimson riding habit with a mannish jacket, a stock at her neck, and her hair tied back like a man's beneath her three-cornered hat. She had pistols at her saddle and a sword at her side. She looked the great lady of the north, and indeed, thought Prudence, why should such a woman be seen as less than a man?

A nursing mother from the estate would feed Diana's child as well as her own while Diana was away.

"I'll be uncomfortable," she told Prudence, "and will have to squeeze out milk, but I want a message sent to all men who trample the innocent in their greed up here in the north."

They attracted notice all along the road, especially as the running footman went ahead. He didn't announce anything, but everyone knew an important person must be coming, and they lined the road to watch.

The grooms had been told to share the bare bones of the story with some—that the Earl of Malzard rode to bring a miscreant to justice. Most of the watchers had to return to their work, but a few followed to see the fun, lengthening their train.

"Perhaps we should have banners," Prudence said when they stopped to water the horses.

"Declaring 'Death to All Demons'?" Cate said. "I wish I'd thought of it."

"You're enjoyng this."

He grinned. "Yes."

"Madman."

He kissed her there, in view of all.

By the time they approached Darlington about twenty people came behind, a few on horseback, but most on foot. Near the town, the road was lined with people of all ages, all wondering at the unusual sight. More began to follow them then, keen to see the show.

Someone recognized Diana, and the word spread. "It's Lady Arradale!" Diana bowed to people, smiling.

When they entered the town, someone recognized Cate.

"That's the one as bloodied Draydale's nose!"

The name traveled through the crowd on a dark murmur. "Draydale, Draydale, Draydale . . ." Oh, yes, many knew how vile Henry Draydale could be.

They rode to the marketplace, the heart of the town, and took up position there. The running footman took out a paper and in a carrying voice declared to the crowd, "His lordship the Earl of Malzard, Viscount Roecliff, Baron Malsonby and Preel, comes here to accuse Henry Draydale of this town of divers crimes and cruelties: that in respect of the lead mine at Briggleby, he did threaten others, and order violence against one, that they should not bid on the mine, and thus he purchased it at less than its fair value; that he sent men to terrify the commons holders near Briggleby so that they dared not object to a road being built through their common land; that he paid witnesses at the trial of Samuel Greenock to gain a conviction; that . . ." The list rolled on, and this was only what Cate's people had found in scratching the surface.

Prudence saw Tallbridge appear at the back of the crowd, Susan and Aaron at his side. Was Tallbridge implicated in any of the crimes? She prayed not.

Eventually the footman got to recent events: "That he caused damage to be made to a carriage in hope of serious injury or death to the travelers; that he ordered the burning of a house in White Rose Yard, Northallerton, without concern for the lives of those living there; that he caused a man of that town, one William Larn, to be unfairly arrested for theft; that he did strike a woman in anger, that woman being precious to the Earl of Malzard, and now his countess, here before you."

At this point, the footman took a well-deserved deep breath and declared, "For all these crimes and many others, Henry Draydale is summoned here to account for himself, and surrender himself to justice."

There was a great pause and silence, everyone waiting as if Draydale might appear. The next plan, she knew, was to ride in procession to Draydale's house and repeat the accusations at his door.

As expected, Draydale didn't appear.

The running footman declared the intent to ride to his house, but just then, someone cried from the back of the crowd, "He's running. Draydale's off in a chaise and six!"

Part of the crowd in that direction turned to give chase, their cries sending shivers down Prudence's spine. Despite everything, she hoped they didn't catch him.

Cate spoke then, his voice strong. "Let notice of his crimes be posted around Darlington, and in Northallerton, Gisborough, Stockton, and the many other sites of his cruelties. And let none befriend him, unless they wish to embrace the same accusations. If any have details of other cruelties and crimes, his or another's, send them to me."

Diana moved her horse forward and spoke in a clear, carrying voice: "I am Diana, Countess of Arradale. This is not my land, but you know of me, and you know I stand for the good of the people of the north." Did she model herself on Good Queen Bess? Prudence wondered. "I declare Henry Draydale outlaw in the north."

It was all a magnificent piece of theater, and probably had no force in law in this day and age, but it would put an end to Henry Draydale here and all around. Word would spread, as word did, and make him shameful throughout the land.

"Where will he go?" Prudence asked, as the crowd began to disperse, talking excitedly.

"Not far enough. I'll find him."

"Be careful, Cate. Vengeance can eat the soul."

"I merely mean to bring him to justice for the crimes that are on the book. And I will. But I'll leave the prosecution to others. He's not worth my attention beyond this."

"I feel the same."

"Then let's return home."

"I'd like to speak to Aaron and the Tallbridges."

"Of course." Cate directed the horse that way and then helped her off.

"Well," said Susan, for once lost for words.

"We're very well, thank you," Prudence said, and lightly embraced her. She turned to Aaron, who seemed torn between awe and annoyance.

"I'm pleased to see you comfortably situated, Prudence."

"Then sound it."

He frowned. "It's only that I worry about you."

Prudence shook her head, laughing, and let the matter drop. Aaron would always tell a story of his own choosing.

Cate was speaking to Tallbridge. "I must apologize again for the destruction of your carriage, sir, but as you'll have heard, it wasn't entirely my fault."

"A nothing, my lord," Tallbridge said, bowing. "We delight to see you safe. May I offer you the hospitality of my house?"

He was being most urbane, but Prudence hadn't missed his intent glance at Diana, still mounted—rather, Prudence thought, amused, like an equestrian statue.

She was sure it was deliberate, and equally sure that Tallbridge lusted to have her as a guest in his house.

"Alas, sir," Cate said, "we must be on our way back to Keynings. But we hope to accept your hospitality some other time. And, of course, you and your daughter and Prudence's brother are welcome at Keynings at any time."

Tallbridge bowed, obviously pleased with the lesser prize.

They set off back to Keynings in good humor, waiting a couple of miles to take time to feed and water the horses. Later, Diana and Perry separated from the group to run an impromptu horse race.

"You want to do that too," Prudence said.

"Yes. Would you mind if I switched horses with one of the grooms for a while?"

"Of course not."

Cate made the change, appropriating the man's plumed hat as well, and raced to join the others, riding magnificently, his laughter on the wind.

There was nothing for it. She'd have to learn to ride.

Chapter 37

Keynings looked lovely in the late afternoon, and Prudence realized that it was already home for her. Not yet her perfect home, but home, and she could be at home in it.

She saw Hetty out in the garden with the children and waved, and nearer the house Artemis was with her daughters, all three of them, along with nursemaids, one of whom carried a baby. Diana immediately turned her horse in that direction. When she got there, she dismounted, took her baby, turned discreetly, and set to feed her, just like a farmwoman.

Prudence hoped she'd soon have a similar confidence to do exactly as she wished.

She, Cate, and Perry dismounted at the front doors, and the other riders took away their horses. As they went into the house Cate said, "I suppose I should go to Mother and give her an account of today's events. She won't approve."

"I'll come with you," Prudence said, "and make sure she does."

"And I'll escape," said Perry with a laugh, and did so.

The dowager was not admiring, but she said, "Such dastards must be dealt with. It will have done no harm for you both to have been seen in Lady Arradale's company. I hope tomorrow will be a more orderly day and she will dine with us. I knew her parents, you know. They lacked a son. It was a great sadness to them."

"Like Henry the Eighth," Cate said, "they might have taken comfort in their daughter if they'd lived to see her reign."

"Henry the Eighth should have been much more judicious in his choice of wives. A foreign papist was a bad beginning."

Prudence managed to keep silent, but when they escaped, she asked, "Does she not realize that Henry was a papist at the time?"

"I think it's the 'foreign' she objects to. She feels our current king would have been wiser to marry an Englishwoman, but the queen's ability to produce children, including healthy boys, is mellowing her. I'm sorry. My mother's not an easy woman."

"But forthright. That, I can adjust to."

"And when you produce healthy boys, you will be the sun and moon to her."

"That might be the more terrifying prospect! But we've rid ourselves of pandemonium, haven't we? And all our demons are defeated?"

"Yes, and thus we should be rewarded."

"Rewarded?"

"Tonight," he said, his meaning unmistakable.

"Tonight? But . . ." They'd arrived at her bedchamber door. She glanced around to be sure no one was nearby. "We can't."

"We can. There are pleasures that carry no risk of a child."

"There are?" she exclaimed. "Why didn't you say so before?"

                    *   *   *

He came to her in his robe, and nothing else. She too
was in a robe, with her plain nightgown beneath. She'd
left her hair loose.

"Pale honey," he said, gathering some in one hand
and letting it drift down. "By candlelight."

She'd waited for him sitting by the window, watching
the last traces of the sun leave the sky and the first stars
show.

He moved a chair beside hers, and then took her
hand, interweaving their fingers. "Night is the time for
demons, but it's also the time for the sweetest love."

The word *love* shimmered in the air like forbidden
fruit. No, she wouldn't demand too much of this. Their
reward would be rich enough.

"Dusk is a peaceful time of day," she said.

"Unless you're a small creature trying to avoid the owl."

She looked a warning at him. "I'll have only paradise
tonight, not *Paradise Lost*. Why is simply sitting here
like this so sweet?" She answered herself. "Because
everyone wants to touch, to be close to someone. Or
does everyone? Do you?"

"I haven't. Or perhaps I've not known it." He kissed
her knuckles. "I can't imagine being married to anyone
but you."

"Nor can I, but if you'd married Bland, Bumble, or
Fizz, you might have come to love her in time." She'd
touched on the forbidden fruit. He didn't seem to notice.

"Perhaps, but I've known enough marriages of that
sort where the couple merely tolerate each other Unlike us."

He kissed each of her fingers, one by one, where they
alternated with his. She drew their hands to her own
lips to copy the gentle touch, enjoying his smell, the soft
roughness of his skin, the fine hairs tickling her lips.

"But for you, I probably would have married one of them," he said, "or one of the other candidates from the list. I was determined to do my duty."

"Instead, you married me, and brought pandemonium into Keynings."

He nipped one of her fingers. "Avoiding a worse kind of hell. I doubt I'd make a placid husband when driven to distraction."

Saucily, she asked, "You're sure *I* won't drive you to distraction?"

"Only in the best possible ways. Come to bed, my wife."

They approached the bed, where he slipped off her robe. "A lady in a demure nightdress. How enchanting. But it will have to go. You permit?"

Prudence's heart was racing and her mouth was dry, but she managed, "I permit."

He unfastened the six buttons slowly, his fingers brushing her chest, and then he eased the cloth aside so he could kiss one breast, and then one nipple, sending a shudder through her.

"Isn't that delightful?" he murmured. "And no risk of a baby."

His robe was hanging open over his chest. She gave in to temptation and put a hand there, where he was hot and smooth and hard with muscle. As he paid attention to her other breast, she stroked, exploring the mystery of his skin.

"There are no bars between us tonight," she said.

"Yes, there are. The bars of our intent, but as I said, barriers themselves can add to delight."

He slipped the nightgown off her shoulders and down, until it puddled at her feet, leaving her naked. She covered herself with her hands before she thought of it. He gently captured them and held her arms out.

"You are magnificent, my warrior queen. A classical body to match your classical face."

"Agrippina," she reminded him, and he laughed.

He shed his robe and stood there, letting her look as he'd looked at her. He wasn't bandaged anymore, but she could see his wounds, old and new. All the same, he was perfect.

"You're magnificent. A classical statue incarnate. You shame those statues in the hall."

"Roe had copies made of ancient statues, but with any damage repaired. Impossible with mine."

"You're a warrior, your scars your badges of honor." She took him into her arms for an embrace even more wonderful than they'd shared before, skin-to-skin, heat-to-heat, but tender, in a fiery way.

Smiling, his eyes bright with delight, perhaps with her, he picked her up and carried her to the bed.

"I remember when you carried me upstairs in Tallbridge's house. It excited me, but frightened me."

"Frightened you?"

"Because you were so strong."

"Do I frighten you now?"

She knew she should say no, but she told the truth. "You're a man. I'm still not well accustomed to men. Especially men like you."

"Men like me?" He laid her on the bed, then walked around to the other side.

"Men like you," she repeated, taking in every detail of his magnificent body. "But I do see the advantages. If you were to come closer, I could become more accustomed."

He laughed and lay down on the sheets, not bothering to cover himself. "Become as accustomed as you wish, my lady."

She did so, touching and exploring for the pleasure of it, hoping it pleased him.

He lay quiet for a while, and then a hand slid between her thighs, a finger exploring there.

She shifted, startled, but then said, "Oh."

"Oh," he said, smiling, leaning to put his lips to her nipple again. It was gentle play to wreak such havoc, but perhaps it was his hand lower down, or both. . . .

"What is this?" she asked.

"A gift of the gods with no repercussions. Surrender, my love."

"Your love?"

"Of course."

"You could have said that before," she complained, and hit him as she had when he'd confessed to being an earl.

But he only laughed and commanded her into delight until she was lost in it, touching, gripping, and kissing any bit of flesh that came near her mouth.

His fingers slid deep inside her instead of his manhood, as he swept her into a dark heat that whirled around her and in her, driving her into raging need. She was grunting—grunting!—then shouting. Then a wave of pleasure swept through her, carrying turmoil away and leaving hot, shuddering satisfaction.

"Oh, my," she said. "Oh, my."

"Oh, my darling," he said, smiling, kissing her. "I knew you'd be a lusty lover."

"I was?"

"You were. Are. Always."

"Say it again."

"Always?"

"That you love me! Or did I imagine it?"

"I love you. You know that."

"You never said it."

"I must have done."

"No."

"You haven't said it to me," he pointed out.

"I was too shy."

"Perhaps I'm shy."

She hit him again, laughing. He caught her hand and kissed the palm. "You still haven't said it."

"I love you. I adore you. I think you the best of men."

He smiled, but almost as if embarrassed.

"You are, Cate. I knew it—part of me knew it from the first. It's why I let you in my house and supported your story in the church. I always knew you were a good man."

"And I knew you were the only woman for me...."

They kissed again, stroking, laughing, and she realized he was hard again. "You've pleasured me, but what of you?"

"There's a messy bed." He moved over to her side. "In time, we'll move to yours. And in the morning, there's the bath."

"Who gets to use it first?"

"We both do. There are so many games we can play as we wait—in bed, in the bath, in a boat, on the swing, even. And after the waiting's over, my delicious, lusty wife, in our paradise, our home, I'm going to delight in every way, all our days, till death us do part."

Author's Note

I took the seed of this story from Amanda Vickery's excellent book *Behind Closed Doors: At Home in Georgian England* (Yale University Press, 2009). As in her other book, *Gentlemen's Daughters*, about women of the gentry class in the same period, she mines the letters and accounts of women of the time to illuminate their lives.

It is full of details about the lives of men and women within the home, including the obvious truth that even those men most in favor of republican rule and liberty, in Britain and America, rarely wished to extend those principles to their homes. The women of this period, and for some time later, were usually under the rule of men, and their lives differed according to the indulgences of these men.

It was most galling when the ruler of a woman's life was her brother, and unless her father had made provisions for her, a woman could be completely dependent on his whim. Many made the obvious complaint that nothing separated them except their sex, yet the son had money and independence while they had nothing.

The book offered a glimpse into the life of one particular woman. When the father died, leaving the family impoverished, she and her mother sacrificed, scrimped, and saved so her brother could qualify as a lawyer and support them in the genteel way to which they were accustomed. When the brother achieved his qualifications and became well-to-do, however, he ignored their pleas for their reward. The mother died, and the daughter harangued him for justice.

In the end he arranged her marriage to a colleague.

Sound familiar? Remember, this is a true case.

This one worked out badly, however. The husband was a brute, and eventually the woman's only recourse was to flee, even though she had to leave her infant daughter behind. She went to court to seek justice and—believe it or not—her brother acted for her husband, and she was left to live on a pittance, never seeing her daughter again.

I decided to rewrite the story with a much better ending, and I hope you've enjoyed it.

The eighteenth century could be a harsh time for women, and I don't think we should ignore those problems in historical romance, but nor should we forget that it was a hierarchical age, and men also had to bend to others—employers, a magistrates or judges, or people of higher rank in society. As you might have seen in *The Secret Duke*, even Rothgar has to tread carefully around the younger Duke of Ithorne, and they both must bow to the king.

Cate himself is an example of other forms of control. The army always was and still is authoritarian and hierarchical, and he doesn't do well at obeying the rules. As a younger son, he was raised to know that his older brother would have nearly everything, and he would have to make his own way. The only difference between his and Prudence's situations is that the Georgian world presented men with many opportunities to make a living and even a fortune, whereas it presented few to women.

And last, he has no real power to resist his fate. When his brother dies, he becomes the earl, whether he wishes to or not. Thus he must take up the onerous responsibilities and devote his life to them. His only escape would be through shameful neglect of his heritage and all who depend upon him. What he needs above all is a help-mate, and in the end, his unlikely countess is exactly the right one.

This book takes part in my Malloren world, ruled over by the Marquess of Rothgar. The main series of Malloren novels begins with *My Lady Notorious*. The book featuring Rothgar and Diana is *Devilish*. You can find out about those books and all the rest on my Web site: www.jobev.com.

My first romance was published in 1988, so there are quite a few.

There's a new countess book in 2012, and there are some details following this letter. There will also be vari-ous reissues between now and then. If you like e-editions, did you find the special reissue published as a lead-in to this book? *The Demon's Bride* is a sexy, spooky Geor-gian novella with a wickedly gorgeous hero.

To receive news of all new and reissued work, please sign up for my occasional newsletter on my Web page.

I enjoy hearing from my readers. You can contact me at jo@jobev.com. Please put something in the subject line or the message could be lost as spam. You can also find me on Facebook, and I occasionally tweet.

May every book you read leave you smiling.

All best wishes,
Jo

Please read on for an exciting preview of
Jo Beverley's next historical romance,

The Scandalous Countess

Coming soon from Signet

Imagine you are twenty years old and by a stroke of fate become both a widow and a scandal. . . .

That's the premise of my second countess book.

Georgia, Countess of Maybury, is an acclaimed beauty, a leader of style and fashion in Georgian England, and enjoys a retinue of adoring men.

When her husband the Earl of Maybury is killed in a duel, however, everything changes. She's a grieving widow, but as she and Dickon have no children, the earldom and all its properties now belong to his uncle. She has lost her beloved homes, but also her reputation.

The beau monde is wondering if Maybury and Sir Willoughby Vance truly fought over an insult to Maybury's driving skills, or whether Vance had been "Lady May's" lover. After all, she is a known flirt, and loves to break the rules.

Georgia's family sweeps her off to her family home, Herne House, in Worcestershire, but as she emerges from her grief, she realizes she's been returned almost to the schoolroom. She has no money of her own, no freedom, and her father expects to run her life.

That won't do. For three years she was a wife and a countess, and by law she has control of her own money.

She determines to reclaim her life against all the odds. Above all she needs a new husband, but he must be exactly right.

When her father tells her she should marry Lord Dracy, she's shocked and disbelieving. He's a mere baron, and a scarred, rough-edged man who's spent most of his life in the navy and has now inherited an impoverished title.

He absolutely will not do, but she'll need all her wits to achieve her goals and circumvent her domineering father's will. And all her resolution to resist a surprisingly intriguing man . . .

I hope this interests you, and that you'll enjoy *The Scandalous Countess* when it's published in 2012.

You can find out all about it and any other Jo Beverley books at www.jobev.com.

From

JO BEVERLEY

—

The long out of print novella

The Demon's Bride

Now available as an eSpecial*

Rachel Proudfoot has enough trouble resisting the temptation of rakish Lord Morden without supernatural intervention. When she plays the traditional role of the demon's bride, however, a mighty earth spirit wants to use them both to return to the world.

Available online wherever books are sold or at
penguin.com

Also Available

FROM

JO BEVERLEY

The Secret Duke

When Arabella Barstowe is kidnapped, she believes her life and virtue are forfeit—until she's rescued by the notorious rogue Captain Rose. Bella never expects to see him again. But years later she learns the wicked truth behind her abduction, and she seeks out the only man who can help her take revenge.

What she doesn't know is that Captain Rose is just a disguise for the formidable Duke of Ithorne, who is intrigued to hear from the mysterious woman from his past. Their lives are soon entangled by danger and a growing forbidden passion.

**Available wherever books are sold or at
penguin.com**

S0159

New York Times Bestselling Author
Jo Beverley

Now back in print: two long unavailable
yet beloved romance classics

Lady Wraybourne's Betrothed
Jane Sandiford has been raised to be a dutiful daughter, and
she accepts an offer of marriage from handsome Lord
Wraybourne. But when her new status takes her into the
world of Regency Society, she begins to think there should be
more to marriage than duty.

The Stanforth Secrets
Widowed Chloe Stanforth only wants to leave her home to
start a new life, especially when the new owner is a man she
felt far too strongly about during her marriage. But murder
and mayhem mean she must stay and solve both those
mysteries, and the ones in her heart.

ALSO AVAILABLE
The Stolen Bride
Emily and the Dark Angel

Available wherever books are sold or at
penguin.com

"Wickedly, wonderfully sensual and gloriously romantic."
—Mary Balogh

"A delicious...sensual delight." —Teresa Medeiros

New York Times **Bestselling Author**

Jo Beverley

THE SECRET DUKE
THE SECRET WEDDING
A LADY'S SECRET
LOVERS AND LADIES
LADY BEWARE
TO RESCUE A ROGUE
THE ROGUE'S RETURN
A MOST UNSUITABLE MAN
THREE HEROES
SKYLARK
WINTER FIRE
SECRETS OF THE NIGHT
DARK CHAMPION
ST. RAVEN
LORD OF MY HEART
MY LADY NOTORIOUS
HAZARD
THE DEVIL'S HEIRESS
THE DRAGON'S BRIDE
DEVILISH
SOMETHING WICKED
LORD OF MIDNIGHT
FORBIDDEN MAGIC

Available wherever books are sold or at penguin.com